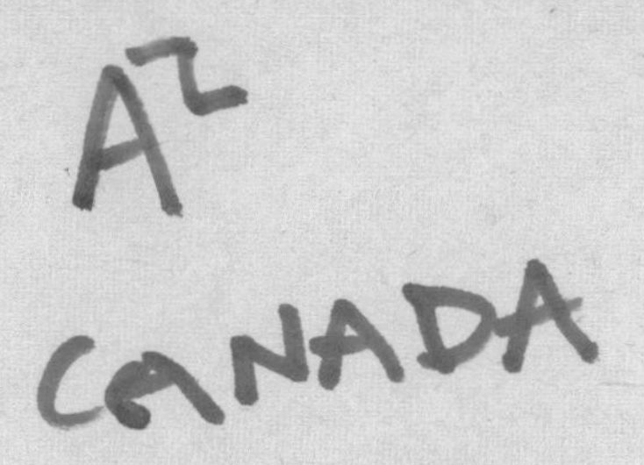

A BIG, BRAWLING NOVEL—
A MAN TO SET
THE WEST ABLAZE

Hellfire Jackson—some hated him, many feared him, but none dared turn their backs on him.

Hellfire Jackson—a man with a message written in brimstone and trouble across the vast frontier.

Hellfire Jackson—a novel to hold you spellbound.

HELLFIRE JACKSON

BY

GARLAND ROARK

AND

CHARLES THOMAS

POPULAR LIBRARY - TORONTO

All POPULAR LIBRARY books are carefully selected by the POPULAR LIBRARY Editorial Board and represent titles by the world's greatest authors.

POPULAR LIBRARY EDITION

Library of Congress Catalog Card Number: 66-17433

Published by arrangement with Doubleday & Company, Inc.

Doubleday & Company edition published in August, 1966

With the exception of actual historical personages, the characters are entirely the product of the authors' imagination and have no relation to any person in real life.

PRINTED IN CANADA

To Jean and A. E. Holtz, Jr.

CHAPTER 1

The horseman in buckskin pants and hunting shirt carefully scanned the road ahead and sent probing glances into the pine forest flanking El Camino Real, the King's Highway. Behind him a middle-aged Negro rode a mule and led a pack animal. A week out of Natchez, Mississippi, they were in upper western Louisiana in the outlaw-infested strip called No Man's Land.

The big man in buckskin had been warned of the danger here. He had been told back in Tennessee that since the year 1803 the area between the Arroyo Hondo on the east and the Sabine River on the west had been claimed by both Spain and the United States. By compromise, to await a treaty, it became the Neutral Ground. Without any government, the strip was ruled by fugitives, outlaws, and renegades. When Mexico won her freedom from Spain in 1821, the lawless element continued to dominate the area. They preyed on travelers, and spilled across the Sabine River into the eastern part of Mexican Texas. Even in this year of 1831 a traveler wasn't safe.

A movement in the brush ahead caused the Tennessean instinctively to rein his mount to a stop. When a deer ran across the road, he nudged his sway-backed horse forward again.

A wind sighed up in the pines, and the freshness of spring hung over the land. Wild flowers bloomed wherever the sun penetrated the dense stand of virgin pine. As the road twisted down into the bottom land of the Sabine River, oak, hickory, sweet gum, and pecan trees, tangled vine and brush in every shade of green clogged the forest and vied with the pine for control of the wilderness. Quail, deer, and rabbits were plentiful. Big cottonmouth moccasins lay on creek banks absorbing the sun's warmth. A crane lifted slowly ahead. A hawk sailed past and jay birds screamed at barking squirrels.

As the pair rode on, the forest on their left opened abruptly to reveal a natural clearing of sloping green meadows dotted here and there with large post oak trees. Beyond lay a fringe of woods that followed a creek which curved toward the road on its way to join the Sabine. To the south white overlapping thunderheads encroached on the blue sky and moved on the wind northeast. The scene faded as once again the jealous forest closed in. The road narrowed and it seemed that brush and undergrowth sought to reclaim it for the wilderness.

The Negro berated the pack mule for stopping to nibble at grass, then said, "How come a sorry old road like we's on done called de King's Highway? It ain't made out o' gold and pearls and sich."

The man on the horse replied absently, "From what I've heard, Wash, over one hundred years ago the King of Spain sent his soldiers up here from Mexico, probably to look for gold. All the way from the Rio Grande River to Natchitoches, Louisiana. They tell me this road is nearly six hundred miles long."

"Yassuh, but I'se hopin' we ain't goin' all de way on—"

"Quiet, Wash. We're dropping down into the swamps where we could be ambushed."

The road became muddy and the ruts made by wagons deepened. This was the river approach. Horatio Jackson felt a surge of eagerness. He wanted to ride fast toward the Sabine, the boundary between Louisiana and Mexican Texas. He stubbornly held to the steady gait, however, for he was not a man to alter his code of self-discipline one iota just to humor an impulse.

The twisting road sloped down toward the river, into and out of bogs. Rounding a bend, Jackson's horse shied away from an object in the middle of the road. Seeing an oblong box, Jackson dismounted and picked it up. No doubt it had been dislodged from one of the wagons of the train ahead. He secured it to his pack and got into the saddle again.

"We goin' to keep it?" the Negro asked.

"If the people ahead of us don't claim it, Wash."

"Ain't yo'all wonderin' what's in it, Rev'ren'?" No reply forthcoming, he said, "Might be some new boots, and then it could be a fine pair o' pants, the Sunday go-to-meetin' kind, and a frocktail coat to go with it. All jes my size, and a tall hat throwed in."

"Don't forget a red velvet vest and a gold-headed cane, Wash."

"Lawdy me, you joshin', Rev'ren'!"

Jackson once more cautioned Wash to remain silent. He nudged his horse into muddy water backed up over the road from a creek that had overflowed its banks. Although it was shallow, they proceeded cautiously until the trail emerged and bent into another of its countless curves. It was midafternoon when the trail opened to reveal the swollen Sabine River.

Jackson stopped his horse and gazed across the muddy stream at the land he had traveled so far to reach.

"There she is, Wash. We're looking at Texas."

"Don't look no different than this side, but we sholy come a long way to see it. Now I'se hopin' we don't come back dis way a-runnin', Rev'ren' Jackson."

They moved on. The road now twisted around a dense thicket to the crossing. There they stopped again. Jackson's expression underwent a change as he saw a group of men on the opposite bank. They were shouting instructions to the driver of the last of three wagons as the ferry touched the riverbank. Whether the men were settlers entering Texas or ruffians, Jackson didn't know. His eyes thinned to active slits as he speculated on the company he could scarcely avoid on his initial crossing into the untamed Mexican province.

There the big adventure would begin. Across the river he, a self-appointed Moses, would find either a Pharaoh's Egypt or a Promised Land. Perhaps Texas was both. In any case, he expected no miracles. At times he had felt the Lord's hand on his shoulder and heard the Almighty saying, "Go to Texas, Horatio Jackson." At other times he wondered if he had only imagined in moments of zealous thought and prayer that he had been called by the Lord to go to Texas. Mortals were vain, he realized.

The ferryman was now shouting at him from across the river, naming a fee for the crossing. Jackson yelled back, advising that he'd swim it.

"She's right tricky, stranger!"

"I've swum worse," Jackson replied. Lowering his foghorn voice, he said, "Wash, we'll get busy making a raft. And once we cross into Texas don't address me as Reverend. Call me Marse Jackson."

Andrew Jefferson Washington scratched his graying head in bewilderment before removing ax and hatchet from the pack mule. He knew his chore, and he took the hatchet to cut and strip vines with which to tie the logs his master would fell.

"How come yo'all don't want to be called Rev'ren' Jackson when we gits to Texas? A preachin' man is a rev'ren', ain't he?"

"Just do as I say, Wash. Understand?"

"Yassuh, but I'se in a habit, and it ain't goin' to be easy."

"Then you'll labor at it, Wash."

Little time elapsed before they transferred Bibles, religious tracts, a few surveyor's instruments, and camping equipment to the raft. Covering the Lord's and man's wares with bearskins, they shoved off some fifty yards upstream from the crossing, both men on their mounts, one on each side of the raft. The current was strong in midstream and logs and brush swirled in the eddies. The difficult crossing finally negotiated, they reached the Texas side below Gaines Ferry and the road. Jackson helped Wash transfer the cargo to pack mule, and when it was done he removed his hat and bowed his head. The Negro did likewise.

2

The last wagon to be ferried across the Sabine joined the other two at the ferry keeper's place a few hundred yards from the river. As it ground to a stop, a young woman alighted and said to the couple she was traveling with, "So this is Texas." Then she was asking the owner of the wagon, Jonathan Mundy, how far they were from Stephen F. Austin's colony on the Brazos River.

"Quite a piece," he said, unhitching his team.

Jane Wells knew no more now than before. "Quite a piece" could be one hundred miles or a thousand. But it really didn't matter; her Aunt Sally wouldn't expect her in Brazoria until she arrived there. So that was that. She turned to the back of the wagon where her trunks and boxes were stored. A minute later she discovered one of her boxes was missing. She recalled distinctly having placed it on her trunk only that morning. Mrs. Mundy had not seen it. Mr. Mundy said it might have fallen from the wagon on the uphill climb from the Sabine; why didn't she go down there and look for it?

Jane had long since learned to expect little if any help from Mr. Mundy. Lifting her shoulders, she said, "An excellent idea, sir," and turned toward the river. Once around the bend in the road, she felt the wilderness closing in on her. All she had heard of outlaws, wild animals, snakes, and alligators sharpened her fears of this unknown country. But she refused to turn back and let Mr. Mundy laugh at a "scared female." She followed the twisting road downhill until the river came into view. There was no sign of the box.

Suddenly she heard a man's voice. It lifted clear and strong from somewhere near the river. Then she saw him. Slipping behind the screen of brush, she listened curiously as he said:

"Lord, we thank Thee on our arrival in Texas, thank Thee for helping us get this far. Lord, we've forded rivers and creeks to get here, and You know it. You saw us do it, Lord, after You spake unto me, saying, 'Carry My word to the foreign land called Texas where American people who came from a Protestant country are forced to live under laws that forbid Protestant worship.' Well, here we are, Lord, in obedience to Thy command, much as Thou said in the Scripture —if You recall it was in the Book of Acts, thirteen, two— and I quote—'The Holy Ghost said, Separate me Barnabus and Saul for the work whereunto I have called them.' "

"Amen! Praise de Lawd!" the Negro shouted.

Jane was a little surprised and shocked to learn that this stranger was entering Texas to defy the religious order. Although she was not Catholic, she respected the laws of any land, if only because they were laws. She knew that Stephen F. Austin, to whose colony on the Brazos River she was going to teach school, had given the oath of loyalty to the adopted Mexican government and had nominally accepted the Roman Catholic Church for himself and his colonists.

Now more curious than before, she parted the leaves for a look at the misguided stranger who prayed so earnestly. She saw a man of large frame who stood well above six feet. His shoulders were broad and his face was big boned and his ginger-brown hair was long. By his dress and the weather-brown skin of his smooth-shaven face, he was a woodsman, and he looked to be in his early or mid-thirties. He wasn't exactly handsome, unless one admired the rough, frontier type of man. Looking at him, trying to assess him, she could not quite adjust a buckskin-clad man to the preaching profession. Nor could she place him in the category of willful lawbreaker. Yet he was saying:

"Now, Lord, let's get down to facts. You know what I carry on that old pack mule. You know the welcome a self-appointed Protestant preacher is going to get in Catholic Texas in this year of 1831. Mighty little, Lord—"

Jane did not wait for the end of the prayer. Holding the hem of her calico skirt ankle-high, she picked her way through the ruts and mud back to the house of James Gaines, the ferry keeper. The box she had gone in search of had no doubt been lost in or beyond the Sabine, she decided. Too bad, for it contained several yards of silk, lace, and ribbon, precious things which she could not replace in Texas. Perhaps she could prevail on Mr. Weatherly, owner of the lead wagon, to send his two strapping boys in search of the box. However, she had sooner do without the makings of a fine dress than suffer the disrobing stares of the big uncouth wagoner who openly declared his intention of finding a wife if only to take advantage of the league of land the Mexican government offered a married man to settle in Texas.

"Oh well," she said, covering her disappointment with a

toss of her head, "I'd do well to help the ladies prepare supper and forget the dress."

As she walked toward the wagons one of the horsemen who had watched the caravan cross the river left the group and moved toward her. A tall dark man, dressed in immaculate black, he removed his hat and bowed from the waist.

"*Bon jour*, mam'selle," he said. "A thousand pardons, but I am an observing man. You have lost something, no?"

As she paused to look at the jade-and-pearl eardrops he wore, he twisted the end of a thin black mustache and said, "Captain Jean Émile Fozatte, mam'selle. And I have the pleasure of addressing—?"

"Jane Wells, sir," she replied. "Yes, I lost a box back on the trail." Before she could move on, the handsome man lifted his shoulders, smiled, and said:

"Captain Fozatte is flattered to serve the lovely mam'selle *au plus fort*." Breathing a courteous *"Au 'voir,"* he executed a bow and turned abruptly toward a group of rough-looking men.

Jane watched him ride toward the river at the head of the band, then turned toward the wagons as perplexed as curious. "Imagine a man wearing eardrops! First a buckskin-clad preacher asking the Lord's blessing for breaking Mexican laws, then this. What next?"

She was not kept waiting long for the answer to her question. The sound of voices in argument jerked her gaze to the source. Where the road humped up to the ferryman's clearing, she saw the preacher and his Negro facing the Frenchman's group. James Gaines was moving hurriedly toward them, and men from the wagons were following him.

As the preacher turned his horse to ride past the men, one of Fozatte's riders reined in to block his way. Jane heard the preacher say, "I'm a peaceful man, gentlemen, up to a point. Now I'll do as I said, give the property to its rightful owner and nobody else."

The property could be her box, she was thinking. It had to be, since the Frenchman had only minutes before ridden out ostensibly to serve her—*au plus fort*, whatever that meant. She had neglected French in favor of Spanish in order to prepare for a teacher's job at San Felipe de Austin. But the box! It wasn't worth the trouble it was brewing down the river road. Nor would she allow it.

Upon reaching the scene, she saw a small pistol in the Frenchman's hand. It pointed toward the big preacher, who was saying, "All right, mister, you've got the advantage, so I'll get the box from my pack mule."

"Better still, m'sieur, your slave will hand it over."

"He's no slave. He's a free Negro who chose my company up in Missouri." Then he was saying, "Wash, hand him the box."

Fozatte saw Jane then. "Ah, mam'selle, Jean Fozatte lost little time in finding the thief who stole your property. He will be duly tried and punished, I assure you."

Before she could voice protest, James Gaines said, "Hold on there, Captain. You forget I'm the alcalde, the appointed justice of the peace, on this side of the river."

"*Non,* M'sieur Gaines, I neither overlook the fact nor your illustrious pursuit of duty. Nor do I wish you to overlook a point, *mon ami.* The box was found and claimed by this thief on the other side of the Sabine."

"That's the second time you've called me a thief!" the accused man said.

Gaines rubbed his bearded jaw, hooked a thumb in his belt, and said, "Captain Jean, I beg to advise here and now that while your point is well taken, you must admit that the property named was recovered on this side of the river, that it's here now. Which fact puts the matter under my jurisdiction. Right?"

Fozatte lifted his palms. *"À la bonne heure, M'sieur le Juge."*

"He means 'Well and good,' " the preacher advised. "So I'll say my piece, Mr. Justice. I found that box and intended, and still intend, to give it to its rightful owner."

"Who are you, and why did you come to Texas, stranger?" Gaines demanded.

"I'm Horatio Jackson, from Jefferson County, Tennessee, late of Arkansas Territory, where I was employed as a surveyor by the Army in which I served for several years. I came to Texas to make a living as a surveyor."

Jane Wells was thinking, "Such deception! Maybe he did steal my box," when Gaines asked to see Mr. Jackson's tools of trade. To her surprise, he unstrapped a canvas roll from his pack animal and produced surveying instruments. Then it dawned on her that a man who deliberately came to violate the provisions of the Mexican colonization program would of course enter Texas under the guise of something else. So he pretended to be a surveyor.

She wondered about it. Next, she was examining the man himself, and she felt that her opinions regarding his honest face and strong, earnest prayer had suddenly betrayed her better judgment. This served to pique her further, and she decided to dislike this Jackson.

Alcalde Gaines was saying, "Well, Mr. Jackson, I can't challenge your entry but I can tell you the prospects for surveyin' land ain't too bright. Not in this department of Texas, at least."

"And why not, Mr. Alcalde?"

"Gaines is my name, Mr. Jackson. James Gaines. I was appointed alcalde when the District of the Sabine was organized in 1824. Now with that brief introduction, which should prove that I know a little something about this part of Texas, I'll answer your question. The reason surveyin' won't pay in East Texas is because the Fredonian Rebellion of a few years back made ownership of land right uncertain. The Edwards grant was revoked, leaving the colonists caught between claims by the Cherokees and the descendants of Gil Y'Barbo and his colonists who came to East Texas some seventy years ago. Land titles are in a mess, as you'll find out."

"All the more reason for surveys, Mr. Gaines. Surely the government wants to settle land disputes."

"Government?" Gaines smiled. "The government ain't like it is back in the States. It's down in Mexico. Saltillo is where the government sits on laws for Texas."

"Then maybe I'll go down there."

"Yeah, you do that. But back to this fracas here, how do you plan to find the owner of the box, Mr. Jackson?"

"I'm sure it fell off one of the wagons you ferried across this afternoon. Why don't we go find out?"

Jane moved through the circle to Gaines's side. "The box belongs to me." As all eyes fell on her she felt a flush of color rise from her neck. "It contains blue silk, white lace, and blue satin ribbon. Well, open it and see!"

"I don't doubt your word, ma'am," Jackson said. "Now I'll be pleased to take it to your wagon."

"Never mind!" Jane picked up the box and moved off. Suddenly she stopped, whirled, and said, "I suppose I should thank you for fetching it here, Mr. Jackson. And you, Captain Fozatte, for going in search of it. Well, I thank both of you, but most of all I'm grateful to Mr. Gaines for stopping the trouble."

Jackson watched her go, thinking that if she was short on gratitude she made it up in spirit. Along with this observation, his masculine eye approved all it saw, from the clear, direct blue eyes, that came alive and looked level with a man, to the small feet that had left tracks in the mud down by the river. Her sunbonnet failed to hide the obstinate brown ringlets at her forehead and cheeks even as her plain calico dress could not conceal a small waist and nicely turned figure.

"I didn't get her name," Jackson said.

"Wells. Miss Jane Wells," a wagoner replied. "She's travelin' with me and the old woman down to Austin's colony on the Bra-zos."

Gaines laughed. "It ain't pronounced Bra-zos, mister. The 'Bra' is like in 'brag,' and you newcomers who called this river the Say-bine might like to know the 'Sab' is like in 'Sabbath.' You say it Sab-bean and you say it right."

Only the Frenchman failed to smile. He continued to eye Jackson. Gaines had seized upon the common mispronunciation of Texas rivers to relieve the tension. Aware that it had been lost on Fozatte, he said, "Now that any misunderstanding has been cleared up, maybe you'll shake hands with Mr. Jackson, Captain Fozatte."

The Frenchman pulled at a mustache thoughtfully. An eloquent shrug preceded his flashing smile. *"Mon Dieu!* Why not?"

Jackson looked at the extended hand. "Twice you called me a thief, stranger, both times with a gun in your hand. The Lord told us to forgive our enemies, but He didn't tell us to submit to false accusations. Now you think it over, Captain, and if and when you figure more is due me than just a handclasp, you'll find Horatio Jackson ready to listen."

Jackson eyed Fozatte a moment, saw his lips drawn to a tight line and his eyes to slits that glittered and emitted a furious stare alive with promises of unpleasant things should they ever meet again.

Nudging his horse forward, Jackson said, "Let's go, Wash."

"Yas-suh! I'se ready, Rev'ren' Jackson!"

James Gaines, ardent Catholic and Mexican official, gave a start. "Hold on there, mister!" he said. "I thought you said you were a surveyor."

Jackson turned his horse and faced the alcalde. "That's right."

"Then how come your nigger called you Reverend Jackson?"

"Because I tried to become a minister, sir."

"But you're not? Is that what I'm supposed to believe?"

"If you care to believe the truth, you are. My church refused to ordain me a minister of the gospel. So I'm a surveyor by profession."

As Gaines scratched his head and eyed the puzzling newcomer, even as Fozatte, his followers, and the wagoners were doing, Jackson broke the silence by saying:

"Mr. Gaines, I've been in Texas less than half an hour and I've been accused of being a thief and a liar and tried before a Mexican official, even had a pistol aimed at me. So, with your permission, I'll be on my way to see what the rest of Texas has to offer."

"You're free to go, Mr. Jackson. No hard feelings, none whatsoever. But you're welcome to stay for supper. Susanna serves up mighty fine corn bread, peas, and pork."

"Thank you, sir. As hungry as I am I'm tempted to partake of your hospitality. But on second thought, the way I'd lay into your peas and pork might provoke charges of grand larceny."

They watched Jackson ride off, saw him pass the house and wagons, tip his hat to Miss Wells, and disappear around a bend in the King's Highway.

Stroking his beard, Gaines said, "A strange fellow, Captain. Whether preacher, surveyor, liar, or thief, he's got a way about him. He rebuked you good and proper, then laid a little honey on his tongue to give me a dose of the same medicine."

The Frenchman raised his hand and looked at it. "He refused my hand! *Mon Dieu,* no man does that to Jean Fozatte!"

"Leave him be, Captain. That's an order from the alcalde."

CHAPTER 2

As was his habit, Jackson made camp some distance off the road that night. He had no desire to wake and find himself surrounded by rowdies. Twice since leaving Natchez for Texas he had hosted uninvited riders of the night and suffered their threats, oaths, and drunken brawls. On this evening, the memory of the promise in the Frenchman's eyes was all too fresh, so he ordered "dry camp," no fires, and he and Wash ate jerked deer meat and washed it down with water from a spring. He thanked the Lord for the remaining crumbs of corn pone and the hardened dried meat in the same sincere manner Wash had heard when the fare was roast turkey and all the trimmings. Following his "Amen," Jackson said:

"Our boot soles might be easier to chew than this old jerky, Wash, but we'll save them for hard times."

"Yassuh. But when yo'all passes up po'k, peas, and co'n bread for this, I figgers hard times done come."

For answer, Jackson began talking about the future and the abundance of fruits of the land. Soon the vines along the roadside would be heavy with big ripe berries. A little sugar, grease, and flour would turn the berries into a delicious cobbler. There would be wild plum thickets, and poke plant to boil and taste every bit as good as turnip greens. Game was plentiful and fish were waiting to be caught.

When a big moon peeped through the tall pines and scattered shadows over the ground, Jackson stretched out on his blanket and eyed the yellow ball that seemed to rush past white wisps of clouds. Night insects and frogs vied with one another in their various songs, and somewhere in the distance a panther screamed. Closer, a whippoorwill sent his call through the trees.

"Listen to that old whip'will, Marse Jackson. Know what he sayin'? He say, 'A chip fell out o' de white oak.' "

"I hear him saying, 'Dick married a widow.' "

Wash listened. "Why, he sholy am!"

"He says whatever you want to put in his mouth, Wash. Just like the bullfrogs saying either 'Jug o' rum' or 'Come to Texas.' This is God's big outdoors, and it talks to a man."

"Hit sholy do."

"It talks strange things into a head, Wash. Fascinated me since I can remember. Sort of claimed me ever since. Changed my whole life, I reckon. Drank my first whisky with a bunch of fellows in the woods. Fished when I should have been trying to live up to what my father and other people expected of me."

"Yo' don't say! Yo'll never tol' me about dat, Marse Jackson."

"Well, I'm not too proud of it, Wash."

"Naw, suh."

"I was quite a disappointment to my father, as well as to all the important men who saw in me promise of greatness in state and national politics. John Schuyler Jackson once boasted that his son would one day be Governor Jackson of Tennessee. He did his darnedest to make it come true by sending me to college and preparing me for a career at the bar.

"But a lot of things got in my way, Wash," he mused aloud.

"How come?"

"Well, the more a big strapping youth of twenty learned, the more confused he became. Oh, I knew my 'wherefores' and 'whereases' as well as the next lawyer, but I also enjoyed the company of my drinkin' friends. There was a brawl, Wash, and we crossed over into Kentucky to fight a duel with pistols. Well, there I stood with the smoking gun in my hand. Even though the man lived, something in me died—"

"You shot a man? Naw, suh!"

"Then in 1819 when I turned twenty-one my father made me his law partner. But law as a career? I wasn't cut out for it, Wash. I should have won my first case in the Nashville court, but to the surprise and disappointment of my father I lost it. My father urged me often to pattern after the rising, popular lawyer Samuel Houston."

Looking up at the moon, Jackson said, "Houston was elected to Congress in 1823, one year after I left my father's law firm and enlisted in the Army as a private. After two and a half years in the service, I was discharged. For the next year I worked as a field hand for a family in Missouri, spent my wages on whisky, and kept company with a rough crowd. I avoided church, for religion was to me something people conjured up as a balm for their fears. An avowed disbeliever, I used my misspent legal talents to argue that there was no God."

"I do declare! Don't soun' like you, Rev'ren'. No it don't."

"That was me, Wash. I wasn't even a good field hand. Got kicked off that job for neglecting chores in order to hunt and fish. It was after a bunch of us broke up a church meeting one day that I fled down into Arkansas Territory and fell in with a group of Army surveyors. Being pretty good at mathematics, I stayed with them and learned to survey."

He told Wash how he had made friends with the Cherokees. He had hunted and fished with them, had learned from them how to trail and cut sign and how to wrestle Indian fashion. They had called him a brother and given him the name of Red Fox. And the old chieftain, Tail-of-Gray-Pony, had wished to adopt him as his son.

"Can you imagine that, Wash?"

There was no reply. The Negro had fallen asleep, leaving Jackson alone with memories of the past, one of which stood out above all others. . . .

2

The surveyors had moved on and "Red Fox" Jackson went with them to a small Arkansas town. There one night in June of 1828 he had let a local girl he was squiring about talk him into taking her to a church revival.

As they approached the lantern-lit tabernacle, a thatch roof over poles, and open on all sides, he said, "On second thought, Miss Emmaline, I don't relish sitting through all that religious hogwash."

"Mr. Jackson, sir!" she replied, indignant. "Maybe you belong back with the heathen Indians you talk about." Then she gave him to understand that he could either escort her to the revival or consider his company undesirable to her in the future.

He pondered the choice before him and studied Miss Emmaline with the eye of a man who had been a long time in the wilderness. Right then she was a handsome woman, despite the fact that she was overly plump and her nose turned up, taking her upper lip with it. He decided to suffer the ordeal at the tabernacle.

They sat on a hand-hewn bench some five rows from the platform. Brother Jeremiah Whiteside came to the pulpit, parted a long black beard, folded his hands across a protruding middle, and spoke to the Lord. Ten minutes later he said, "Amen," and the crowd said, "Amen! Praise the Lord!" and Miss Emmaline said in a rapturous whisper, "He's truly a godly man, Mr. Jackson," and Horatio said under his breath, "He's a humbug."

A hymn followed, and Horatio admitted that the preacher had a voice that would carry on a fair breeze all the way to the Cherokee village. Having a good voice himself, he joined in just to show Brother Whiteside that he wasn't the only man who could shake the rafters with song. Besides, it helped drown out Miss Emmaline, who couldn't carry a tune. His vanity backfired on him, however, when the preacher lifted a restraining hand and, in the ensuing quiet, asked that "the good brother with Miss Emmaline" come forward and lead the next stanza and chorus. Embarrassed, but not to be outdone by any backwoods preacher, Horatio marched to the platform and gave his best through that song and three more which he had sung as a child.

Returning to his seat under the beaming eyes of his companion, he listened while the preacher opened his Bible, adjusted his spectacles, and said, " 'Vengeance is mine; I will repay, saith the Lord.' " Next, " 'With what measure ye mete, it shall be measured to you again.' " Then—and Horatio was sure that the minister's eyes were fixed upon him—" 'There is no peace, saith the Lord, unto the wicked.' "

Following another long prayer, Brother Whiteside really warmed up. He brought the Lord and His wrath into the very midst of the sinners to drive out the devil and his host of imps. "The devil is amongst us!" he shouted. "In you, brother!

In you, sister!" He pointed a finger at every person there, and he preached fire and brimstone until one could almost smell the acrid smoke of hell. But there was hope and there was salvation, he said. He pointed to the sky and exhorted the Lord not to close the pearly gates of heaven until every sinner present had an opportunity to wrestle with the devil and repent of his transgressions.

Amid the shouts of "Amen! Glory, glory be!" from the congregation, Miss Emmaline clutched at Horatio's arm and shouted also. Horatio sat a little stunned by it all. He was curious, fascinated, and confused. He felt a battle raging on the platform between the preacher and old Satan, and he felt the presence of the leering red devil, and he wanted to join in the shouting. Restraint was difficult, for he now realized that the devil actually existed, that poor Brother Whiteside was fighting him with all his might and calling on the Lord for much-needed help. Well, well, Horatio was thinking. It did beat all how some men tackled the impossible and then asked for help. Now he was wondering how Whiteside would get his foot out of the trap.

At that moment the preacher raised his arms and eyes and cried in triumph, "The gates of heaven are opening to you, beloved! How can you escape the devil and enter? By confessing thy sins and declaring for the Lord. Will you come forward while we sing?"

The singing began. The arms of Brother Whiteside were outstretched in invitation and his voice pleaded over and over: "Come, sinner. Come." And now Miss Emmaline was asking Horatio to accept the Lord.

Horatio felt a mighty force at work inside him. He tried to shake free of it. "Jesus is calling you, Horatio," she said. He wanted to run. His feet would not obey. He trembled and the whole world seemed to swim about him, to envelop him. He was being hypnotized and he knew it. He felt a surge of joy, of strength, such as he had never before known. The chains that bound him seemed to part. Then, as if in a dream, he was moving toward the pulpit.

"I come," he said. "Lord, I come."

Next morning Horatio awoke wondering if the great experience had been real or a dream. If real, would it last? Fearing it was a temporary thing, a fleeting emotional wave that had engulfed him, he began to study the Bible. The more he read the more convinced he became that the Lord had touched him, had singled him out for His work on this earth. The feeling persisted and he prayed for guidance from above. At last the Lord pointed the way.

Two months later he set out for Tennessee. In Nashville he presented himself before a body of churchmen and told them that he was a candidate for the ministry, that he had heard the call to carry the Lord's work to the Mexican province of Texas. He saw eyebrows lift. Then they were asking if he was ignorant of the fact that Protestant ministers were forbidden in Texas. Yes, he knew that, but hadn't Christians been forbidden in Rome in the time of Paul? They eyed the big man in buckskin and placed further questions:

Who was he, where had he heard the call, and what were his qualifications? Jackson told them the truth. After due consideration the churchmen decided that his request was most unusual, that while he was a man endowed with strength, and purpose, and a soul "which gleamed with noblest affection," his background and appearance coupled with his strange call to Texas forced the body in the best interests of the church to refuse him.

"Well, gentlemen, I don't give up easy. I'll apply elsewhere and keep at it until I become a licensed minister."

True to his promise, Jackson applied before another body of churchmen in eastern Tennessee. Again he was refused because of his backwoods appearance and the "erratic vision" that pointed him toward Texas. When privately advised by one of the leaders to present himself in proper attire next time and to omit any mention of his backwoods life, Horatio replied:

"Brother, I accept your advice in the spirit it was given, but I reckon we just don't read from the same Bible."

In the fall of 1829 layman Jackson went to Tennessee again. Once more rebuffed by the church, he went to Missouri. There Andrew Jefferson Washington, who had found the life of a free Negro burdened with responsibilities he was unable to cope with, had asked to become Jackson's slave. Jackson refused on the grounds that he was at heart opposed to slavery. After again being refused admission to the ministry, Jackson got on his horse and rode toward Arkansas Territory. Next morning he awoke to find Wash frying bacon over a fire. When taken to task, the Negro replied, "Ain't no harm to play like I'se yo'all's nigger, Rev'ren'."

The pair rode on together, down into Arkansas, on to Alabama, and back to Natchez, Mississippi. There Jackson attended a revival and found Brother Whiteside again. Upon learning of Jackson's many rebuffs in his attempt to become a minister, he tried to dissuade him from going to Texas. Failing, as had all others, he suggested that Brother Jackson modify his demands and request the churchmen to make him a colporteur, a seller of religious tracts and Bibles, in the province of Texas. There he could hold religious meetings in secret and work toward the realization of his ultimate ambition.

Jackson took hope. Soon he was made a colporteur. Without money to purchase religious literature and Bibles, he returned to Arkansas with Wash and joined the surveyors again. When he had earned money to purchase Bibles, tracts, a pack mule, and meager supplies for the trail, he and Wash went down to Natchez, then crossed the Mississippi River into Louisiana. He was at last on his way to Texas.

3

Horatio continued to lie there, staring up at the big moon that seemed to hang just above the tall pines. He joined the past to the present and pondered his future for some time. All the while the creatures of the night talked on near by and in the distance. Knowing the habits and ways of the birds and animals, he read much in all he heard. But they revealed nothing of the future. Then suddenly the incessant noise of insects ceased. The birds and animals were silent also. He knew the wild country, knew there was a reason for silence. He put his ear to the ground and listened. The fall of hoofs against the hard-packed ground told of riders in the night. Then this sound vanished, to tell him that the riders had stopped, perhaps to search the trail for tracks.

"Our tracks, maybe," he said to himself.

His surmise was not five minutes old when he heard horses and the creaking of leather on the road. Then men were talking. Finally one of them raised his voice, saying angrily, "If their tracks end here, you fool, they must have taken to the woods! *Mon Dieu,* yes!"

There was no mistaking the voice. Fozatte was on his trail, his purpose obvious. Jackson was hoping his own horse and mules would not disclose their whereabouts when Wash sat up and said, "Who's dat, Rev'ren'?"

"Quiet! It's the Frenchman! And stop calling me Reverend!"

The night riders left the road and walked their horses into the bush and woods, toward Jackson's camp. They came closer, to almost within a hundred feet of the camp before turning in another direction. Half an hour later the horsemen rode back toward the Sabine. When the hum of night insects sounded again, Horatio said:

"Well, Lord, since it looks like Your servant Jackson has sure enough got himself a bear by the tail and can't turn loose, I'd appreciate it if You'd coax the critter to head fast for safer ground."

CHAPTER 3

Jackson and Wash pushed west that night. Midmorning found them approaching Ayish Bayou. Weary from loss of sleep, Jackson looked at his animals and decided to pitch a camp off the road once they put the brush thickets of the bottom land behind them. Topping a ridge, they gazed at overlapping hills, all covered with tall pines. Seeing a column of smoke ahead, they rode on and soon came to a large clearing. A long house of logs and pine slabs, together with several cabins, a cotton gin, log barns, and cattle grazing in the fields, looked inviting. The smoke they had seen from a distance lifted from one of the rock chimneys. When the tantalizing smell of roasting meat finally won over caution, they moved warily toward the small settlement.

Several Negroes appeared to look at them, and by the time they reached the long porch fronting the house, a white man who looked to be in his mid-fifties came out of the house. He shook Jackson's hand and welcomed him to Elisha Roberts Campground.

After introducing his wife, Martha, and bidding her set a table for the traveler, Roberts said he had known several families of Jacksons back in Tennessee. Following brief conversation on the subject, he recalled having met Horatio's father in Nashville. This was cause for another welcome to a fellow Tennessean, as well as for open curiosity regarding Jackson's entry into Texas. Upon learning that the newcomer was a surveyor by profession, he shook his head in dismal manner and told Jackson about the various conditions that made land ownership uncertain.

"So you see, surveying is a useless trade in East Texas, Mr. Jackson."

"That's what Mr. Gaines told me yesterday."

"Well, I've been here twelve years. Now back in 1818 and

on up to the Hayden Edwards Colonization grant, which ended in the Fredonian Rebellion at Nacogdoches, a surveyor was welcome in East Texas. But he'd starve to death now. Maybe down in Austin's colony he'd find work. But did you say you were at Gaines Ferry yesterday?"

Jackson gave an account of his meeting with Gaines and the Frenchman, and of the latter's search for him in the night. When he had finished, Roberts said:

"That Fozatte is a man to steer clear of, Jackson. And if you're headed toward Nacogdoches, watch out and don't take the south fork. It skirts Nacogdoches for a mighty good reason, which is why it's been called Contraband Trace or Smugglers Road since way back before you were born. Fozatte is quite a smuggler himself. As a lad, he was one of Jean Lafitte's pirates and smugglers down on Galveston Island. He brags about it. He's fought a dozen duels, so I've heard. He's dangerous, and doubly so when he's running slaves up from the coast. So is Hominy Baines, another smuggler, horse thief, and outlaw from the States."

Horatio shook his head thoughtfully. "The Good Book says that 'Whoso diggeth a pit shall fall therein.' "

Roberts eyed Horatio narrowly. "Are you sure you came here to survey land, Mr. Jackson?"

"Are you an official of the Mexican government?" Jackson replied quickly.

"Yes, I'm alcalde of the Ayish Bayou District."

"Then I'm a surveyor, Mr. Roberts."

Their glances met and held a moment, and neither man missed the twinkle in the other's eyes. Then Roberts gave Jackson a friendly slap on the shoulder and said he heard Martha's call to come and eat.

"She sets a fine table, Jackson, one that you might enjoy saying thanks over. Been a long time since we've heard the food blessed in good old Tennessee language."

Inside the house, Jackson looked at the pine floor and saw a Negro girl sweeping it with a broom made of sedge straw. The furniture was made from hand-sawn pine, and the seats of the chairs were of deerskin and rawhide. Only the sofa had been imported.

The food was simple, but worthy of Horatio's sincere thanks to the Lord and his mortal hosts. Huge chunks of beef, roasted brown, were piled on a platter, and there were bowls of fresh turnips and greens and lye hominy, as well as peach preserves, fresh-churned butter, and all the buttermilk one could drink. The staff of life was corn bread called "pound cake" by the colonists, because the corn was ordinarily pounded into a rough meal. Roberts had his own gristmill, however, and the bread was of finer texture.

"A man's got to be handy with tools out here," Elisha said. "We make our own wagons, saddles, shoes, churns, and more." He praised the skills of his "contract laborers."

"What do you mean by contract laborers?" Horatio asked.

"I was referring to my slaves, of course. Since you don't know the law, I'll explain. The Constitution of Coahuila and Texas prohibited slaves when Austin got his grant to settle a colony in 1824, so Austin prevailed on the legislature to pass a law which legalized labor contracts. This was a neat way of evading the intent of the Constitution. Then in 1829 the Mexican government passed a law freeing the slaves. When nobody paid any attention to that, Mr. Austin tried to get the colonists to really set the slaves free. Naturally everybody protested and did nothing about it. Then last year the Mexican Congress decreed that no more Americans, white or black, should come to Texas, but they're still coming and we don't stop them. What's more, Mexico established customhouses along the Texas coast and levied duties on all foreign imports. And now I hear the Mexicans are sending troops to enforce the customs laws and collect fees. I smell trouble. What do you think about it, Jackson?"

"I don't know enough about it to answer that," Horatio replied. Forking another piece of beef onto his plate, he said, "It seems that every generation feels it is going through a revolution of one kind or another. We all sense some new development in history, like a cloud on a horizon that keeps changing its shape. Maybe that's what's happening in Texas, Mr. Roberts. Fact is, I think trouble is bound to come to Texas."

Elisha Roberts removed his pipe from a corner of his mouth and said, "On account of customhouses and troops?"

"These things could bring it to a head, but I reckon it was already there, has been there, brewing, since 1824. Us Americans are a stubborn, independent people to start with. We don't like laws that take even a little of our freedom away from us, such as Mexican laws that forbid trial by jury and the right to worship as we choose. But our hankerin' for land and wealth sort of makes us overlook these things and take the 4428 acres of land for thirty dollars which the Mexican government gives to a married man to settle in Texas and say we're good Catholics. We're not exactly honest with the Mexican government, and we're not honest with ourselves. Therefore we sow seeds of trouble when we pretend to think like Mexicans."

"I never thought of it that way, Mr. Jackson."

Horatio grinned. "Oh, you thought about it, all right, Mr. Roberts. You just never admitted it."

"Reckon you could be right," Roberts laughed, stuck the corncob pipe back in his mouth, passed a dish of sweet-potato cobbler his wife had dished up to his guest, and said, "Continue, Mr. Jackson."

"I've talked too much already. Always do, I suppose. A man finds one of his kind who's a good listener and he don't know when to shut up. But a man's a strange critter. He'll track a bear and risk his neck for its skin. He'll tread where he oughtn't to, and go against his own good judgment because he's too stubborn to quit."

"That's why you came to Texas to preach, Mr. Jackson?"

"Now I was talking about Texans and possible trouble with Mexico," Horatio replied. "And the way I see it, the Texans aren't about to turn and run if trouble comes." Glancing at Mrs. Roberts, he said, "Ma'am, I don't know when it was that I tasted such good food. And I'm right ashamed of the way I went after it."

Rising, he faced his host. "Now how much do I owe you, sir?"

Roberts said, "Just say a prayer for us every now and then."

"I pay as I go, Mr. Roberts, so we'll just kneel right here and now."

2

The three wagons bound for San Felipe de Austin were still some two miles east of the Ayish Bayou settlement when Jonathan Mundy stopped the wagon and opened the canvas flap behind the driver's seat. After inquiring about his wife, who had been ill since their stay at Fort Jessup in Louisiana, he asked Jane Wells to drive while he stretched his legs.

Jane welcomed the opportunity to leave the interior of the groaning canvas-top. Spring was in the air. The late afternoon sun played on the pines and sent shafts of light deep into the forests. Ahead, a redbud tree held her gaze with its great clumps of tiny magenta-colored blossoms. Minutes later Jane braked the wagon to a stop and got to the ground to gather a few clumps of the blossoms. The lead wagon stopped also, and Mr. Weatherly voiced his displeasure at the delay—which caused Mr. Mundy to display his irritation. Now wasn't it like a woman to stop a whole caravan to pick a few flowers? He said more, and Jane politely told him that he'd said enough, that she was not a servant but a passenger who had paid her fare.

Mundy stroked his red beard thoughtfully. As though policy dictated his reply, he said, "Accept my apology, Miss Jane. Reckon this wild country and them riders made us all jumpy. Never knew whether that Frenchman was going to rob us or not. I'm right thankful he turned off the trail a few miles back."

Left alone, Jane breathed a weary sigh. The long trip was rough on a woman, and San Felipe de Austin was still far away. Then she was wondering what it was like down in Austin's colony, and next she was thinking about her Aunt Sally, who should have been a man, for she was every bit as strong as one and did the work of a man. But "Aunt Sal" had a big heart. In the fall of 1826 she had filled her wagon with tools and set out for Texas to help the colonists down on the Brazos.

The sun was slipping behind a blue cloud just above a distant hill when the Ayish settlement came into view. Jane was taking in the scene of prosperous-looking fields, tilled land, barns, and houses when one of the mules stumbled. The animal continued to limp, and the two wagons ahead left the Mundys far in the rear.

Night had fallen when the wagon finally joined the others at Elisha Roberts Campground. Jane stepped wearily to the ground, turned her head toward the big house, and sniffed the aroma of cooked food. She was hungry, and she was tired of the same company. She had enjoyed helping Susanna Gaines last evening, if only for relief from the same desultory topics of conversation. Now she began to wonder what she would find here.

Nora Mundy was calling her. Where was Jonathan? My, but she was weak! Did Jane think they could find another mule, or would they have to remain behind in this awful wilderness, and would Jane please ask the people here to prepare her a broth? She preferred chicken broth.

"Very well, Miss Nora." As Jane turned toward the house, a tall man appeared at her side. Startled, she looked up into the face of the preacher-surveyor who had returned her lost box the day before.

"Evening, ma'am," he said, removing a battered hat. "I was told by Mrs. Weatherly that Mrs. Mundy is ill."

"Yes," Jane replied curiously. "However, I don't imagine she's in need of a surveyor, Mr. Jackson. And she's hardly sick enough to have you read her title clear to a mansion in the sky."

Jackson's brows lifted and a grin spread across his face. Before he could shape a reply, she turned and walked toward the house, leaving him staring after her. "Well, well, Horatio!" he said. "Like you observed yesterday, there's a right-spirited woman."

He studied her with mounting interest until she disappeared from view, then looked at the wagon and asked if he could talk to Mrs. Mundy.

A quarter hour later, Jane emerged from the Robertses' house with a bowl of steaming broth and a plate of corn bread. Suddenly she stopped and stared incredulously at what she saw under the porch lantern. "Impossible!" she said. Yet there was Mrs. Mundy, accompanied by Mr. Jackson, moving up the porch steps. And if Miss Nora's expression reflected her true feelings, she had made a startling recovery. Smiling at Jane, she looked at the broth and said:

"My dear, I won't be needing that. Mr. Jackson here thinks I should eat hearty."

"But, Miss Nora, are you able to be up?"

"My goodness, yes, child! How can a body count one's many blessings and appreciate the wonders of this great land of Texas flat on one's back?"

As Jane looked from Mrs. Mundy to the buckskin-clad curiosity who was preacher and surveyor, Horatio Jackson cocked a brow at her and, to confound her further, gave her a sly wink of an eye. Then Mrs. Roberts appeared and urged Jane to hurry and eat, for Elisha had prevailed on Mr. Jackson to lead everybody, including the slaves, in singing religious songs."

"Thanks, Mrs. Roberts. I'm really not very hungry."

The moon was larger than it had been the night before, and it stood higher in the heavens. Jane watched it climb, saw it struggle against the onslaught of large and small clouds that sailed in from the south. As it continued to shine, she soon forgot Jackson and her own pique. A moon was made for dreams, however vague, and she sat on the grass with her back to a wheel of Mundy's wagon and let half-formed dreams speak for themselves.

Perhaps she should have taken the St. Louis lawyer's proposal of marriage more seriously. Her Aunt Minerva, with whom she had lived since her father's death in 1826, had thought so, as had many of her friends. True, Joseph Pearce, scion of a wealthy river shipper and landowner, had been both handsome and attentive; a good catch, beyond any doubt. Moreover, and her aunt had hammered home the fact, a woman of twenty-one was practically an old maid already; she should be married and the mother of at least two children.

Jane had tried to convince herself that she loved Joseph. She had almost done so, but not quite. On the other hand, she had never fully convinced herself that she did not love him. Even now, she wasn't sure. Joseph had written to her in Natchez, begging her to return. She read his letter daily. She wished to return to him and then again she had no desire to see him. She was a strange, stubborn, vacillating woman who didn't really know what she wanted.

"Which is why I came to Texas," she said pensively. Then almost wonderingly, she added, "Probably to marry some uneducated pioneer and live in a log house with a dirt floor and raise six children, and all the while wishing I had married Joseph."

But she knew herself better than that, and she blamed the last thought on the moon. No, Jane Wells would never seriously wish she had married someone other than the man she took to be her husband, because when and if she said the marriage vows it would be for love and for always, regardless of circumstances. However, one could not help dreaming about a fine house and luxurious furnishings.

But dreams were wishes, and wishes were foolish, and the moon wasn't to be trusted. Besides, she was hungry, and the night air was rather cold. She rose and went to the rear of the wagon for a shawl.

While searching her small trunk, she heard Mr. Mundy talking to someone about a mule. The voices moved closer, and Mundy was telling the other man what a fine mule Old Blue was. Just a little lame at present, but within a few days he would be as good as new. And he would "swap Old Blue for the mule the nigger rode, and ask nothin' to boot. Now how does that strike you Mr. Jackson?"

Jane listened. Now Jackson was saying:

"Strikes me that you're either mighty ambitious, Mr. Mundy, or you take me for a fool. Now I'm a swappin' man, but when I think about tradin' a healthy mule for a lame one, I'm also thinkin' about lookin' at the mule first and then listenin' for some money to boot."

"You say that to me? About the finest mule ever to come out of Missouri? Why, look here, Jackson, I was offered forty dollars for Old Blue by the quartermaster at Fort Jessup. Man, I'm takin' a real skinnin' when I offer to trade Old Blue for that starved, one-eyed mule o' yourn."

Jackson was soon examining Old Blue. After due reflection he said, "You mean he offered you forty dollars? It's hard to tell which one of you was the craziest, the soldier for offerin' such a sum or you for not takin' it, Mr. Mundy."

"I see you don't know mule flesh, stranger. Where I come from folks hearin' you talk that way would wonder whether you was seein' your first mule or was a half-wit."

"Sure. I lived in Missouri myself, Mr. Mundy, and long enough to know a mule like yours can't last long. Not with those teeth."

"What's wrong with his teeth?"

"Nothin', except they're about ready to fall out."

Black and forth it went, in the finest tradition of the art of horse trading. Each man praised his own animal and energetically pointed out the flaws, real or imagined, in the other's. To have done otherwise would have branded them novices. A crowd gathered, for this was rural sport at its best. Mundy soon painted Jackson's mule as a worthless creature, hopelessly blind, sway-backed, stubborn as a woman, all "balk" and no "go," and probably ready to "lay down and die."

"He might be thinkin' about that, all right," Jackson said dryly, "considering what you did to your mule. Probably been callin' him Old Blue since you were knee high to a duck. At least he looks that old. Poor old fellow, he's plumb wore out, worked to death, disillusioned, and weary of it all. Why, he couldn't make it to Nacogdoches if he was drivin' and you was pullin', Mr. Mundy."

Jane could not help noticing how Jackson kept dropping his *g*'s. Perhaps he considered it in his favor to assume a backwoods speech in keeping with his appearance. In any case, he was drawing laughter at Mundy's expense. Then Jackson was walking away, and Mundy was saying:

"Hold on, friend! I'm out of my head, but I'll be charitable and give you a dollar to boot!" Jackson kept going. "Two dollars!" Mundy went to five hurriedly and, getting no response, said, "Ten, Jackson!" Jackson stopped and asked if he heard fifteen. Mundy fumed and said the mule wasn't worth that with bridle and saddle thrown in, and Jackson began to walk away again. "Twelve, and that's my limit!" When he got up to fifteen dollars, Jackson returned.

"All right, Mr. Mundy. I'm being cheated good and proper, but I need the money." Turning toward Roberts and the audience, Jackson said, "Now don't you fellers laugh at me too much for lettin' this wagon man skin me bone-deep."

As the audience departed for the benches in the campground area, Mundy led Jackson's mule toward the barn. Then Jackson called Wash, who was mourning the loss of his blue-lipped mount, and said to the Negro:

"Look, Wash, here's the trouble with Old Blue. Now keep your mouth shut and don't remove this rock from the hoof until after the Mundys leave here."

"Not till then? How come, Rev'ren'?"

"Didn't I tell you not to call me Reverend in Texas, Wash? And you'd better remember that. Now about that rock in Old Blue's hoof. Since the Lord didn't send me to Texas to make enemies, it's better for that old skinflint Mundy to think he bested me in the trade."

Jane had heard enough of the conversation to understand what had happened. And now this crowning deception! Just what sort of adventurer was this gangling, cunning, unpredictable man who had worked a miracle of sorts with Mrs. Mundy and, next, had mulcted Mr. Mundy of fifteen dollars? While she grudgingly admitted her admiration for anyone who could do that to the selfish wagoner, she could never admire a false prophet.

Her puzzled gaze followed Jackson on to the moonlit clearing bordering the wagon camps where a crowd was assembling. A strange man, indeed, she mused. Twice in as many days he had crossed her path, each time handing her a double-barreled surprise. She could not help asking now just what he would come up with next.

Jane soon had the answer to this question. She saw him in the moonlight, standing on a tree stump before the assembled pioneers, their families and slaves; and she heard him telling them that Alcalde Roberts had invited him to sing and read from the Scriptures.

"Now I don't reckon the President of Mexico or the Pope could object to that, folks, especially when both of them exhort the people to love God and each other and deal justly with one another." He drew a round of laughter with what he said next: "And since their ain't a priest or a Mexican general in these parts, I reckon it's up to this old Tennessee boy to take the stump tonight."

Producing a Bible, he raised it and said, "My good friends and neighbors, this Good Book tells us in these words, 'For where two or three are gathered together in my name, there am I also.' "

A man cried, "Amen, brother!" Then Jackson was asking everyone there to join in and sing with him "Hark, My Soul, It Is the Lord."

As he began to sing loud and clear, Jane cocked her head and listened. When her critical ear could detect no flaw in his fine baritone voice, she said in open amazement:

"Why, that mule-trading hypocrite can really sing!"

Minutes later she reluctantly made her way toward the gathering.

CHAPTER 4

Dogwood trees were in full bloom when Jackson reached the hill overlooking the old pueblo of Nacogdoches. Masses of snow-white blossoms under the sheltering trees met his eye as a good omen. It was one of those years, he had been told by a settler, that the redbud, dogwood, and wisteria burst into blossom almost simultaneously. Perhaps this also augured well. In any event, he had met with no trouble since leaving Elisha Roberts' place two days after the wagons bound for San Felipe had departed.

However, the sight that held his gaze now could mean trouble unless he exercised caution. Below him, nestled between hills, was the gateway to Spanish Texas. From his position he could see the Mexican tricolor of green, white, and red waving over the Stone House, a building which had held in the past such famous prisoners as Philip Nolan and Peter Ellis Bean. He had at last reached the Mexican stronghold of Nuestra Señora del Pilar de Nacogdoches.

"There she is, Wash, all peaceful and quiet. But don't let it fool you. Mr. Roberts said this was the place where the powder keg has always been, with the fuse handy. The King of Spain wanted this town and the King of France wanted it, and Mexico aims to keep it. This town was the target for all sorts of filibustering expeditions—Philip Nolan's, the Gutérrez-Magee, James Long's—all trying to take over Texas, all empire-minded.

"Well, we aren't trying to raise a flag to replace the Mexican eagle, 'cause there happens to be a whole garrison of soldiers down there. And over yonder—that must be what's left of the old mission Mr. Roberts mentioned. They called it Nuestra Señora de Guadalupe. This town is Catholic, so don't make the mistake of calling me Reverend. Understand?"

"Yassuh."

"And be sure to keep our Bibles and Protestant literature covered. Now let's mosey on down the hill and lay in a few supplies."

Arriving at Plaza Principal, they watered the animals at the public well. Jackson then tied them to a hitching post, left Wash to look after them, and sauntered down the street. Near a general store several Mexican soldiers were engaged in conversation with a priest; and within earshot, settlers discussed the weather, the prospects for crops, and, of course, politics. A few were openly critical of the Mexican President Bustamante for allowing the establishment of customhouses along the Texas coast, because duty on goods raised prices on necessities as well as luxuries.

"I for one," Jackson overheard a colonist say, "ain't payin' the duty prices. Not while Cap'n Fozatte sells cheaper down on Smugglers Road—"

"Quiet, Henry! Colonel Bean just passed."

"Yeah. And he's a fine one. Leavin' to command the new Fort Teran the Mexicans are building. No tellin' who they'll send here to replace Peter Bean. But back to Fozatte, I got word that he'll be down on the road soon with some real fancy goods."

Everywhere he turned, Jackson heard men discussing the customs duties imposed by Mexico, the colonists' opinions of Fisher and Bradburn, Americans appointed by the Mexican government to enforce the customs laws. There was also talk of Cherokee Indian uprisings in East Texas.

Men turned to eye Jackson, and several spoke to him. "You from Tennessee or Kentucky, stranger?" one asked. "Tennessee, eh? So am I. Well, I guess you know there's no land for a newcomer around here. Might find some swampland down toward the coast."

Jackson passed Mexicans in large, wide-brimmed hats and wearing bolero jackets. A fat Latin woman, clad in bright red skirt and black blouse, her gold looped earrings dangling, tried to sell him a basket. From another he purchased tortillas and *cabron*—"Fresh roasted this day, señor!" With the first bite, his eyes began to water and sweat ran down his face. "Why you cry, *amigo?*" she asked, and he replied, "Because you put all the pepper in Mexico on your roasted goat, señora." She laughed, and her children and her relatives laughed when Jackson rushed to the well and tried to quench the fire.

"Por Dios! Qué hombre!"

A tall man in immaculate Army uniform paused at the

sounds of merriment. To the fat woman, he said, "*Qué hay?*" The woman did not look up at the officer as she replied, "*El Americano, señor. Mamo el tramojo.*" She laughed, and the officer said crisply, "*Por qué?*" The woman, her gaze still on Jackson, answered, "*Chile caliente. Buena!*"

"*Basta!*"

The Mexican woman turned quickly to see who dared to reprimand her. Upon recognizing Colonel José de las Piedras, Commandant of the 12th Permanent Battalion, she paled. Then she was gesticulating and talking rapidly. She had meant no harm, and the illustrious colonel knew she was a poor woman and a good mother.

"*Si, si,* Amelia! I know! I know! But we must be kind to the Americanos. They are good people. Now you apologize to the offended *hombre* and I shall forget the incident."

Only then did Piedras level a curious eye at the big American whose mouth was scorched. As he studied Jackson, his black brows arched, and he was comparing the man to the description of a religious offender, whom a colonist had described as a tall buckskin-clad man with ginger-brown hair. The informer, a wagoner on his way to the Austin Colony, had reported that the man had held Protestant religious services at Roberts Campground and had sold a few Bibles also; that his name was Jackson.

Piedras shrugged. "A matter for Colonel Bean," he said. As for himself, he had no desire to disturb the peace in this predominantly Anglo-American town. The establishment of a customhouse at Anahuac, on Galveston Bay, had stirred up enough dissension here already. So as long as the suspected preacher abstained from theft, murder, and smuggling, he was free to go his way. However . . .

Recalling that the informer was still camped on the banks of Banita Creek just beyond the church, Piedras decided it might be wise to warn this Señor Jackson about the religious laws in effect. Accordingly, he walked to the well and introduced himself to the big man.

"*Buenas dias,* Colonel. My mouth's singed, but my name's still Horatio Jackson. My business? Why, Colonel, I'm a surveyor by trade."

"And by choice, señor?" Piedras twisted the end of a black mustache as he asked the question in friendly, almost jocular manner. Before Horatio could reply, he said, "There are few secrets in this country, *amigo mio.* I hear you preached a fine sermon up on the Ayish Bayou."

"Well, Colonel, I—"

The other lifted a hand. "Say nothing to incriminate yourself. And do nothing in Nacogdoches to cause either of us embarrassment." Smiling, he said, "Now that we have reached an understanding, perhaps you will join me in a glass of wine."

"I don't touch it, Colonel, but I'd be happy to cool my burned tongue with milk." As they walked toward a saloon, Horatio said, "Now I'm wondering just who could have told you that I preached a sermon up on the Ayish."

"That, Señor Jackson, must constitute one of the few secrets I mentioned."

As they neared the door of the saloon, the Mundys and Jane Wells walked past the place. Horatio paused, tipped his hat to the ladies, spoke to Jonathan Mundy, and introduced them to Colonel Piedras. When Mundy admitted to having already met the colonel, Jackson began to wonder if it was he who had told Piedras about the Ayish Bayou religious service. Something in Mundy's expression, the intentness of his gaze, as though he were trying to convey a message to the official, almost confirmed Jackson's suspicion. It also provoked a feeling of hurt at being betrayed by one of his kind. Perhaps he had misjudged the man. He decided to fish for the answer.

Placing a hand on the wagoner's shoulder, he augmented this gesture with an engaging smile. "That was a fine gathering we had up at Ayish, Mr. Mundy. I felt that the Lord was amongst us, didn't you?"

Mundy opened his mouth to speak, but no sound was forthcoming.

Horatio inquired of Mrs. Mundy's health. Then, with a promise to drop by that evening, he raised his hat and followed the colonel into the saloon.

Once inside, he said to Piedras, "Well, Colonel, seems one of your few secrets revealed itself. And, the Lord willing, I'm going to make a convert of that man if it takes me the rest of my life to do it."

"*Bueno,* señor! But please, not in the Department of Nacogdoches!"

2

Jane had been silent all the way back to the wagon camp. She could not quite fathom the strapping man who pretended to be a surveyor, who prayed earnestly, spoke the Scriptures with seemingly inspired zeal, sang in a manner to stir one's soul, then with no shame whatsoever entered a saloon. A baffling man, indeed, one who broke the law and had the unmitigated gall to admit it in the presence of the military head of the district.

She looked at Mr. Mundy, who seemed every bit as displeased as preoccupied. He sat on a tree stump. With harness to mend, he just sat there, glaring at the lazy creek. Now Jane was wondering again why he had turned red of face when Jackson mentioned the Ayish Bayou services. She could understand his surprise and subsequent anger when Mr. Weatherly, who, while riding past them on the plaza, had laughed and told Mundy that the mule he had traded to Jackson no longer limped. It was quite obvious that Mundy didn't enjoy being the loser in any trade.

Nor did Jane wish to admit that Horatio Jackson emerged the better man in other ways. Yet, despite her positive dislike of any person who practiced deceit, she did admit it. However, the admission served only to emphasize her poor opinion of Jackson. And when he visited the camp that evening, she would not see him. And that was that!

With her mind made up, she joined Mrs. Mundy in preparing venison stew, corn pone, and coffee. With nightfall, everything was ready, though the awaited guest had not arrived. Another hour passed, and still Mrs. Mundy said they should wait a little longer. Mr. Jackson would come, for he had promised to do so. Mundy scoffed, reminding her that she had seen the "preachin' man" enter the saloon, that he was probably good and drunk by now.

"I don't believe it!"

"Maybe you don't want to believe it, Nora. Maybe you favor a man like him over me. You a married woman at that, cravin' the likes of a deceivin', Psalm-singin' hypocrite! Why, a shame on you, woman!"

"The old devil's got a hold on you, Jonathan Mundy! You know I don't crave for no man! I crave of the spirit, and I ask for upliftin' and cheerin' for the soul, 'cause a mortal needs a song and the Word same as corn bread and water. So I'd be right obliged if you'd speak up and say you didn't mean them hurtin' words."

"I ain't a retractin' man, Nora."

"So you ain't. But you're sure a stubborn one. And more'n likely you're goin' to be a single one."

"What you mean by that, woman?"

"That unless you tell me you spoke them terrible words to me out of pure rile and didn't mean 'em, I'm stayin' right here and you can go on to San Felipe by yourself."

"I didn't come to Texas for no single man's grant of land, Nora."

"Then you better start retractin' right now, Jonathan Mundy!"

Jane had heard enough. She left them and walked toward the Weatherlys' wagon, wondering why Jackson had broken his promise to visit them. While she didn't care in the least, she told herself, she did think he should be ashamed of himself for adding false promise to his host of shortcomings.

3

As Jane Wells silently reprimanded him and watched the late moon lift lazily over the hill east of Nacogdoches, Horatio Jackson sat the saddle some ten miles northwest of the town. For company, he had a body of Mexican soldiers and a dozen outraged Anglo-Texans, all riding toward the Cherokee camp in the vicinity of a creek called Arroyo Loco.

The mission he was on had had its beginning late that afternoon when a settler named Peters, from up on the Santos Coy Survey, galloped up to the Stone House and demanded an audience with Colonel Bean. Upon learning that Bean had departed for San Antonio two hours earlier, Joshua Peters appeared in the plaza and let it be known that the Cherokees had stolen his three-year-old son. A crowd soon gathered, and within minutes men left to get their horses and guns. It was high time, they declared, to drive the "ornery, thievin' savages" out of East Texas.

A corporal of the 12th Permanent Battalion rushed to garrison headquarters and asked to see Colonel Piedras at once. The colonel had departed not a half hour earlier with a troop to chase a band of smugglers, so Lieutenant Ariola heard the corporal's story of impending trouble and ordered a platoon readied.

Jackson arrived at the plaza and saw the crowd. A small man who seemed to carry some authority was advising the men to do nothing rash; rather, they should determine the extent of guilt on the part of the Indians, then let the authorities handle the matter. A colonist challenged him saying:

"Ain't no time for peaceful talk when the Cherokees steal our children, Mr. Sterne."

Jackson eyed Sterne with respect, for Elisha Roberts had told him about Adolphus Sterne, a young Jewish merchant of Nacogdoches, civic leader, and friend to all, especially the needy. In 1826 he had smuggled munitions in barrels of coffee out of New Orleans to aid the Fredonians. When the rebellion was put down, the Mexican authorities had sentenced him to be shot. He had been spared through the influence of the

Masonic order, of which he was a member. Now Sterne was saying to the irate colonist:

"Nor is it time for a war we don't want, Rufus. Trouble will bring more troops and slow the plowing and planting. So don't go out and start shooting until you're sure that's the last resort. First talk to the Cherokees."

"Talk? Who the hell talks Cherokee, Dolphus?"

"I do," Jackson spoke up.

Sterne looked at Jackson. After taking him in from head to foot, he finally asked, "Who are you?" Upon learning that he was Horatio Jackson, once a lawyer in Tennessee and next a surveyor in Arkansas, Sterne extended a hand and said, "Welcome to Texas, Mr. Jackson." Next he asked where the newcomer had learned to speak the Cherokee language.

"In a Cherokee camp, sir, where I learned to wrestle with the bucks and a lot more."

"Since you appear to be a man capable of taking care of yourself, and since Colonel Bean received official notice from San Antonio that I'm the new alcalde, I hereby appoint you the man to negotiate with the Cherokees. Do I hear any objection?"

"We never saw this man before, Dolphus."

"Neither did I. But look him over now."

The men did just that. Then they demanded some assurance that he wasn't a "damn'd Injun lover," and that he would represent them and not the Indians. "Well, what about it, Jackson?" one asked.

"Well, it seems I was appointed to negotiate. Now since I know the Cherokee, I'll say this much, men, they've got laws the same as we have, and if one of their tribe violates a law he's punished. What's more, if the whole tribe had been in on the stealing of Mr. Peters' boy, they wouldn't have stopped at that. They'd be raiding right and left. So if you want me along, I'll go. If you don't just say so. It won't hurt my feelings."

They decided to accept Jackson. Several minutes later Lieutenant Ariola and his troop appeared on the scene. . . .

And now it was past nine in the evening. The Cherokee camp lay ahead at the edge of a large clearing near a creek. A fire burned and several Indians were seated about it. When their dogs began to yap, Jackson reined up short and said:

"It might be better if you fellows waited here while I go powwow with them."

"All right," one of the men replied. "But if you ain't back in half an hour, I'm ridin' in a-shootin'."

Jackson said, "What's your name, mister?"

"Bill Rogers. Why you ask?"

"So I'll know who to mop up this red dirt with just in case anybody comes a-shootin'."

With that, he rode off at a slow trot. At the edge of the Indian camp, he slowed his mount to a walk and approached the campfire with an arm upraised, to indicate that he came in peace. As the Cherokees swarmed about him, he spoke to them in their tongue. He was Red Fox, a close friend of the Cherokees in Arkansas. He was here on a special mission. He brought no gifts, unless a continuation of the peace with the white men was a gift.

He seated himself on the ground and they did likewise. Then he asked if their leader, "The Bowl," was among them. No, Chief Bowles was absent. He was hunting beyond the land where the sun went to rest. Then who was the sub-chief?

"I, Antonio Yellow Bear. Now what brings Red Fox to our camp to speak of peace as though it runs from us like a fleet deer? Did we not come to this land and help the Me-hi-canos end trouble among the white men in the Fredonian Rebellion?"

"True," Jackson replied. "But peace is like a leaf in the wind. The reason, a man named Peters, who lives a few miles from the village of Nacogdoches, reports that his son could not be found after Cherokees passed his place this afternoon. He says they stole his boy."

"He lies!"

"No, he does not lie," Jackson said. "He could be mistaken, but he does not speak with forked tongue. Why not look into the minds of your people, Antonio Yellow Bear? Both you and I know that only the great spirit is without any fault."

The Indian's eyes burned into Jackson's and he said he would have an answer for Red Fox on the next sun. He leaped up and glared in hostile manner when Jackson advised that he could not wait that long, that he must carry a reply to the angry whites within the hour. The offended leader spoke his unyielding opinion of the selfish, domineering whites who treated the redmen as though they were dirt under their feet; who cheated and robbed the Indians, sold them the water that crazed them, and molested their women. If that was the price of peace, then the Cherokee would prepare for war.

"Who speaks this way?" Jackson demanded. "Is it The Bowl, great chief of the Cherokees? No. I hear the voice of a boy who has yet to gain the wisdom of a man, much less that of a chieftain."

Antonio Yellow Bear picked up his hatchet and ordered a

tribesman to hand one to Red Fox. Horatio accepted the tomahawk, then flung it aside. "I came in peace, a brother. I leave in peace. The child whom The Bowl left in charge can save his hatchet for the Me-hi-cano soldiers and white men who will come."

Standing by his horse, Jackson said, "What shall I tell them, Antonio Yellow Bear?"

"Tell them to return when the sun is straight over our heads."

"Tell them yourself. They are on the edge of the clearing yonder."

"Then tell them to wait until the moon is directly overhead on this night, Red Fox."

Jackson rode off, aware that he had another battle ahead. Sure enough, it began with his announcement. The settlers wanted no part of waiting several hours. Better to ride down on the Cherokee camp with guns in hand and let the "varmints" know they meant business. Didn't *el teniente* agree? Lieutenant Ariola wasn't sure. After all, the alcalde had warned them all against unnecessary violence. He did not wish to offend the civil authority, nor did he relish the wrath of Colonel Piedras, who was trying to keep peace in the Department of Nacogdoches.

"The devil with excuses!" gaunt Bill Rogers exclaimed. "What the hell are we here for anyhow? I say we ride down there guns a-poppin'."

"I say we don't," Jackson replied. "Better to give Yellow Bear time to find the boy, if he's in the Cherokee camp."

"You're mighty damn cocky for a newcomer, Jackson." Turning to the Texans, Rogers said, "He's probably in cahoots with the savages, ready to split a neat ransom with them."

The words were hardly out of his mouth when a hand grasped his shirt collar. "Now I'm a peaceful man, Mr. Rogers, but I don't tolerate talk like that. So I suggest you either apologize like a man or fight like one."

Rogers studied Jackson a moment. Then, quick as a cat, he lunged forward, arms swinging. Lieutenant Ariola tried to stop them, but the men restrained him. They liked a good scrap and, since the pair were evenly matched, this promised to be a real Donnybrook. It was just that while it lasted. It ended all too soon, however, when by some trick or skill Jackson caught Rogers by the arm and sent him flying through the air. When Rogers finally came around, he got up and said he'd give Jackson a whole dollar to show him how he'd done it.

"You mean again?" Horatio said. "Where you want to land this time?"

This evoked laughter, which to Jackson was a good omen. The fight had broken the crowd tension, an ominous thing in time of trouble. While he had gone against his own teachings, he had served the Lord and man with a little violence that might prevent bloodshed on this night. So maybe the Lord would realize that it was a good trade all around, that is if the men had decided to curb their impatience for a while.

"Well," Horatio said, "all in favor of giving Yellow Bear the time he asked for raise your hands."

Joshua Peters spoke up suddenly. "Hold on a minute. Them bucks could use that time to get my boy a long way from here. What do you say to that, Jackson?"

"I say you could be right. But I also say Yellow Bear didn't speak with a forked tongue. As your representative I accepted the time limit and he believed we would keep our word. And faith is a two-sided thing in dealing with people, Mr. Peters."

"Jackson's right about that, all right," Bill Rogers said. "I vote we wait, Joshua."

Soon the dissenters agreed to go along with Jackson. Peters, while not convinced, found himself outnumbered. He conceded with a grudging statement that Jackson had better be right, for if the Indians used the time allowed them to move his boy to some other place Jackson would answer to him personally.

When the moon reached its zenith, Horatio said it was time for him to return to the Cherokee camp. He would take Joshua Peters with him. The man called Rufus demanded that they all go, but Jackson refused on the grounds that the Cherokees were a proud people and that it would not be a good policy for the whites to make a show of force.

Upon reaching the Indian camp, Jackson got off his horse, leaving Peters mounted, and moved through the circle to where Yellow Bear sat. He asked no questions, said nothing whatever. Finally Yellow Bear led the way to a teepee, threw the flap back from the opening, and entered. Jackson followed and, seeing no one but a fat woman sitting cross-legged on the ground, he asked to see the boy.

"Boy at his home by now. I send him there by my braves."

"Then why bring me here?"

"Squaw there stole boy. We take her before council, then drive her from tribe."

Jackson eyed the woman. Knowing her people and their unyielding laws, he pitied her. He knew what happened to a banished squaw. She would be refused by her own kind and shunned by whites simply because she was Indian. He asked why she had taken the white boy, and she told him that she was unable to bear a child of her own; that she had borrowed the small boy to hold close to her heart; that she had meant to return him to his people soon.

Jackson left her and went directly to Peters. After relating all Yellow Bear and the woman had revealed, he said, "The Cherokees may steal a little but they don't lie. Your boy is at your place."

"By God, he better be! I'll soon find out."

"Yeah, you do that, Mr. Peters. And when you find him safe and sound, think about that Indian woman's punishment. She'll have to live like an animal in the woods until she either goes crazy or dies."

"Serves her right."

"Accordin' to Cherokee justice it does just that. But you aren't Cherokee."

"What the hell you drivin' at, anyhow?"

"I was only leadin' up to a fact. A pure and simple fact, Mr. Peters. Her crime was nothing more than love for your boy. You think on it."

Peters glared at Jackson a moment. "I still don't know what you're drivin' at, Jackson."

"You wouldn't like it if I told you."

"Wouldn't like what?"

Meeting the man's glance, Jackson said, "I was thinkin' of you more than the Indian woman, I reckon. You havin' her on your conscience in the dead of night and bein' unable to do a thing about it. Sayin' to yourself you could have saved her life by doin' what the Good Book says about forgivin' thine enemies and lovin' thy neighbor and becomin' a good Samaritan and—"

"Look here, Jackson, I didn't pass judgment on that squaw!"

"Course you didn't. And I'll be the first to agree with you that an Indian woman wouldn't be much help to Mrs. Peters with the chores and burdens until you good folks taught her how with kindness and patience. Why, she might even do a little thievin' at first. But it comes back to what I said, Mr. Peters, that you wouldn't like the idea if I told you."

Horatio watched Peters ride off into the night. He then searched out Antonio Yellow Bear and asked permission to talk to the Indian woman before she was banished from the tribe.

4

The sun was just peeping over the hill east of Nacogdoches on the following morning when Jackson rode into town. He had spent the night with one of the colonists after the party had stopped by Peters' house and learned that the boy had been returned to his home safe and sound.

Having left Wash, the mules, and his wares in the care of Adolphus Sterne for the night, Horatio felt it was his duty to call early and thank the man for his generosity, as well as to report to Sterne on the adventure of the night. He found the house and saw the owner on the long porch engaged in conversation with several freight wagoners. After they had departed to unload stores in the log building behind the house, Sterne invited Jackson to take breakfast with him.

Jackson's host was already informed on events of the night. After complimenting the newcomer for his service to all in the handling of a delicate situation that could have resulted in hostilities, Sterne invited Jackson to make his home in Nacogdoches. He saw little future for a surveyor, however. Perhaps Jackson would entertain ideas of practicing law, say if only as a steppingstone to the political opportunities which would surely be forthcoming in Texas.

While they were thus engaged over platters of fine food, Mrs. Sterne announced a visitor. Joshua Peters wished to see Adolphus on the porch, and he seemed rather upset.

"Didn't you invite him in, Rosine?" Sterne asked.

"No. And for a good reason, as you'll find out."

Sterne went outside. When he returned several minutes later, he looked at his guest and said, "Mr. Jackson, it might be a good idea for you to stay away from the plaza today. Peters is looking for you, and he's mad as a hornet."

Jackson nodded knowingly, and Sterne said, "So you did send the Cherokee woman to his house! Well, it seems Mrs. Peters decided to keep her despite her husband's objections. And Joshua, having lost a battle at home, is anxious to take you on."

Jackson lowered his coffee cup to the table, lifted bushy brows, and, in response to Sterne's chuckle, said, "I don't ordinarily wear out my welcome in a community in one day."

So saying, he rose and thanked his hosts for the fine food and hospitality and promised to ask the Lord to shower them with blessings. Outside, he scanned the wooded area and road and told Wash they would take to the brush and skirt the town. He stood a moment as if pondering his decision, then mumbled something about seeing Miss Jane at a more propitious time.

A half hour later Wash asked Jackson why they were sneaking through the woods and creek bottoms to avoid going through town. Horatio grinned, "It's like this, Wash. There are times to stand up and give a good account of one's self before the multitude. Then there are times, like now, when it's better to light out fast for some other place."

CHAPTER 5

Jackson and Wash emerged from pine thickets a few miles east of Nacogdoches and followed an old wagon trail that wound northeast. Bits of conversation overheard the night before had caused Jackson to alter his plan of riding down to Austin's colony on the lower Brazos.

The men had talked of thriving American settlements in the Tenehaw Bayou area, some thirty or forty miles from Nacogdoches back toward the Sabine River. About ten miles north of Elisha Roberts Ayish Bayou District was a community called Nashville. The Latham and Osborn families were upstanding citizens, the men had said, and Ben Osborn operated a store and Indian trading post, had a gristmill, and planted cotton. Jackson summed up his reasons for pointing toward the Neutral Ground in a few words:

"We'll work our way into Texas all over again, Wash."

"Yassuh. Hope we don't git the hide skint off our haids and then some befo' we even start down to Mistuh Austin's place. But who dat comin'? Could be de outlaw man Hominy Baines they tell yo' all to watch out fo'."

Horatio instinctively left the road for the cover of pines and underbrush. When a wagon and several horsemen moved on toward Nacogdoches, Jackson and Wash returned to the road. They plodded on until the sun overhead reminded them they were hungry. Although game was plentiful, a shot might attract the company of ruffians. They topped a high hill overlooking the rolling country before shooting a rabbit. Wash cooked it over a low fire while Jackson kept watch on the road in both directions. Following a "mighty lean meal," as Wash defined it, they moved on toward Attoyac Bayou.

Late that afternoon a log house appeared in a clearing. Young corn grew in long rows, and near the house a vegetable garden bordered a leaning barn. Jackson was eying the place with thoughts of hiring out for board and keep a few days when the quiet was broken by sounds of profanity. It lifted strong from a patch of corn behind a screen of trees and was directed at a mule named Damon. Poor Damon was every kind of "a goddam lop-eared son of a bitch"; and he'd pull the plow else Abner Bowser would club the hell out of him. The mule still refused to move, and Bowser began to fling whip and a string of spicy oaths that were amazingly wicked and original.

Horatio grinned. "You know, Wash, if I could preach with that sort of practical eloquence, I could chase the old devil out of Texas in no time."

He dismounted and walked to the field. There he introduced himself to the tall, big man with aggressive nose, red beard, and eyes that flashed like blue lightning. "Now, Mr. Bowser, you set a spell and think up some new cuss words to call old Damon while I turn a furrow."

"Who the goddam hell are you, stranger?"

"A mule tamer from Tennessee, that's who."

"Ain't you now?" the man said, handing Jackson the reins. "Go at it. Git that walleyed critter goin' if you can."

Horatio put his hands to the plow and let go with a Missouri mule driver's yell. Damon's ears lifted. The yell was repeated. Then Horatio began to sing: " 'Rock of Ages, cleft for me, Let me hide myself in Thee—' "

Damon began to move. He kept going. Horatio continued to sing, guide the plow around stumps, and turn the rich soil up to the corn. " 'Nothin in my hand I bring. Simply to Thy cross I cling—' " Verse after verse rang over the field, and a woman came out of the house and stared and listened, and several young boys and girls moved curiously out to the corn patch. And Bowser stood with whip in one hand, scratching his red beard with the other, saying over and over:

"Well, I'll be goddammed!"

Jackson and Wash helped milk the cows that evening. Jackson took ax in hand and reduced a log into wood for the crude stove. Mrs. Bowser set a fine table that night, fried chicken and flour gravy, turnips and greens from the garden, corn pone, and buttermilk.

"Eunice, set the milk pitcher 'fore Mr. Jackson," Bowser said to his wife. "You, Samantha, and you, Mary, fetch more turnipin greens. Make haste now." Turning to Horatio, he said, "What you think about them damn Mexicans settin' up customhouses down on the coast?" Then, to a boy who looked to be seven or eight, "Hiram, how many times I done told you to wipe your nose? Want your bottom whaled good, boy?"

Next, he was telling about pulling up stakes in Kentucky back in 1824. There he had known Benjamin Edwards, brother of Hayden, who secured an *empresario* contract from Mexico in 1825 to establish eight hundred families in East Texas. Bowser had been among the first to cross the old Neutral Ground. He had built Eunice and the children this fine house, one of the first to have a plank floor.

"Well, the Edwardses got mixed up in Mexican politics, land titles, and all, and defied the Mexican militia sent by the governor. That was the Fredonian Rebellion. Since then, I ain't sure I own any land at all, but I'm damn sure ready to fight to keep it."

When Bowser went out to feed the hogs after dinner, his wife said to Jackson, "You know that's the first time a blessing was ever said over a meal in this house. Abner just don't tolerate with God. Not a bit he don't. The only reason he let you say grace was on account of the chores you done. But he's a good man, Mr. Jackson, a good pa and honest. A mite strict and harsh, but he don't mean no harm."

Jackson nodded. He looked at the children, then at Eunice Bowser, still a fine-looking woman, who would no doubt go on bearing babies for an infidel. He was thinking the Lord needed to get a foot inside the door here when she said it was the first time that six of her nine children had ever heard a religious song.

"I don't count but eight," Jackson said.

"Ruth's in bed. She's ailin'. Got fever and pains down in her chest."

"Maybe I better look in on her, Mrs. Bowser."

"You good at doctorin', Mr. Jackson?"

"I've doctored a little here and there."

Jackson found Ruth, a girl of perhaps eleven or twelve, suffering a severe chill. The Negro mammy attending her was frightened. "She ain't doin' no better, Miss Eunice." Jackson placed a hand on the girl's forehead. Fever was high, and she coughed. Her breathing was short and gasping. He diagnosed it as pneumonia.

"Bring me raw eggs," he said. "And fix up some powdered mustard stirred with vinegar and flour—for a poultice on her chest. And I'll need some axle grease to put on first, else it'll blister her skin. Might boil a hog hoof for tea."

"Don't have any powdered mustard, Mr. Jackson."

"Then fetch red pepper and turpentine."

Jackson watched over the girl all that night. He fed her raw eggs, kept her wrapped in quilts, gave her juice squeezed from baked onions, as well as sassafras tea, and he knelt and prayed for her. Mrs. Bowser and the Negro mammy remained in the room also. Abner Bowser came in often to check on his daughter's condition. Upon finding Horatio praying aloud on one of his visits, he said:

"Prayin' ain't gonna do no good, Jackson."

Horatio said, "Excuse me a minute, Lord," and looked up at the man. "How do you know prayin' is no good? Ever try it?"

"No. Don't believe in it."

"Then you need prayin' for a lot more than your sick daughter, sir. But right now I don't want to burden the Lord with more than one thing at a time." Bowing his head again, he said, "Now where did I leave off, Lord?"

Before dawn spread its gray light over the hills, Ruth's fever broke. Her breathing became easier, and she fell asleep. Jackson thanked the Lord for stepping in to lend a hand to humble folk doing their best. But mortals couldn't quit now, he told Mrs. Bowser. So while he went out on the porch and caught a wink or two of sleep, he'd appreciate it if somebody would stand by to give the patient water and change the poultice. Turning from the bedside, he said:

"As it says in the Scripture, 'God will help her, and that right early.' "

Abner Bowser could restrain himself no longer. "Hogwash!" I don't believe that's in the Bible."

Horatio stopped still, squinted an eye shut. "Now maybe I'd show you if you could read."

"How come you think I can't read?"

"Oh, reckon I thought you might have grown up too stubborn to learn to read." All the while Jackson was thumbing through the pages of his pocket Bible. Then, putting a finger on the verse he had spoken, he said, "Right there, Mr. Bowser, in Psalm Forty-six."

Bowser eyed it. Rubbing his beard, he trained his blue eyes on his wife. "By God, Eunice, it's there, all right! But it don't mean a damn thing."

Horatio felt a surge of anger then. He wanted to take Bowser apart and persuade him with hard fists to accept Jesus as his Saviour. But he realized this would avail him nothing. He felt the challenge, and he vowed to one day make a convert out of this man. So he said with all the calm he could muster:

"There are ways of convincing a mule and there are ways

of convincing a man. Seems in Texas you have to strike a happy medium." Before Bowser could reply, he said, "Now if you'll allow me an hour's sleep, I'll finish plowin' that corn. The other patch needs weedin' and plowin' also, so I'll stick around a few days and help you catch up."

2

Several days later Jackson said farewell to the Bowsers. All but Ruth stood on the porch, and she waved at him from her window. Eunice wiped a tear from her cheek; and Abner, whose fields were weeded and plowed, welcomed Jackson to stop by any time. He did not know that Horatio had given his wife a Bible and songbook or that he had promised to pray for Abner.

Bowser was much in Jackson's mind that day. After he and Wash crossed Attoyac Bayou, he remarked on the man's good qualities. "Which are many, Wash. But his head is like old Damon's. I tried my very best to arouse in him curiosity about God and heaven and hell. He shut me up every time. Seems I have a lot to learn before I make a good preacher."

"Yassuh." Under Jackson's sharp glance, Wash said hastily, "I mean naw, suh."

They rode on up hills and down them. That night they made camp off the road and slept in a small clearing in a pine forest. With the first light of dawn, they moved on east. Shortly after sunrise they came to a log house and sniffed the tantalizing aroma of ham frying. Several horses and a number of wagons attested to visitors, which at that time of day pointed to sickness or death perhaps. Horatio told Wash to wait there and keep watch while he followed his nose to the skillet and whatever brought the settlers to this place.

The first man Jackson met was Ben Osborn, from the Nashville settlement. He was not a large man, but there was something big about him; it was in his expression, in the tolerance of brown eyes, in the strength and purpose of firm mouth, chin, and square jaw. It was in his voice as he gave Jackson the only welcome void of suspicion he had received in Texas since he had left Ayish Bayou.

Osborn said, "Jackson? Are you by any chance the Jackson Elisha Roberts spoke of?"

"Could be, sir. I've met him. A good man."

"Then maybe you came at the right time, Mr. Jackson. Seems Uncle Ned Zachary is on his deathbed. He's eighty-eight, and he keeps askin' for a preacher to say a few prayers for his soul and listen while he unburdens himself."

Jackson looked about him. Men stood with grave faces and women were stifling sobs and wiping their eyes. One tall, gaunt man was saying Uncle Ned had lived a full, useful life back in Kentucky; he had his shortcomings, as did all men, but he always stood up for a friend or a cause, be it with tongue or rifle.

Taking his Bible from a pocket, Jackson said, "Lead me to him, Mr. Osborn."

"Maybe you'd rather eat first, Jackson."

"Later, sir. The Lord ain't to be kept waitin'. But the Negro on a mule out there could use a bite to eat if it isn't asking too much."

Osborn introduced Jackson to the friends and relatives gathered there and led the way to the other room of the cabin. The hard-packed dirt floor was clean, and the logs were neatly whitewashed and chinked with clay. On a four-posted bed lay a man with long white whiskers. His watery gray eyes snapped alive as he squinted at Jackson.

"And who be he, Ben?"

"A preachin' man, Uncle Ned. Name's Jackson."

"Don't look like one. Where you from, son?"

"Tennessee, sir," Jackson replied.

"Runnin'?"

"No. Came to Texas by choice."

"Know the Scriptures? Do, huh? Right off, what's the first book o' the New Testament? . . . Matthew, ye say. Right, as I recollect. Now say me a verse from the Bible, real quick."

" 'Jesus wept.' "

"He'll do, Ben. That is if he don't pray that short. A man needs a good boost up to them pearly gates. You agree, Jackson?"

"That I do, Uncle Ned," Jackson replied, taking a chair at the bedside. "Now tell me what's heavy on your heart."

The old man blinked his eyelids and gazed pensively at the canopy. He told of cheating Indians back in 1781, or it could have been 1782. Anyhow, he got the pile of furs dirt-cheap. And he had lusted for an Indian woman, and had broken all the Ten Commandments but one or two. He named them. Finally he said:

"Them's my sins in order, Brother Jackson. Leastwise, near as I recollect."

Jackson eyed him. "Uh-huh."

"You sound a mite dubious."

"Oh, I was just thinkin', Uncle Ned. You see, when you get to the gates up there it ain't me who'll be checkin' on what you say against what you actually done."

"Reckon I never thought o' that."

"Which is why I mentioned it, Uncle Ned."

"Yeah," the old man said thoughtfully. "Course I ain't never had no experience in this sort of thing."

After more or less doubling his list of transgressions, and reminding Jackson that he'd prefer it if his sins didn't get on every Tom, Dick, and Harry's wagging tongue, he said he'd like a sample of Brother Jackson's prayers. Horatio obliged him, long and earnestly. When at last the Amen came, the old Kentuckian began to shout praise of the Lord. Jackson shouted with him, and soon all the friends and children and relatives joined in the shouting. Tears were shed and everybody was happy that there was no longer any doubt about the direction Uncle Ned's soul would take when he breathed his last on this earth.

Uncle Ned passed away in peaceful sleep that night. Jackson helped the neighbors dig the grave, and he preached the burial sermon. He lifted his voice with hymns Uncle Ned had asked for, and he prayed a good quarter hour after the body was lowered into the grave. He named scores of blessings the Lord had bestowed upon the Anglo-Texans, and he prayed for wisdom and patience and tolerance and restraint on the part of Texans in their dealings with the Mexican government's representatives.

When it was over, Ben Osborn called Jackson aside and handed him a small purse. It was from the Zachary family in appreciation for all he had done for them in their time of trial and sorrow. "It's worth a lot out here to have the kind of funeral you're used to back in the States. Many of us have to read funeral services for our loved ones and friends, and being laymen we naturally feel incapable. As Uncle Ned himself once said, we're silently apologizing to the deceased as we bury them."

As Jackson accepted the money, Osborn invited him to come to the Nashville settlement and maybe do a little preaching. "A Protestant minister would be fairly safe from Mexican officials there. We're close to the Neutral Ground, however, and the outlaws and smugglers like Hominy Baines and Captain Fozatte don't have much love for a preacher. But the folks from all around, Granny Creek, Tenehaw, Sip, Patroon, and Ayish Bayous, get might hungry for the gospel."

"Odd, I was headed for your place, Mr. Osborn." Jackson related his experience in Nacogdoches and in the Cherokee village. "Some of the men, including Lieutenant Ariola, spoke highly of you and John Latham. But I'm not an ordained minister. I'm a colporteur and I travel as a surveyor, which I am by trade."

"We measure a man by his deeds out here, Jackson. So the invitation still stands."

"Thank you, sir. Now down to the practical side. I find it hard to eke out a living selling Bibles and tracts. Wash and I have to augment this by earning our board and keep wherever we go. We plow when there's plowing to do, hoe, swing an ax, doctor a horse, and I tend the sick as best I can. In short, we do what's needed. Think your people could use us for a few weeks?"

"Well, you might do better than board and keep for yourself and your slave."

Jackson was quick to inform Osborn that Wash was not a slave, but a free Negro who had attached himself to him. "Now while I don't believe in slavery, I don't preach manumission or deal in abolitionist talk. My job is gathering souls for the Lord, be they white, brown, or black, that and keeping the ones gathered from straying. The latter, sir, ain't easy."

Osborn chuckled. "Well, if the people in my area don't hear the gospel preached pretty soon, there'll be more strays than you can shake a stick at. Suppose we head for my community, Jackson, and see if you can pen up a few of them."

3

Jackson spent his first day in the Nashville settlement at Osborn's store. There he met a number of settlers and helped unload and store supplies out of Natchitoches, Louisiana. Osborn introduced him to a few men as Brother Jackson and when Horatio asked why it was Mr. Jackson to some and Brother Jackson to others, the storekeeper said he knew whom to trust with news of a preacher in their midst. It would be up to Jackson to win the others over to his side after the word got around.

"And since most of the folks here have never seen preachers turn a hand to more than thumbing the leaves of a Bible or lifting a fork to their mouths, it won't hurt you none when there's talk about a working preacher."

Horatio remembered this next day when everybody it seemed went to a house raising, as it was called. A couple from Georgia had selected a cabin site about two miles south of Nashville. To welcome them as neighbors, the settlers would in one day's time fell logs, notch them, and build a cabin. The work began early. Wagons kept coming. Men chopped trees and the womenfolk, who had baked bread, cakes, and prepared dishes of every description for the occasion, spread a feast on the ground.

Jackson swung a mighty ax that morning. At noon, when all gathered to eat, Osborn called on Brother Jackson to ask the Lord's blessing on the food and the people assembled there. Horatio obliged him. He took his time, for he was not one to overlook an opportunity to preach even in prayer to a large gathering. There were many blessings to give thanks for. He kept on naming them; and once beyond that, he called God's attention to the fact that here on this spot was evidence of the fulfillment of Jesus' second great commandment "Thou shalt love thy neighbor as thyself."

Finally he said, "Amen," and Osborn told them they had heard a sample of Brother Jackson's thanks; and "come Sunday" they could sample his preaching at the clearing on his place a mile north of Nashville. "Preachin' begins at ten in the morning, followed by dinner on the ground. Brother Jackson invites you all to bring your children and colored folks. And the way he's eyin' Mrs. Thompson's berry cobbler, some of you ladies might take the hint and fetch more."

Sunday came, clear and bright and warm. Lula Osborn had ironed Horatio's Sunday shirt and suit the day before and Wash had trimmed his hair. As they rode out to the clearing, Jackson told Ben Osborn that he felt a little nervous in the region of his stomach, for this was to be his first real sermon preached on Texas soil and in violation of Mexican law. To which his friend and sponsor replied dryly: "Well, Brother Jackson, if the Mexicans come, you won't have far to go to the Sabine."

A score of wagons were already there when they reached the clearing. More were on the way. Slaves stood deferentially aside, and colored mammies tended children, and rugged pioneers stood in groups, each dressed in his "go to meetin' and funeral suit." The women wore their calico, gingham, silk, and lace and bonnets saved for special occasions. They created a pretty picture of color, and Jackson remarked on the blessing of women in this old world; they not only put up with men, they scrubbed and cooked and looked beautiful and proud for them. As the wagon ground to a stop, Mrs. Osborn reminded her two daughters that "pretty is as pretty does," and they shouldn't forget it. Then she pinched their cheeks to put "a rose" in their complexions.

By ten o'clock the June sun was bearing down with a promise of a hot day. The few men who wore coats looked uncomfortable and joined the crowd in the shade of oak and pecan trees. Jackson took his place in the open, where a tree stump would serve as a pulpit. He stood surveying his audience, debating on whether to shed his coat now or later, whether to drop half his *g*'s or all of them, and whether to use "isn't" or "ain't." Even among the frontier clergy there were two schools of thought on the subject. Some advocated religious dignity first, last, and always; others thought a preacher should speak the way the people spoke.

Wagons were still arriving, and more clattered down the road. The people were really turning out on this day, Jackson observed. Whether to hear him or suffer him for the spread of food to follow, it was all the same. They were here and he was saying in silence, "Lord, by this day Thy servant shall be known in Texas. Old Jackson will sure appreciate Thy help."

Raising an arm, he said in a voice that vibrated like a bugle through the crowd, "The Lord is with us today, brothers and sisters. Now let Him hear you praise Him in song." So saying, he began to sing:

" 'A-maz-ing grace! how sweet the sound, That saved a wretch like me! I—once was lost, but now am found—Was blind, but now I see!' "

Both arms moving to the tempo of the old song, his deep voice lifting loud and clear, he led them through the second stanza. Pausing, he cried forth, "You darkies back there! Let the Lord know you're here! You folks from Granny Creek and Sip Bayou, sing out! The crops look good and the watermelons are fattenin' on the vine! Yes, sir, and because of the Lord's amazing grace! Now sing out, everybody."

" 'Thro' man-y dan-gers, toils and snares, I have al-ready come: 'Tis grace has brought me safe thus far, And grace will lead me home.' "

When the five stanzas were ended with "Amen," he told them the Lord couldn't help but hear that kind of singing, that on a good wind their praises in song would likely cause some consternation in hell. "So let's worry the old devil with another one."

After two more songs Jackson lifted a hand to heaven and began to pray. He talked to the Lord, and he beseeched, and he praised, and he gave thanks, all in the same energetic manner in which he sang. He sweated, and he wished to shed coat and tie. But he wasn't ready for that. Following the long prayer, he read from the Bible. Then he snapped the Good Book shut and opened his sermon in a moderate tone of voice:

"There's a story about a preacher up in the cold part of

Canada who made converts of a lot of them Eskimo folks after every other clergyman had failed. When asked how he did it, he said he preached and tried everything he could think of but got nothing but disinterested blank looks from them until one cold night he got to talkin' about hell's fire. Well, he said, they began to sit up and listen, 'cause hell's fire sounded good and warm to them frostbit Eskimos.

"Well, we ain't frostbit here today, brothers and sisters."

"Amen!" a man in the crowd shouted.

"And in this shimmerin' heat under God's blazin' sun, I reckon I ought to dwell on the cool hand of Jesus on our sweatin' brows, or those rivers of cold spring water a man down in hell's furnaces knows are flowing up in heaven. But instead I'm going to preach about that hell where sinners go, not for one day, no. Not for one week, no! One year? No! Did I say ten years? I did not! Did I say a hundred years? No! I say forever, FOREVER!"

Jackson brought a fist down hard to his palm. Lowering his voice, he said, "You know how hot a blacksmith's fire can get. Turns a horseshoe red hot. Drop it in the tub of water and it steams and sizzles. That's hot! That's mighty hot!"

"Amen!"

"Well," Jackson ran a forefinger across his forehead and flung sweat. "Well, a blacksmith's fire is like unto wintry snow compared to the fires of hell!" Bringing his arm down and pointing a finger at his audience, he said, "And don't you dare doubt it, brother!"

With that, he removed his coat and placed it on the stump. In low tones he told the men to shed their coats also. "Because, my friends, it's going to get hotter."

He predicted rightly. Both he and the sun had only just warmed up. He talked of the roads that led to hell, the sins of mortals, and he always came back to the fiery pits, toward which men cheated and sinned their way. With one hand pointing up into the cloudless sky, he spoke of God's amazing grace. Then, swiftly dropping the other hand toward the searing flames of hell, he said, "Which, my friends? Which do you choose?"

He preached on. The audience responded with "Amen!" often, and Ben Osborn got to his feet once and shouted, "Praise the Lord and Hellfire Jackson!"

Horatio talked softly at times and at other times he shouted. He read verses from the Bible, emulating an angry God, and read other verses with tearful entreaty. Then he prayed, and next he admonished all who had sinned against the Lord and man to come forward while they sang and in their own hearts "give the Lord the facts straight."

After many came forward to grasp Jackson's hand and say "I confess," the final prayer was spoken. Then the service was over and the people were talking and giving Jackson another kind of handclasp. A settler from Tenehaw Bayou told Jackson the weather had warmed up considerably since ten o'clock. "And if you hadn't stopped preaching hell's fire when you did, there wouldn't be nothin' left of the food but ashes."

"Well," Jackson replied, grinning. "I'm hopin' Mrs. Thompson's berry cobbler ain't burnt to a crisp."

CHAPTER 6

By the time the oak, sweet gum, and hickory trees turned from green to shades of brown, red, and gold, it was mid-November. Mornings were frosty, days were clear, and nights were cool. The smell of autumn was in the air, and a blue haze hung over the hills of East Texas. The odor of wood smoke evoked anticipation of winter evenings about a fireplace and the sounds of corn popping in a skillet and the happy laughter of children as they cracked pecans or hickory nuts. Sweet potatoes had been bedded down under mounds of soil. Firewood piled up outside attested to the ringing of axes against hardwood earlier. Pine knots had been gathered to start fires. Now men eyed fat hogs while awaiting a norther to bring in "hog-killin' " time.

By this time settlers in the Redlands above Nacogdoches, in the area of Nashville, Palo Gacho, Patroon, Sip, and Tenehaw Bayous, had learned that the big man with a big voice who sold Bibles and quoted the Scriptures not only preached hell's fire and damnation, he tackled a man's chore with the same zeal. Men remarked on the way he swung an ax: "Why, you'd think he saw a devil in every tree." He knew how to notch a log for a cabin, turn a neat furrow, repair harness, build a rock chimney, doctor the sick, tree a squirrel, possum, or coon, and render coon fat into lamp oil. He turned in a day's work for his board and keep, and the way he called on the Lord to bless the food left little doubt that the Lord heard and obliged "Hellfire" Jackson, a man who stayed a day or two or maybe a week at one place before moving on to another.

When Ben Osborn had got to his feet and shouted, "Praise the Lord and Hellfire Jackson!" on that hot Sunday in June he had unwittingly given Jackson a permanent and popular sobriquet. Frontiersmen liked nicknames as much as they enjoyed their politics, and they soon forgot that Jackson had any other name. What's more, Hellfire expressed in one word the evangelistic character of the Pineywoods preacher. Also, it had a certain militant ring that suggested total harmony with the Anglo-Texans' grievances against Mexico late in 1831.

Before the first frost and change of colors in the trees, the colonists became more discontented with the Mexican decree of 1830, which banned further Anglo-American migrants into Texas and brought to Texas convict soldiers to enforce customs collections at Velasco, Brazoria, and Anahuac.

Early in the year a Colonel Bradburn, a Virginian in the Mexican Army, appeared as head of the military in Texas. When he closed the port of Brazoria, because he could collect no duties from the stubborn Texans, colonists from the Gulf to Gaines Ferry angrily called Bradburn a renegade. They chose to overlook the fact that they had also adopted Mexican citizenship in order to settle upon an *empresario* grant. And they had seemed a little piqued when Hellfire Jackson dryly reminded them of their "pardonable inconsistency."

Jackson was forced to admit, however, that they were justified in objecting to the outrageous $2.12½ tonnage fee levied against Texas shippers. And the very fact that a man who preached the gospel said it was cause for discontent served to fan the political fire in East Texas, especially since Mexico had promised the settlers in 1824 freedom from taxation for ten years.

Shortly after the first norther struck the Pineywoods in December an incident down at Velasco, near the mouth of the Brazos River, heaped fuel atop the fire. It happened at a time when another American by the name of Fisher, who had replaced Bradburn as Mexican customs authority on the Brazos, established headquarters at Anahuac and advised Texas shippers at Velasco that in order to get official clearance to leave port they would have to come to Anahuac for his signature. Since this necessitated an overland trip of about one hundred miles, the unreasonable order triggered the first open resistance to Mexican authority by Anglo-Texans:

Jeremiah H. Brown, captain of the schooner *Sabine,* refused to obey Fisher's order, and ran the ship past the fort at Velasco in an exchange of fire on to the open sea. Bound for New Orleans with Texas cotton, Brown was told by shipowner Edwin Waller to convert part of the proceeds of cargo into two cannon and to bring them back to Velasco.

Several weeks passed before news of the Velasco affair reached the Department of Nacogdoches. It came when Horatio "Hellfire" Jackson had returned to Natchez, Mississippi, to replenish his supply of Bibles and tracts and to once again try to become an ordained minister. He failed in the latter and left Natchez for Texas still a colporteur. He reached Elisha Roberts' settlement on a crisp day late in February of 1832.

Wash's remark, "Right here is where we got this old mule from Mistuh Mundy," evoked a memory of more than a mule and a trade from Jackson. Pretty, spirited Miss Jane Wells had entered his mind often since he had last seen her in Nacogdoches on the day Joshua Peters' boy was taken to the Cherokee village. She popped into his head when he rode under the sun and camped under the stars; unbidden, she eyed him with womanly challenge and womanly judgment in her glance. She was good company for a man's thoughts as he sat a saddle or looked into a campfire.

As he stared at the spot where Jane and the Mundys had camped, a pensive grin spread across Jackson's face. "By Jove, it's over two hundred long miles down to Mr. Austin's colony on the Brazos but it wouldn't take much promptin' to set me in that direction!"

Unaware of developments on the lower Brazos, Horatio joined Elisha Roberts at the big smokehouse and spent the afternoon helping the alcalde butcher hogs, hang hams to smoke, and grind pork into sausage. That evening Roberts stared into the blaze in his fireplace and told Jackson why the schooner *Sabine* had run to sea in violation of Mexican orders. Now what did Jackson think of that?

After voicing his surprise that any government would trust its colonies to such irresponsible adventurers as Bradburn and Fisher, Horatio said, "I see trouble ahead, Brother Roberts. What else can we expect when this arrogant Fisher issues utterly impossible orders to stubborn Anglo-Texans? What's more, it seems likely that when the news of the schooner *Sabine* reaches Mexico City more troops will be sent to Texas."

That night Jackson penned a letter to Jane Wells. Several days later, when the sun warmed the land and a first hint of spring was in the air, he said to Roberts, "Since I feel it's my bounden duty to help Mr. Austin and his colonists if and when trouble starts, I reckon I'll be headin' down toward the Brazos."

2

Jackson and Wash took the road up to the Nashville settlement in order to avoid trails frequented by outlaws. At every place they stopped Jackson found settlers anxious to learn more of what was happening down on the Brazos. Had Captain Brown of the schooner *Sabine* been arrested by the Mexicans? Did it look like war? Was Mexico trying to undo the liberal colonization law of 1824 that gave Americans land and freedom from taxes for ten years in order to get them to settle in Texas? Certainly the Mexican decree of 1830 which ordered the freedom of slaves in Texas, and which the Texans bitterly protested and ignored, that also prohibited more Anglo-Americans from settling in Texas, pointed toward a reversal of opinion by the Mexican government. And the levy of taxes on all foreign imports seemed to guarantee it.

"Me, I'm ready to look down a gun barrel at the Mexicans. How you feel about it, Hellfire?"

Jackson looked at Ezra Benson and four of his neighbors seated about the fireplace. "Well, it does breed distrust and insecurity between the Mexicans and Texans, all right. But back in Tennessee, Ezra, I'll venture you got every bit as hot under the collar at election time. Course you don't get to vote here, which is a mistake on the part of the Mexicans, since they don't give American settlers a chance to loose tempers and tongues at a candidate they don't like and get it out of their systems until the next election.

"However, Ezra, I wouldn't be too hasty with gun and temper. Seems Mexico passes a lot of laws that somehow don't get enforced in Texas. So it balances up. That is it has up to now. But if Mexico provokes war, then war she'll get."

"Meanin' we should bide our time?"

"Right, Ezra, and be ready if and when trouble starts. It may not be soon, but it's bound to come."

The men were less militant when Horatio left them. He moved on, knowing that the subject would come up again at the next place he stopped. His surmise was correct. He rode toward Abner Bowser's place. There he tried to talk the Lord into Bowser, but the man was too busy cursing the Mexicans and their antecedents to listen to the Word of God.

Next day, on the road to Nacogdoches, Jackson told Wash that talking to Bowser was like preaching to a rock wall. "Maybe the Lord is using him to test me. If so, I've been found wanting. Could be God is humbling me, saying, 'Horatio, don't get it in your head you're a good preacher until you can crack a tough hickory nut like Bowser.' "

"Yassuh. And what yo'all say to dat?"

"I'm just askin' Him to show me the way to do it. I'm askin' in all humility, Wash."

That afternoon they reached a fork in the worn trails. The road to the west led to Nacogdoches. The one to the south skirted the town and led down to Smugglers Road, which Elisha Roberts had warned Jackson the year before to avoid. Jackson debated on which direction he should go. Wishing to avoid Mexican officials who had no doubt heard of his holding Protestant religious services in East Texas, he decided to by-pass Nacogdoches.

"We'll just have to ride careful and keep our eyes peeled for any sign of smugglers, Wash." This they did that afternoon and camped without building a fire that night. With morning they were unable to find tracks or any sign of recent travel over the desolate, twisting wilderness trail of smugglers, so they resumed their way west with less caution than they had exercised the day before.

Late in the afternoon they came upon an abandoned campsite at an intersection of the road and a trail leading to Nacogdoches to the northeast. Since the camp appeared to have been deserted during the winter, Jackson felt reasonably sure that he had reached the rendezvous of smugglers at a time when they were engaged in the transport of illicit goods elsewhere. But just to be on the safe side, he decided to make camp off the road a little farther ahead. Leaving Wash to build a lean-to and get a fire going, Horatio took his rifle and went in search of game. He found something else.

He had no sooner topped a small hill a quarter mile up on the Nacogdoches road than he heard a squirrel barking. As he raised his rifle to fire, the creaking sounds of a wagon drew his attention to a curve in the brush-choked road. Then, off to his left, he saw other wagons and men unloading them.

"Smugglers or outlaws!" he said to himself. He had heard that the dangerous outlaw Hominy Baines was in the Nacogdoches area. While he wasn't sure that the wagoners were not settlers on their way down to the Gulf of Mexico, he did not care to risk his life in determining just who they were, so he worked his way cautiously down the hill and through clumps of brush back toward his camp.

Arriving there he found the lean-to completed and a fire burning. Wash, however, was gone, as were the horse and pair of mules. Now sensing immediate danger, Jackson kicked dirt on the fire and dashed into the woods. He had scarcely crouched behind a tree, from which point of vantage he intended to watch for developments, than something struck him from behind. Then all went black.

When he regained consciousness, Jackson found himself bound by rope to a tree. Several forms swam dizzily into and out of his vision before taking on shape. They sat with backs to him near a campfire, all drinking. Beyond the men, Horatio saw Wash, also tied hand and foot and propped against the trunk of a pine tree.

Jackson shook his head in an effort to ease the pain inflicted by the blow that had felled him. As his head continued to throb, he scolded himself for his own carelessness. He had not only known better than to risk the dangers along Smugglers Road, he had relaxed his vigilance. There was a verse in the Book of Proverbs that seemed made to order for him: "Seest thou a man wise in his own conceit? There is more hope of a fool than of him."

Jackson could only say, "Amen."

One of the men said, "What are we going to do with them, Captain?"

"Sell the slave and shoot his master."

Jackson could not believe the man was serious until he heard him add "*Mon Dieu,* yes!" to the soft-spoken verdict. Then Jackson felt a cold chill running up and down his spine, for he knew his captor was the notorious smuggler, slaver, duelist, and ex-pirate who ruled the strip called No Man's Land with gun and sword.

If there was any doubt in Horatio's mind as to the man's identity, it was quickly dispelled when light from the campfire played on jade-and-pearl eardrops. Soon the Frenchman arose and moved to within a few feet of Jackson. Standing with feet planted wide apart, he twisted the end of a thin black mustache and eyed his prisoner a minute before saying:

"It is mos' regrettable that you have crossed the path of Captain Jean Émile Fozatte again, m'sieur. Indeed, for I have sworn to kill you."

"Me? For what? I have done you no harm."

"No harm, you say? *Sacrebleu!* You call the injure to one's pride, the insult, no harm? No man refuse the hand of Fozatte and live. *Non!* But there is another reason. Our wagons of smuggled goods are here and we cannot spare the life of a man who could carry the news to the authorities. So you see, I am mos' serious, M'sieur Jackson."

He paused. Jackson said nothing. Then Fozatte ordered his subordinates to bring in Jackson's pack mule and determine the value of the loot he would take from his enemy. When only surveying instruments, Bibles, and pamphlets were found, Fozatte showed both surprise and disappointment. Next, he asked why M'sieur Jackson carried such worthless goods.

"I sell Bibles and I preach the word therein."

"*Mon Dieu,* no!" Fozatte exclaimed before throwing his head back for a hearty laugh. At last he said, "That you violate the Mexican law for so small a reward I do not comprehend." When Jackson told him that the repentance of one sinner caused a rejoicing in heaven, and that this was his reward, Fozatte eyed him pityingly. "A man stupid enough to believe such rot do not deserve to live."

"And a man who does not believe in God is not ready to die, Captain."

"You have the sharp tongue for a man about to die, m'sieur." Drawing his pistol, Fozatte said, "The time has come."

Jackson stared at the gun pointing at his head. The hammer had been drawn back. It awaited only the mere tightening of a finger at the trigger to send a bullet into his brain. Aware now that Fozatte actually intended to kill him, he tried to put down the awful sickness that was coming upon him. Failing, he looked up into the cold eyes behind the pistol and said:

"Can you give me a little time to pray, Captain?"

Fozatte shrugged his shoulders. "Very well, m'sieur, since it is the custom to grant a doomed man a last wish. But maybe you like a little wine instead, no? Or the Irish whisky, which make you die laughing."

"I'd rather pray, Captain."

Fozatte shrugged. "*Le diable t'emporte!* So pray then."

"Thank you," Jackson managed to say. Closing his eyes, he turned his face to the heavens and sent up the most earnest petition he had ever voiced. He spoke loud and clear. He told the Lord of his life as a sinner and blasphemer. He recounted his sins and told of his repentance and named the many joys and blessings that followed in his service to the

Lord. He asked forgiveness of his sins and the sins of Captain Fozatte and his men.

Five minutes went by, then another five, and he was still praying; for his friends now, and he named them; for Jane Wells and for Wash, who had been faithful to him, and for the sinner Abner Bowser; and for Texas and Texans in their struggle sure to come with Mexico; for understanding among men and for peace on earth.

Peering through the slits of his eyes, Jackson saw Fozatte. He was still standing with gun in hand at his side, while his henchmen sat around the fire, some staring into the blaze, others with hats in hand and heads bowed.

"Lord, I reckon I've prayed for everybody I know and then some. Now in conclusion I ask Thee not to smite the men gathered here for the foul deed their leader is about to commit. And don't smite their leader, Lord. Do not tear the earth apart and amid their cries of anguish send them plummeting down into the fiery pits of eternal hell. Instead, dear Lord, I beseech Thee to show them that a wrathful God can also be a merciful God."

Minutes later Jackson said a reluctant "Amen," looked up at Fozatte, and said, "Reckon I'm as ready to go as I'll ever be, Captain."

The Frenchman stood silent, a hand at his mustache, a curious and puzzled expression dominating his face. After a minute of intent scrutiny, he looked at his pistol, raised black brows, and sent a glance at his followers.

"What do you think, *mes amis?*" he said. There was no reply, and he slowly faced Jackson again. "A thousand thunders!" he exclaimed. "How can one kill so good a man?"

3

Horatio and Wash rode all that night in order to put as many miles between them and the smugglers as possible. While Jackson agreed with Wash that he had escaped death by a miracle of God, and said in his prayers of thanks that if he ever entered the pearly gates of heaven he would look up Daniel and say "Brother, we've got something in common," he realized that mortals like Captain Fozatte could and often did change their minds.

The Frenchman's words as he cut the bonds binding them were still fresh in Jackson's memory: "Next time I may not be so generous, m'sieur." This was fair warning, and Jackson vowed that he would be more careful in the future. Better to ride with the caution and alertness of an Indian, for other than Fozatte there were other desperadoes to avoid. And at times when he felt secure he should take warning and double his vigilance.

Wash listened and thought about it. "You is sholy right, Marse Jackson. Mighty right." Then he seemed to sum up the history of man's troubles, tragedies, and mistakes through the ages in his own simple words: "Yassuh, right now we knows we gotta do dat, but pretty soon we forgits."

Upon reaching the Angelina River to the west, they found the stream swollen and stretching far out into the bottom land. Aware that a crossing was next to impossible, Jackson decided to go back to the Nashville settlement and wait for the spring floods to subside. Several days later he and Wash rode into the settlement.

Ben Osborn was glad to see the evangelist. What's more, he was hungry for the kind of "gospel preachin' that's got more bite than bark." He thought it would be a good idea to spread the word that there would be a camp meeting on his place as soon as the planting was complete in the area. Jackson thought about it, and said he was planning to go down to San Felipe de Austin, to which Osborn replied, "Down amongst them Catholics and Karankawa Injuns when the Redlands is your circuit? And maybe you didn't hear me when I said camp meetin', Hellfire."

Jackson had heard, all right. And he was impressed, for he had never presided at a camp meeting. While he aspired to this, he could not forget that he was not an ordained minister. However, as lay evangelist or missionary, he could assist the minister of Osborn's choice. But how did Mr. Osborn plan to handle such a big affair? There were no tents or houses for the people who would come to camp for days, no pulpit or seats for them.

"Well, there will be," came the reply.

Ben Osborn was as good as his word. By mid-April a big pulpit, hand-hewn benches to seat two hundred people, as well as tent, board, and log houses covering an acre of ground, and accommodations for wagons and animals awaited the Anglo-Texan families who came from all parts of East Texas.

Jackson had not only helped fell trees and saw boards, he had ridden to Louisiana to engage an ordained minister. He returned without one, because Protestant churches in the United States refused to send preachers to Texas in violation of Mexican laws which forbade them. He returned with more Bibles, but with misgiving, for news of the camp meeting had spread rapidly and there was small doubt that the

Mexican authorities had heard about it. Colonel Piedras had warned him once, politely, but he was wondering just how polite the genial colonel would be next time. On this score he was not kept waiting long. But first Jackson encountered opposition from another source.

On an afternoon before the camp meeting opened, Horatio approached a creek crossing between Ayish Bayou and Tenehaw only to find his way blocked by a band of ruffians. They were drinking from jugs, and the foul odor of whisky was strong. Their leader, a huge red-whiskered man, grinned, executed a mock bow, and asked Jackson if he had ever heard of Hominy Baines. Before Jackson could reply that he had, the man brandished a whip and said, "Git down, Rev-'ren', and we'll decide whether to horsewhip you or just give you fair warnin' not to hold that camp meetin'." Ten minutes later Jackson rode off with a double warning ringing in his ears: the outlaw was sending word to the Mexican authorities about Jackson's preaching in violation of the law; and if the soldiers didn't break up the meeting, Hominy Baines would.

By the following evening some fifty families were camped at Ben Osborn's place. Under the brush arbor men, women, and children were gathered to worship. Expecting trouble, Osborn and Elisha Roberts placed guards outside. When Hominy Baines failed to appear that night or the next, the settlers labeled the threat an idle one made under the influence of liquor, and withdrew the guards.

Just before the meeting on the third night Osborn informed Jackson that Abner Bowser had come to his store for supplies and, with nothing else to do that evening, had decided to see if Hellfire could preach as well as he handled a mule.

"Praise God, Ben!" Jackson said. "I'm going after that man tonight. Going to use David's slingshot on him and try to bag that unbelievin' Goliath for the Lord."

That evening, just after Jackson concluded the opening prayer, he and the congregation were startled to see a dozen uniformed visitors enter and take seats. The arrival of Mexican soldiers cast a pall over the meeting. The first song, a popular one, sounded weak and spiritless. After cutting it short by three stanzas, Jackson faced the gathering and said with more assurance than he actually felt:

"We are honored to have with us this evening Colonel Piedras and members of the 12th Permanent Battalion. We welcome our protectors to this meeting of law-abiding citizens who like to sing praise to the Lord and listen to gospel reading. And right here let me say that if more of us gathered to sing and pray there would be less horse stealing, arguments, fights, and whisky drinking in this wonderful province of Texas."

A vigorous "Amen!" sounded in the audience. As others followed, the tension seemed to lessen. Horatio felt better until he thought of his sermon topic, David's battle with Goliath, which the visitors as well as the settlers might interpret as a victory of the outnumbered Anglo-Texans over the powerful forces of Mexico. This could prove both embarrassing and disastrous. If harmony was to prevail, he should find a topic more suited to the occasion. And in a reach for harmony, he would preach harmony. He began by saying:

"Tonight I'm going to surprise the old devil with what he least expects. If he's anywhere near this settlement, brothers and sisters, he's going to get his ears singed good and proper, 'cause I'm going to reveal one of his secrets—how he sows seeds of dissension amongst us and creates a lack of understanding between men and races and nations and causes hate and war and suffering."

Jackson lived up to his nickname in the hour that followed. He aimed his sermon in two directions, the Mexican colonel and Abner Bowser. But he knew before he had preached a quarter hour that he could not shoot both ways at once. Bowser would keep, the Lord willing, so he would do well to aim and fire his best blast in politic manner at the colonel. This he did and concluded his service with a long prayer for peace and understanding among men.

With his "Amen," Colonel Piedras and his soldiers approached the pulpit. As Jackson, Elisha Roberts, Osborn, and other colonists wondered if the soldiers were planning to jail them all, Piedras said:

"Señores, I must remind you of the law which forbids public gatherings without official sanction by the authorities, as well as the law that prohibits all but Catholic worship."

Horatio and his group nodded, exchanged dismal glances, and waited for the order for their arrest. Piedras continued, saying:

"Now that I have fulfilled my duty on that score, I shall enter into my report the following observations: No horses were stolen, nobody was murdered, and there was no talk of revolution. Therefore, I see no conflict with the intent of our laws." Facing Jackson, he said, "Especially in tonight's sermon. But tell me, *Reverendo,* had I eavesdropped instead of coming inside, would I have heard the same sermon?"

Jackson rubbed his jaw and considered the question. Aware that much hinged on his reply, that his own honesty was up for notice by the colonists, and that Piedras was a most discerning man, he said, "Well, Colonel, yes and no. By yes, I mean I'm always after the devil. Never stop fighting him. But when you arrived and I thought this might be my last sermon in Texas, I sort of bent the barrel of my gun and aimed it in another direction."

When Piedras laughed and said he liked an honest man, Jackson felt like a man who had jerked a foot out of a bear trap just as the jaws were closing on him.

4

The feeling that he was accomplishing something in Texas, that the Lord had not sent him on a vain mission, stayed with him all the next day. His only regret was that Bowser had returned to his home. When he stepped to the pulpit that evening he was a man inspired. The devil had better watch out on this fine spring night; had better double his armor or retreat to where he couldn't see a pine tree. And that was the way Hellfire Jackson preached for twenty minutes.

Then he saw something that caused him to freeze with arm upraised and voice hushed in midsentence. In his relentless pursuit of the devil, he had forgotten the imps. It was a little late to correct the error, for Hominy Baines and his ruffians had arrived as promised. The Philistines had entered the temple!

When the outlaw approached the pulpit and warned the people to remain in their places while he gave the preacher a taste of his whip, the colonists rose up in protest.

"Do as he says!" Jackson shouted. "I'll have none of you harmed if I can help it." Facing the red-whiskered Baines, he then asked why he wished to break up a religious meeting. The outlaw promptly gave his reasons: He had no use for religion or preachers, and he would tolerate no meeting here. Furthermore, he had given the "preacher feller" fair warning not to hold the camp meeting.

Again an angry murmur ran through the crowd, causing Jackson to lift a hand and say, "Mr. Baines gave me a fair warning, all right." Sparring for time, he said, "Now, Mr. Baines, let me tell you something. If you take the whip to me tonight, it will avail you nothing, for Hellfire Jackson will be right here preaching tomorrow night."

"Then I'll be here to give you another whippin', mister. And that's a fact."

Flicking his whip, Baines stepped to the platform. Horatio studied the man closely and saw mean purpose in his bright blue eyes; saw a man of huge frame with the strength to back up the promises he had made. For a run of seconds Jackson toyed with the idea of using all he had learned from the Cherokees in the art of rough-and-tumble fighting. A look at the colonists who would rush headlong to his aid, then at the dozen drunken ruffians who would shoot them without compunction, caused him to abandon any idea of resistance that would surely result in bloodshed. He decided to try another approach.

"Mr. Baines," he said, "with a dozen bullies to back you up, you're a powerful brave man. Now I'm wondering just how brave you'd be if just you and me settled this with fists and no holds barred, say after the meeting tonight. Well, what about it?"

"Fine and dandy, Jackson, except there ain't goin' to be no meetin' tonight. And besides that I promised to horsewhip you, and I am going to do just that."

Seconds later Jackson received his second surprise of the evening. He did not see a tall man in black step from the shadows into the tabernacle, but he and all there heard the visitor say with quiet authority in his voice:

"I beg to differ with you, M'sieur Baines."

As Jackson whirled and stared incredulously at what met his eyes, Hominy Baines darted a glance at the man who dared to challenge him. Tensing all over, his eyes narrowed to mere slits, he stood out a moment of surprise then another in which sharp resentment and mean cunning vied with the innate wisdom of his kind. His one hand tightened on the whip as the other instinctively dropped to his pistol and as quickly jerked away from the gun.

"Sure now, Captain," Baines said, forcing a grin across his face. "But I don't recall a time when I ever tried to butt into your business."

"True, *mon ami,* which proves you are a mos' wise man. Indeed, for you are alive, no?"

In the minute that followed, Jackson and every person there felt the presence of trouble sure to explode any second. It was in the duel of glances between outlaw and smuggler. Then it slowly faded and the Frenchman put his back to Hominy Baines, almost in a gesture of contempt. Facing the audience, he said:

"It is the wish of Captain Jean Émile Fozatte that my good frien' M'sieur Jackson continue the services, after, of course, my other good frien' M'sieur Baines speak to you his regret for the interruption."

Jackson found it difficult to reconcile his rescue from trouble to the man who only a few weeks before had come close to putting a bullet in his head. With the departure of Baines, he resumed his place at the pulpit still trying to adjust the surprises of the evening in his mind. Finally he said:

"I don't know where I left off in my sermon, but following a special prayer of thanks this humble man is going to talk about miracles."

CHAPTER 7

Some two hundred miles south-southwest of Nacogdoches as the crow flies the town of Velasco sweltered under the late May sun. The mighty Brazos River, which emptied into the Gulf of Mexico just below the town, seemed impervious to the unseasonal heat. It flowed on wide and serene, still a muddy yellow as a result of spring floods. It slid lazily in with small boats and rafts from Brazoria, about six miles upriver, and from San Felipe de Austin, seat of Stephen F. Austin's colony, another fifty miles beyond. Past sandbars and shoals, the river moved eternally toward the Gulf, unmindful of trouble with Mexican customs collectors who had closed Velasco, the most important port in Texas.

On this sultry afternoon Jane Wells stood at the door of the Velasco schoolhouse near the river waving at children who shouted, " 'By, Miss Wells! See you next fall!"

When they had all gone, she turned her gaze on the empty schoolroom. It was too quiet, and she was suddenly very lonely. With a final nostalgic look about her, Jane picked up her books and left the log-and-plank building that served the town as school and public meetinghouse. Once outside, she gazed up at fluffy white clouds sailing fast upriver on the prevailing wind off the Gulf of Mexico. The weather promised fair for the trip up to San Felipe on the morrow. She moved on, now taking in the scene of town, wharves, and river.

Commerce seemed at a standstill. Wagons no longer creaked under heavy loads of lumber and hides toward schooners waiting to transport Texas products to New Orleans. Missing also were the sounds of slaves singing as they unloaded boats from upriver or ships from the Gulf. An inbound schooner drew her attention. Though heavy with goods, the vessel had her sails spread full and she moved at a fast clip on the brisk following wind. She was the defiant small ocean-going *Sabine* that came and went with or without permission from Mexican authorities. Captain Jeremiah Brown, the first Texan to defy the blockade and to bring a cannon to Texas, commanded the sleek craft.

Instinctively Jane's glance fell on the Mexican fort which had fired on the *Sabine* months earlier. In the center of a circular redoubt of sharpened uprights stood a bastion topped by a parapet. The cannon were visible. She had heard the fort's swivel gun bark the day the *Sabine* ran past with cotton for New Orleans. She had also seen its bite when a shell exploded in the topsail rigging. But Captain Brown had sailed on despite the tangled wreckage. While she admired "Jere" Brown, as did all Anglo-Texans, she could not quite sanction his warmongering actions. Now she was wondering if she would once more hear the blast of cannon from the fort. But no attempt was made to stop the *Sabine*.

Moving on toward the street fronting the wharf-lined river, she gazed at the Brazos and watched screaming gulls bank in graceful motion toward the eddies and currents in search of food.

Near the American Hotel, men raised their hats and spoke a "Good afternoon, Miss Wells," before resuming talk of Santa Anna's pledge to defend the Mexican Constitution of 1824, which upheld the rights of the states. Jane heard one man say that any Texan who failed to back Santa Anna was a butt-headed fool. "Ask William Wharton. Ask Edwin Waller, who owns the schooner *Sabine*, which way the wind blows best for us. Me, I'm for chasin' Bustamante's convict soldiers from the fort all the way to Velasco Bar, and I hope Santa Anna overthrows Bustamante."

"Bustamante! Santa Anna!" Jane said to herself. The former was President of Mexico and had been in power when the Mexican Congress passed the law of 1830 which prohibited further American colonization of Texas and established customhouses in Texas. The Anglo-American settlers naturally resented these harsh acts and were quick to favor the dashing idol of Mexico, General Antonio López de Santa

Anna, who had rebelled against the administration and was trying to overthrow President Bustamante.

Jane knew little of the political and revolutionary characteristics of the Mexican people, and still less of the unpredictable, explosive riverbank and street-corner politics of the Anglo-Texans. And all she heard now at every turn, from trapper in buckskin, farmer in homespun, bandy-legged sailor, clerk, river boatman, and frontier lawyer, seemed a prediction of serious trouble. Perhaps they were justified in their views. She supposed they were, though she could neither understand nor condone their desire for war and violence.

"Small wonder Mr. Austin always looks done in," she said in silence, moving on toward her aunt's blacksmith shop.

The ring of hammer on anvil sounded louder. Jane wondered how her Aunt Sally could do the work of two strong men from dawn to dusk day after day. It continued to amaze her. But "Bucktooth Sal," as she was called by her host of friends, enjoyed being a blacksmith. Moreover, she had a sense of humor, a flair for Brazos politics, and the knack of turning a profitable trade. She was considered as good a judge of horses and mules as any man on the Brazos, and when she asked a top price for an animal the buyer knew he was getting his money's worth.

Jane lived with her aunt in a two-room log house near the blacksmith shop. On this afternoon she saw a mule tied to the oak in front of the shop that reminded her of the one Jonathan Mundy had traded to Horatio Jackson up at Ayish Bayou the year before. She had thought of Mr. Jackson often, each time with the same curiosity regarding his total honesty as when he had bested Mundy in the trade. He had had a way about him that seemed to lift him above the ordinary run of men one met on the trails. She continued to wonder about him. Maybe he was the man new settlers in from East Texas called Hellfire Jackson.

"And maybe that's his pack mule," she said, directing her steps toward the blacksmith shop. Approaching the shed, she heard the clang of hammer on red-hot horseshoe, saw her aunt thrust the shoe in a tub of water, heard the sizzling, and saw the steam. Then Sal turned, brandished the horseshoe at the end of the tongs at a sailor, and raised her foghorn voice with:

"Why you webfooted, barnacle-brained idiot, don't you set there and tell me this Santa Anna would be no different from old Bustamante! You may be bald-headed as a capstan but you ain't got the brains of one, else you'd know that it was

Bustamante who sent the customs collectors and convict soldiers here!"

Seeing Jane, she lowered the tongs, worked her lip down over the bucktooth, and wiped the other hand on her leather apron. "Hello, Jane. Was just tryin' to convince Cap'n Joe here which side his bread was buttered on. Done it polite though. Didn't I, Cap'n?"

"Aye, that ye did, if threatenin' to ram a hot horseshoe down my hatch is polite!"

"Now, Cap'n, why'd you have to say that, knowin' how anxious Jane is about my good manners?"

Jane smiled. "I came just in time, didn't I, Captain Herrick?" Turning to her aunt, she said, "Whose mule is that out there?"

"Belongs to the Whartons. Why?"

"Just curious."

"Coon oil! You ain't never been curious about a mule before, girl."

"Belay, Sal!" Captain Herrick bellowed. "I'll be glad to take Miss Jane up to San Felipe in the mornin', just to get her away from you and your influence. And we get under way with the tide. That suit you, ma'am?"

"I'll be ready," Jane replied, turning to go.

"Hold on a minute, Jane," Sally ordered. "A letter came for you today. A man brought it down from the Redlands."

"Probably from Martha Roberts at Ayish Bayou," Jane said, accepting the letter. Then she saw the handwriting in bold masculine scrawl: "To Miss Jane Wells, Colony of Empresario S. F. Austin, San Felipe de Austin on the Brazos." Curious now, she went on to the log house before breaking the seal and learning that it had been written at Elisha Roberts Campground almost three months in the past by Horatio Jackson.

The message began with an apology for his failure to join her and the Mundys at supper on Banita Creek in Nacogdoches back in May of 1831. He told of joining a group of settlers riding out to rescue the child of a settler from the Cherokees on that afternoon. She read on:

> Since that time I have pursued my vocation, that of surveying, to no avail in Texas. I have been asked to practice law, a profession for which I was educated back in Tennessee, but feel that my calling is to preach the gospel in this province, despite Mexican opposition to Protestant worship. So I sell Bibles and tracts and preach

when and where I am invited to do so, and make myself useful and welcome by the sweat of my brow—at the plow or with ax, hammer, adz, and saw in hand wherever I go, believing my reward is service to mankind. Thus far I have found the people receptive, the authorities tolerant of my clandestine efforts, and the Lord kind.

It is now late February of 1832 and I have just returned to Texas from Louisiana where once again my efforts to be ordained a minister have met with failure. But I shall try again, as it has been my ambition for several years to pursue the work of a missionary with the sanction and recognition of the church.

The foregoing constitutes a general summary of my activities in the Redlands, and I pray that mention of my not illustrious adventures and vicissitudes since our last meeting does not bore you. Perhaps you recall where we met last—before a saloon in Nacogdoches, where I entered but not to partake, I assure you, Miss Jane!

In closing, please allow me to remark on the pleasure I derived from meeting so fair and fine a lady as you. Be assured that my humble prayers for you and all the good people in Mr. Austin's colony, who are caught up in political troubles and oppression, are constant. I plan to ride down to San Felipe and offer my assistance to the Texans with the coming of spring, maybe by the time the dogwood and redbud trees bloom. If so, perhaps I could fetch you a bouquet of blossoms!!!

Yr. Obedient Servant & c.,
Horatio Jackson

Jane's brow lifted, then knit together. Biting her lower lip, she looked at the letter again. " 'So fair and fine a lady,' " she said. " 'Perhaps I could fetch you a bouquet of blossoms.' "

She was wondering if she would have accepted the flowers from this strange man who continued to puzzle her. Although he revealed his true purpose for coming to Texas in his letter, if she could accept this as true, he still defied satisfactory assessment. In his favor, he was not of the ordinary mold but totally different from anyone she had ever met. On the debit side, and the suspicion persisted, he seemed to be hiding behind the mask of surveyor and missionary while setting the stage for some undisclosed adventure.

"Filibustering perhaps," she said. Then she scoffed at the idea. "However, men do strange things."

Jane was preparing the evening meal when Sally entered the house and declared her uncompromising opinion of men and mules. "They got so much in common, girl, makes a body wonder why the Lord failed to give a man long ears and two extra feet. Now who was your letter from, Jane?"

"The preaching surveyor I told you about last year—Horatio Jackson."

Bucktooth Sal grinned. "You mean the feller that skinned old Jonathan Mundy in the mule trade?"

"The same," Jane replied, forking ears of corn from the oven.

"What did he have on his mind?"

"He said he was coming down to the Brazos to offer his assistance to the Texans caught up in political troubles and oppression."

"Good for him!" Sally exclaimed, slapping her thigh. "We can use a few men with spirit."

"Spirit? Seems we've got a full share of that. Our warlike attitude can only invite trouble with Mexico."

"Lord help us, child! I'm right glad school's out. Maybe you can get that pretty head o' yours out of books and look at a few plain facts. Like trouble us Texans didn't start but sure as hell have got to finish sooner or later. And you can lay to that! But what else did this Jackson feller have to say?"

"That I was a fair and fine lady," Jane fairly snapped back at her.

"Can't see nothin' wrong with his judgment there, girl. Course he don't know you very well, but he'll learn."

"Learn what?" Jane stood with a steaming platter in each hand, her eyes sharp and demanding.

"Was fixin' to say if he's comin' a-courtin' he'll learn what all the other blades that tried to spark you found out, that it takes more'n a scorchin' Texas summer to thaw you out."

"Prittle-prattle! The way you carry on, Aunt Sally, one would think I was violating some law by not trying to jerk a proposal of marriage out of every man who calls on me."

"Just say it's odd as all tarnation. But skip it and tell me what else he wrote."

"That was about all," came the crisp reply.

Bucktooth Sal grinned. "Short letter, wasn't it? But I like a man who speaks brief, don't you, girl?"

Jane somehow managed to suppress the retort on the tip of her tongue and placed the food none too gently on the table. She could hardly wait for the morning trip upriver to Brazoria and San Felipe, where Stephen F. Austin managed to hold the warmongers in check and her friends would not be conspiring to send her to the altar.

Such were her thoughts when her aunt gave her a sly

smile and said, "How old a man is your friend Jackson, girl?"

To Jane this was too much. Placing hands on hips, she tossed her head defiantly and raised her voice with, "I don't know and I couldn't care less!"

2

Even as Jane gave vent to her feelings, a large man in buckskin pants got off his horse up in the upriver municipality of San Felipe de Austin, entered a small store, and asked where he would find the residence of Mr. Stephen Fuller Austin. Upon learning that the *empresario* had just returned from a meeting with the Mexican governor of Texas at San Antonio de Bexar and was probably "worn to a frazzle" from the trip, the man advised that he would call on Mr. Austin next day. But perhaps the storekeeper could direct him to a schoolteacher, a Miss Jane Wells.

"Wells? Wells? Oh yes, I recall now, stranger, she's the schoolmarm down at Velasco. But I didn't get your name."

"Jackson, Horatio Jackson."

"Where you from Mr. Jackson? The Redlands, eh? Well, are folks up there for Santa Anna and the Constitution of 1824—which will give us statehood—or still in the same old rut? Now I say—"

At that moment a priest entered the store. A man of strong face and proud bearing, he greeted the storekeeper cordially, acknowledged the introduction to Jackson by word and hearty handclasp, made his purchase, and departed. Jackson learned that he was Father Michael Muldoon, who had so impressed Mr. Austin down in Saltillo the year before that he had been invited to come to San Felipe as missionary for his colony.

Curious, Jackson asked questions and was told that the good and popular Irish padre had won the respect of the colonists by marrying Negroes without exacting any fee from them or their masters, by attending the sick and unfortunate in all parts of the colony.

"But he's right pompous, I'd say," the storekeeper went on. "Can't remember all the titles he gave himself when he arrived. It's in the issue of the *Mexican Citizen* I saved." Fishing through his papers, he finally placed a copy of the newspaper before Jackson. "There it is. Read it and you'll see what I mean."

Jackson read the official notice in which Padre Muldoon styled himself "Parish Priest of San Felipe de Austin and Vicar General of all the Foreign Colonies of Texas Already Existing or That May Be Hereafter Established, Invested with Plenipotentiary Papal and Episcopal Powers, and Faculties to Administer Confirmation."

Jackson raised bushy brows and rubbed his jaw thoughtfully. "High-sounding, all right," he declared. "Maybe he forgot to add the three words he left off. Else he could be working mighty hard to annex them."

"Yeah? What three words?"

"Pope of Mexico," Horatio replied dryly.

The storekeeper repeated the padre's new title and after a deep laugh offered to put the welcome newcomer up for the night. Jackson readily accepted. When Wash was quartered in the hayloft and the store was closed, Horatio joined his host for a few hours of night fishing on the banks of the Brazos.

Next morning Mr. Austin's secretary, Samuel May Williams, told Jackson that Mr. Austin would see him shortly after lunch. Finding the *empresario* still closeted with visitors at one in the afternoon, Jackson took a chair on the porch to await his turn. While seated in the shade, he saw Padre Muldoon emerge from the house, pause in brief study of him, and, without any word or sign of recognition, walk away. Jackson wondered about the priest's strange behavior. Mr. Williams, who had witnessed the incident, appeared on the porch.

"Mr. Austin will see you now," he said. Then, a twinkle in his eye, he added, "Sorry the Pope of Mexico stayed so long." As Jackson started, Williams said, "Father Muldoon is a sensitive man, fast to make friends or enemies."

Jackson shook his head dolefully. "And I reckon I'm the kind of man who shoots off at the mouth when he should be listening. But this sort of worries me, Mr. Williams. I meant no harm, and I'm going to look him up and tell him so."

The secretary to Austin advised against this. The joke was on every tongue by now; better to let it run its course and later communicate his apologies through Mr. Austin.

The matter of Father Muldoon weighed heavily on Jackson's mind as he was ushered into the presence of Stephen F. Austin. Then he was shaking hands with the small, thin, pale man, with high forehead and dreamy hazel eyes, who was by far the greatest man in Texas.

That this busy person of renown had granted him audience and was now honoring him with firm handclasp was enough to cause Jackson to feel proud and humble. Now Austin was asking where he was from and why he had come to Texas. The reply, that he was a surveyor who wanted to be a Protestant minister and a man who had studied law in Tennessee, led to talk of other men from that great state. The host casually reminded his guest that he had come to Texas several years too late as a surveyor and no telling how many years too early with his aspiration to preach Protestantism.

After further discourse Austin remarked on the strange fact that his secretary had not mentioned Mr. Jackson's application for a colonist's league of land, and Jackson replied that however strange it might seem he had not come here to seek gifts but to offer his assistance to Texans caught up in political oppression.

Austin's brow lifted a trifle, and a hint of a smile appeared on his face. "Oppression?" he said. "Perhaps a better word is 'misunderstanding.' I have been married to Texas for many years, Mr. Jackson, and my aim had been, and still is, prosperity for my people, understanding and harmony between Anglo-Texans and the Mexican government, from which we obtained a generous contract for colonization."

He talked on, slowly, quietly, recounting the many obstacles and troubles encountered in the tasks of settling the colony. Indians, floods, fever, land squabbles, allocating grants, the system of records, relief from tariff duties for the progress of trade, the matter of slaves to work the plantations versus Mexican laws which prohibitied slavery, these problems and more had preceded the recent disquiet arising from the customhouses.

"Lately," he said, "my troubles have been chiefly with colonists who forget they pay no taxes to the Mexican government but wish to take up arms because of excess tonnage fees imposed by Mexico. While justified in their objections to the highhanded methods and the exorbitant tax, they also forget that such matters, as the past proves, call for mediation instead of muskets. At least for the present."

His gaze drifted often, Horatio noticed, to the big window of his cluttered study. Outside, hummingbirds hovered over upturned honeysuckle petals, and the sounds of jays and cardinals mingled with the songs of Negroes engaged in various tasks.

"The slavery question, Mr. Jackson, presented a much graver problem than customs fees—" His voice trailed off, lifted again with, "There would be no plantations without the Negroes, and the law prohibited slaves. But we worked that out amicably, as you know."

"Yes, but didn't you try to get the colonists to free the slaves two years ago?"

"I did. I have no use for the institution of slavery. However, I have often been caught between personal ideals and what is best for my colony. You know which won. But back to your words 'political oppression.' There is little of that really. But there is an abundance of misunderstanding. With patience and an attempt at understanding among our people, we can as in the past, I believe, arrive at proper compromise and arbitration on all issues."

Jackson was impressed by this man. Against his wishes, he was forced to admit to himself that Austin had backed up his policies by deed and accomplishment. Rubbing his chin, frowning, Horatio studied the firm jaw and short upper lip of the *empresario* and tried to adjust all he had heard to all the militant colonists advocated.

"Mr. Austin, how do you stand on the Santa Anna and Bustamante issue?"

"In my position, Mr. Jackson, would you abandon a well-tried policy of silence, of aloofness, in matters dealing with Mexican political struggles?"

"Seems when the shoe pinches the foot, it's time to do something about it, sir."

Austin smiled tolerantly. "You can stretch a shoe, Mr. Jackson. Our present need is for harmony between Texans and Mexicans, two peoples of conflicting emotions, background, and economy. Each is to the other a curiosity. For example, Mexican leaders are horrified at the plight of the North American Negro. They overlook the fact that the Indians of Mexico, though free, are subjected to a more cruel bondage. These leaders on the other hand find it difficult to understand why it is that our colonists who paid taxes in the United States cry out in protest when they are asked to pay tonnage fees levied by Mexico.

"I leave for Saltillo tomorrow to attend the legislature of Coahuila. There the tax question will assail me again. In answering for my people I cannot tell the legislature that Texans choose to ignore and evade the question. I can only appeal once more for relief from taxation. However, that is beside the point. The examples cited are to acquaint you with natural differences which stress the need for a closer understanding, amicable and charitable, between two peoples."

Jackson rubbed an ear. "Now maybe it would help some if Mexico would allow the Texans to worship as they please. What about that, Mr. Austin?"

"I think true religion is an individual matter, Mr. Jackson. Believing this, let me say I felt no qualms whatever in accepting the Roman Catholic state church nominally for my people and myself as an expedient to colonization. Nor did the colonists. While I dislike sectarianism, I also feel that every man has an obligation to keep his word and promise. Don't you?"

Jackson could only admit that Austin had adroitly silenced him on the religious issue; for the time being, at least. While he wished to argue the matter, to lay his own convictions before the *empresario,* he realized that this was not the time for it. He was rising to go when Austin said:

"I appreciate your visit to offer assistance to Texans, Mr. Jackson. I believe you said 'Texans caught up in political oppression.' " Touching fingertips absently, his eyes still on Jackson, he said, "Now if you still feel that the people are oppressed, follow the dictates of your mind and heart. On the other hand, if you believe that my policy of seeking relief from taxes and laws effecting our economic and social welfare by peaceful and lawful means is the proper course to follow, then you might feel that you could better serve the people by advocating patience, restraint, and understanding."

Austin observed a pause, then added, "The latter course will not make you popular, Mr. Jackson. But think about it."

3

Jackson did think about it. Upon leaving Austin, he joined Wash and said they were going fishing. After the Negro dug worms and caught grasshoppers to use for bait, they rode to a quiet place on the bank of the Brazos.

Horatio had long since learned that a man thought things out better with a fishing pole in his hand. He could relax and gaze pensively at ripples in the water; let his mind ramble in search of answers.

The setting seemed made to order on this day. The south wind off the Gulf sang a perpetual song through the moss-laden branches of live oak trees. They sat in the shadow of the oaks, amid patches of sunlight that animated the grass and yellow earth in green and gold. Across the river, trees and brush shimmered in the afternoon heat and a pair of red-winged blackbirds were winging their way across the Rio Brazos de Dios.

Horatio Jackson saw little of the scene about him and he forgot that he held a fishing pole in his hand. He was too busy tackling the question the quiet, patient colonizer had placed firmly in his mind. It continued to lodge there, like a cocklebur, and stir up arguments aplenty. If the Mexican customs officers' unfair demands backed up by convict soldiers didn't constitute oppression, what did? However, was it wise for

Texans to rise up in open defiance of Mexican authority without first trying to remove the customs thorn by peaceful means?

"Throughout the history of the human race the free mind of man has looked for the truth," Jackson meditated aloud. "Truth in its real meaning, not as we want it to be."

Wash rolled his eyes from fishing line to Jackson, blinked his eyes, and resumed watch on the cork. "Truth is dese fish ain't bitin', Marse Jackson."

"Now is Mr. Austin unaware that the inherent natures of the people of Mexico and Texas make understanding impossible and conflict inevitable?"

"You got a nibble, Rev'ren'!"

"Or is it possible that he is far wiser than all of us and has found the key to that understanding between Mexicans and Anglo-Texans?"

"Got more'n a nibble! Look at dat! He done took it under! Now he turn loose! Where yo' all at, Rev'ren', suh?"

"You know, Wash, Mr. Austin went down to Mexico in 1823 and helped the first Mexican Congress draft the Imperial Colonization Law. It was a good one for both Mexico and the colonists. After six years he got it renewed. Maybe he is right in what he wants me to do."

"Yassuh. And I hopes I'se right in thinkin' maybe dat fish you let alone am goin' to hit my hook right soon."

A cloud drifted across the sun, its shadow moving on upriver. A crane flew by and then another. Wild bees hummed lazily. Wash closed his eyes and the pole soon slipped from his hands.

"But how can he be right if all his patience and efforts toward understanding and peace are rewarded by customhouses and forts for quartering convict soldiers?"

The answers, like the fish, continued to elude him. When late in the afternoon they rode back to San Felipe, Jackson was still undecided on how he could best serve the cause of the colonists. The problem hung heavy on his mind as they approached the town's boat landing. He paid no attention to the small schooner coasting in on the feeble southeast wind until Wash caught his sleeve and exclaimed:

"Looky who on de boat deck, Marse Jackson!"

Horatio looked. He jerked his horse to a sudden halt, stared with disbelief a moment and then with acceptance of what he saw. A wide grin spread across his face. Forgotten were Stephen F. Austin and all he advocated as his gaze held fast to Jane Wells.

CHAPTER 8

As Captain Herrick worked the schooner toward the landing with every inch of canvas he could muster to catch a dying breeze, Jackson continued to stare at the young lady who stood with one hand on the ship's rail, the other delicately holding the skirt of her pale green dress. Her hair fell from a matching green bonnet, flashing more golden than brown in the light of the late sun. Then she was looking at the small crowd lining the pier, and next straight at Jackson. She seemed to stiffen, though her blue eyes remained fixed on him. As he lifted his hat to her, she suddenly put her back to the rail.

A sober expression crossed Jackson's face. "Well, well!" he said under his breath, trying to overlook the fact that he had been snubbed. He was endeavoring to convince himself that he liked spirited women as well as spirited horses when he saw an opportunity to gain her attention. The schoonerman needed help from shore now. The craft was falling short of the pier and standing still as the weak wind and steady Brazos current fought it out for the hull. Oblivious of the crowd forming on shore, Jackson nudged his horse forward and cried out to the schooner captain to heave him a line.

"Bless ye!" Captain Herrick yelled. "The blarsted wind she's backin' fast, so show lively!"

The line he flung fell short of the bank, though Jackson rode out and retrieved it and gave it a hitch about his saddle horn. The tug of war began. Sails hung limp and it was horse versus current, neither willing to give an inch, until a cat's-paw barely filled the sails before falling away. The brief push helped momentarily, and slowly Jackson's horse pulled the boat toward the pier.

Horatio did not miss Jane Wells's glances at him as the townspeople on the riverbank and the few passengers and crew on deck cheered him on. Although she seemed caught up in the excitement, she refrained from voicing her feelings. He noticed also that she showed no surprise when a man on the pier bellowed forth:

"Why, if it ain't Hellfire Jackson! Come on, pray the schooner in, Rev'ren'!"

Nor did Jackson miss the quick glance Jane darted at the black-robed priest who stood at the edge of the crowd. So now Father Michael Muldoon knew who he was, Jackson reflected. Well, if a rose didn't have a thorn in the stem a man could look for a bee in the petals. That was life, and so was battling it out with the current of the Brazos a reminder that there was zest to life; especially under the challenging eyes of a vivacious woman.

With the schooner tied to the wharf, Captain Herrick helped Jane ashore. As Jackson parted the crowd and stood near her, Padre Muldoon greeted her, advising that he had promised to deliver her to the plantation owned by her friends. Jane thanked him, and said she would be ready as soon as the baggage came ashore. Only then did she look up into the big-boned face of Horatio Jackson. Her expression seemed to hover between pique and reserved friendliness, and her full red mouth tightened a trifle, as did her eyes.

"Welcome to the Brazos, Mr. Jackson. However, you're a little late with the promised bouquet." As Jackson detected a faint chill in her voice and winced, she suddenly gave him a warm smile, condescending in a way, he thought, and proceeded to introduce him to Father Muldoon.

"We've met," the priest said, forcing a smile that somehow failed to reach his eyes. "But I didn't know at the time he was Hellfire Jackson, the Redlands preacher we've been hearing about." His look seemed to say more, that now he could understand why the Protestant rabble rouser had given him the name "Pope of Mexico."

"Well, Padre," Jackson replied, "I reckon I'm the man, all right, except for the fact that I'm not an ordained minister."

"Not ordained!" Muldoon exclaimed. "Then by what authority could you conduct religious meetings even outside Catholic Texas?"

"By the authority of God's call, Father Muldoon. That and the desire of the people of rural areas to hear His Word read and hymns sung in His praise, even by an itinerant lay evangelist."

"Well said, Mr. Jackson. But by whose permission do you preach in the province of Texas?"

Jackson rubbed his jaw and assumed a serious expression. "Permission? Well, it's like this. Since I'm not recognized as a preacher by any church, what I say can hardly be called preachin'. And that being true, Padre, I'd be a conceited fool to presume I needed permission. Now don't you agree?"

As the priest cocked a perplexed brow, Jane laughed. "Better watch him, Father. You've heard about the trader who bested Mr. Mundy up in East Texas. Well, he's the man."

Muldoon eyed Jackson with fresh respect. "So you're riding Jonathan Mundy's mule!" An Irish smile lit up his face. "By what miracle? But never mind, just get behind me, Satan, before I shake your hand and call you friend!"

Jackson watched Jane and the padre depart, wondering as he did so if he had passed up an excellent opportunity to make a friend of Father Muldoon by not taking advantage of the priest's moment of friendliness to correct the "Pope of Mexico" misunderstanding. Evidently he had, for the priest had quickly shed his smile and iced over again.

"I was too carried away with Miss Wells, I reckon, to grab the padre's hand and shake off our differences."

"Yessah, reckon yo'all was," Wash said dismally. "Now dat all de folks knows you is a preachin' man, I'se hopin' dem men comin' our way ain't goin' to cause us no trouble."

Turning an alert glance on the group of settlers approaching him, Jackson recognized several men who had attended his songfest and Scripture reading at Elisha Roberts' camp. Following handclasps and an exchange of hearty greetings, the men came to the point. They would like to hold a camp meeting for the Brazoria area within the next couple of weeks if Jackson would preach and sing for them.

"Me? What about Father Muldoon?"

The colonists said they liked the padre. He was a fine man and a good pastor, but as a preacher he read too much Latin and talked over their heads. "While we took the Catholic faith to get land in Texas, what we're hankerin' for, Hellfire, is the old-fashioned kind of preachin' we got back in the States. The kind of gospel we hear you been preachin' up in the Redlands."

Horatio weighed the invitation carefully. First, he did not wish to offend Mr. Austin by holding Protestant services almost in the *empresario's* back yard, or get into trouble by openly violating the law. Next, he had no desire to widen the breach between himself and Father Muldoon. Beyond these things, he had not yet come to any decision regarding the kind of assistance he should give Texans, or whether or not he still felt they were victims of Mexican oppression. Politically, he rode the fence. On the other hand, he had been called to this land to go wherever he was invited to spread the Lord's message by word, song, and deed.

Jackson said at last, "Well, gentlemen, the cat's out of the bag and everybody knows who I am by now. Anyhow, you invited me into your midst, so I feel it's my duty to accept, no matter the consequences."

A half hour later Jackson called at Austin's house and asked for a brief audience with the colonizer. Mr. Williams advised that Austin was very busy preparing for his departure for Saltillo, Mexico, early next day, but that any urgent message would be conveyed to him.

Horatio rubbed an ear and palmed his chin. While he considered what he had to tell Mr. Austin was relatively important, he could scarcely label his message urgent. So rather than bother the man who shouldered the problems of all Texans, he asked Mr. Williams to advise the *empresario* that he had accepted an invitation to preach at a camp meeting in Brazoria.

Austin's secretary said, "He has already been informed of that, Mr. Jackson."

"Lord a-mercy! Now who could have beat me here with that news?"

"I believe you once referred to him as the Pope of Mexico." When Jackson recovered from the shock, Williams said, "I hope you realize what you're doing and proceed with caution."

Jackson left the house and stood with hands on hips, his gaze fixed on the dying band of orange that separated land and sky. "You know, Wash," he said dolefully, "we've been on the Brazos less than one day, and already I've carelessly made an enemy of a powerful priest, and let Mr. Austin confuse the political issues in my head. But I didn't stop there. Not Hellfire Jackson. No siree. I had to go and bite off what could be a real chunk of trouble by agreeing to hold a Brazoria camp meeting."

"Yassuh. Yo'all's sholy got a talent, Marse Jackson."

2

Several days later Horatio and Wash rode into Brazoria. They paused often to watch the activity along the river and to gaze in wonder at the bustling town that boasted forty or fifty houses, a few of them brick, a large hotel, several stores, mills, cotton gins, blacksmith shops, and other buildings. The sounds of hammers and saws and axes mingled with shouts of boatmen and songs of slaves along the wharf. Houses and sheds were being built of logs, split lumber, and slave-made bricks. As Jackson and Wash rode toward the center of town, a well-dressed man stepped into the street and hailed Horatio:

"Are you a carpenter, mister?"

"I can saw and swing a hammer."

Jackson and Wash spent one week helping the man from Connecticut and his sons erect their house in Texas. The owner was a Yale graduate, and his wife was the kind of woman who spread her finest china and linens in the open for every meal. Believing in polite living even in the wilderness, she required her family and servants to bow their heads for grace and to mind their manners. Horatio realized that she was more an exception than the rule among newcomers to the province, that her influence would be felt in Texas of the present and future. It was a good omen.

Jackson found Brazorians as friendly and hospitable as industrious. But since Brazoria was a large port in the center of the most populated colony in Texas, her citizens were quick to feel any change in Mexican tariff regulations. They were acutely interested in the political wind blowing up out of Mexico. It had already slowed river and ocean shipping, so it was only natural that they were angry at the arrogant Colonel Bradburn, ranking Mexican military officer in Texas. Stationed at Anahuac, in upper Galveston Bay, he had reinforced the garrison at the closed port of Velasco with one hundred twenty-five soldiers sent to Texas by President Bustamante.

"So you see," they told Jackson, "the presence of troops again means either another attempt to collect outrageous tonnage fees or suppression of our support of Santa Anna, and maybe both."

"Could be," Jackson said, pondering the whole thing all over again, wishing himself to enter the spirit of all this.

"Right," the man went on. "Now as we see it, a little timely action to oust Bradburn over at Anahuac, as well as the garrison down at the mouth of the Brazos at Velasco could have its advantages, Hellfire. It might cause Santa Anna once he gets in power to grant Texas full statehood, lift the ban on immigration, and allow us Texans free trade."

"Correct," another man put in. "Things are hot and smoldering over at Anahuac, I hear tell. Trouble sets on a powder keg, ready to bust loose any time now. And it won't stop there."

Jackson tried to forget political troubles and busied himself helping the colonists prepare for the crowds expected at the first camp meeting on the Brazos.

There was much to be done before the morning service of Sunday, June twenty fourth, when he would open the revival. The large tabernacle, with open sides and brush-and-thatch roof, was not quite finished. Benches had yet to be made, as well as the pulpit platform. Work on the corrals for stock and sheds for families who would come by wagon and oxcart had also been slowed by days of rain. But the hot June sun finally won over stubborn clouds off the Gulf, and Jackson once more set the pace with hammer, saw, and ax.

That was the physical side. He rolled up his sleeves and fell to it with genuine enjoyment, for in sweat and labor he found escape from a number of things that nagged at his peace of mind. However, he could not forget that the local alcalde had suggested that he refrain from holding Protestant services. While genial Señor Eduardo de Herrera had voiced no threat whatever, his courteous approach implied as much. Beyond this, there was Father Muldoon to pacify, if possible, and this called for a most diplomatic preface to his opening sermon. Next, with the political wind blowing increasingly warmer, not even an evangelist could sit astraddle the fence on the Brazos for long. Therefore in the week remaining before the camp meeting he should and must make up his mind and take a stand one way or another.

"Do I go along with Mr. Austin or with the majority of the colonists?"

In an endeavor to answer this most important question, Horatio broached the subject often and weighed each man's opinion. Some were pacifists, some were warmongers, but even the former were tired of Colonel Bradburn. And so it went, back and forth, with valid arguments for settling issues by arbitration and by, again the popular term, "timely action."

Some days earlier Jackson had seized upon the question as an excuse for writing Miss Wells at Peach Bluff Plantation. To his surprise, one morning a riverman handed him a letter from upriver. He read avidly the brief message:

Mr. Jackson, sir—

In reply to yours in which you weigh mediation versus impetuous action as a proper course for Texans in these troubled times, I implore you to consider maturely the advantage of a peaceful settlement of any and all differences with Mexico as demonstrated by our great leader, Colonel Stephen F. Austin. Your personal stand is important in this matter because of the influence you can in your position as (minister?) exert, and for this reason I write. The news that you are holding a camp meeting comes as a decided shock! Such defiance indicates that your sympathies are with the warmongers. True?

Respectfully & c.
Jane Wells

Postscript: If you wish to discuss the above further, I shall reach Brazoria on the nineteenth, and c/o Oak Island Plantation.

3

Toward midafternoon of Wednesday, June twentieth, a tall, broad-shouldered man clad in a maroon-colored coat, silk cravat, and tan trousers—clothing he had obtained by trading Bibles and some of his surveying equipment—tied his horse to a tree before the main house of Oak Island Plantation. In his hand was a bouquet of wild flowers. Removing his hat, he walked up the path to the porch of the long one-storied house. A Negro servant met him, and soon returned to advise that Miss Wells would join him on the porch shortly.

Horatio Jackson nodded his head, eyed the bouquet skeptically, and admitted to himself that he was a little nervous. "Maybe it's the way I'm rigged out," he mused. "Or maybe I'm expectin' a wet wasp with an anxious stinger."

He waited, feeling more uncomfortable with each passing minute. His gaze alternately drifted to the prairie meadow dotted with wild peach and mesquite and back to the breezeway or "dog trot," as it was called, that divided the house into two parts under one roof. Then he suddenly tensed, rose from the rawhide-bottom chair, and stood blinking his eyelids in the manner of a man who might be looking at a woman for the first time. This was true in a way, for in his opinion Miss Jane had never appeared quite so pretty and exciting before.

She stood in the breezeway, her direct glance full upon him. The shadows gave her an ethereal look that, like moonlight, seemed to intensify beauty in any woman. Nor did the fact that she used chalk on her face and neck, as was the fashion, take anything from her. The brown ringlets at her forehead, the curve of her mouth, despite the determined set of her lips, wouldn't allow it.

He managed to bow. "Good afternoon, Miss Jane. If I

may be so bold, I'll say these lovely flowers I fetched aren't half so lovely as you."

Jane's brow wrinkled an instant, as if she hardly knew what to make of this man who should be in buckskin instead of broadcloth, and who addressed her in the words of a suitor. She accepted the wild flowers, however, remarked on his thoughtfulness, and asked if he would escort her down to the boat landing where she wished to post a letter to her aunt in Velasco. All the while her blue eyes met his, swept on past him, and returned as if to challenge his right to call on her.

Horatio winced under her imperious glance, but quickly rallied to hand her down the steps. He liked her in lavender, and he thought the lavender silk bow that tied her bonnet on and nestled under her chin added just the proper feminine frill to complete a picture he would long remember.

After a dozen or so steps, Jackson remarked on the fine location of the plantation.

"Yes," she replied. "Isn't it?"

"Indeed." That was the extent of their conversation.

They paused in the shade of a vine-covered arbor that gave a view of the placid, muddy Brazos and the dense growth of sugar cane on the opposite side. Beyond lay a clearing representing a great outlay in labor, and in the background large live oak trees rose from patches of shade to touch the bleached June sky. It was a pretty scene, and it reflected the industry of the Anglo-Texans, and it brought home the fact that the ideal was land, a permanent and prosperous community for man, a place to build homes and raise children.

It wasn't a bad idea, he decided, eying Jane surreptitiously. She was long-limbed and graceful, and honest, perhaps a little too honest.

As they moved slowly down the red clay bluff to the landing, he guided her past prickly pear and thorny growth. For something to relieve the oppressive silence, he said, "I got your letter, Miss Jane."

"Well, I hope it helped you make a decision." Getting no reply, she said, "Well, did it?"

"No ma'am."

Her eyes were wide, brightly curious, then demanding. "So you're a war-party man! Why not admit it?"

"Because I'm not, that's why," he replied tartly. "I'm straddlin' a fence trying to get off and can't. I talked to Mr. Austin and I approved his ideas, and I talked to the shippers and men on the streets and I agree that they've got reasons to get their tempers up at the Mexicans."

She laughed lightly. "Really?" After posting her letter in a box for access to any boatman, she stood on the pier gazing downstream. "Well, would it surprise you to know I feel the same way, Mr. Jackson?"

"Then you're ridin' the fence with me!"

"I never straddle an issue, sir. While I feel at times that Mr. Austin is too mild and the colonists are too headstrong and rash, I can also be in sympathy with the views of both without letting myself get caught in the middle."

"Well, well, ma'am! Now that's a trick I'd like to learn. Just how do you do it?"

"It's very simple," she said, glancing up at him. "One day boys in my school were playing with an iron hoop. Jonas, a strapping, overgrown boy, decided to keep it when it was Edwin's turn to roll it. Though small, Edwin clung to it and demanded that his right to it be recognized. Jonas then said, 'And if I don't let you have it, just what'll you do?' The small boy had a choice. He could fight, and he was justified in doing so, but with the certain knowledge that he would take a beating besides losing the hoop. Or he could hold his temper and threats in check and appeal to Jonas' sense of fairness. Now suppose you were little Edwin, which choice would you have made, Mr. Jackson?"

"Well, it's hard to hold your temper in a case like that. And a boy don't worry too much about the odds when he knows he's right. But tell me what little Edwin did."

"Why, he did just what you would have done. He fought and took a beating. And he lost the hoop."

"Maybe so," Jackson spoke up. "But he had the spunk to stand up for his rights!"

Jane was smiling now, rather teasingly, and shaking her head as if she found humor in despairing of him. Suddenly he seemed to know why, and he frowned and reddened in his embarrassment, for he realized that he had been so quick to champion little Edwin's cause that he had forgotten there was a moral to the story. In that moment she gave it to him and it struck like a stinger when she said:

"Oddly enough, Mr. Jackson, when I took Jonas to task, he said, 'Miss Wells, I didn't want to fight Edwin. If he hadn't hit me, I would have given him the hoop.' "

Jackson stopped still. Ramming his hands in his pocket, he eyed her severely. "I reckon poor little Edwin was Texas. Right?" Meeting with only a slight shrug of her shoulders and a perfectly serene look, which he took to be an expression of triumph, he said gruffly, "Now that we know who's got the hoop and why, ma'am, I'd be gratified to have you enlighten me on another subject. In your letter you say my holding a camp meeting comes as a decided shock, and that such defiance indicates my sympathies are with the warmongers. Just how in blue blazes do you—?"

"Why, Mr. Jackson, you sound angry!"

"And you sound mighty superior, ma'am. Fact is, every time we've met you seem to rub me under your feet with what you say and the way you look at me. But about my camp meeting, just how does my preaching make me a warmonger?"

"On second thought, Mr. Jackson, it seems more likely you were born with a warlike disposition." There was no humor in her smile as she said, "Now if you'll be so kind as to see me back to the house, I'll relieve you of my undesirable company." As he simply stood there in mixed bewilderment and anger, she tossed her head defiantly. "Now, Mr. Jackson!"

He did not move, he just studied her, half in anger, half in admiration of her face, the spirit in her eyes, and her easy, graceful motions. "I—I didn't say you were undesirable company. All I said was—well, what I meant to say is the way you bristle up at me for no good reason at all riles me considerable. And what's more, you lay the ice on thick the way you say 'Mr. Jackson.' And you don't approve of my preaching, and my—"

"All right! So I don't approve!" She faced him, hands on hips, eyes narrowing and flashing, and lips tightening into a firm line. "You ride under false colors—a preacher under the guise of a surveyor! You excuse yourself for violating Mexican law by saying the Lord sent you to Texas. Why, that's sacrilege!"

Whirling, she took a step toward the bank. Before she could walk past him, he caught her shoulders and held her roughly. "You're wrong, ma'am!" he fairly yelled at her.

Her eyes alternately widened and narrowed. Then she was staring at him, no longer trying to free herself from the grip of his large hands. What he was saying, or perhaps the sudden calmness of his voice, held her motionless and attentive. "You may not approve of me or what I'm doing but I'm not sacrilegious. I heard the call to come to Texas. I didn't want to come. But I came, came feeling the way, groping for the light." Slowly his fingers released her shoulders. "I'm still groping, ma'am."

For a run of seconds she studied him, suspiciously at first, then very curiously, as if he constituted a puzzle that defied solution. His glance did not waver under her close scrutiny but held firm and steady.

"Perhaps I've misjudged you. I'm sorry if I have, Mr. Jackson."

"Then wait until you're sure before you say so."

Turning from him, she walked the length of the pier slowly, pausing to gaze out over the water before returning. He saw her eyelashes fall, flutter a moment, then lift. She said:

"Then I'll wait until after the camp meeting."

Something in her tone of voice sounded like mockery, but as he searched her expression he could not find the slightest trace of it. Rather, he saw challenge, strong and deep. In silence she seemed to declare her doubt of any man's true worth and to dare him to prove her wrong.

"We'd better go," she was saying when the challenge of her seemed to splash over and through him like a warm wave. He tried to escape it and at the same time to cling to it, even as a sudden yearning for a colonist's league of land, for a home, and plantation, and a wife, flashed into his mind. A wife named Jane!

He took the step separating them, caught her slim waist, and, unmindful of the startled look in her eyes, drew her roughly to him, tipped his head, and found her mouth with his.

He felt her struggling, and she was moving her head from side to side to escape him. Her mouth was firm, too firm. Then she was no longer trying to free herself from his embrace and he felt for an ephemeral moment her lips dissolve and her hand touch the back of his neck. But he wasn't sure. He could never be sure, for she was pushing him away from her.

Horatio Jackson was suddenly afraid, very afraid. He broke and ran, ran as fast as his legs would carry him, to his horse. He fairly leaped into the saddle and, without a backward glance, sent the animal racing toward Brazoria.

Oak Island Plantation was a good mile behind him when he reined the horse to a standstill, dismounted, and sat on a cottonwood stump to ponder his rash act and its consequences. "Jumpin' Jehoshaphat!" he said over and over. Whether what he had done was a crime or sin, he was still too frightened to know. If it was a sin, he had been trapped by a mighty fast devil who came like a bolt of lightning out of the blue.

"Only it was lavender, Lord."

A bracing Gulf breeze pushed cottony clouds up the Brazos and stirred the surface of the river. The scene held and there seemed a sigh of trouble on the wind. And weaving in and out of wind, water, and sky, out of Austin's request that he preach patience and restraint, was the lavender dress again and the beautiful woman he had held in his arms. What a woman!

Suddenly Horatio Jackson could contain himself no longer. He got to his feet and let go with a yell before sailing his hat high in the air.

CHAPTER 9

It was late Saturday afternoon in downriver Velasco. The June sun sank behind a blue cloud bank, silvering the ragged edges and hurling white shafts high into the bleached sky. For a time the reflected light played on scores of gulls banking and screaming about the rigging of a schooner pushing cautiously across Velasco Bar for port entrance. Then the sun peeped through a tiny hole in the distant cloud screen and for an instant shot the surface of the sea, the bosoms of gulls, and sails of the small schooner with sunset colors.

The parapet of the Mexican fort at Velasco accepted also a brief coat of orange-red, as did the handsome officer who trained a telescope on the incoming schooner. As the sun retreated behind the cloud, Lieutenant Colonel Domingo de Ugartechea said to his subordinate:

"It is the schooner *Austin,* Juan. Señor John Austin has returned from Anahuac."

"*Por Dios,* he is the rabble rouser, Colonel. That *hombre!* Such a difference in him and the kind Señor Stephen F. Austin. But they are not related, which explains it in a way. Now I am due at the blacksmith shop to get my saber, Colonel. I hope to return before the schooner arrives."

Several minutes later Lieutenant Juan Pacho of the Velasco garrison wrinkled his nose at the acrid smell of seared hoofs and charcoal smoke that met him at the entrance of Bucktooth Sal's shop. Mules and burros staked out in back were greeting the end of day with the usual jackass serenade, and Señora Sal was answering the beasts with a thunderous order to stop their "damn'd racket."

A most unusual woman, Lieutenant Pacho admitted for perhaps the hundredth time. She provoked no end of wonder. It seemed that fate had played a huge joke on her by not making her a man. Now she was bending over the forefoot of a horse.

"*Buenas dias,* Señora," he said. "Is my saber ready?"

"Well bust my britches, if it ain't Lootenant Juan! No, it ain't fixed yet. Now you can sit and wait for it, or you can cut your tortillas with a jackknife."

"I'll wait." Seating himself on a nail keg, he asked about Señorita Wells.

"Yeah, Lootenant, you always askin' about Jane. Right interested in her, ain't you? Well, when you come a-totin' a full colonel's pay in yer pocket—that is, if Santa Anna don't reduce you Bustamantes to convict soldiers first—old Sal might invite you to set down to sowbelly and *chile verde* one fine night. But don't count on it."

Pacho shrugged and grinned. He was used to this. "When does she return from Brazoria?" he asked.

"Won't know till I see her up there tomorrow. I'm goin' up to the camp meetin' this preacher they call Hellfire Jackson is holdin'. That is, if he's not foamin' at the mouth by then. Cap'n Herrick says he was roundin' Oak Island Bend Wednesday afternoon and seen this Jackson on the bank jump up and yell and throw his hat treetop high. Course he could a been practicin' up for the services."

"Camp meeting? I'm surprised that Señor Austin sanctioned Protestant services, Señora."

"Why not? Padre Muldoon can't do it all. Besides, law or no law, us double-barreled Texans is gettin' damn'd tired of Mexican oppression, religious and otherwise, Lootenant. You said yourself we were gettin' a raw deal. Now if you'd back up talk with action, it might help."

"*Sí*. But, Señora, saying and doing are two different things."

"Yeah, I know, Juan boy, but don't be surprised if we Anglos do some doin' any day now."

Several minutes later a Mexican soldier reached the blacksmith shop on the run. After giving Pacho a crisp salute, he said Lieutenant Colonel Ugartechea wanted the lieutenant to return to the fort at once. To Pacho's question he replied:

"I do not know, *Teniente,* but something was said about trouble at Anahuac."

Bucktooth Sal dropped the forefoot of the horse, wiped her hands on the grimy leather apron, and stared at the soldier, then at the genial lieutenant. Seeing the troubled expression forming on his face, she moved to his side.

"What did I tell you, Juan lad, you and Domingo Ugartechea? Well, you can bet the Santa Anna sympathizers are fittin' a rope to Bradburn's neck for the hangin' he needs." As Pacho departed for the fort, she cried after him, "Wouldn't want to see it happen to you too, so you better declare for Santa Anna!"

Several minutes later curiosity got the better of Sally. After finishing the chore at hand, she flung the leather apron aside and struck out for the American Hotel to find out what had happened at Anahuac. She was not the only person with the same idea. Farmers, boatmen, sailors, merchants, clerks, sawyers, and hangers-on crowded the street and wharves to await the end of the conference between Captain John Austin's group and the Mexican colonel at the fort. Although speculation was rife as to what trouble was brewing at Anahuac, the Texans were in accord on one thing—they had a "bellyful" of Bradburn.

At around half past eight, Captain John Austin and Captain William Russell, together with William Houston Jack of San Felipe, left the fort and joined the curious colonists in front of the American Hotel.

Besieged with questions, Captain Austin loosed a booming "Belay!" Out of the silence this evoked, he said, "Our esteemed friend Colonel Juan Davis Bradburn—" laughter rang out with that, "had the gall to arrest Patrick C. Jack for organizing a militia around Anahuac. When Pat's lawyer, William B. Travis, went to get him out, Bradburn arrested him too. Well, William Jack rode like Paul Revere and got a rescue party, and on the tenth of June they captured one of Bradburn's patrols. Now while a citizens' army charged the fort, three of our Texas schooners, our *Austin*, also the *Waterwitch* and *Red Rover*, began the blockade and siege of the fort."

Captain Austin's pause evoked a clamor of "What happened, John? Go on!"

"Quiet!" he thundered forth. "We blasted that fort with our Kentuckys, the only arms we had aboard, until Bradburn felt singed enough to ask for a parley. He said if we would release his soldiers he would free Travis and Jack. We complied. But did that ornery, lyin', cheatin' renegade Bradburn? He did not!"

An angry murmur ran through the crowd. Captain Austin continued, saying, "So we decided to set sail for Brazoria and get the cannon up there that Cap'n Brown brought in on the *Sabine* and go back to Anahuac and bombard the fort. Blast Bradburn out of Texas!"

Nothing could have pleased the audience more. When the cheers finally died down, John Austin said his delegation had called on Lieutenant Colonel Ugartechea for the express purpose of requesting the amiable colonel, whom they all liked, to declare his loyalty to the Constitution of 1824 and its champion Santa Anna to the extent of permitting the

Texans to carry the cannon unmolested past his fort; that Ugartechea had replied that he could not in honor violate his oath as a soldier and denounce President Bustamante, nor could he allow the cannon past his fort for that reason and for another—Colonel Bradburn had ordered him to get possession of the cannon at all costs.

"I say to hell with Bradburn! As sure as tomorrow's Sunday, we'll go up to Brazoria for the cannon and volunteers!" Austin added, "And unless our friend Ugartechea meets our demands upon our return, we'll turn the cannon on the fort yonder!"

Bucktooth Sal led the cheering. When it died down, she lent fresh energy to the spirit of rebellion with a yell that carried across to the Mexican fort:

"*Viva* Santa Anna!"

From Fort Velasco came a shout of defiance: "*Viva la Republica! Viva* Bustamante!"

2

Dawn of Sunday, June twenty-fourth, broke fair over the Brazos with the usual summer promise of a hot and humid day. Few Brazorians worried about the heat, however. They were more concerned with looking their best at the opening services of the camp meeting. There broadcloth, silk, linen, and cotton would mingle with homespun and buckskin. A festive air hung over Brazoria that morning, for after the singing and preaching dinner would be served on the grounds. Every family would contribute to the feast. Cakes and pies had been baked. Goat, venison, pork, and beef had been cooked in pits. And wagons now creaking into town from plantations and scattered farms carried baskets and boxes of fried chicken, fresh-cooked garden vegetables, sweet jams and jellies, as well as beribboned young ladies to catch the eyes of young blades.

The day promised more, something new and exciting to the Austin Colony, the first open-and-declared Protestant church services on the Catholic Brazos. There was a hint of defiance about it, polite but laden with a curious and pleasant suspense. Now how would Padre Muldoon react to the challenge? Was this the beginning of freedom of worship in Texas? Would Mexico retaliate by revoking the land titles of all who attended the forbidden Protestant services? Would Mr. Austin ask the frontier preacher to leave his colony? "*Quien sabe?*" as their Mexican neighbors said with a shrug,

"Who knows?" Whatever the result, the colonists anticipated the cause with rising interest.

By ten o'clock that morning the throng of milling men, women, and children exceeded all expectations. When they kept coming, arriving in oxcarts, wagons, on foot, and on mules, burros, and horses, logs were skinned of branches to serve as seats for the overflow crowd. By eleven, when the war-minded John Austin and his party from Velasco were a little more than an hour away from Brazoria, even the log seats were occupied and people were standing.

Jackson had never expected anything like this. In numbers the gathering far surpassed the meeting up at the Nashville settlement. He stood on the rostrum, dressed in his Sunday best, a proud and grateful man, an humble servant of the Lord. His eye swept the crowd, slowly, carefully, in search of something or someone. Finally the search ended, and he seemed to breathe with certain relief. Then for several seconds he traded glances with Jane Wells, who refused to let him outstare her.

Jane regretted that her Aunt Sally had failed to arrive as promised, for she would have no doubt enjoyed Hellfire Jackson's type of gospel preaching. Jane had come with Angela Wilson, whom she was visiting. Angela, about Jane's age and a striking woman with honey-colored hair, seemed quite fascinated by Mr. Jackson.

The musicians were now taking seats upon the platform, and Jackson was placing his Bible on the cottonwood altar. While the two fiddles and banjo were being tuned, Jackson saw everyone staring toward the street. As he looked in that direction, he gave an inward start and said to himself, "Here comes trouble, Lord! I'd sooner face Hominy Baines!"

Moving slowly toward the brush-and-pole tabernacle was a procession led by Father Muldoon. Chanting, holding a crucifix above his hand, the padre came on, followed by another priest and the alcalde of Brazoria. Behind these men were the Mexican customs collector for the ports of Brazoria and Velasco, and two Mexican soldiers. A score of persons, Mexican and Anglo, completed the religious procession.

Father Muldoon halted at the edge of the tabernacle, blessed the gathering in Latin, Spanish, and English, then slowly surveyed them in silence. It was evident that every landowner there felt the padre's gaze and thought it both accusing and threatening, for faces reddened, glances fell, and there followed an uneasy clearing of throats. "The power of silence," Jackson was thinking.

Father Muldoon invited all who wished to keep the religious covenant made between colonists and the government to join his procession on its way to Mass at the little church. Horatio felt that the burden imposed on his audience had been shifted to him when embarrassed landowners sent appealing glances his way. Aware that it was incumbent on him to do something, he also found himself wondering if Father Muldoon had him neatly trapped. He wished to shout defiance, but was quick to admit that rashness would not serve him here. Then an idea popped into his head. Lifting a hand, he said:

"Father Muldoon, we all appreciate your thoughtfulness, your visit, and your invitation to Mass. It was right hospitable of you, and I for one feel we would be remiss in our Christian duty if we failed to reciprocate. So, since you're already here, we invite you to stay. You can hold your Mass first and I'll preach next."

Before the priest could reply, Horatio forced a broad grin on his face and said, "I know it's unorthodox, Padre, but then it ain't every day that a priest comes callin' at a frontier camp meeting. And before you say no, Father, let me remind you that dinner on the grounds, the finest and fanciest victuals a body ever said thanks over, follows the services. Now what do you say to that, Padre?"

"Unfortunately I have no choice but to decline the invitation to hold joint services here, Mr. Jackson." Then, with a twinkle in his eye that said he wasn't about to let a transient frontier preacher get the better of him in his home territory, Father Muldoon said, "However, being a good Irishman with a healthy appetite, I'll counter your offer with a real sporting proposition, Mr. Jackson. I'll stay for your services provided you'll attend my Mass directly following this meeting."

"You mean after we eat?" Jackson asked.

"I do not. Your stomach is no more privileged than mine, sir. You'll suffer with me and eat after Mass with the Pope of Mexico."

A ripple of laughter and then hearty guffaws told Jackson that he was slugging it out with a man of quick wit who was parrying his every thrust with admirable skill. Then, like a veteran fencer, the priest caught him off guard with a deep-throated chuckle and a remark that scored another round of laughter from the listeners:

"Furthermore, Mr. Jackson, since noon Mass means twelve o'clock, I'll thank you to oblige me—and the folks with appetites—by trimming your sermon down to one hour."

Jackson agreed to this, though he was unable to resist injecting a little humor of his own by saying it took at least one hour to dent the souls of pioneers from the States, and that the real devil-chasing took place in the next hour.

As Jane listened and laughed with each man in the exchange of quips, she wondered at her mixed feelings, asking herself whom she actually favored in this duel in which religious and political issues were barely masked by surface humor. Certainly the meeting was significant if only because it was the first open test of the Mexican ban on Protestant worship. However, personalities seemed to take precedence over issues, and throughout the song service she vacillated between the popular priest and the unpredictable backwoods preacher.

Then once again the latter resorted to prayer. Earnest prayer, Jane admitted, trying to reconcile the man who petitioned the Lord to the one who had embraced her as vigorously a few days earlier. She gave up and joined the congregation in another song. Soon the man who had earned the name Hellfire was running long, bony fingers through his shaggy mane and opening his Bible.

"The first verse in the first chapter of the first book in God's Bible tells us: 'In the beginning God created the heaven and the earth.' Who denies this? You, brother?" Jackson asked, pointing a finger. "You, sister? Does the Baptist deny this? Does the Methodist say it's not true? Does the Presbyterian? Does the Catholic?"

After reading the second verse, he once more thrust his finger forward and demanded in louder tones: "Do you doubt this, brother? Do you, sister? Does the man of Baptist faith? The Methodist? The Presbyterian? Does the Catholic?"

Following each verse through the tenth, he asked the same questions. Before reading verse eleven he removed his coat and mopped his face with a handkerchief. Then, pausing to wait while a mother made a hasty exit with her lusty-voiced baby, he read the eleventh verse, in which the Lord called upon the earth to bring forth grass, herbs, and trees. Again he asked the same question, but with more force and vigor. His arm rose higher, came down faster to level a finger at the congregation and demand if this brother or that sister doubted the Scriptures. Did the Baptist, the Methodist, the Presbyterian, and last, the Catholic?

Since the third verse the congregation had replied to his questions with, "No, brother!" with a few scattered shouts of "Hallelujah! Praise the Lord!" thrown in for good measure. Following the last mass reply, Father Muldoon stood and in true frontier camp-meeting style cried, "Hallelujah!" and then said:

"And if it pleases the Lord, could Mr. Jackson put the Catholics first just once?"

"Aye, Padre!" Jackson boomed forth, his voice rising above the undertones of mirth. "And the Good Book tells us the earth brought forth grass, herbs, and trees. Now that was the beginning. It goes on, but we'll stop there and say the Catholics, Baptists, Presbyterians, Methodists, and all other creeds accept the Holy Word. That they do, and yet they jaw back and forth, all claimin' their belief is the only one—

"Yes, sir, the only one!" Jackson threw off his tie and opened his shirt collar. "They get right het up about it, they do, like they each believe they got the only prayers God listens to! Why, you'd think each had an entirely different God! Now what would it be like if they did? Well, things might be a sight different, my good brothers and sisters. The Catholic God—honorin' your request to be first, Padre—might have said on that day the Lord was makin' trees that He wasn't particularly fond of the kind of leaves that grew on the live oak tree yonder, that He preferred the leaves the persimmon tree was sportin'. Then the Methodist God up and protests, sayin', 'Now look here, I'm all for puttin' magnolia leaves on that old moss-covered oak!' 'Oh no,' says the Baptist God, 'none o' that for me! I like a fuzzy leaf, like the cottonwood.' And so it would go among them, and if they were like us militant, mule-headed mortals, who refuse to give an inch in our set beliefs, that old oak yonder might still be lookin' around for leaves."

"Amen, Brother Hellfire!" a bearded man yelled.

"Who says 'Amen'? Persimmon-leaf or magnolia-leaf Christian?" Lowering his voice, Jackson said, "The forest of worship is full of trees, my beloved brothers and sisters. And we mortals of all faiths wag our jawbones and tongues like prophets and claim to have the only tree in the forest, which is utterly impossible, my friends, when all rise from the roots found in the Holy Bible. Therefore, one tree, one faith, one church, cannot be the only religion and road to eternal salvation, can't be the only tree in God's forest."

Bringing his fist down hard on the pulpit, he cried to the top of his voice, "It can't and it ain't!"

Jane was wondering with rising trepidation whether or not Jackson intended to openly denounce the Catholic Church next when he settled her fears by saying, "You think on it, my good friends and righteous Christians, while I take the rest of the time allotted me to speak to the sinners and bigots, and say in the words of Jesus, in the Book of Matthew, 'Ye blind guides, which strain at a gnat, and swallow a camel. Woe unto you, scribes and Pharisees, hypocrites!' "

He talked on, holding his audience spellbound with the kind of sermon for which he was becoming famous. He waged total war against the old devil and sin. He preached hell fire and damnation, and he told the sinners to clean up their souls and leave whisky alone and stop coveting "you know who, you young blades and old goats!" If they didn't get right with God then they could expect His wrath in more ways than their mortal minds could conceive.

"Yes, sir, ye scribes, Pharisees, hypocrites! Admit that your souls are hungry for the Holy Spirit! Well, this is the time to find it and this is the place to find it, right here in this refuge from the old devil."

As he banged the Bible with the palm of his hand, something stirred in the brush-covered roof above the platform. A moment later a copperhead snake emerged, dropped, and hung with its tail anchored to a limb in the roof. When women in the congregation screamed and pointed, the two fiddle players looked up and, seeing a snake poised directly over their heads and eying them speculatively, flung fiddles high and fairly leaped over their chairs. As they hit the ground running, the banjo player let go with a yell of "Goddam snake!" and took a frightened swing at the unwelcome visitor before diving for the aisle. Just as he landed in the lap of a plump lady on the first row, Jackson grabbed up the banjo and cried out:

"The devil dared to join us! There he is wagging his finger in our faces!" He swung the banjo. The snake dropped to the platform and wriggled toward Jackson. "By the grace of God, you ain't chasin' Hellfire Jackson from the pulpit!" He was dancing gingerly about, however, swooping in and out like an Indian, and hovering over the now retreating copperhead.

Suddenly he grabbed it by the tail and swung it like a whip. There was a resounding crack. Then Jackson flung the headless snake aside and returned to the pulpit.

"Old Nick came after you sinners, all right. You saw him, saw a servant of the Lord exterminate the symbol of hell. But he'll come in another form, 'cause he's after you and he won't give up! Now, ye scribes, Pharisees, hypocrites, blasphemers, coveters, liars, cheats, and just plain homemade sinners, soon as the music and singin' start—and I hope the musicians are still amongst us—you better walk down the aisle, get on your knees, and get right with God!"

A great number did just that. As the singing continued past noon, and Father Muldoon waited outside for Jackson, many of those who knelt and prayed leaped to their feet and shouted their praises to the Lord.

Jane bit her lip and wrinkled her brow. She did not know just what to make of Mr. Hellfire Jackson. While she had to admit that he could sway a multitude and turn one's very soul inside out for minute inspection, she continued to believe he was something of an opportunist. The way he had used the snake incident to frighten scores of people into public repentance seemed to prove as much. She could not be sure of this, however, any more than she could positively label him a crowd pleaser pure and simple who, like a weather vane, obeyed whatever wind was blowing at the time. But of one thing she was reasonbably sure, he could not forever hide the real Mr. Jackson behind a mask; something, some person or event, would serve to uncover him before the week-long camp meeting ended.

Such were her thoughts when sounds of shouting down at the river claimed her attention. Just as Jackson concluded the benediction, Jane and everyone there felt a sharp warning of trouble on the wind, for the yells from the wharf were plainer now:

"Down with Colonel Bradburn! We've come for the cannon and volunteers!"

CHAPTER 10

That afternoon Jackson was forced to look the problem facing him squarely in the eye. He could no longer straddle a split rail on the issue now demanding a decision on the part of every Anglo-Texan: Justified defiance of Mexican authority or patience and restraint in accordance with Stephen F. Austin's wishes. Which? What was the proper course, mediation or muskets? Which would benefit Texas more in the long run? Should the colonists submit to further mistreatment from Colonel Bradburn or strike back and let Mexico know once and for all that Texans would not tolerate Mexican oppression?

Jackson mingled with the people on street corners and along the river. He lent an ear to Captain John Austin and Captain William Russell, and to William H. Jack, who told in detail all that Bradburn had done to strain the patience of peace-loving Texans. Gaunt men in homespun listened, raised shag eyebrows, and rubbed cheeks girt with stubble. What they heard seemed to strike iron against flintrock and spark flashes of anger in their eyes. And John Austin, ex-Connecticut Yankee and ex-filibuster, fanned the sparks with further talk:

"The very idea of Bradburn confiscating our supplies, declaring our land titles void, placing prominent citizens in jail without any reason whatever, and forcing us to go overland to Anahuac to get clearance to sail our ships! Can we go on tolerating this? Next he sends word to Colonel Ugartechea to take our cannon. Why, he's dangerous to have around, an absolute monarch without scruples, reason, or any respect or regard for us or our rights!"

A colonist poled a cheek with tongue, then said, "I volunteer, Cap'n Austin. I'll go get my blue whistler."

Another asked when the volunteers would go downriver, and Austin replied, "Before midnight. We plan to sail past the fort at Velasco, our cannon cold or hot, boys, early tomorrow morning."

"On board what? Cap'n, that little schooner o' yourn might tip her stern under with a cannon aft. Besides that," the man laughed, "she won't ship enough men to aim a cannon."

"Don't plan on using her, Zeke," Austin replied. "See that big schooner docked over there?" He winked an eye. "She'll be in our hands tonight."

Jackson eyed the fine schooner *Brazoria.* She was tied up fore and aft to the dock, sails neatly furled, her unsuspecting crew snoring through *siesta* in the shade of her deckhouse. To seize the vessel would be an act of piracy, he realized, and with Stephen F. Austin down in Saltillo there would be no one to prevent it. Unless he, Hellfire Jackson, could prevail on the outraged colonists. "No, not me!" he protested to himself. "Why should I, when I'm almost ready to join up with them?"

Everywhere he turned, men were recounting their grievances against Bradburn. Fists struck palms resoundingly, and voices lifted with no patience left in them. "What the hell we got to lose, boys? Nothin', 'cause we've already lost our rights." This was the tone, the temper, of Brazoria that afternoon. Walking away from the milling throngs, Jackson said to himself:

"The Lord's going to play second fiddle to rebellion at the tabernacle tonight. I might just be the only mortal there."

Feeling the need of help from both the Lord and man in choosing sides, he was torn between a desire to lose himself in prayer and curiosity about what a man of the cloth had to say. Deciding to visit Father Muldoon first, he made his way to the little church in the center of town only to find no less than a dozen colonists in the shade of a moss-draped live oak tree talking up a good war while waiting for the Catholic padre to join them. Recognizing Jackson, they gathered about him, demanding to know how he felt about open resistance to Mexico. Did he agree that they should chase Bradburn out of Texas?

"Now hold on there, boys!" Horatio cried, lifting a hand. Grinning, he backed a step and said, "Bradburn is one thing, war's another. Like a poet once wrote—Byron, I believe it was—'A thousand years scarce serve to form a state; An hour may lay it in the dust.'" Under their glances of disappointment and wonder, he said, "But then the New Testament tells us in the Book of Galatians, 'Stand fast therefore in the liberty wherewith Christ hath made us free, and be not entangled again with the yoke of bondage.'"

"Sure, Brother Jackson, but how do you feel about us and Bradburn?"

"You come to the tabernacle tonight, and I'll tell you, friend," Jackson replied, even as he said to himself, "That is, if I know how I feel by then."

Past the wharves, Wash asked if it was a sin to fish on Sunday. Even as Jackson replied, "No more a sin to bait a hook than to harbor the desire, I reckon," he saw a small craft rounding a bend. Recognizing Jane Wells, he watched the boat come on under a lugsail. As it touched in, he stepped to the pier and took Jane's hand. With the wind molding the dress to her shapely body and tossing the brown ringlets about her forehead, she smiled up at him briefly, just long enough to let him feel an instant of wild triumph. Then her blue eyes met his. They were like cold porcelain, and he felt a confused stirring half of curiosity and half of disappointment.

"Thanks," she said, stepping to the planking.

"It's my pleasure, Miss Jane. My pleasure indeed. I saw you in the tabernacle today."

"Yes." She pursed her mouth and narrowed her glance on him with a certain mischievousness of eye. "And I'll be there tonight with my aunt from Velasco. It will be very interesting to see which way you lean in the political emergency, Mr. Jackson."

"You mean a preaching man has to take sides in the pulpit, ma'am?"

"Surely you know Texans, sir! But just how do you lean, toward militant John Austin or peaceful Stephen F. Austin?"

"You be at the meeting tonight and I'll tell you then, Miss Jane."

A minute later her friends claimed her. She gave him a half smile, somewhat defiant, and left him. When she disappeared, he continued to see her in memory and remember the kiss he had stolen from her. Then her question sounded again: Just how did he lean, toward John or Stephen Austin?

Half an hour later Jackson emerged from prayer on a wooded bluff overlooking the Brazos and joined Wash on the riverbank. Fastening a grasshopper to his hook, he tossed the line out into the stream and sat down to watch the cork. Nothing happened, so he leaned back against a tree trunk and gazed up into the blue June sky.

"You know, Wash, I'd like to throw off all restraint and join the folks in crying 'Down with Bradburn!' He deserves being run out of Texas. Should be ridden out on a rail, I'd say."

"Yassuh, he sholy do!"

"And where a man's heart is, he is also. And my heart and mind are both sayin' to me right now, 'Horatio Jackson, get yourself aboard that schooner *Brazoria* tonight and help take Forts Velasco and Anahuac from Bustamante's soldiers.' Reckon that's what I should do, Wash."

"Yassuh. Reckin you ought to."

"I prayed on it, long and earnest. Got no answer from up there, so I guess the Lord is leaving it up to me to make up my own mind."

"Yassuh."

"And while I still believe Mr. Austin can settle the matter peaceably, and that armed resistance to Bradburn could bring harm to Texas, maybe I should show the people I'm with them right or wrong."

"Now you's talkin'!"

"That's the proper thing to do. Join the people in time of their trouble. Fight their battles with them, share their sorrows and grief, else partake not of their joys and harvests. I love these people, Wash. I belong with them in person and in spirit. I can't escape that."

"Co'se you can't, Rev'ren', suh. Co'se you can't!"

"Nor could Stephen F. Austin escape that very thing. He's

not here to ask them to keep the peace, to counsel with them to avoid war with a powerful enemy. If he were here he'd ask them to stow their tempers, empty their powder horns, and put their rifles back over the doors and mantels while he negotiated Bradburn out of Texas."

"Yassuh, he sholy would!"

"He might actually convince these Brazorians that he could settle the matter peaceably. He's earned the right, and therein lies his greatness. Deeds are his bid for their full respect and total obedience in matters affecting the welfare of all Texans. But am I his spokesman in his absence? Could I be even if I felt it my bounden duty to do so? I don't think so."

"Reckin not, Marse Jackson."

"And even if I tried, the people probably wouldn't listen to my pleas for their patience and restraint at a time like this."

"Naw, suh."

"Well, maybe they won't, Wash, but they're sure going to get the chance. My mind's made up."

2

The sun was playing in and out of a bank of clouds hanging raggedly over the western horizon when Samuel May Williams, secretary to Stephen F. Austin, called at a home in Brazoria and asked to see Mr. Horatio Jackson. When informed of this, Jackson was reasonably sure the prominent visitor had come to forbid him to hold public Protestant worship that evening. Putting on his coat, he went outside.

Williams seemed cordial enough. Grasping Jackson's extended hand, he said, "I hear you gave a good account of yourself this morning, Mr. Jackson. But that was before John Austin's war party arrived. Tonight, you'll likely find a crowd more interested in action than religion. You're aware of this, I'm sure." He paused and Horatio assured him that he was well aware of the fact. "Then I'll come to the point, Mr. Jackson, and ask whether or not you're supporting the popular demand for this thing they call timely action."

"Are you here to stop me if I am, sir?"

Williams smiled. "I am not."

"Then I'll tell you that I'm going to preach the three P's tonight, sir. Peace, patience, and policy."

"I'm relieved to hear that, Mr. Jackson. I came here hoping for a champion at this critical time. Since you'll have a large audience this evening, and since Mr. Austin has written to me expressing his wish for patience and loyalty in the face of the Anahuac disturbances, perhaps you would quote him verbatim at your night service."

Without waiting for a reply, he extended copies of pages from Mr. Austin's recent letters. "He writes from his heart," he said. "He is to present a memorial to the legislature of Coahuila asking for statehood for Texas. Trouble will ruin his chances."

Jackson read avidly. Here was a fountain to help quench the flames of war; fresh and to the point from the *empresario* himself. The message gave him hope, the first he had felt since his decision; gave him courage when he needed it most.

"Thank you, Mr. Williams. Mr. Austin's wishes fill a blank place in my sermon. I'll be happy to quote him."

Williams studied him a moment. "Without asking any favor in return, Mr. Jackson?"

"None whatsoever, sir. And now, for the record, you might find it expedient in this game of politics you and Mr. Austin are forced to play with Mexico to warn me again about holding Protestant services in Catholic Texas."

Williams smiled, winked an eye, and extended his hand. "Yes, I might. Consider it done, Mr. Jackson."

3

Evening brought in a weak breeze off the Gulf to relieve the oppressive heat of the June afternoon. Stars seemed to sail through the thin clouds coasting lazily upriver. Crickets and frogs sent up their night songs in an incessant overtone to usher in a fat moon edging the land over toward Anahuac. Few lights were seen along the river and in the houses as night fell. The only competition the old moon met in Brazoria that evening emanated from the site of the camp meeting.

The tabernacle was again filled to overflowing by Texans who had come from all parts of Austin's colony to hear the gospel preached and sung in good old-fashioned manner. Hellfire Jackson had captured their fancy that morning. His pulpit demeanor, the battle with the devil who appeared as a snake, and his badinage with Father Muldoon, all vied with the coming of John Austin and promised military action for the chief topic of conversation during the afternoon. The evening service promised to be every bit as lively, for the word had spread that Hellfire would speak his mind on the Mexican question. And if he lived up to expectation, both Bradburn and Bustamante would get their ears singed good and proper.

Jackson stood on the platform surveying his audience. Beribboned little girls sat staring up at him, and men with beards and hands calloused by hard work were awaiting his message. Mothers and grandmothers were equally interested in his stand and he saw concern in their faces, a wish for peace. Pretty young ladies who cast furtive glances at prospective beaux were more anxious to join him in song. And there sat Jane Wells with her Aunt Sally. He had overheard the latter's remark upon entering: "By thunder, this Hellfire looks much a man, Jane!"

Then he was asking the congregation to raise its voice through the stanzas of "Amazing Grace." He gave his best. He cried, "Lift the rafters, Texans!" They did just that. At the end of the third verse, he threw off his coat and raised his arms. "Let old Bradburn hear you all the way over in Anahuac!"

All the while the full import of his decision, one which the pacific statesman Stephen F. Austin had said would not make him popular, nagged at his brain and caused him to pray silently for the courage to go through with it and the eloquence to turn the militant crowd from the evils of war. When the song ended, he continued to feel the need for courage. But the time had come for spoken prayer.

"O Lord God, almighty and merciful, whom the heavens fear and worship, who has made even the callous heart of man respond to the touch of Thy spirit, we beseech Thee to stir amongst us on this momentous night when men must think of the uncertainty of life and the quickness of death, and the reward for meekness and love and understanding against the reward for hate and rashness and a thirst for blood. There is a sickness and a heaviness of pain in our hearts, a burning anger at those who arrogantly deal us injustices and heap more injustices upon us—"

"Amen!" The shout rose from the benches.

"Lord, the story is simple and short. You probably recall all the trouble the Egyptians gave Moses and his people. It's in the Book of Exodus, Lord. Well, it's not that bad in Texas yet, and we pray it never will be. But you can't blame these folks here in a way for getting their tempers up. After all, they were invited to this province of Texas—INVITED HERE, Lord! —by the Mexican government to settle this land. They came here used to the security of a stable national government and state governments to boot, not the political insecurity they found here. And what else awaited them in Texas, Lord? Orders and decrees based on the idle and arrogant whims of irresponsible renegades in the hire of Mexico, that's what!"

"Amen, Hellfire!"

"Lord, You know how Mexico needs a colonial policy. And Thou knowest also that she has neglected Texas! So—"

As "Amen!" lifted in a chorus, an idea suddenly formed in Jackson's mind. Aware that there was luck in prayer, that the colonists would not walk out during prayer, he was tempted to pray his sermon through to the end. However, since it wasn't exactly fair, he discarded the thought and said:

"So, Lord, can these Texans be censored for getting riled up? What did You say, Lord? Sure, I'm going to deal with both sides of this matter. And now, with Thy permission, I'm going to shorten this prayer and ask Thy blessing on the reading of Thy Word. Amen."

Jackson looked at the congregation, then opened his Bible, and said:

"I read from Saint Matthew, chapter fifteen. In verse fourteen Jesus is speaking to his disciples about the Pharisees, saying, 'Let them alone: they be blind, leaders of the blind. And if the blind lead the blind, both shall fall into the ditch.' Now hear me, brothers and sisters, and think on that. Ponder it, chew on it, while I dwell a minute on this Promised Land —Texas, my friends. On it you settled, beloved. What have you done with Texas? I'll tell you what—you clawed with your fingernails and by the sweat of your brows crops of corn, sugar, and cotton out of a wilderness, houses and homes from the forests and brush. Look at your hands and see the marks of labor. Look at your fields and gins and stores and families and see the fruits. It wasn't easy. No it wasn't. But—"

"Amen!"

"But who led you? Was your great *empresario* blind? Oh no! Were you blind to follow him here? Oh no! Then who's blind? Now listen to verse fifteen." He lifted a hand. " 'Then answered Peter and said unto him, Declare unto us this parable.' That's what Peter said to Jesus about the blind leading the blind. 'Declare unto us this parable.' "

Horatio rolled up his sleeves, a sign that he was warming up physically, religiously, oratorically.

" 'Declare unto us this parable!' All right. Let's look about us for blind leaders. I don't see anybody that's blind. You, brother, you're a leader. But are you blind? Why, I'll venture a guess you could shoot the whiskers off a squirrel at fifty yards. But Jesus wasn't talking about eyesight, brother. He was talkin' about our hearts and our minds—our souls. About what's right for our families, wives, and children. About us gamblin' the welfare of all, the community itself, on a foolish whim put in our heads by blind leaders of the blind."

Jackson leveled a finger at the congregation and asked if Moses had been a blind leader. He told of the worship of idols by the Israelites, of the Lord's wrath, of His words to Moses—" 'And behold, it is a stiff-necked people.' And the idol worshipers were slain. They were, brother, and the people knew Moses was a good leader.

"But Peter said to Jesus 'Declare unto us this parable.' Now here we are in Texas and old renegade Bradburn over in Anahuac won't even allow us land titles. He makes us pay duty on imports when we were promised free trade by Mexico to settle this land. He won't even keep his own promises, much less Mexico's promises to us. He makes us mad as hornets and he causes us to load our rifles and ready for war and forget what our Moses who brought us to this Promised Land, Stephen F. Austin, counsels us to do, causes us to forget we are but a few against one thousand Mexican troops in Texas and another seven hundred stationed at Matamoros.

"Bradburn is blind! He is leading the blind!"

"Amen, Hellfire!"

"Hold on there! He's not the only one who's blind, brothers, sisters! No he ain't! Right now our Moses, Mr. Austin —Stephen F., not John—is in Saltillo making a bid for statehood for Texas. And we Texans are worshiping war as the Israelites worshiped idols!"

Jackson saw men exchange glances and he heard the murmur of voices in the back pews; murmurs of disapproval. One man arose, either to depart or to voice protest, though his wife tugged at his coat until he sat down. When another man leaped up and opened his mouth to say something, Jackson pointed a finger at him and shouted:

"You there, brother! Either sit down and hear me out or come up here and you take over the pulpit!"

When the warmonger sat down again, Jackson said, "Any man or group of men who fans the flames of war in you, who convinces you that a few can whip one thousand Mexican soldiers, who causes you to risk all you've worked for in Texas, constitutes a blind leader amongst you. And the Bible says—right here in Matthew fifteen, verse fourteen— 'And if the blind lead the blind, both shall fall into the ditch.' Now—"

"Whose side you on, Hellfire? Bradburn's?" a settler shouted.

"Yours, blind man, that's who! Now you listen to this. I'm going to read what your Moses, your leader Mr. Austin— Stephen F., not John—wrote to his secretary, Mr. Williams. Quote:

" 'If things can be kept quiet in the colony all will end right and prosperously. What is needed there is a *dead calm.* The object (statehood) is a very important one, and it is best to bear almost anything rather than jeopardize *all* by rashness and ill timed passion and imprudence.'

"And listen to this, ye blind men. He writes this: 'Do try to impress this on every one, and especially on those in Brazoria who are rather warmer than they ought to be, tho perhaps not much more so than rigid justice requires. Imprudence and rashness, even if just cause is given, will totally defeat everything and ruin all.'

"That's from the Moses who led you all to this land of Texas. Now, 'Declare unto us this parable.' Peter said that to Jesus. And in verse sixteen, which I read now, 'And Jesus said, Are ye also yet without understanding?' "

Jackson paused, hoping for a show of support from the crowd. When only one woman cried "Amen!" he said, "Am I all of a sudden deaf or have the showers of 'Amens' from the pews turned into a drought? Or have some of you hotheads unloaded your guns and don't want to embarrass your blind leaders? I sure hope so. In fact—"

"Down with Bradburn!" a man cried. He stood, and he was Jonathan Mundy. Then Jackson saw others who had picked up the cry being silenced by their womenfolk. He said:

"Now I'd invite Mr. Mundy and his cohorts to come up here and bray forth their battle cries but I don't want to ask their wives to lead the blind to the pulpit."

A ripple of laughter sounded. As it died away, Jackson was quick to realize that he had stirred up a nest of hornets that would continue to harass him as long as he preached. Knowing he was trapped, he knew also that it was time to retreat to the safety of prayer. "Now let us pray." Raising his face, he said:

"Lord, some of us know Thy Word in the book of Micah. We listen to it again. It says, 'They shall beat their swords into plowshares, and their spears into pruning hooks; nation shall not lift up a sword against nation, neither shall they learn war any more.' That's Thy Word, O God, though I reckon you forgot to mention right there the blind leading the blind in violation of Thy command. Pardon me for reminding You of the oversight, Lord, as we cry out to Thee, asking if we should beat our plowshares into swords in disobedience to Thee or counsel patience and restraint as Mr. Austin, Stephen F., not John—don't get 'em confused, Lord—asked us to do."

As he continued to pray, his face upturned, his arms lifting and falling, the flame of ardent conviction and religious zeal burning stronger in him, the congregation grew a little restless. He prayed on, tenderly, mightily:

"Texas, O Lord, is like the Garden of Eden, like a land flowing with milk and honey. Texas, true to a heavenly vision, was placed like an apparition before Stephen F. Austin. He saw it, Lord, saw a Promised Land here in Texas. Did he just stand there with his hands in his pockets and do nothing? Did he turn his back on the vision his father had before him? Did he say, 'Lord, I ain't up to it'? Did he say, 'Let somebody else do it'? Did he say, 'Lord, it's a far piece down to Mexico to work out a fair deal for everybody'? No siree, he didn't! Then what did he do? Why, he went down to Mexico and worked out a mighty fair deal for the colonists. Free land! And no taxation for ten years! Imagine that, Lord! Then he came to Texas. He led the way. Did he fail? He did not! You remember, he won with arbitration and peace, and not by the sword.

"Well, Lord, look at the results if You've got a minute. Fields of cotton and sugar cane and vegetables and fat, sweet watermelons and towns and businesses and houses, and no taxes! The Promised Land! Canaan! Now, like the people of Moses, who turned from Thee, Lord, to worship idols, are these Texans about to say, 'Now our leader is too peaceful. Is he a fuddy-duddy who won't fight?' Some want to fight, Lord. Yes. Want to take on a thousand soldiers, despite Mr. Austin's bid for a dead calm in the colony at this time. Counsel them, Lord, tell them to read the Book of Exodus first. Tell them if they don't have a Bible that I'll sell them one right cheap. Tell them to draw their militant mule ears back in their heads and think like men made in Thy image and shed their guns and get back to their plows as Stephen F.—not John—Austin wants them to do at this time."

Jackson closed his prayer a few minutes later, said "Amen!" and ran an eye over his audience. The congregation sat still and quiet. He took hope that by some miracle of the Lord he had reduced the militant majority to a minority. But he wasn't sure, and he wasn't about to allow the warmongers any time to rally and turn on him. He said quickly:

"Now we'll all join in and sing 'Highbridge,' beginning with the verse ending in, 'Fit us to die and dwell with Thee.' Sing it out, brothers and sisters, in praise of the Lord. Lift the rafters—"

He got no further. A tall man, with sun-reddened face and shock of hair the same color, leaped to his feet, brandished a fist, and cried out, "You got your say in, Hellfire Jackson, but it ain't doin' you no good! I'm still goin' after old Bradburn!"

Jackson yelled, "Sing out, folks!"

Other men were now rising. "Down with Bradburn!" they cried. "Let Jackson pick flowers with the women!"

Jackson sang on, pretending to ignore them. Although he had expected some opposition, he had not expected anything like this. And he felt a deep hurt. As the present seemed to take on a nightmarish quality, he continued to sing as though deaf to the chorus of lively protest from the roused and offended gentry. Nor did he stop singing when they walked out of the tabernacle, leaving scarcely two dozen women who had refused to be stampeded, together with their children, to join him in the hymn.

Then, as if he were holding on to the one sure thing in a terribly shaken world, Hellfire Jackson lifted his voice higher and proclaimed almost defiantly to the night and Brazoria—

" 'Long hast Thou reign'd ere time began, Or dust was fashioned into man; And long Thy kingdom shall endure, When earth and time shall be no more.' "

4

Jane sang with the small group, trying as she did so to forgive her aunt for walking out with the angry war enthusiasts. Forgetting Bucktooth Sal, she continued to sing stanza after stanza but with little attention to the hymn itself as her first feelings of pity for the big, foolish frontier preacher turned into something akin to admiration. While she resented this favorable impression of the man now forming inside her, she was forced to admit that he had dared to oppose the lions of war instead of joining them. Here was positive proof that he was not the crowd pleaser who obeyed the prevailing wind. And however unpopular he was now, he had stood a man of his convictions, mystically dedicated. Such a person, she thought, would not flicker out but would end like a great oak under a bolt of lightning.

Such were her disturbing thoughts when Jackson finally gave the signal to cease singing. The moment of silence preceding the closing prayer seemed timed to the whooping and yelling down at the river. Men were crying, "We've got the *Brazoria,* lads! Now let's put the cannon aboard!"

Jane saw Jackson's shoulders sag under the weight of all the shouting portended. Then he winced, as though he were listening to a celebration of his own defeat.

CHAPTER 11

All Brazoria, it seemed, turned out to see the seized schooner of the same name make ready for the night run downriver to Velasco. Captain John Austin was unanimously elected commander in chief of the army of volunteer riflemen and Captain Russell was named to the command of the pirated schooner *Brazoria.* Under the dancing glare of torches and to the cheers and *vivas* of the crowd, men sweated and hauled at ropes to put the cannon aboard.

Not far away from the scene of excitement Jane Wells, who had waited until all the women and children departed the tabernacle, walked slowly toward the platform where Jackson sat slumped in a chair staring forlornly at nothing. He looked done in but got to his feet and thanked her for staying on when the hotheads deserted him. And when she said, "Well, you tried, sir," he stared into space and replied, "Yes, I tried hard. Even got the Lord caught up in this thing with me." Awakening suddenly to the fact that she for once appeared friendly, he eyed her dubiously, then with more hope than he dared to admit even to himself.

"You mean you feel the same way I do about patience and restraint and such?" With her nod and direct glance, Jackson struck a palm to thigh, grinned, and exclaimed, "Well, dad gum! Your charity, ma'am, occasions gratitude and pride beyond words!"

His exultation of the moment was cut short by her quick reply of "I agree with Mr. Austin on the matter of getting what's best for Texans by peaceful means, Mr. Jackson. That's why I remained when others left. My charity ends there, however, for I think you acted foolishly on two counts."

Jackson palmed his chin and said, "Uh-huh. In the first place, I tried to slip one over on the folks. Right? And in the second place—well, what?"

"With a thousand and one subjects for a sermon in that Bible, you could have easily avoided the political issue."

He studied her, and his eyes snapped with something like malice. Then he leaned toward her and stabbed a palm with forefinger. As she took a backward step, her own eyes round with wonder, he said:

"You're wrong about the latter, Miss Jane. Very wrong. Now I hope you're accessible to the truth, for I'm going to tell you something about any man who lives in pursuit of an ideal. He can't waver, he can't throw in with the crowd just because he wants to, and God knows he often wants to. He'll go hungry and cold and wet, but singleminded he must be, aware that any deviation from the thing he knows is right begets internal conflict, which destroys the ideal and in turn the man himself. Now what has tonight got to do with it? Just this, Miss Jane—

"As I wrote you, and told Mr. Austin, I came to the Brazos to offer my assistance to Texans. Oppressed Texans, I said. Mr. Austin planted an idea in my head. I tried to shake it off, like a mule with a bothersome cocklebur in his tail. And I wanted to be popular, to go along and gobble gravel with the rest of the geese. So I fought the idea tooth and toenail until this afternoon. And that's why I had to choose the political issue, because it was my way of assisting Texans. Now do you understand?"

She stared back at him, her eyes like scales that weighed his every word for truth and essence. "I don't know," she replied to his question. "Sure it sounds good, but—"

"But what? Say it, ma'am. Don't spare me. Nobody else did."

"All right, I'll say it. You resort to trickery at times, seem a little too shrewd and versatile. At least it's a shock to one's conception of what a preacher should be to find a man like you who appears to entertain a curious pride in his deception."

"Well, now! But look here, ma'am! I—"

"Let me finish, Mr. Jackson. Now to illustrate what I mean, look at the way you bested Mr. Mundy in that mule trade. Or the mysterious manner in which you suddenly lifted Nora Mundy out of her state of utter depression. And in your morning sermon today you preached right at Father Muldoon, as everybody realized, when he couldn't strike back. Oh, I know he came uninvited and flung the challenge." She paused for breath. "But tonight you did beat all! You kept those war-minded men guessing and then, when they caught on, you held them through prayer they couldn't walk out on."

She laughed. She could not help it. In another moment he was laughing with her, quickly snatching at the relief from trouble and serious thoughts her turn of emotions gave him.

And when laughter subsided and they looked at each other, it started all over again.

Then they were suddenly sober. The warm feeling between them seemed to vanish and in its place a wall of doubt and wonder and awkward suspense rose up to separate them further. He tried to smile, and he opened his mouth to say he'd be pleased to see her home. But no words formed. He felt a strong desire to express his true feelings toward her, though he knew that even as they trembled on his tongue he could not, dare not, voice them. What had happened? He wondered. Why didn't the laughter return? Then she was eying him strangely, now sharply, as if she possessed the faculties to read a man's mind.

"I'll thank you to escort me to the plantation skiff, Mr. Jackson."

It sounded so formal. Then, despite his attempt at lightness to offset cool, stiff courtesy, he heard himself saying all too seriously, "Yes, I'd be happy to, Miss Wells."

After dousing the last torch in a keg of water, he led Jane into the night. As though oblivious of the sounds of celebration from the river, they walked in silence, watching the moonlight cast its magic upon the land and houses and trees. It silvered edges of deep indigo and etched outlines of roof tops and vanishing meadows, even as it turned familiar objects by day into ghostly apparitions.

Shadows seemed to peer at them from the darkness under the trees, and suddenly all the world became a shadow as the moon slid behind a cloud. Then Horatio and Jane were staring up into the sky, caught up in some vague enchantment as the drifting cloud released the moon. As the meadows and streets again turned into a flowing silver stream, they slowed their step and then stopped still, as if by common consent.

As they seemed to stand there in harmony with the night and each other, Jackson felt a quickening of his pulses. His hand tightened involuntarily on her arm and he heard above the song of the night the hammering of his heart. It sounded louder as under his half-bold, half-timid glance her plae face blurred momentarily into focus. Suddenly aware that the scene, setting, and company presented an opportunity that might soon slip away never to return, he fought down his incipient fears, cleared his throat noisily, and said:

"Miss Jane."

"Yes, Mr. Jackson."

"Why—why—er—" he faltered. "I was just thinking—" Not only did his courage fail him then, he suddenly realized that he had no earthly idea of what he had really intended to say. "Yes, ma'am, I was thinkin'—thinking, I mean, what a lovely night it is after all—under the moon, you know. Understand?"

"Mr. Jackson," she said frostily, her sharp glance digging into his, "another of your foxy attempts to deceive and influence people that I forgot to mention is the way you sound your g's on occasion and at other times drop them altogether." Then she said, "Why?"

As startled as disappointed, Jackson gazed up at the now useless moon and replied. "Hadn't thought much about it, ma'am. Reckon it's a part of me I carry around like an anchor. There are times to hoist it on deck and times to drop it. Among my own kind of folks I'm at home, so I drop my anchor—and my *g*'s."

"For effect?" Jane said almost accusingly.

"And comfort, ma'am. Works both ways."

They were walking again, and once more there was silence between them. He was a little unhappy with her for breaking the spell under the moon, for being acutely curious and critical. Picking on the way he let go his *g*'s! The very idea! And at a time when he had been building up to praise of her beauty and to certain romantic confessions. He supposed it wasn't his night, that the sooner he handed her aboard the plantation skiff the better off he'd be.

Then she was telling him that she and her aunt would be leaving for Velasco next afternoon, and he was voicing his regret and asking if he might come to see her there. She wasn't sure, since her plans were to sail for New Orleans once the shipping tension eased.

A minute later both Jackson and Jane forgot all but the scene of men, wharf, ship, and river. The second cannon was being hoisted aboard the *Brazoria.* Torches flared, highlighting the sweating backs, arms, and faces of men struggling with blocks and tackle. Amid grunts and groans from the workers, cheers and all sorts of advice from the onlookers, the cannon approached the deck.

Shortly after Jackson and Jane stopped at the edge of the crowd to watch, a great strapping man with club beard, black eyes, and flat, lean belly walked past them. Suddenly he spun on his heel, craned his head forward, and boomed forth:

"Well, bend me on fer a to'gannels'ls, if it ain't the jackleg preacher! Maybe he's here to pray the holloware off'n the decks, lads! How 'bout it, Mr. Hellfire? You here to slow us down with another sermon?"

Jackson decided to take Jane on to her waiting skiff. They had taken only a few steps when the big man loosed a guffaw and blurted forth: "If'n old Hellfire hadn't preached so long we'd be a long way down the Brazos, boys! Reckon he's a Mexican lover, but that ain't no greaser woman with him, by God!"

Jackson stopped in his tracks. Jane urged him to ignore the man, advising that he was a schoonerman and bully suspected of piracy and slave-smuggling. In any case, Velasco people steered clear of Charley "Hog-Trough" Jones. As Jackson reluctantly moved on toward the skiff, something happened that seemed to rub salt in his evangelistic wounds. A cheer went up for Father Muldoon. Wondering why, if the purpose was to humiliate him further, Jackson was about to ask the question of Jane when Captain Austin cried from the *Brazoria*'s stern:

"Father Muldoon is going with us down to take the fort in Velasco if we have to! Right, Padre?"

The padre answered in a voice all could hear, "That I am, John."

A minute later Jane's aunt reached the skiff. Standing with arms akimbo, eyes squinted almost shut, she looked Jackson over while Jane made introductions. "Well," Bucktooth Sal said, shaking her head hopelessly, "he's a heap o' man, Jane, and he don't look like a feller that's scared of old Bradburn. Too bad he won't fight like he can preach, but for your sake, Jane, reckon I'll shake his hand anyhow."

Jackson held forth his hand. Seconds later he thought it was in a vise which was slowly crushing the bones to pieces. After getting his hand back in one piece, he said, "I'm glad to meet you, ma'am, however painful." Turning to Jane, he asked if he might call on her the following afternoon. "Maybe I could see you home after morning services at the tabernacle."

Jane's aunt placed a ham hand on his shoulder. "Hellfire Jackson, I feel sorry for a grown man who can't see a damn'd inch in front of his nose. Don't you know that after the way you rubbed the fur against the grain tonight, there ain't likely to be no mornin' services?"

2

Bucktooth Sal came very close to predicting the truth. But before the time came for religious services on that morning of June twenty-fifth, 1832, the issue had been resolved at Velasco and history had been made. It began before daybreak near the mouth of the Brazos. . . .

With about forty rifles and the pair of cannon aboard the

Brazoria barking predawn diversion fire, eighty-five riflemen on shore under Captain John Austin set up a palisaded embankment within thirty yards of Fort Velasco. All looked well afloat and ashore for the Texans until dawn broke with such a heavy fire from Lieutenant Colonel Ugartechea's men that not a Texan dared to raise his head above the embankment to return it. Attack and advance were out of the question. However, the Texans could still shout, and the "*Vivas*" for Santa Anna drew from the Mexican garrison enthusiastic "*Vivas*" for the Republic and "*el Supremo Gobierno.*" The exchange of lead and cheers ended at eight o'clock that morning when a torrential downpour wet the powder of Captain Austin's men and forced them to withdraw.

All the while the *Brazoria*'s cannon had been slugging it out with the Mexican nine-pounder bastion swivel. When the *Brazoria*'s moorings were shot away, she drifted on the tide toward the fort, grounded herself, and was left high and dry no more than one hundred sixty yards from the fort. That was her position when the "dumplin' mover," as the Texans called the downpour, came. Fortune seemed to favor the Mexican forces at the time, since the fort's one hundred twenty-five men were opposed by only forty riflemen after having beaten off the Texans' land attack.

However, Captain Russell's men, shielded by cotton bales on the *Brazoria*'s deck, took careful aim at every Mexican of Ugartechea's gun crew. They fired fast and true, and so hot was the fire that the Mexicans were unable to stand up and train the swivel on the *Brazoria.* When a Mexican hand or wrist appeared, Texan snipers loosed a bone-shattering volley.

Only one man of the garrison was allowed to aim the swivel gun. Respecting and liking Domingo de Ugartechea, they refused to shoot at a man brave enough to expose himself to their fire. But when Ugartechea was unable to score a clean hit on the grounded schooner the fighting seemed to be approaching a deadlock.

At 10 A.M., while Austin and Russell were wondering how they could dislodge the Mexicans, rousing yells from deck and shore drew their attention to the fort. However difficult to believe, they saw a white flag being hoisted above the fort. The Mexicans had surrendered!

Before it was time for the morning services at upriver Brazoria to begin, Ugartechea had endorsed Santa Anna and was preparing to leave Texas with his troops. His losses were seven killed and nineteen wounded. The Texans lost seven men and more than twenty were wounded.

But at 11 A.M. on that Monday morning no news of the battle had reached Brazoria. Only the torrential downpour had moved upriver to darken skies and spirits. At around half past ten Jackson reached the campground and discovered a dozen wagons making ready to depart. The men gave various excuses for leaving before the camp meeting ended. They named the weather, malaria, crops or slaves needing attention, among other things, though Jackson began to wonder if he had as Jane's aunt put it "rubbed the fur against the grain" and lost himself a congregation. He refused to believe that these people who had come to stay a week were leaving on the second day of the meeting.

As he watched the oxen and mules pulling wagons out of the sticky Brazos mud, an old canvas-top lumbered past him. A towheaded boy of about seven or eight sat at the rear of the wagon. Eying Jackson a second or two, he said:

"The rooster must have got your biscuit this mornin'." It was a way of saying a person looked mighty unhappy.

"Yes," Jackson said. "I reckon he did, sonny."

"What's a jackleg preacher?" the boy asked.

"Why you ask that, sonny?"

" 'Cause pa said you—"

"Jimmy Smith!" A man's voice from the driver's seat cut the lad's reply to Jackson in half. "Shut your trap, boy!"

Jackson watched the wagon a minute or so before turning toward the tabernacle.

Only a few women and children attended worship that morning. Fewer still came to the evening services. Jackson blamed the muddy streets and roads, and late that afternoon when the news of events down at Velasco reached Brazoria he thought the victory celebration stole his audience. So he shrugged philosophically and decided that since there was nobody left for the Texans to fight they might fill the tabernacle on Tuesday. This too turned out to be wishful thinking. The handful of boys and girls on hand at 11 A.M. fell short of a Sunday-school group. That night he sang and preached to only ten little old ladies, who thought Hellfire Jackson whom they had heard so much about was strangely lacking in religious zeal.

When it was over, Horatio walked outside the tabernacle and sat stonily, his eyes on the town and river in the moonlight. Both were lacking in certain virtues, he thought. The river he could understand and forgive, for it was a formless thing; but not the town, which seemed too aloof and unkind, too austere, to extend love and friendship or even fair play. A man gambled and lost, a man adopted a cause and lost, but that was life and people accepted it. "Unless you're a preacher," he said, almost swearing himself a revenge in silence. "You take the unpopular side and you're finished."

He sat there grave and silent, though inside he seethed with growing resentment toward the whole undisciplined lot of fire-eating adventurers who called themselves Texans. Political opportunists, land grabbers without principle, Catholics, Protestants, or pirates—depending on which was most convenient at the time! Such were his thoughts and his violence of feelings, against which all the words of forgiveness and love that he preached sounded lame and out of place. He wanted to tell these shortsighted, hardheaded, bigoted Brazorians a thing or two. And by damn he wouldn't be talking up peace! Not this time.

The more he thought about it, the angrier he got and the more often he told the Lord that he had a bellyful. He told the Lord that on this night Hellfire Jackson was less a preaching man or even a passable Christian and more a mistreated Samaritan caught up in a nest of Philistines and Pharisees, and that he was "riled up and rarin' to fight."

He walked belligerently down to the river in search of Charley Hog-Trough Jones. Upon learning that the bully of the Brazos had not returned from Velasco, he asked the hangers on to pass the word on to Mr. Hog-Trough that Hellfire Jackson was ready and anxious to take him on any time, any place, in fistic combat or rough-and-tumble fracas, and no holds barred.

Planter, riverman, and storekeeper exchanged surprised glances, wondering if they could believe their ears. Maybe, they thought, this pulpit advocate of peace was also a drinking man on a bender. In any case, he was sure as hell a contradiction. Besides that, he was knotting big hands into fists and challenging the toughest, roughest fighting man between the Sabine and Rio Grande Rivers, poor fellow.

"Sure, Brother Jackson," a man replied, "we'll pass the word on if you say so. But how come a peace-pushin' parson like you is all of a sudden so anxious to go agin what you been preachin' and get yourself chewed up and spit out besides?"

Jackson struck a warlike pose, narrowed his eyes to slits, and pointed a forefinger at the colonist. "It's really none of your business, mister, but since you ask it's like this—if I can't preach to the best of you folks down here, because I ain't afraid to air my opinions, then I'd just as soon fight the worst of you."

CHAPTER 12

It was late July and Austin's colony was some two hundred miles south and west of Horatio Jackson. It evoked memories he'd just as soon forget, he told himself, breathing deep of the East Texas air. There was a welcome in the bracing odor of pine, in summer landscapes of red hills and tall trees and lazy creeks. Ahead, down the long hill, lay the shaded Arroyo Loco on the Nacogdoches approach. Crossing the road was an ageless narrow trail worn hard by moccasined feet and flanked by vines and thick underbrush. It wound between walls of trees and disappeared.

"God's country," Jackson said aloud, causing Wash to jerk his eyes open and mumble something. "No Brazos prairie grass, mesquite trees, and prickly pear to contend with up here." Moments later he added, "Except in a man's mind."

Sleep through the midday heat had eluded him. He rolled up his blanket and stared into the cool of the forest, knowing in his soul that the time he had spent in the south had drained him of strength of body and spirit and purpose. He had gone to the lower Brazos with zeal and the will to conquer. He had left the Brazos a man shaken to his very roots.

He walked into the forest, his face muscles alternately taut and relaxed into unconscious dourness, the same now as when he had stood on a street in Brazoria or Velasco short weeks ago, his resentment then turning easily into quiet fury. Only now he was trying to restore his lost faith in people instead of nursing grudges and feeding vindictiveness. He was in his second long week of wrestling with Horatio Jackson, making every effort to convince the rebellious excolporteur and lay evangelist that the Lord had not dealt him a low blow.

"What a fool you were, Horatio!" he said to himself. "What a fool!" He had gone to San Felipe under false colors, actually; had gone to refresh his memory of a girl's wavy dark hair, full red lips, and the disturbing depths of spirited blue eyes; that he had done, all the while telling himself he was there solely to serve the Lord and the people. Honest up to a point, yes. But honest all the way, no. As though he could fool the Lord!

Too bad Jane had sailed for New Orleans the day before he arrived in Velasco in quarrelsome humor. She might have been more indulgent than the rank and file who, seeing him alone and cantankerous, passed him by as they would a drunken sailor. A man who had chased the devil so diligently over the hills of East Texas as to earn the name Hellfire was himself being chased by a lively devil, and for all eyes to see. And by that time the whole fabric of the man seemed changed. Throaty chuckles and dry humor that supplemented profound and inconsequential talk were no longer a part of him. These happy virtues had been replaced by a forbidding expression and matching silence.

Whether fortunate for himself or Charley Hog-Trough Jones, Jackson never found the big man who became a symbol of his defeat on the Brazos and therefore a devil at which to strike back. He had watched every inbound schooner with the hope that Jones was aboard.

Bucktooth Sal had taken him on as helper at the blacksmith shop. He sweated over the forge, nailed shoes to the feet of mules and horses, hammered viciously at hot iron as though the sparks he sent flying were red devils of torment cast from his soul. He had to eat, so he worked for Jane's aunt and argued with both the buxom woman and the Lord for a couple of weeks. He became quite intolerable at times, and Sal told him so. He glared at her and at her customers out of eyes blurred by both sweat and hostility. Finally one afternoon he flung the hammer aside and told Sal he was leaving.

He had no sooner saddled his horse than cheers, shouts, and guns popping sounded down the street. A courier from Anahuac had arrived with news worth celebrating. As Jackson and Sal reached the hotel they heard, "*Viva* Cunnel Piedras!" Jackson's brows shot up. "Piedras?" he asked. "Why are they cheering him?"

"For good reason," Edwin Waller, owner of the schooner *Sabine,* replied. "Colonel Piedras decided the trouble in Texas was due to the unreasonableness of Bradburn. Anxious to make peace with the Texans, he marched his troops down from Nacogdoches to Anahuac, free Travis and the other colonists, and dismissed Bradburn. So we're rid of old Bradburn!"

Horatio shook his head in dismay. Wanting to say "Well, I'll be damned!" he turned away just as Waller said:

"So you see, Jackson, our bit of timely action paid off."

Horatio could only nod his head and wonder at the turn of events that had not only ridded Texas of customs collectors but had backfired on Hellfire Jackson as well.

Jackson recalled how glad he had been to put the Brazos and its people behind him and cut through the wilderness toward the blessed red-land country. The wind whispering in the tall pines was music to his ears and the sight of rolling hills, overlapping in blue in the distance, harmonized with the soothing songs of the open. There he called almost every plant, bush, and tree by name. Here he fished and basked in the sun and shade like an alligator, and stared at the moon like a coyote and bayed out his heart to a blue-eyed woman who stirred a little sugar into the bitter memories of defeat.

This kind of life had partially restored him. He had risen with the dawn, with the hope of a bountiful nature in his heart. His thoughts began to move in wide circles, always returning to that one big religious defeat at Brazoria. "You get too big for your britches and you get spanked back to your size."

But that did not account for all of it, for he had honestly believed that Stephen F. Austin's policy of peace would serve Texans better in the long run. Not only had he believed as much, he had had the courage to declare himself in public.

"Knowing as you did it, Jackson, you were going to get your britches dusted good and proper. Fact is," he told himself, "you just weren't man enough to take it." Although Bucktooth Sal had said the very same thing, he had been unable to accept it then. Now he could, and he felt meek and ashamed. But there was more, and he would never forget Father Muldoon's kindness and words of experience during his period of trial.

"Serve and guide your flock gently," he had said. "But never drive your flock." Now in the Redlands, Jackson could understand this. He had cracked the whip of his own convictions in a purely political, not religious issue in an effort to drive his congregation around to his way of thinking.

"So you drove your flock off," he said. "Then you got all red-eyed mad and chastized them for not comin' back! Lordy mercy, Jackson, you were one more poor excuse for a preacher!"

2

That night the four-footed predators in the area where the old San Antonio Road crossed Arroyo Loco paused to listen intently to the strange cries of an animal new to the forest.

They did not know that the vigorous yells that bounced from hill to hill were shouts of joy from the throat of a man creature who had slunk off into the shadows and foraged beyond the sounds of "Praise the Lord from whom all blessings flow!"

Hellfire Jackson had made up with the Lord.

3

Jackson was up with the dawn. After splashing about in the creek, he returned to camp, built a fire, and nudged Wash awake. "A beautiful morning," he said, dancing a jig. "The Lord has hung out a veil over the hills and valleys. And our feathered friends will sing us a welcome all the way to Nacogdoches."

Wash stretched his muscles and grimaced. "Hope so, 'cause I don't 'member nothin' but trouble in dat place, Marse Jackson. Come to think about it, we's sholy got a talent fo' trouble, ain't we?"

"Well, maybe we did have, but things have changed, Wash, like that colored preacher said when a big hungry bear was chasing him and his flock through the church-house door, 'Our trouble is behind us!' "

"Heh! Heh! My, but you all is sholy peart and joyful this mawnin!"

"And thankful to be alive, Wash, despite the fact that we're out of Bibles, money, salt pork, and flour. Thankful and trusting, knowing the Lord will provide."

The advance of morning on this the last day of July, 1832, found them on the trail. The day was a benison, blue overhead, green on all sides, and streaked with shafts of golden sunlight. As the pines fell away to allow a brief view of rolling meadows, the sun seemed to fall richer with promise on the deep lush grass. There was a vibrant beauty and energy in the scene and song of day yet fresh and cool, something that guided his thoughts to a pair of fine eyes, blue, flecked with gold, in an oval face. Miss Jane's! He thrilled again to the touch of her lips in that stolen kiss. He felt music, gay and fast, and he lifted his voice in an old song:

"Would you wear red, my dearest dear,
Would you wear red, Jenny Jenkins?
No, I wouldn't wear red, for it's the color of my head;
I'd buy me a filly-wolly, dilly-dolly,
Sic-a-juicy, double rosy, Annie Laurie dress—

"Would you wear blue, my dearest dear,
Would you wear blue—Jane Wells?

No, I wouldn't wear blue, fot it's a color too true;
I'd buy me a filly-wolly, dilly-dolly—"

Wash said suddenly, "I smells ham!"

"The Lord will provide," Jackson replied before picking up the tune and—" 'I'd buy me a filly-wolly, dilly-dolly, sic-a-juicy, double rosy, Annie Laurie dress.' "

Jackson's faith in the Lord's willingness to provide was rewarded when they came upon a log house a few miles west of Nacagdoches. Jess Curtain, a ramrod-straight, weather-tanned Tennessean, with hard blue eyes and bald head, said he had a cookstove and ham in the smokehouse. Now did the stranger know how to swing an ax? Jackson fell to work. Curtain watched the chips fly and the stack of wood grow larger. When fried ham, redeye gravy, and hot biscuits were set before the big traveler who had earned them beyond any doubt, the host joined him and said:

"Well, if it's steady work you want, Mr.—er—Jackson, is it?—reckon we can find a place for a man and his nigger—that is if he's God-fearin', honest, and for Santa Anna and the Constitution of 1824. But why don't you eat?"

"Pretty soon you'll be askin' me why I don't quit eating, sir. But first, if you don't mind, I'd like to say grace."

He had no sooner done this than Mrs. Curtain, a small woman with friendly face, said, "Mr. Jackson, are you by any chance the man everybody calls Hellfire Jackson?"

"I am, ma'am, all six feet and more of me includin' a hollow stomach." Stealing a glance at her surprised husband, he said, "I reckon you could rightly call me a God-fearin' man, all right, tol'ably honest, I'd say, and definitely in favor of Santa Anna and his 1824 document. And besides that, ma'am, I vote your biscuits and peach preserves the finest between the Brazos and Sabine Rivers."

"Bless you, Reverend! You do make a body rejoice. Eula May Peters still speaks grateful of you. You recall the time you done her a favor by sendin' her the Indian woman who had stolen her boy?"

"I recall," Jackson said, making a wry face. "Joshua Peters didn't like it, and I've steered clear of him since."

"Brother Jackson, I would be mighty grateful to you if you'd advise with Jess here and tell him not to go into Nacogdoches today with his gun loaded and his temper up."

"Look here, Sarah, I don't need no advisin'! And chances are Brother Jackson feels the same as me and all other Texans who know which side their bread's buttered on. Unless the colonel declares for Santa Anna and the Constitution of 1824, then I'm for drivin' him and his four hundred Mexican soldiers out of Texas. Even if it means war."

Jackson's eyes blinked fast, and his jaw hung slack. With a forkful of ham poised halfway to his mouth, he said, "Colonel who? And what's this about war?"

"Colonel Piedras, that's who," Curtain replied.

"Piedras?" Jackson lowered the fork, his appetite suddenly gone. "Oh, no! Why, he—" He stopped himself in midsentence, and when the host asked what he was about to say, Horatio replied, "Nothing. Nothing at all."

As Jackson listened avidly to Jess Curtain's account of the storm brewing in Nacogdoches, he could not help thinking of all that had happened down on the Brazos in June. He had flung himself into the middle of that cyclone of aroused opinion, had bucked the gale winds only to find himself buffeted about like a straw. And now he was wondering if he had reached East Texas to find himself caught up in the same thing all over again. He made a silent vow to keep his mouth shut and avoid the issue; if necessary he'd get on his horse and ride all the way to Mississippi.

One thing was bothering him, however, and he asked Curtain if he and the men said to be gathering for a march on Nacogdoches were sure that Colonel Piedras had refused to declare for the Constitution of 1824. Of course he was sure, Curtain replied; why did Jackson ask?

"Because I was in Velasco when some of the Texans in the Anahuac affair returned to the Brazos and said that Colonel Piedras had no sooner thrown Bradburn out of office than he told them he had no argument with Santa Anna's Plan of Vera Cruz, which upholds the 1824 Constitution."

Curtain's agate-hard eyes seemed to drill into Jackson's, as though he suspected and accused his guest of being pro-Mexican.

"Well, thanks for the fine meal," Jackson said, rising to go. Then, under Mrs. Curtain's pleading gaze, he forced himself to say to her spouse, "Maybe the colonel still feels that way, Mr. Curtain, but can't go against his oath to President Bustamante. Anyhow, I'd find out and think a spell on how fair he treats everybody up here before makin' war."

Curtain said nothing. The flinty sharpness of his eyes and tight set of mouth spoke for him. Jackson's glance fell under the onslaught, not because he felt any the less right in what he had advised but because he had broken a vow to keep his mouth shut only seconds after making it. Aware that Curtain was about to lose his temper, Jackson hurriedly took his leave.

Once on the road, he told Wash that they would stop in

Nacogdoches only long enough to purchase supplies for the trail, which wouldn't take long considering that he had less than a dollar to his name. A little powder and lead and coffee, and they would strike out for Ayish Bayou. It would be good to talk with Elisha and Martha Roberts again, people who would not take personal offense at his opinion that Texans could gain more by resorting to peaceful means than a show of force.

He kept his word. Despite his desire to call on Piedras, who had befriended him in the past, he rode down the long hill on the west of the *pueblo* to the store in the Stone Fort, spent his last cent, then rode up the long hill on the east side and put Nacogdoches behind him. Pausing to look back on the scene of fort, church, stores, and houses nestled between the hills, he said:

"Looks real peaceful, don't it, Wash? But don't let it fool you. While trading for a dab of coffee and flour, I got the feeling I was straddlin' a powder keg, short fuse lit and sputterin'. It was too quiet, no men on the streets, in the stores, not even in the saloons."

"Yassuh, I was wonderin' where everybody was at, Marse Jackson. Do beat all, don't it?"

They nudged their mounts into a trail pace and continued east, still wondering why the streets of busy Nacogdoches, the largest municipality in Texas, had been deserted. They had ridden less than two miles when the answer appeared up the road.

"Well, now!" Jackson exclaimed, reining his horse to a stop. "Look at that, Wash! If there's one man in that camp, there are a few hundred! And lookit who's ridin' out to greet us! Elisha Roberts himself! And there's his son-in-law, Philip A. Sublett!"

The pair from Ayish Bayou cried a welcome. "If it ain't Hellfire Jackson himself!" They shook hands, slapped backs, and exchanged questions: Where had Jackson been and why? And Horatio asked about their wives, Martha and Easter Jane. Then another man rode up and gave Jackson a friendly slap on the shoulder.

"Henry Augustin!" Horatio cried.

As they rode toward the camp and the East Texans recognized the tall, lean, big-boned lay preacher, there came a succession of spontaneous cheers. Colonists, leaders from Tenehaw Bayou, the Nashville settlement, and from down on the Neches, all crowded about to shake the hand of "good ole Hellfire Jackson, the dam'dest devil-chasin' preachin' man west o' the Mississippi!" They brought him helpings of roasted venison hot off the fire and asked that he hold services for the whole camp that evening. The Nacogdoches people who knew Horatio voiced their approval also.

Horatio's spirits soared under the deluge. Here was manna from heaven, the bread of life. What more could one ask than to be liked, and loved, and wanted by his friends, his own kind of people? Here was warmth that filled a heart to overflowing, that evoked a tear of joy and a prayer of thanks. Indeed, life was rich and worth living, and no sane man would do anything to change it.

While Jackson was buoyed to the skies by such sentiments, two prominent citizens of Nacogdoches came forward to request that he humor the men by preaching to them. They were Adolphus Sterne, business and civic leader of Nacogdoches, and the town's alcalde, Encarnación Chirino. Sterne said a sermon in camp would do much to sustain order among the restless colonists. Moreover, they just might decide to march on Nacogdoches and give battle to Piedras that very night unless their passions were diverted.

Jackson finally gave in. With Bible in hand, he got on the tree stump nearest him and began singing a lively hymn, keeping time with both hands in motion. Men joined in here and there, moving closer in pairs and groups. A few shouted wildly, others fired guns in the air and asked if they'd gathered here to form an army or hold funeral services. To which Jackson replied, "Unless you quiet down prompt, old Hellfire's liable to hop off this stump and skin you alive before preachin' your own funeral, boys! How about that?" he asked the crowd. "Do I hear 'Amens' out there?" The "Amens" came. Soon even the offenders found themselves responding to a brand of preaching that had a split-rail flavor. A few, however, persisted in heckling.

"Hey there, preacher, ain't you gonna give Cunnel Piedras hell tonight?"

Jackson leaned forward. "Just a minute, friend," he said, thumbing through the Bible. Then, snapping the book shut, he pointed a finger at the questioner. "You there with the fidgets, the Good Book don't say a thing about a Cunnel Piedras!" Following the round of laughter, which advised that he had scored over the heckler, he launched into his sermon again with: "But the Good Book does say, friend—"

When his sermon was finished, Jackson was besieged by handshakers and well-wishers. He knew full well that he had never preached a more popular sermon in his life. He had purposely injected wit and humor, sadness, threat, fear, and hope into his sermon, mixed them and stirred them for crowd-pleasing flavor. He had preached the Bible he told himself, not political issues. Now he could be on his way to Natchez, where he would try once more to become an ordained minister. And what happened to Colonel Piedras or the Texans would not involve him.

At half past nine that evening Jackson and Wash rode out of the war camp toward the Sabine River. At around midnight they made camp under the summer stars. Several hours later Jackson put the toe of his boot to Wash's ribs and told him to get up.

"What fo', Marse Jackson? Where's we goin'?"

"Back to the camp, that's where."

CHAPTER 13

Breakfast fires were burning when Jackson and Wash reached the Texans' camp. He was building a fire when settlers from down on the Neches invited him to join them. While partaking of their coffee and bacon rind, he listened to their talk of war. They were rather impatient for action. Upon learning that the civic and military leaders were now moving to a spot overlooking a ravine to hold a conference, Jackson excused himself and ambled off toward the ravine.

Approaching Mr. Sterne, Jackson asked if he could talk with them briefly. Sterne spoke to the leaders before waving an invitation to Jackson to join them. When all were seated on the grass, Horatio said:

"Now I don't mean to be hornin' in where I'm not invited, men, but the hospitable gentlemen who invited me to breakfast said everybody might be marching on the Red House this morning. That right?"

"That's Colonel Piedras' headquarters," a bearded man replied. "So that's the place to go."

"One minute, *amigo*," Henry Augustin spoke up. Eying Jackson curiously, he said, "That's what we came out here to discuss, Hellfire. But why do you ask?"

"Curious, I reckon. Maybe a little puzzled. Colonel Piedras happened to befriend me on two occasions. Impressed me as the kind of man who'd bend like a willow branch to work with Texans. Am I wrong?"

Alcalde Chirino, a handsome man and leader of the Nacogdoches group, came up with a considered, "No. The colonel is a fine man and officer. However, the *comandante* shouldn't have ordered us to lay down our arms when we hadn't brandished them. And his stand for Bustamante is not only unpopular it is not for the best interest of Texas."

"Maybe so." Jackson rubbed an ear and darted a glance up at Chirino. "But I thought it was Bradburn who worked against us."

"Indeed it was, Jackson."

"And wasn't it Colonel Piedras who kicked Bradburn out?" With the reply that this was true, Jackson said, "Maybe you men are either overlooking a fact or are mighty anxious to by-pass it."

Several of the leaders began to eye Horatio coldly, a few with open hostility. "Just what the devil are you leading up to?" one of them demanded.

"What I heard in Velasco from the Texan courier who was in Anahuac when Piedras sent Bradburn running. Care to hear it?" The leaders were curious, and Jackson repeated what he had told Jess Curtain a day earlier, that Piedras had stated that he had no argument with Santa Anna's Plan of Vera Cruz, which supported States' rights and the Constitution of 1824 in opposition to Bustamante's centralistic views.

"So," Jackson said, "maybe somebody should ask him how he feels. You wouldn't want to start a shootin' war for nothing, would you?"

"No, we wouldn't," Adolphus Sterne replied. Sublett, Chirino, Augustin, and a few others voiced agreement to this. Captain Bradshaw, who headed a company from the Neches settlements, said then:

"I agree to that, but with reservations, gentlemen. We must remember that Anahuac and Velasco have already declared for Santa Anna with gunpowder and lead. Now, unless Nacogdoches does likewise, she'll not only lose her leadership in Texas but will earn the disfavor of Santa Anna when he becomes President of Mexico."

"I agree with Captain Bradshaw," Captain Davis from Ayish Bayou remarked slowly. "The only Mexican garrison left in Texas is in Nacogdoches. And Piedras has a big one. So I say we call on him in force, ready to fight today if he refuses to declare for Santa Anna." Turning to James Bullock of the Ayish settlement, he said, "What's your opinion, sir?"

"I'm for putting it to a vote."

All there supported this idea and without further ado it was voted that they should confer with Piedras before opening hostilities. Elected to call on him were Augustin, Sublett, and Isaac Watts Burton. It was their job to persuade the colonel once again to declare openly for Santa Anna.

Jackson took hope then, for he believed the handsome, genial colonel was a man who could be led but never pushed into making a decision. He said as much to Sublett and Augustin, asking them to reserve threat of battle as a last resort.

"Why don't you go with us, Jackson?" Sublett asked. "Remember when you preached to the colonel at the Nashville camp meeting?"

"Yeah, I remember," Jackson replied, rubbing his jaw. "How could I ever forget, me a-squirmin' like I was settin' on a cactus? But about me callin' on him with you, you decide that after I tell you men I'm definitely against settling the matter with guns if he refuses to declare for Santa Anna."

A strained silence fell over the group of leaders. Some looked startled, others angry, and still others disappointed. Feeling the need of an excuse for his friend, Sublett said, "Reckon we understand, Brother Jackson. You being a preacher man, you'd naturally be against fighting."

"A most likely observation, Philip. But that's not my reason, and Hellfire Jackson is not about to hide behind it."

Following an exchange of amazed glances, Adolphus Sterne asked Jackson if he cared to state his real reason for avoiding battle.

"Mr. Sterne and gentlemen," Horatio began, "I'm just as much in favor of Santa Anna and the 1824 document as you are, as Stephen F. Austin is. But, like Mr. Austin, I believe in going after what's best for Texas and Texans through negotiation and parley, as in the past, and without spilling the blood of Texans unnecessarily. As at Velasco, gentlemen. We lost seven men there, had nearly four times as many wounded. For what? To get rid of Bradburn, that's why. Say the cause justified the loss. But don't forget that it was less the blood Texans shed and more the friendship and understanding of Colonel Piedras for the Texans that got rid of Bradburn. Now I ask you, was death and bloodshed necessary? You, Mr. Sterne—you, Alcalde Chirino—you, Captain Bradshaw—and all you gentlemen—answer me that."

There was no reply, just thoughtful silence. Jackson broke it, saying, "Reckon we're a funny lot, us Anglos. We overlook the fact that Santa Anna ain't the president yet."

Again the men exchanged glances. Horatio broke the silence by saying, "Considering the way I feel about it, gentlemen, I'll release you from the invitation to go with you to call on Colonel Piedras."

With that, Jackson thanked the leaders and left them. When he crossed the ravine and looked back they were still staring after him. A wave of hope surged through him. Perhaps, and he put it in the form of a brief prayer, these Texans of the Redlands were ready to adhere to Mr. Austin's policy of peace and avoid further bloodshed.

"Lord, I hope so. You better take a little time out up there and help me on this."

He repeated the fervent wish when the trio appointed to confer with Colonel Piedras rode toward Nacogdoches at around ten that morning. He said it again shortly after four when the three emissaries returned to the Texan camp.

2

Jackson sat under a post oak tree eating watermelon. The day had begun hot and dry and before noon the heat had driven the Texans to scattered positions in search of shade. Scarcely a breath of air stirred the tall pines. Even their tops, which usually swayed lazily back and forth, seemed too still, and the soft murmur of wind through the upper branches was missing. Nature seemed minus all motion other than the dancing of heat waves over the fields and overlapping blue hills off in the distance.

Elisha Roberts sent one of his slaves to his wagon for another melon. Pocketing the seeds for planting in the year to come, he said this was his fourteenth summer in Texas and, he reckoned, the hottest. Did Jim remember a hotter one? James Bullock couldn't recall a hotter summer, though he had been in Texas only eight years. But he'd seen it a "darn sight dryer"; in fact he remembered when it was so dry the fish up on the Attoyac Bayou carried gourd dippers of well water. And Roberts, refusing to laugh, said, "Well, now, that must have made 'em sweat, Jim!"

Jackson laughed. "I reckon I could lay both of you in the shade, but since a man of my callin' is supposed to be truthful I'd better not tell how hot and dry it got on a place we were surveyin' up in Arkansas in June of 1827. But you're friends, so I'll chance it. Anyhow it was close to suppertime and I sent Wash out to the cornfield—there were twenty-six acres in corn, I recall. Told Wash to pick us some ears for roastin'. Pretty soon he came runnin' back, the whites of his eyes big as saucers, and him a-pointin' and gaspin' something awful. Then he told me the ground was white as snow. In that heat all the corn had popped."

When laughter subsided, Bullock slapped Jackson on the

shoulder and looked at Roberts. "You know, things have come to a pretty pass when a preacher can sit here and tell a bigger lie than all of us put together. I reckon we—"

Suddenly Bullock was on his feet. "They're back!" he exclaimed, moving toward the three horsemen across the meadow.

"It's Philip, Isaac, and Henry, all right," Roberts said. "Back from their confab with Colonel Piedras. They're ridin' mighty slow, Jackson, like maybe there's going to be a scrap."

"Or maybe peace," Jackson said.

"I'm going over there and find out."

Horatio watched Roberts and Bullock out of glare-slitted eyes until they reached the horsemen. The whole camp, on all sides of the clearing, seemed to rise up and stretch itself out of *siesta,* to cut its first yawn short and erupt from the shade in a dash for the three returning riders. Jackson continued to stand with back to oak trunk and absently lick melon juice from the blade of his hunting knife.

"Well, maybe there won't be war," he was saying when a mighty roar went up from the group surrounding the horsemen. Hats were flung into the air and men were leaping about, shouting, "To hell with Piedras!"

At nightfall the camp was still in an uproar. The leaders had experienced difficulty in restraining the five hundred Texans who had been all for marching on Nacogdoches late that afternoon. Even now loud yells of "Down with Piedras!" mingled with cries of "We want Bullock!" or "Elect Bradshaw commander!"

Jackson ate with Roberts and Sublett, saying nothing as his gaze took in the dozens of bivouac fires, all dancing like yellow puffballs in defiance of the dark, hot night. Closer, loud guffaws and anti-Piedras talk rose above the babble of voices and songs about a campfire from across the meadow. Close by, jugs passed from hand to hand, and men imbibed freely, sliced off succulent pieces of roasted beef, mutton, or pork, and washed down big mouthfuls when the jug came around again.

The night was oppressively still, making it even hotter. The smell of human sweat joined that of horses and mules, and mingled with odors of wood smoke, tobacco, alcohol, and the aroma of meats cooking on open pits, as well as occasional heavy scents of polecat. Over in the Nacogdoches camp a pair of huge-shouldered, hard muscled bullies were stripped to the waist and circling each other warily to settle a bet as to which was the better wrestler. The spectators urged them on, mopped sweat, and placed bets.

At the camp next to Roberts' a man loosed a foul oath, let go a kick at a hound heavy with undropped pups. A howl followed, and the owner of the dog was soon throwing hard fists at the offender.

On this hot night some of the men were mean from the heat. It was the night before a battle, and pulses beat faster and anger flashed easily, like tinder to a spark. The night was a fuse, Jackson observed, and salt sweat in a man's eyes did nothing to put it out.

"And the colonel looked at us, Jackson," Sublett was saying, "looked us right in the eye one by one and said as polite as you please, 'Gentlemen, señores, your information is correct. I did say at Anahuac I favored the liberal Constitution of 1824, also that I had no argument with Santa Anna's Plan of Vera Cruz. However, I did not declare in favor of this usurper and political chameleon Santa Anna. Watch him, señores! He uses the Constitution as a ladder. When and if he gets to the top, he'll discard it."

The hound had started a free-for-all. Even the pair engaged in wrestling a minute earlier were swinging fists around the neighboring campfire. A man fell to his knees. A blow on the jaw flattened him, and Roberts said of the man who struck him down, "You'd think Rufus Granger a tough one the way he's actin' tonight. Now Rufus is fair and upstandin'." The fight ended, and Philip Sublett was saying:

"Then Colonel Piedras said to us, 'You men wish me to come over to Santa Anna's side? I, an officer in the Mexican Army, sworn to uphold the government of Mexico, should turn against *El Presidente* who heads the government! Where is my honor then, *amigos?* Would you, gentlemen, any of you, do such a thing?' "

"What about his order to all colonists to lay down their arms?" Jackson asked. "Did he have an answer to that?"

"Yes, and it didn't set well with us. He said that late in May he had received orders from the general *comandante* in Mexico, one Mariano Guerro, to put an end to the Anahuac disturbance and to order the colonists in East Texas to put down their arms. 'But,' he said to us, 'I did not obey the latter order then, for I felt that conditions here did not warrant this. And when I did suggest that there be no show of arms here it was merely a token obedience to orders.' "

"Well, that was fair enough, Philip. So what was it that didn't set well with you?"

"This General Guerro's order. It's typical of Bustamante and—"

A crier on horseback drowned the rest of Sublett's reply

with repeated calls for the army to assemble in the central clearing to elect a commander. Trailing the crier were cheers for this leader or that one to win the command of the Texan forces. The Neches River crowd yelled for Captain James Bradshaw, and the Ayish Bayou men shouted their favor of both Bullock and Augustin, and wagons rolled for the meadow amid clouds of dust to serve as voting booths.

Half an hour later the election was proceeding in true frontier fashion. Nominations were made in rousing stump speeches. As the lively affair progressed, Jackson saw Joshua Peters, father of the boy the Cherokee woman had stolen, trying his hand at oratory. He was wondering if Peters was still angry with him when a man stepped on his foot, turned to apologize, and said in amazement, "Well, I'll be doggoned, if it ain't Hellfire Jackson!" He was Jonathan Munds, on his way to Natchez for furniture. He had no sooner moved on than the order came to form voting lines at each of the three wagons. Only those with firearms who intended to serve under their respective leaders and obey orders were qualified to vote.

The five hundred armed Texans voted. They elected James Whitis Bullock to command them, and when the announcement was made they demanded a speech from him. The veteran of the Indian wars under Andrew Jackson and a participant in the Battle of New Orleans against the British gave a good account of himself. They were going to march on Nacogdoches next day, and unless the Mexican colonel came to his senses there would be some shooting and "some of us might get hurt." But the cause was right and just and he wanted the Lord's blessing to go with his band of soldiers.

"Now will Brother Hellfire Jackson come up here and petition the Lord to be on our side as we march to overthrow the oppressor?"

Jackson started, and a sudden sickness formed in the pit of his stomach as he realized that he was caught between what was popular and appropriate to the occasion and what he actually believed. His mind ticked fast for a way in which he could save face with both the crowd and himself. In the ambivalence of his feelings, he got up into the wagon bed and grasped the hand of Commander Bullock, wishing to cling to it instead of facing the sea of faces flickering in the firelight out there. In them he saw his own conscience staring back at him, waiting, demanding perhaps more of him than he could muster.

As he raised one arm and then the other, and a silence fell over the meadow, a voice somewhere in the throng shattered the reverent hush with a shouted warning: "Better watch Hellfire Jackson! He'll be prayin' for the Mexicans, like he done down in Brazoria the night before we took Fort Velasco!"

Jackson lowered his arms. "I prayed for patience, restraint, and a peaceful settlement of political differences, stranger, the same—"

A second voice, this one from down in front, cut Horatio's words short: "Jackson was at my place west of Nacogdoches yesterday and he took sides with this Piedras when I told him about the trouble! I'm Jess Curtain, and my wife heard him too!"

"Yeah! Ask him why he left Brazoria! Have him tell you why all the men walked out of his camp meetin'!"

Jackson recognized Jonathan Mundy and at the same time became acutely aware of the effect the interruptions and charges against him had on the audience. A murmur ran through the crowd, and a colonist demanded that the hecklers be tossed out then and there. In answer to this, several men insisted that Brother Jackson make his position clear to all. Soon Bullock stepped to Horatio's side and said so all could hear:

"I'm the man you elected commander, men. Now I command you to keep quiet until Jackson's through!"

As Bullock spoke, Jackson saw a man push his way to a spot in front of the wagon. There was something vaguely familiar about the face. It was that of a man somewhere between thirty and forty, weather tanned, minus any apprehension or disturbance. He stood at careless ease, but with a poised vigilance in his keen, appraising eyes. As suddenly as Jackson saw the knife he carried, that quickly he recognized the newcomer as a colonel of Mr. Austin's Texas Rangers, a former duelist in New Orleans, at one time a smuggler and slaver in cahoots with Jean Lafitte, and the inventor of the all-purpose frontier knife bearing his name. He was James Bowie.

Now Bullock was saying, "Take over, Hellfire. Preach or pray as you choose."

With silence restored, Jackson told his audience that since a few of their number wished to bite at his heels he would save his petition to the Lord until he got rid of the gnats and coyotes. "Why Jess Curtain turned on me I don't know, unless I ate too much for the wood I cut for him. But the man from Brazoria had a reason. As Elisha Roberts from Ayish Bayou will verify, Mr. Mundy tried to skin me in a mule trade, and it backfired on him. Mabye that's why he said you'd better watch me."

He chuckled and the crowd did likewise.

"Now did Jonathan Mundy think that Commander Bullock

wanted me to trade for a cripple mule with the Lord when he asked me to say a prayer? Is prayer to him a trading proposition? Don't laugh, friends and fellow Texans, for many of us think we're pretty sharp tradin' with the Lord for this and that. A new plow, a fine saddle, maybe a sorrel ridin' horse to boot, O Lord, and I'll obey Thy commandments! I'll love my neighbor as myself—well almost! Thou shalt not lie! You mean me, Lord? Look now, Lord, You know how it is, there are times when the truth would never do! *When the truth would never do?* Think on that, chew on it, my brothers. Is this one of those times? Is the truth out of place here?"

"No!" the crowd answered.

"Are you sure, you whose guns are loaded and waiting? Do you want truth now or is this one of those times when the truth would never do?"

"Preach the truth, Hellfire!"

The newcomer, the man with the famous knife, said nothing, showed no change of expression whatsoever.

"Well, thank you, my friends. You asked for it. You asked, knowin' I'd be one more poor Christian if I preached anything but the truth as I see it, so help me God!"

"Amen!"

"So I'll begin by giving you the truth about what happened down at Brazoria. I called on Mr. Austin and told him I had come to offer my assistance to Texans caught up in political oppression. What did Mr. Austin say?"

Jackson talked on, telling all Austin had said to him about the need for patience, restraint, and understanding, and that "oppression" was not the word, and that all good things had come to Texans through peaceful means and proper compromise on all issues. Texans paid no taxes. Was that oppression? Could they say they had no representation in government themselves? No, because Mr. Austin represented them successfully.

"I hear no argument to all this," Jackson said. "I offered none, because I had none. But I had gone to the Brazos wanting to drive Bradburn from Texas with my Kentucky spitting fire instead of waiting for Mr. Austin to get rid of him. But Mr. Austin sure made me see the light."

After telling of the arrival of John Austin and the war party in Brazoria, of his battle with himself that Sunday afternoon, and of his final decision to support Austin, Jackson gave an account of his sermon at the tabernacle that night.

"What happened? I'll tell you what. Like my mule-tradin' friend Mundy told you, the war lovers, the hotheads, walked out on old Hellfire! They didn't want the truth, not even the truth as Mr. Austin saw it. They wanted war. They went to Velasco and got it. They took the fort, but while doing it got seven of their number killed and twenty odd wounded. But did that get rid of Bradburn? No. Colonel Piedras got rid of the worst enemy Texas ever had, Bradburn!" Pausing, he said:

"By the way, did any of you boys out there ever go to the trouble of thankin' Colonel Piedras?"

Thank Piedras? Someone guffawed. It was infectious. As laughter swelled, Jackson began to take encouragement. It seemed that he was getting through to this unruly gathering. Praise the Lord if he could do it! He felt a quick surge of joy, and he was praying that the Holy Spirit would continue to speak through him to quell the desire for battle in the breasts of these men.

Laughter, however, seemed all too brief. It fell away like a pendulum completing its reach, and that was the end of it. The pendulum swung the other way then and a yell broke the silence over the camp:

"Down with Piedras! *Viva* Santa Anna!"

The crowd picked it up and flung it back at Jackson. When the yelling subsided, Jackson opened his mouth to speak. But the Texans wouldn't allow it. They shouted him down with more of the same until he dropped his arms in despair and turned to leave the wagon.

At that moment James Bowie stepped forward. Climbing on the wagon, he raised an arm in a bid for silence. Something about him, perhaps that quality of self-assurance that in any company always speaks for itself, caught and held the crowd's attention. In the hush that followed he said quietly but with authority:

"Your elected commander asked Mr. Jackson to pray. He's going to get the opportunity to pray right now. Colonel Jim Bowie says so."

A rousing cheer broke loose for the famous frontier fighter. Bowie seemed oblivious of the ovation. He was standing with thumbs in belt, feet spread apart, his eyes on Jackson, who moved to his side with hand upraised and head turned up to the sky. He heard the cheer end, and he saw Jackson tighten both hands into fists before saying:

"O Lord, Creator of heaven and earth, Father of mercy, Forgiver of iniquity, we are assembled here in East Texas on what seems to be the eve before trouble and bloodshed. As Thou knowest, some amongst us are hot and rarin' for a scrap. Well, Lord, here is Thy servant once more caught up twixt the devils of war and the convictions You pounded into my head down on the Brazos. Remember what You said to me down there when I was straddlin' the fence and wantin' to raise one hand in a bid for peace and the other with a rifle aimed at old Bradburn? You said to me, 'Now look here, Jackson, the fact is you're mule-stubborn. A man gets nowhere chasin' back and forth from one conviction to another, for pretty soon he's got nothin' that resembles a conviction. So brace up, Jackson, and remember that that crowd of Brazorians can't do more than skin you alive!'

"Now, Lord, as You know, they almost did just that in words. And remembering that, this humble servant is going to touch mighty light on that verse in Saint Matthew which says, and which fits these warmongers like a glove, 'They be leaders of the blind. And if the blind lead the blind, both shall fall into the ditch.' I'd appreciate it if you'd poke that verse into a few heads here tonight, Lord, 'cause Jackson down here don't aim to have a verse he can't handle any too good backfire on him again.

"So, Lord, this mortal who knows that only in Thy mercy can we escape hell's fire, which is seven times hotter than mesquite coals—and that's hot, Lord—is askin' Thee to touch the minds and hearts of the hotheads amongst us here tonight with that thing called patience, which is a twin of restraint and a forerunner of understanding and peace. An amazing thing, patience, so give us patience, Lord, with that friend of Texans, Colonel Piedras, the patience to understand his position as well as our own; the patience to dwell on the situation here before grabbin' up our rifles; the patience to work things out in peace so that we may enter the pearly gates after a long and useful life of service to Thee and Texas instead of right away because we are in a fidget to stop a Mexican bullet.

"Lord, didn't Mr. Austin say to me that with patience and an attempt at understanding we can arrive as in the past at proper compromise on all issues with Mexico? He sure did. Now, I ask Thee, is it askin' too much of these good people assembled here to once again approach Colonel Piedras and say, 'Colonel, let's talk this thing over again and try to avoid any shootin'?' Reckon it would do any good to remind some of these belligerent Texans that a gun shoots both ways, or that a wise man will shoot at his fellow man only in defense of his rights as a last resort?

"Why, it might at that, Lord. Engrave its meaning, its very charity in our hearts. Tomorrow? *No, tonight!* Reach down and whisper into every ear now, Lord. Say, 'Listen, you hotheads, whom I the Creator sent to this Promised Land of Texas, go parley with Colonel Piedras again.' They're listening,

Lord. Are You getting through a few thick skulls amongst us? Yes, Lord, I believe You are! Praise be to God!

"But wait a minute, Lord! Some of the boys ain't listenin' to You. Now, while I keep quiet a few seconds, would You tell them again to parley once more with Piedras?"

Then Jackson raised his arms and said to the gathering, "Listen! Listen, my friends! The Lord is speaking to you—now!"

A hush fell over the crowd. It held a full minute in which no sound was heard from any man there. Then Jackson resumed his prayer:

"Thank You, Lord. Thanks for comin' down amongst us. Thanks for tellin' us to parley again for peace. However, Almighty and most gracious God, Who hath the power to redeem even these stiff-necked, pigheaded, war-whoopin' Texans, the power to show them the joys of peace over the despair of war, if it is askin' too much of a miracle to change their minds and get them to make another bid for peace, watch over them in battle and bring them home victorious. In Jesus' name we ask it. Amen."

A strange quiet followed the prayer. For long seconds the crowd seemed too still, too quiet. Jackson felt the silence, and he wondered what it portended. Then a voice from somewhere out in the throng broke the spell with:

"I make a motion we call on Piedras again."

"I second the motion!" another man cried.

"I say no, Piedras had his chance!"

Then the argument began. As Jackson stepped to Bowie's side and waited in silence, with strong hope in him, the debate grew hotter. One man pointed at Jackson and shouted, "Jackleg!" All the while Commander Bullock was shouting for order. After several minutes, in which it seemed a battle would break out between the divided groups, Bullock finally got them to listen. He wasted no words, but said while he had the chance:

"All in favor of another bid for peace say 'Aye.' "

"Aye!" It rose strong from the crowd.

"All opposed say 'No'!"

"No!" The sound was equally loud.

"Then we'll count hands!" Bullock cried. "All in favor of another parley raise your hands." The same followed with those who opposed a second meeting with Piedras. As Sterne, Sublett, and other leaders tallied the count, Jackson felt the excitement of a man who waited for either victory or defeat on an issue which could be decided by a single vote. He was tense, and he found himself craning his neck and counting hands as he gripped the wagon seat with tight fingers. He told himself that he needed this victory, and then he asked forgiveness for thinking selfishly.

Then Bullock raised an arm and asked for silence. This time it was quickly forthcoming. Then he named the figures. "For another parley with Piedras two hundred and forty-five! Against another parley two hundred and fifty-three! The 'Ayes' lost by eight votes."

Jackson winced, and said in silence, "Well, Lord, we almost won here, and that's a whole lot better than we did down in Brazoria, wasn't it?"

3

The sun rose in a cloudless sky and Thursday, August second, began as Wednesday had, hot and dry. At around nine that morning a faint breath of air stirred the pines and pushed a few cottony clouds up over the bleached southern horizon. An hour later, as Bullock assembled his Texans, low-hanging clouds hid the sun, and colonists were calling on the elements for a slow soaking rain.

It showered on and off as Bullock's men marched the few miles to Nacogdoches. Approaching the business district by noon, they maneuvered warily at the foot of the hill, waiting to be attacked. When the enemy, estimated to be about five hundred strong also, failed to show himself, the Texans moved cautiously toward the Stone Fort in the center of town. They were stationed just a little north of the old fort when the Mexican cavalry suddenly appeared at full gallop. Just as the sun broke through a cloud, the Mexicans fired, wheeled, and retired but not before Texans' rifles barked out an answer.

In the initial exchange the alcalde of Nacogdoches, Encarnación Chirino, was killed by a Mexican bullet.

The incensed Texans spread out, shouting thier *vivas* for Santa Anna and *el constitución* from the north and east of Plaza Principal. As they took cover in and behind houses and moved forward firing, the Mexicans retreated from the Stone Fort to the Red House, Piedras' headquarters a short distance away on Pillar Street. From this position across the square, the Mexicans charged the Stone Fort, forcing the Texans to retire. Re-forming at the base of the hill east of town, the riders led by Colonel James Bowie drove the Mexicans all the way to the hill on the west of Nacogdoches and again occupied the Stone Fort.

And so it went, the fort changing hands back and forth all that afternoon. Some called the battle a horse race, others dubbed it a battle of *vivas* punctuated by gunfire. But there was little humor in death and bloodshed, and Colonel Piedras, whose casualties far outnumbered the Texan dead and wounded, waited for nightfall to evacuate the government building. After dumping ammunition he could not carry into wells, he left his dead and wounded and moved out of Nacogdoches under cover of darkness.

Jackson had joined the colonists for work behind the lines shortly after the first engagement. The Mexican wounded were many, though they received the same attention as the few Texans. The Stone Fort was turned into a hospital late that afternoon, and men who had shot at Mexicans earlier now assisted Hellfire, a frontier doctor, and the fine old Catholic priest Father Diaz de Leon. They dressed wounds and held their enemies of an hour or two before to the floor while the doctor probed for a Texan bullet.

"You know, Padre," a gaunt colonist said, looking down at a young member of the 12th Battalion who did not survive, "I liked Manuel. Played cards with him. But I won't no more."

Father Diaz nodded and, wise in the ways of mortals, sent the sorrowful Texan to attend another Pedro or Antonio.

The stifling heat in the confines of the building, the smells of blood and vomit, the flies, and the groans and screams of the wounded and the sobs of a señorita who grieved for her lover or the tears of a mother who stared at a son in death, were things Jackson knew he could never put out of his memory. This was the ugly side of human conflict, of man's madness in his reach for glory in battle. And cries of "*Madre de Dios!* Mercy! Mercy!" sounding all about him seemed to make causes hollow and turn victories into defeats.

"The sword and the cross," he said to the padre as the men removed a corpse.

"The will of God," Father Diaz replied.

Jackson worked and comforted the wounded and sent up Protestant prayers along with the good padre's Catholic prayers throughout the night. The gray dawn of August third had scarcely painted the horizon over Pine Hill when Philip Sublett touched Jackson's arm.

"Commander Bullock wants to see you, Hellfire."

Wondering foggily what on earth the commander could want with him, Horatio went to his headquarters. Bullock, Bradshaw, and all looked tired. The leader sat with elbows on knees in sharp study of Jackson before saying:

"You look done in, Hellfire. But we're all a bit tuckered, I reckon. Anyhow, we learned that Colonel Piedras is moving his men toward San Antonio. You know what that means if he gets to San Antone? Means he'll get reinforced and come back up here to chase us out of Texas."

"Sounds logical, I'd say," Jackson said.

"Since you're his friend, maybe you could do us all a favor. Say by going to the Angelina with James Carter and his sixteen men and maybe get in a word to Piedras. Make him see it our way if you can. Feel up to it?"

Jackson rubbed the stubble of his cheeks and exhaled deeply. "Don't think it will do any good, but I'll try."

That was the extent of the conversation. Jackson left with Carter and was soon in the saddle. They followed the old San Antonio Road. The sun burned down hot. Men and horses sweated and little was said among the men that morning. Pine forests flanked the road and scouts rode ahead up the long hills to warn the troop of any possible ambush. After about four hours at a steady trail gait, a scout reported the Mexicans were headed for the Angelina River, that by cutting through the wilderness they could beat Piedras to Buckshot Crossing.

The race through pines, underbrush, and vines, over gullies and around thickets, began. Carter's men reached Buckshot Crossing first and waited under cover of brush and trees. Soon the Mexican advance guard arrived and rode into the water to let their horses drink. Carter ordered them to surrender. Sergeant Marcos of the 12th Battalion had no sooner given the order to resist than the Texans opened fire. Marcos fell, and the Mexicans retreated.

By noon it was learned that Piedras and his men had moved upriver to Linwood Crossing and had stationed themselves at the house of Joseph Durst, a former alcalde of Nacogdoches and a brother of John Durst who had fought with the Texans the day before. Carter led his men toward the Durst house. Nearing the place, Carter wrote out a demand for the Mexicans to surrender, and looked at Jackson.

"It's your quiltin' bee now, Hellfire. We'll be ready either way it goes."

Jackson nudged his horse into a slow trot. Emerging into the open several hundred yards from the house, he was instantly under the scrutiny of the Mexicans camped about Durst's long, whitewashed, log-and-plank cabin. Three uniformed soldiers mounted their horses and rode out to intercept the buckskin-clad visitor. Soon the order to halt sounded, "*Alto,* señor!"

"*Buenas dias, amigos.* I carry a paper to your colonel."

"*Gran Dios,* it is *el señor reverendo!* I remember your sermon up at the *pueblo* of Nashville. Since you are not armed, proceed, and I shall announce you."

"*Gracias.*"

The officer and his men led the way to the long porch. Jackson dismounted, gave his horse to a Negro boy, and waited for Piedras to receive him. He was not kept waiting long. Joseph Durst opened the door and bid him enter.

"The colonel will see you in there, Hellfire. He and I have been doing a bit of jawin' back and forth, so I—"

Piedras appeared. He looked tired. His uniform was torn in places and dusty. Eying Jackson, he extended a hand. "My thanks, *Reverendo* Hellfire, for your efforts to stop the fighting night before last."

"You're welcome, Colonel. Too bad it had to happen, but it did. And since it did, I reckon I'm one of them peace-loving souls who don't know when he's licked and comes up with another bid for peace."

Piedras lifted black brows curiously. "To me? Surely I am in no position to aid you there, Señor Jackson. I did not start the argument that led to fighting. I only got the worst of it after it began."

"Maybe so, but you're the only man who can give the kind of peace to Texas you've tried hard to sustain for several years."

Again the black brows arched. "I? How?"

Jackson handed him Carter's demand to surrender. Piedras read it, frowned, rubbed his cheeks wearily, looked at Durst and then at Horatio.

"First, *Reverendo,* you defended me before the whole Texan camp. Now this. How can you take sides back and forth like a politician?"

"I'm politikin' for peace, that's why. And it takes both sides to achieve that."

"Yes. You're right. My apologies." The colonel read the brief, curt demand once more. Moving to a window, he stood looking outside for a minute or so, his hands joined behind him. Whirling, he faced Jackson.

"What do you imply when you say I am the only man who can give Texas the kind of peace I have long desired?"

"I mean, Colonel, that the people of Nacogdoches and East Texas hold no personal grudge against you. Rather, they like and respect you for many reasons. You didn't tell them how to run their civil government, and you translated the letter of the law in their favor, as you did in my case. You knew how to use your office, your power in East Texas, for the betterment of relations between Anglos and your government."

"*Por Dios!* A lot of good it did me!"

"Hold on there a minute. In our times of adversity we mortals forget much. A lot of good it did you, you say. Do you count your years since 1827 in Nacogdoches, the fruits of your labor, the regard of your fellow man, as nothing? Nearly six years, sir."

"Continue."

"*Gracias.* Now suppose you don't meet the demand I brought and go down to Mexico and come back here with troops and turn this land into hell on earth, then and only then can you say in all truth, 'A lot of good it did me.' As it stands now, your planting is ready to harvest. So how do you want it, sir, the fruits of friendship and tolerance or the ashes of your earned harvest? That's your choice, Colonel."

Piedras eyed him intently out of slits that seemed to exude fire and doubt and a demand for total honesty. All the while it was evident that his mind was actively assessing not only the frontier preacher but the fruits or the ashes of his career. Jackson's gaze did not waver under the fierce onslaught, but held strong. He knew that the slightest withdrawal of attention on his part would provoke distrust. Finally the duel of glances ended. Piedras lowered his head and stared hopelessly at the floor. A few seconds later he looked up and said:

"Very well. Tell the Texans I accept their terms. I shall upon their arrival here transfer my command to Major Francisco Medina. But even as a prisoner, I personally refuse to declare for Santa Anna."

Upon Jackson's return to Carter and his men with the news, Carter asked how he had prevailed on Piedras to surrender. Meeting with no reply, he said, "What the devil happened, Hellfire?"

"Oh, we just jawed and chinned right sociable a spell."

4

Before five o'clock that afternoon Carter's men arrived in Nacogdoches with three hundred and ten prisoners. Major Medina declared for Santa Anna and the Mexican Constitution of 1824 before the Stone Fort. Then Commander Bullock ordered that on the morrow Colonel James Bowie should escort the Mexican soldiers as prisoners to San Felipe, and that Colonel Piedras be taken to San Felipe also and placed in the custody of Stephen F. Austin.

Before sunset of that day of August third, Nacogdoches was a scene of wild celebration. Men who had participated in the series of skirmishes put aside their guns and began yelling and shouting and racing their mounts at top speed through the plazas and streets. The saloons filled to bursting, their walls echoing to war cries and joyous, earsplitting victory *vivas* for Texas, Santa Anna, Jim Bowie, James Bullock, and no end of others. The celebrants, some with bottles in hand, spilled into the streets, where they clapped hands, stamped booted feet, grabbed any man or woman handy and swung partners to the scraping of fiddles and blowing of jugs.

> "Grab yo' partner and round we go,
> Done chased old Piedras to Mex-i-co!
> Hitch old mule to a bustin' plow,
> Done got us a consti-too-shun now!
> Whoopee! Hi! Yi! Yi-ee-ee!"

Jackson listened. The inherent spirit of dancing worked in side him, and he was beating out the full jerky rhythm with every fiber of his body even as he stood still.

The ruts of the street didn't bother the men. They kicked up clods of earth and loosed war whoops and struck hats at thighs without missing a step. Across the street on the plaza, by the central well, a shapely Mexican girl in yellow bodice and coal-black skirt flaunted her hips and sang in Spanish. Whirling, she sent her skirt flying up and up until her bare knees and then her thighs were exposed. The cries of delight were bilingual. A white-haired Mexican stuck out an elbow, which she took with a hand. Her head thrown back, hair flying, she pranced with him. Then a colonist proffered an elbow and the old *caballero* lost his partner until the next time around. A fat señora in a dress as red as the setting sun cried "*Viva* Santa Anna!" and threw herself into the dance with startling celerity.

"Anglo and Mexican!" Jackson said. "Beats all. Fight each other and when its over they celebrate the same thing together."

Jackson strolled over to the Stone Fort, where a casualty list was posted. He bought tortillas and munched on them as he read the long list. The Mexican dead numbered forty-one, the wounded forty. On the Texan side there were three dead and five wounded.

The figures caused his brows to lift. From a military point of view it was indeed amazing. Five hundred troops had been driven from Texas at a cost of only three lives. Horatio added the three to the seven lost at Velasco and shook his head in mixed wonderment and admiration. These Texans were something to talk about.

"Imagine it!" he said to Wash once they had put the scene of celebration behind them. "At a loss of only ten lives the colonists have cleared Texas of all Mexican authority! Not a soldier or official of Bustamante's government will remain in the province!"

Wash replied, "I do declare! I sholy do! Now is we goin' to stay and preach, Marse Jackson?"

"No, Wash." There was a note of regret in his reply. There was also a certain hint of the stubborn man who had twice faced a crowd and gone against that which was popular. "No, Wash," he said, with a sigh that was freighted with disappointment and a bitter memory of having twice been rejected and humiliated. Blowing out his cheeks, he reined up short and looked down on the town from the top of a hill.

"No siree," he said. "You didn't hear anybody asking Hellfire Jackson to stay in Texas, Wash."

"Naw, suh." Wash scratched his graying head and wrinkled his face. "But come to think about it, Marse Jackson, this here nigger didn't hear nobody ax *yo'all* t' come here in de first place."

"Reckon you're right, Wash. But that's past and it's done and gone. The present and short future are what counts now. Every time somebody saw me ridin' up they'd say, 'Now if we'd listened to Jackson, we'd still have Mexican soldiers on every corner.' So you see, Wash, I'd be about as popular in Texas as a polecat at a quiltin' bee."

Wash chuckled and said, "Yassuh," and the pair rode slowly on toward the east, their destination Mississippi, Tennessee, or perhaps Arkansas, anywhere other than the explosive and unpredictable province of Texas, where the *chile con carne* scorched a tongue but wasn't nearly so hot as Yankee tempers.

CHAPTER 14

For several months following the Battle of Nacogdoches little or nothing was heard of the tall, gaunt backwoods colporteur and evangelist who had sawed against the political grain in a summer swath through Texas. But where Texans gathered in the early fall of 1832 to reminisce and relive the incidents of Anahuac, Velasco, and Nacogdoches, there was invariably some mention of Hellfire Jackson. While he had of course been wrong, they said pensively, one had to give credit to a crazy preacher who had the gall to face two big-war-minded crowds with the very opposite of what they wished to hear. But what had become of Hellfire? The question evoked various answers. One rumor had him teaching school in southern Arkansas or nothern Louisiana, and another placed him aboard a Mississippi River steamboat, a stoker between Natchez and New Orleans.

Jane Wells was also curious as to the whereabouts of Horatio Jackson. She had gone to New Orleans in mid-July to visit a friend. The attentions of handsome Gustave Barroon and a rival, Robert Berry, had sent her in a whirl of dining and dancing in the Vieux Carré, the famous French Quarter. Both had polish and a certain well-bred elegance. Compared to them, Horatio Jackson seemed a clod, a gaunt scarecrow of a man. And yet, and rather puzzling to her, when she thought of the pair who had squired her about in New Orleans it was with memories of their world and not the men themselves uppermost in her mind; and to pique her further, they appeared quite ordinary and unimpressive against the gangling man she had once labeled humbug and hypocrite.

Even as Jane wondered what had happened to the itinerant preacher who had crossed her path and earned himself quite a reputation in Texas, Horatio Hellfire Jackson sat in the empty saloon of the stern-wheeler *Natchez Queen,* tied up at the foot of Canal Street in New Orleans, reading the letter he had just penned to her:

Friday, September 14, 1832

Miss Jane Wells
Velasco on the Rio Brazos
Province of Texas
My Dear Miss Jane—

Well, here I am in New Orleans temporarily engaged in feeding a boiler aboard a steamboat plying between here and Natchez. I have somehow managed to convince fourteen sets of Natchez parents that I am capable of tutoring their offsprings at two dollars each per mo. beginning in Oct. This will enable me to lay in a supply of Bibles and tracts printed in English and Spanish for my next trek to Texas. Such dignified employ as a teacher should prove advantageous when I make my next application in November to become an ordained minister. Could you, would you, wish me well in this endeavor?

I was grieved when informed by a citizen close to Mr. Austin that the *empresario* sent me word that he was fully satisfied that Father Muldoon could serve the spiritual needs of his colony. While I realize that such an attitude is in keeping with colonization agreements, I nevertheless felt called upon to address Mr. Austin in defense of the work God has called me to perform. I have therefore written to him that I read the Scriptures and sing only where I am invited; and I exhort the people to walk humbly before God and their neighbors; and it is deplorable that not one family in nine in his colony possesses a Testament or Bible.

I suppose you have by this time heard of my futile stand for peace and Mr. Austin's policies in Nacogdoches. The results were much the same as in Brazoria. But one's wounds heal under the balm of faith and trust. Despite the results, if I had it to do over again I would do the same. I am a very stubborn man, for I went against myself, my own wishes, on both occasions! But do forgive me for revealing my inconsistencies and defeats, dear Miss Jane.

I trust you are enjoying excellent health and spirits, as well one so fair and forthright should. My fond memories linger on the Brazos, and I venture you can guess why!!! Perhaps when you have time on your hands you might pen this admirer of yours a line of cheer and send care of La Bourse de Maspero, St. Louis & Chartres Streets, New Orleans, where it will be sent on to me wherever I am.

In the meantime, *Dieu vous garde* (God keep you).

Tout à vous!!! (wholly yours!!!)

Horatio

Jackson squinted a critical eye at his final expression of sentiment. Out of a minute's debate, his pursed mouth spread into a grin. Then, lest he change his mind, he folded the letter, addressed it, sealed it with wax, and left the riverboat. He would post the letter at Maspero's for delivery aboard the first schooner departing for Texas.

Once ashore, he paused to scan the dozen Negroes still engaged in unloading Natchez cotton. They sang and heaved and sweated. Wash was not among them. He asked an old gray-haired slave why Wash wasn't there.

"Jes' don' know right off, suh. He leave a right smart time ago and say he gwine cool off some. It am tol'ably hot, suh."

"Well, when he returns you tell him I'll be back in an hour or so, Gideon. Understand?"

The yells of teamsters drowned the Negro's reply. Threading his way between barrels, cotton bales, boxes, and no end of upriver stores piled on shore, Jackson dodged a clattering oncoming dray that splashed through a puddle of water and picked his way through the muddy street to a wooden sidewalk which they called a *banquette* here in hot, humid French New Orleans.

Night was approaching and the town began to come alive. Pleasure was a business in the Vieux Carré and it vied with cotton, sugar, shipping, and the slave trade for top position. Relaxation and freedom from restraint and discipline were encouraged, and adventurers, filibusterers, vagabonds, gamblers, and ladies of the brothels found a welcome. To these and the footpads the night belonged, though the Creoles and others of the upper class, the latter a relative thing in the always confused caste system of a gay, passionate, and polylingual people, claimed the evenings as their time of day. They spent lavishly, dressed in finery, and demanded elegance and a cuisine fit for royalty in the cafés. The classes graduating downward aped them in less expensive establishments.

Jackson paused to look back at an oncoming luxury sternwheeler. Her tall twin stacks forward belched black smoke, and her gingerbread topside was painted yellow. Her fancy rails were lined with people from upriver. Planters, tradesmen, land speculators, card cheaters, painted ladies seeking to improve their fortunes, sellers of guns, Irish whisky, and gambling devices: the usual run of passengers, Horatio reflected, all anxious to plant their feet in the wickedest city on the continent.

Slapping a mosquito on his cheek, Jackson moved on toward Maspero's Exchange. He had not gone far when an olive-skinned man dressed in the flashy garb of the New Orleans gambler appeared in a doorway and addressed him:

"Ah, *mon cher cousin,* step inside and win your fortune at *vingt-et-un*. The game of cards, twenty-one or bust, m'sieur, is played fair in my establishment."

"Thank you, sir, but I'm not a gambling man," Horatio replied, without breaking his stride. He had heard enough of the "sure-thing games" and "square dealers" to convince him that even if he were a gambling man he'd stay out of such places. While gambling had been legalized in New Orleans in this very year of 1832, the many victims claimed that the law legalized the fleecing of customers in a hundred and one ways in saloons, bordellos, dives, and cafés at roulette, faro, *écarté,* and brag.

"Lord, the gospel sure is needed here," he said in silence. "Trouble is everybody's too busy serving the old devil to listen."

Farther on, a mulatto in claw-hammer coat of green invited him inside a saloon for a free drink. Jackson did not pause. He turned into a narrow street flanked by two-story houses, all joined together, each with its upper gallery framed in lacy iron. Ladies were coming out on the balconies. Some were wives of rich Creoles. Others were romantic ladies, either paramours of the same wealthy Creoles or adventurers of the evening. One didn't try to determine which was which. If a flower dropped from a balcony as a man passed below he could be sure it was an invitation from one of the latter group to a first prospective customer of the night. In the back streets they were less subtle: No flowers, just voices, and they named a price.

Ahead, in a small yard fenced in scrolls of iron, a banana tree spread its huge leaves. Purple bougainvillaea climbed and hung from a balcony roof. Standing on the upper gallery were a Negro man and fine-looking Negress, both light yellow. Horatio realized at once that they were of the *gens de couleur,* free Negroes of the upper class, many of whom owned sugar and cotton plantations. Some were money brokers, merchants, or musicians. One of this group whom Horatio had met imported rum and molasses from Hispaniola.

Night had fallen over New Orleans when Jackson reached La Bourse de Maspero, or Maspero's Exchange. Entering the place, he paused to adjust his eyes to the glare of light from hundreds of candles and a dozen Carondelet oil lamps. A bar, running the full length of the ninety-foot room, was already lined by men, and the tables on the sanded floor were fast filling. Cigar smoke hung in a layered fog over the huge room. The babble of voices rose and blended into a drone that pounded at an eardrum without relief.

Jackson had no sooner posted his letter at the mail counter than a man rushed past him and came to a panting stop before Pierre Maspero. A minute later the owner was ringing a bell. With silence and all attention upon him, he said in a voice that carried to every ear there:

"News just in from Mexico, *mes amis.* The schooner *Gulf Wave* arrived from Vera Cruz a half hour ago and her captain sends word that the city was celebrating the overthrow of President Bustamante by General Santa Anna. Santa Anna has won!"

Rousing cheers followed. They continued. To a stranger who didn't know that the demonstrative Orleanians chose any event as an excuse for celebration, it would appear that Santa Anna had saved New Orleans. But the fact that lodged in Jackson's mind was that the Texans had gambled their all on the winner. It was worth a shout of "Praise the Lord!" and he let go with just that. It rang to the rafters in a hush between cheers, and it seemed to jerk every eye in the place around to him. Out of this moment of unwanted attention another cry sounded from a corner table:

"Hellfire Jackson!"

In another minute Edwin Waller and Thomas F. McKinney, both Brazos shipowners, were escorting Jackson to their table. Seated there were Joseph Durst, Adolphus Sterne of Nacogdoches, and other Texans, all jubilant, as could be expected. They slapped Jackson's shoulders, ribbed him considerably about his dove-and olive-branch brand of politics in Texas, and demanded laughingly that he " 'fess up to the truth" and say he'd been wrong.

"Hindsight says I was, gentlemen. Foresight said I wasn't then. So it goes to prove a preacher's got about as much business in Texas politics as a pig has in a parlor. Only difference is they fatten the pig before they grind him up for sausage."

Durst laughed with the others, then said seriously, "Well, Jackson's peace talk helped save another battle and quite a few lives when he came to my place on the Angelina and persuaded Colonel Piedras to surrender." After relating a little of Horatio's convincing argument that prevailed on the colonel to forego further hostilities, he said, "And when it was all over and Commander Bullock and the leaders tried to find Jackson and thank him, he was nowhere to be found. Why did you rush off, Hellfire?"

"Thought the Texans might be mad at me for interferin' with their war, I reckon."

Waller dryly commented on Jackson's loss of weight, to which Horatio replied: "You feed a boiler on a stern-wheeler and you sweat from the bone out."

"But why are you stoking, Hellfire?"

"Closest place to hell on this earth, I reckon. If a man's goin' to elocute on the subject, he can sure get inspired feedin' a boiler."

Had Jackson heard about the convention Texans were holding in San Felipe beginning October first? Jackson had not.

"Well," McKinney said, "Mr. Austin is with us, and from the news we just heard, it seems our timing is right. Delegates from all over Texas will meet to pledge their support to the Constitution of Mexico and ask in return for their support—of Santa Anna and his liberal polices—an extension of tariff exemption for three more years to bolster the economy in Texas, permission for more immigration from the United States, the appointment of a land commissioner to issue land titles in East Texas, donation of government lands to maintain primary schools, and permission to organize a state government separate from Coahuila."

"What do you think of that, Hellfire?" Durst asked.

"I say it's good and proper and, I hope, timely. But—"

"But what?"

"I'm just hoping Santa Anna is not what Colonel Piedras said he was, a political chameleon."

At that moment William H. Wharton, Brazos planter and a man of influence in Austin's colony, joined the group. He had just returned from the slave market near the Opera House, where he had heard the welcome tidings from Mexico. Excited over prospects for the future of Texas under Santa Anna, he spoke of buying more slaves and converting much of his Eagle Island Plantation into sugar cane. He ordered oyster stew, oysters on the half shell, and oyster pie, talking of his plans all the while. When his drink arrived, he paused to voice a toast to Santa Anna and Texas. His glance paused on Jackson.

"You don't mind, do you, Jackson?"

"Go right ahead. If I was a drinking man, I'd bend an elbow with you, sir."

Wharton frowned and lowered his glass to the table. "I don't mean to be inquisitive, Jackson, but I thought your colored man was a free Negro who traveled with you."

"That's right, Mr. Wharton."

"Then why is he up for sale at the slave market?"

"Wash? Up for sale? Why, that's impossible!"

"Maybe so, but he's in the courtyard, and they're asking eleven hundred dollars for him."

Horatio was suddenly on his feet. "Then Wash has met with foul play. May the good Lord have mercy on the men who did it."

"Hold on a minute, Hellfire," Durst said, rising. "I'll go with you."

"So will I." McKinney rose. Then Sterne, Waller, and Wharton got to their feet. Leaving drinks and food untouched, they left the Exchange with Jackson and walked briskly toward the slave market in silence.

As they entered the richly appointed lobby, Jackson thought they were surely in the wrong place. Soft sea-green walls, heavy plush curtains, crystal sconces, porcelain urns, and chairs with gold and silver threads woven into the fabric seemed to declare the establishment anything but a slave market. To attest further to this belief, servants in fine attire came with free drinks and cigars. Then a tall black-eyed, mustached man entered.

"Ah, good evening, gentlemen. May I serve you?" Recognizing Wharton and Durst, he said, "The best for my Texas customers."

"Look here, Lester," Wharton said, "we want to see the Negro Wash. I saw him here not a half hour ago."

"Probably sold by now. Business is rather brisk, you know."

"He better not be sold," Jackson said, anger putting a quiver in his voice. As the slave dealer assessed him with a look that seemed to measure a man for a coffin, Horatio added, "If he's not here and free within five minutes, I'm taking this place apart, mister."

Lester smiled, though it did not reach his cold black eyes. "I would do nothing to offend my customers from Texas. But one does not threaten Sam Lester, sir."

Durst said calmly, "One may not, but what about six of us?"

"But I paid a big price for that nigger, Mr. Durst."

"To whom?" Jackson demanded.

There was no reply. Lester politely opened a door and ushered them into a room where a dozen Negro women sat sewing and spinning. One, a young, big-bosomed, slim-waisted woman of pale complexion, rose as they entered, grinned, rolled her eyes, and twisted her hips in unison as she said:

"I'se good at mos' anything you kin think of, gen'mun."

Lester paused. "Feel of her, Mr. Durst. You too, Mr. Wharton. Firm flesh. Lots of work in her." Then, grabbing a servant passing toward the courtyard, he whispered something before once more pointing at the girl.

"I wouldn't do that, Lester," Wharton advised.

"What, sir?"

"Send word to your cronies to have the Negro Wash whisked away before we get there." Even as he spoke, Wharton stepped to the courtyard door and flung it open.

Jackson saw Wash then. There he sat on a keg on a long

platform, one of a dozen Negro men whom the white crier was extolling as "the finest lot of bucks it has been our pleasure to offer you smart buyers." In another second Jackson was in the courtyard moving hurriedly toward the dais. Wash saw him and rose to his feet.

"Thank de Lawd you done got here, Rev'ren'! They tryin' to sell old Wash!"

Instantly the big man addressing the few buyers whirled. "You goddam nigger, I'll teach you to keep your mouth shut!" As he spoke his arm lifted. It came down in a backhand slash that struck Wash across the face. As suddenly he spread legs and arms and thrust his head forward to meet Jackson.

Horatio anticipated his leap from the platform and crouched. He came up under the auctioneer and sent him into a somersault. Horatio moved in as he landed with a thud, rolled, and made a desperate effort to put a boot in Jackson's loin. Just as Wharton cried, "Look out, Hellfire!" a Bowie knife appeared in the other's hand and cut an arc all too close to Jackson's throat. Dislodging the knife with a kick at the other's wrist, he then resorted to an old Cherokee wrestling trick and sent the man into another somersault.

Now the courtyard was in an uproar. Two of Lester's henchmen were trying to whisk the slaves, Wash included, through a door in the high courtyard wall while another pair began to close in on Jackson. Joseph Durst took his place at Jackson's side, fists flying, even as Wharton, Waller, and McKinney cornered Lester and demanded that he "call off his dogs" at once, else suffer the consequences, physically as well as economically. Lester hastened to obey, and the fracas ended as suddenly as it had begun.

Wiping blood from a cut on the cheek, Jackson refused to listen to Lester's apologies for "a most regrettable mistake." With Wash at his side, he left the place in company of the Texans, whom he thanked individually for saving both himself and Wash from rough handling.

Wharton grinned. "Seems you did a little rough handling yourself, Hellfire. I didn't know you were a fighting man."

Jackson touched a cut cheek tenderly and winced. "Ordinarily I am a peaceful man, Mr. Wharton. But this wasn't the time to preach peace, patience, and restraint."

"I'se mighty grateful, Rev'ren'," Wash said humbly, " 'cause ole Wash he was one mo' scared nigger."

The Texans laughed, and Wharton said, "Bet you were at that. But did you know he was a fighting man, Wash?"

Wash chuckled. "Naw, suh, I sholy didn't. But after what I

done seen tonight, suh, the ole devil he better watch out, 'cause Marse Jackson liable to get tired o' fussin' at him and throw him clean acrost de Miss'ippi River."

2

Several days later Jackson and Wash left the riverboat in Natchez with their pay and moved up the hill. When they stood overlooking the wide Mississippi, Horatio eyed the *Natchez Queen* below and spoke a farewell to the craft, voicing a wish never again to stoke a furnace. Next he surveyed the stores and streets of notoriously wicked Natchez-Under-the-Hill, as it was called. Shaking his head hopelessly, he remarked on the need of God's spoken word down there as well as in New Orleans "where the devil sure had me outnumbered, Wash."

"Yassuh, 'cept it's dat way ever place we goes. But where's we headed now?"

"To Brother Whiteside's place, where we left our horse and mules. And I'm hoping they earned their keep, Wash, since I need all my hard-earned money to pay for the Bibles and tracts I ordered."

"Well, suh, if'n yo'all gits hard up, reckon that thirty-forty dollars you's totin' for me might come in handy, Rev'ren'. The way I sees it, ain't no use bein' rich if'n I can't be o' some service."

"Reckon not," Jackson replied.

They passed large houses of brick fronts with white columns, all surrounded by gardens and spreading trees draped with Spanish moss. These were the homes of wealthy plantation owners and shippers. Jackson paused before a church and gazed from the freshly painted pillars up to the tall spire. In a way he envied the preacher who addressed his fashionably clad congregation from an imported pulpit each Sunday in that imposing edifice; collection box overflowing and long, comfortable pews and hymnbooks that hadn't been thumbed long enough to rub the print off "Blest Be the Tie That Binds." In another sense, he felt a certain pity for any preacher who partook of fried chicken every Sunday at the home of a rich deacon or elder who told him how to run his church.

"Fried chicken and factions," he said under his breath, moving on toward the modest home of Reverend Jeremiah Whiteside, the man who had baptized him up in Arkansas several years earlier and who had since become close friend, adviser, and sponsor. Seeing Whiteside on the shaded porch in a rocking chair reading his Bible, Jackson hailed him.

Whiteside got to his feet, peered over his nose spectacles, stroked his beard, and cried a welcome. Soon the pair were shaking hands and firing questions at each other.

"Pull up a chair, Horatio. I'll ask Janie Faye to fetch a cool glass of tea. You look like you could use one." After attending to this, he returned to the old rocking chair, folded hands across his protruding middle, and inquired of Jackson's runs downriver and back and his opinion of New Orleans.

Horatio gave a brief account of his several trips as stoker and concluded with the trouble at the slave market. "Now my opinion of New Orleans is none too good, sir. Probably the same as that of any man who serves the Lord. It's a Sodom on earth. Somebody speaks to you, calls you *mon cher cousin,* and you turn around to see the devil himself giving you one of those *à la Creole* smiles. In one hand is a deck of marked cards, in the other Irish whisky, and at his side is a half-naked, leering woman. Reckon I prefer a place like Texas, where a man don't find old Nick behind every tree stump."

Whiteside smiled. "Oh, he's there, all right. That's one of his tricks, Horatio, adjusting himself to the environment, whether in a dive or on the back pew at church. But are you thinking of returning to Texas right away? I thought you were supposed to begin tutoring in another week or so."

"I'm thinking on that, Brother Whiteside. My mind says stay here and tutor, but my feet urge me to head for Texas."

The older man palmed his bearded chin. Eying Jackson critically, he said, "Trouble with you, son, you won't stay still long enough to knock the callouses off your hands and look like a preacher. How do you ever expect to be ordained?" Not waiting for a reply, he said, "Maybe if the Lord and man together could prevail on you to remain in a civilized place a few weeks, you just might stand a chance with the church body meeting upriver at Vicksburg in late October."

"In October you say?" Jackson replied with a show of interest.

"Yes. But I doubt if you could stay planted in one place that long, Horatio. You'd probably hear those Texans calling you to defy Mexican law again and strike out for the wilderness before the Vicksburg meeting." Observing Jackson's thoughtful expression, he went on, saying, "Supposing you remained and met with the churchmen, more than likely you'd shock the dignified body with some expression or other more backwoods than ecclesiastic. Well, what about it? Do I sponsor you or watch you riding for the Sabine atop that sway-backed animal out there?"

Jackson pursed his mouth and stared at the branches of an

oak with unfocused eyes. "Well, sir," he said after a minute of silence, "I reckon that old horse needs a little more rest."

"I'm glad to hear that, Horatio. But I'm warning you right here and now that if I hear you drop a *g* in your speech or come up with an 'ain't' before that Vicksburg meeting I might just lose my temper and order you to straddle that horse and go to that synonym of hell they call Texas."

3

In the weeks that followed, Jackson began tutoring his fourteen pupils by day and in the evenings reviewing subjects for his own examination before the church body in Vicksburg. Reverend Whiteside aided him in the latter. He placed questions on the Bible, ancient and modern history, and mathematics until Horatio was weary, then reminded him that the men who would soon examine him expected and demanded quick, accurate answers. And always with Jackson's nod of understanding he would fire another question. Perhaps it had to do with some minor event of the American Revolution or again with a verse from Isaiah or Amos.

"You know, Brother Whiteside," Jackson said one night, "if I was half as hard on my scholars as you are on me, I'd find myself lookin' for another job." To which Whiteside replied crisply, "Now what did I tell you about dropping your g's?"

The tutor who was being tutored left the house each morning wearing a coat, as was proper, and walked to a building in downtown Natchez. One room of the structure, which housed a store and a few offices, served as Professor Jackson's rent-free private school. He always stood in the doorway to greet the young gentlemen and ladies who alighted from carriages with the aid of domestic slaves. When all were assembled, he said a prayer, bid them be seated, then spoke briefly on the advantages of being Americans and Christians. He began with history because it was more interesting than grammar, French, or mathematics. Poetry reading and elocution followed geography and Bible.

Professor Jackson introduced other subjects which were not on the prescribed curriculum, and before the end of the first week his popularity with the pupils exceeded his fondest expectations. As the second week drew to a close, the cause of his popularity provoked concern on the part of parents and, on the first day of his third week, a visit from the mothers in a body. They arrived several minutes before the class in Bible, the last for the day, ended. Rather surprised and curious,

Jackson concluded the lesson with a prayer, dismissed the class, and thanked the ladies for their visit.

"This is more than a visit, Professor," a lady who was evidently their spokesman informed him. "We are here to demand that you adhere to the courses of study which met with our approval. We are not interested in educating our children in the ways of the Indians and frontiersmen."

"Indeed we are not, Professor Jackson!" another spoke up frostily. "I wish Harold to grow up a polite, cultured gentleman, not an uncouth person with a reputation for throwing a knife or hatchet at a tree. Furthermore, I positively do not sanction his walking a mile to school instead of coming by carriage simply because you have instilled in him the idea he quotes from you, sir, 'God gave us legs to walk with.' "

Jackson smiled and said politely, "It is kind of you, Mrs. Carstings, and all you ladies, to come directly to me with your suggestions. I appreciate your interest. Now Harold is a good scholar and a young gentleman. Did you know that since he started walking he can outrun 'most any boy his age in Natchez? One moment now, ma'am, I know you're not sending him here to learn to run or to bury a hatchet or knife blade in a tree at ten paces. I know you realize also that young gentlemen grow up to be adult gentlemen, and that in the process they must compete with others and grow in confidence in their own ability to do things in manly fashion—"

"Sir, you talk just like John Carstings!"

"Thank you, ma'am" Jackson grinned. "Now I'll venture you've noticed an improvement in Harold's French and mathematics."

"Well, yes, but—"

"Know why, Mrs. Carstings? Now this a secret between us—wouldn't have Harold hear this, ma'am, let him learn it later—since he's learned he can run and fling a hatchet better than most, he is also out to compete in learning."

"Really, Professor?" She looked startled, next dubious, then partially convinced.

When Mrs. Carstings left off, the mothers of the girls took over. One said her daughter's dancing master almost suffered a stroke after watching her do a Cherokee dance. A most unladylike performance, and as such wasn't to be tolerated. She was supported by a chorus of protests, which Jackson let run its course before saying quietly:

"You know, ladies, I demonstrated that dance during the class in Bible."

"Bible? Heavens, sir, surely you jest!"

"No, ladies, I do not jest. I was talking about thanks due the

Lord for the many blessings bestowed upon us. It wasn't too interesting to the young folks. In fact, they were letting it go in one ear and out the other. So I wasn't teaching, I was just talking, and none of you are paying me all of two dollars a month to just talk. So I decided to drive my thought home by example. I began to chant and went into an Indian dance. Believe me, that caught their attention. Then I told them what it meant."

Jackson paused to allow perplexed and impatient glances full exchange among the women. Sure enough, as he had anticipated, curiosity got the better of them and provoked a question:

"Just what does it mean, Professor?"

"It was the harvest dance. The Indians were giving thanks in their way for the blessing bestowed on them, thanks for the harvest of corn, pumpkins, and all."

"But savage and pagan, sir!"

"Yes, ma'am, by our standards. But let's admit that sincere thanks to our Creator is one of the many great lessons from the Bible, and it's for the young as well as us grownups. Anyhow, the Indian dance and chant got the idea across where a long sermon might have failed."

Jackson glanced at the mother whose daughter had shocked the dancing master. "Now, Mrs. Brooks, maybe I should tell you that your Sarah named more things she was thankful for than any of the others. In fact, she came up with fourteen blessings she was aware of, and they weren't at all childish. Thought you might like to know, ma'am."

Mrs. Brooks was both surprised and pleased, though she tried to hide the latter. Jackson knew why. She did not wish to go against the majority by condoning the very things they had come here to protest. Aware that he had blunted a few spears, he didn't overlook the fact that it was far wiser to appear the modest loser here. Indeed, he told himself, these women had not called on him to be silenced. No siree, they had descended on him to convince him of something. So he said:

"But I grasp your point, Mrs. Brooks, that I do. And yours, Mrs. Carstings." Addressing others who had voiced complaints, he remarked on the need for watchfulness and concern on the part of parents in every phase of their children's activities, especially their education. "So from now on, ladies, I'll leave the dancing to the dancing masters and the hatchet throwing to the Indians."

That evening Jackson related his experience of the day to Jeremiah Whiteside. The older man laughed and complimented Horatio on the manner in which he had handled the women.

"You're beginning to learn a few things that can further a man's progress in his every endeavor, Horatio. A little policy goes a long way in dealing with people. And a preacher who hasn't got it won't last long. Now I hope you remember that when we go up to Vicksburg next week."

"I'll try to, all right, in keeping with honesty, of course."

"I thought you'd say that, Horatio Jackson. But remember this, a man can be as honest with his mouth shut as with it wide open and tongue wagging about the Lord calling him to preach in Texas."

CHAPTER 15

Late October on the Gulf Coast of Texas seemed but for an autumn haze over the land an extension of the long hot summer. While a breeze out of the north had blown in cool and refreshing a week earlier, it had been no match for the jealous wind off the ocean and was soon pushed back up the lazy Brazos.

On this late afternoon Jane Wells looked up from the stack of history papers she was grading and gazed through the window at trees across the river. They had lost none of their summer green, though the setting sun touched the leaves with colors of gold and orange. It was a quiet time of day, and she rose and moved to the door. Only the clang of her aunt's hammer on anvil and a faint yell of a passing boatman broke the silence over Velasco.

The peaceful scene of river, trees, and meadows seemed to Jane in perfect harmony with the political quietude of Austin's colony. Since the disturbances of summer that ended with the Battle of Velasco, Bradburn's dismissal, and the surrender of the Nacogdoches garrison, tempers had cooled and issues so important in June and early July appeared to slumber. The very men who had grabbed up rifles and turned them on the Mexican troops had turned to crops and shipping with the same energy they had applied to war. Cotton gins hummed and slaves sweated and sang and ships took on Brazos cotton and lumber and produce for New Orleans, departed, and returned without any molestation from Mexican customs officers. No soldiers manned the fort that had belched fire at the Texans four months earlier. All was placid, too calm, she thought, but wonderful while it lasted.

Jane left the house and walked slowly past the orchard to her aunt's private pier. Returning, she paused to pick flowers that defied the season.

The rosebush she had planted near the window more than a year ago continued to bloom. The roses held her attention for some time, reminding her of the bouquets Robert Berry had sent her in New Orleans during her visit there last summer. This in turn brought to mind the blossoms promised by Mr. Jackson in his first letter but never delivered; and next she was thinking of his recent letter posted in New Orleans, in which he flung French in romantic manner. His *"Tout à vous!!!* (wholly yours!!!)" simply failed to strike any semblance of harmony with the man himself. An expression in Cherokee or Choctaw would be more compatible to his type and personality, she was thinking.

"Oh well," she said, rising. "He should have my reply by now, however brief it was."

Dismissing Jackson from mind, she brushed a ringlet from her forehead and went inside, debating on whether to finish grading the examination papers now or at school next day. She wasn't in the mood for that now and, besides, it was time to prepare supper. Her aunt would be hungry as usual and there was no telling whom she might bring with her to argue politics or horseflesh.

The sun had scarcely disappeared when she heard Sally telling someone to keep quiet until she got her "say in." Then her aunt and Captain Herrick entered the house in hot argument. Both were so engrossed in the subject that they forgot to speak to Jane or ask if supper was ready. Smiling, Jane turned to the stove again and listened.

"So I repeat the question, Cap'n! What good will come of the convention Mr. Austin held three weeks back when—?"

"Quiet! If you'll listen, Bucktooth Sal, I'll tell ye! And I'll appreciate it if you wouldn't yell when ye next butts in. I ain't deaf, y' know."

"Might as well be. All bone for a brain. It's a wonder to me you can navigate a dory, much less a schooner. But since you're my guest, I'll be ladylike and listen while you bray your fool head off."

Captain Herrick scratched his bald head and appeared

astonished. "Maybe she ain't feelin' well, Miss Jane," he said, taking a chair. "Else she's in shoalin' water with a cranky helm and rudder and knows it."

"Could be," Jane replied. "But hadn't you better take advantage of the fair wind she allows you—while it lasts?"

"Aye! Now I was sayin' the convention o' Texans was a good thing. Shows we're all o' the same mind in resolutin' for tariff exemption for another three years, askin' Mexico to allow more 'mericans to come to Texas, petitionin' for land to support schools, and permission for statehood."

"All of the same mind, you say?" Bucktooth Sal fairly shouted at him. "What about the San Antonio delegates? Didn't they refuse to attend the convention? Didn't they say the meeting was unauthorized and therefore illegal?"

"Well—yes," Herrick admitted.

"Right, you webfooted swamp crane! And didn't Mr. Austin decide the petition for statehood was premature after all? And has Mr. Wharton, elected by the convention to present the proposals to the Mexican government, done anything about going down there? He ain't and he won't. Know why? I'll tell you why. 'Cause Santa Anna hasn't taken over down there yet, even though he won."

Now Herrick sat strangely silent and Bucktooth Sal struck the table with a palm. "So tell me what good was the convention? Speak up Cap'n!"

Jane turned from the stove and whispered in Herrick's ear. He grinned, eyed Sally wisely a moment. "What good ye say? It's alluz good when free men band together and declares for what they feel is right and—" He looked at Jane.

"Just," she said for him.

"Correct, and that's what us Americans did with England. But the—"

"Parrot!" Sally flung at him. Looking at Jane, she said, "Two against one, eh? Well, I'll tell you both what I told Bill Wharton today, which is he ought to go see Santa Anna. But he ain't goin', and that's that, which is proof the convention ain't worth two whoops in hell!"

"Aunt Sally! Watch your language! Now, Captain Herrick, finish your speech."

"Thanks, Miss Jane, for stoppin' her 'fore she blows boiler and stack. What I was about to say was that the convention was mighty important because it was the first time that Texans got together as a—a—" Again he turned to Jane for help, and again she aided him, saying:

"The first time Texans met together as a united group from all parts of the province."

Herrick eyed Sally exultantly, as though he had said it. "And fifty-eight delegates guaranteed it, Sal, and you can't whistle that fact down."

"Speakin' of delegates, Jane," Sally said, ignoring Herrick, "guess what Bill Wharton told me about Hellfire Jackson. Or are you interested?"

Jane lifted brows and shoulders and proceeded to place plates on the table. She did not see her aunt wink an eye at Herrick, nor did she seem aware of the gathering silence until curiosity got the better of her. "Well, I'm waiting, Aunt Sally."

"Yeah? For what?"

"For whatever Mr. Wharton said, what else?"

"Made her fish for it, didn't I, Cap'n?" Sally laughed and struck Herrick's shoulder. Meeting Jane's sharp glance of reprimand, she sobered and repeated William Wharton's account of Jackson's fight at the New Orleans slave market. "Hellfire was takin' on all comers to keep them from sellin' old Wash. Now who would a thought old peace-preachin' Jackson was a fighting man?"

"It does sound odd," Jane said, setting food on the table. "But go on."

"Ed Waller and Thomas McKinney and a couple of men from Macogdoches were on Jackson's side, but it was old Hellfire that was tossin' men like they was horseshoes. That I would like to see. Yes, sir. But that ain't all Wharton said. Where's the corn bread, Jane?"

"Coming. But did Mr. Jackson leave with his Negro?"

"Did he? He did. Now where was I? Oh, yes, what Wharton said about the folks up in Nacogdoches wantin' to send Hellfire to the convention as a delegate."

Jane stopped still, then said, "Ouch!" as her hand touched the hot corn bread. "You mean they wanted him, Mr. Jackson, for a delegate?"

"Sure. But they couldn't find him."

"But why him? I thought—"

"To reward him for what he done after the battle up there, that's what. But are you goin' to stand there till that corn bread gets cold?"

"I'm sorry, Aunt Sally." Serving the bread, Jane asked, "Just what did he do to earn their gratitude and that honor? In his letter to me he sounded very disappointed about the outcome of his stand for peace in Nacogdoches."

"Well, he was old peace-at-any-price Jackson, all right. But after the battle he done more than tend the wounded. He rode out at the request of the Texan commander and talked

Piedras into surrenderin'. So his peace talk finally paid off. It stopped another battle."

Jane sat down and stared incredulously at her aunt. Then she looked a little bewildered. "Why, he didn't even mention that in his letter! Now I wonder why."

Bucktooth Sal nudged Captain Herrick. "Got her curious, ain't he? Now they say when a man can do that to—"

"Aunt Sally!" Jane exclaimed. Then she rose from the table and walked out into the night.

2

On that same evening Horatio Jackson appeared before the body of churchmen in Vicksburg, Mississippi. He was dressed for the occasion, uncomfortably so, but at Brother Whiteside's insistence. He looked and felt unearthly gaunt in snug pantaloons, tight black coat, flowing blue cravat, and stiff white collar that sawed at his neck almost up to his ears. And if fancy attire wasn't enough to make him squirm and wish for buckskin and a campfire on the trail, the intent if not critical scrutiny of the six men who held his close future in their hands more than made up for it. Indeed, for they seemed to be dissecting him as they one by one assailed him with questions.

Whiteside sat with them, stroking his beard thoughtfully. He seemed as much a part of the richly appointed surroundings as the plantation owner who had made the mansion available to his pastor for this meeting. Only Horatio stood, and he felt, as he told Whiteside later, "like a crane with both feet caught in a bog while they scattered my feathers as fast as they could reload muskets."

Jackson breathed easier once past the examination in ancient and modern history. If they ran true to form, mathematics would follow, and he could breeze through that like a duck gobbling up June bugs. However, one of the examiners, a short paunchy man, with pale face and a head so bald that it bounced the light from the chandelier like a mirror, wasn't quite satisfied with Mr. Jackson's knowledge of ancient history. It was all of twenty minutes before the body picked up mathematics, and another half hour had passed when the examination in Bible began.

"How many books in the Old Testament, Mr. Jackson? . . . Thirty-nine is correct. In the New Testament? . . . Twenty-seven is right, sir. Name the books of both in order." When Horatio had done this, he was asked to quote a verse from the Bible dealing with the company of fools.

Jackson winced, rubbed an ear, and said, "Just bear with me a minute, gentlemen and brothers, and give me some comfort in this trouble—as you'll find in chapter fourteen, Book of John—for this aspirant seems to be knee deep in quicksand at the moment."

The bald man smiled. The other stared coldly. A brow or two lifted. Silence was heavy. Whiteside sat tense.

"Now I recall," Jackson said, blowing out his cheeks and inhaling deeply. "Thirteenth chapter of Proverbs, verse nineteen, or twenty, quote, 'He that walketh with wise men shall be wise; but a companion of fools shall be destroyed.' "

Whiteside breathed easier. The question had been one to baffle him until Jackson came up with the answer. But he was well aware that more would follow before the severest test began, the aspirant's interpretation of various verses and chapters of the Bible. As he predicted, so it was. Although Jackson failed to answer a few questions, he did exceptionally well in impressing on the group his close acquaintance with the Word of God.

"Now, Mr. Jackson, we are interested in how you would preach, using for your text chapter thirteen, Revelation. Proceed, sir."

Jackson tugged at his collar a moment. "That's about the beast rising up out of the sea, having seven heads and ten horns, and on each head the name of blasphemy, and the people worshiping the dragon. Well, gentlemen and brothers, to be honest with you, I'll have to confess that that's the last chapter in the Bible I'd choose for a text."

"Why, Mr. Jackson?"

"Because I'm a mortal and I'd be in the pulpit facing mortals who would expect me to explain something I am not smart enough to handle. A preacher don't last long—"

"A preacher *don't,* Mr. Jackson?"

Horatio saw Whiteside's brow knit. Swallowing hard, Jackson said quickly. "Beg pardon, sir, a preacher *doesn't.*"

"Thank you, Mr. Jackson. It is only that we feel that ministers should always uphold the dignity of the church by adhering to the rules of grammar without fail, whether in or out of the pulpit. Do you agree?"

Whiteside's hand clutched at his beard and his jaw dropped and seemed to hang still as though paralyzed while he waited for Jackson's reply. He saw Jackson grimace.

"Well, sir," Horatio began, "yes—and no. I mean by yes that in your company and in your pulpits and environ the use of 'he don't' is an improper, offensive, inexcusable abrasion on the King's English and is not to be tolerated by a polite, cultured congregation, but there are times—"

"Excellent, Brother Jackson," Whiteside spoke up. "Well spoken," he added, hoping to put an end to it before Horatio put his foot in a trap. "And since it's getting late, I suggest that with the sanction of the examining body we by-pass the side issue, as well as Revelation thirteen. With Brother Jackson's permission, of course."

The churchmen agreed and Jackson, meeting Whiteside's sharp glance, was also quick to approve. Other questions on the Bible followed. Horatio was not found wanting. He was in fact beginning to impress the group. Finally the examination ended. As the presiding minister rose to ask Jackson to wait outside while the body reached a decision, the bald-headed man said suddenly:

"Are you the man known in Texas as Hellfire Jackson?"

"I am, sir."

Amid exchanges of frowning glances and elevated eyebrows, Whiteside's groan was audible. A heavy silence ended with a clearing of throats. Then the bald man asked:

"Why didn't you identify yourself, sir?"

"You didn't ask me, sir. I have nothing to hide, and I'm not ashamed of the appellation bestowed upon me by religious-hungry Texans."

"Naturally, Mr. Jackson. But there are numerous stories in circulation about your violation of Mexican religious restrictions. Is it true that you engaged a Catholic priest in a public exchange of words in Texas?"

"Why, yes. But without animosity, and only after he marched on my tabernacle meeting."

Again the six churchmen looked at one another, their expressions grave. "Is it true that you embroiled yourself in political issues from the pulpit, Mr. Jackson?"

"Only if you define a bid for patience, understanding, and a peaceful settlement of differences on the eve of battle embroiling one's self in political issues."

"According to rumor, you were warned by the Mexican colonel about the ban on Protestant worship."

"Yes, but he sat through one of my sermons after that. He found nothing wrong with my sermon since I didn't preach hate and revolt."

"Naturally, Mr. Jackson. We realize your motives were pure and that credit is due you for exhibiting zeal and courage in the face of overwhelming opposition in Texas. However, it is all rather astonishing and, if one may say so, hardly exemplary of the accepted image of the ministry. With this thought in mind, sir, are we correct in assuming by your presence before this body that your trials in the wilderness are behind you and that you plan if ordained a minister to modify your activities and adhere to the normal accepted pattern of conduct of a minister instead of continuing to be an exception to the rule?"

Jackson's bushy brows lifted, fell, and knit into a frown. His blue eyes flashed and the muscles of his jaws hardened. Taking his Bible from a pocket, he held it in the palm of one hand and stabbed the cover with the forefinger of the other.

"We read from the same Book, gentlemen, but we sure don't get the same meaning from the Scriptures therein. Now I've never found a passage in this Bible where Jesus told his disciples *not* to spread the gospel in all lands. And I haven't run across any passage in this Book where the Lord told Paul *not* to preach in Rome because Christianity was in violation of Roman religious restrictions. Moreover, I have yet to find anything in my Bible that says Jesus chastised a prophet for preaching patience, understanding, and peace instead of war. Nor have I read in this Holy Book any verse that tells us that a sermon preached from a tree stump on the forks of a creek isn't blessed as much as a sermon delivered from a fine polished pulpit in a city."

Raising a hand, he brought it down with forefinger pointing at the group. "So, gentlemen, with or without your sanction, I'm going to Texas where the Lord called me and where a preacher *don't* degrade the sacred office by wearing buckskin instead of the fancy clothes I'm rigged out in now. I'm going to preach the gospel when and wherever I'm invited to do so and in the language most Texans use and understand, and I'm going to make their social, economic, and political problems mine, as a pastor should."

Lowering his hand, Jackson thanked them, turned abruptly, and walked out of the room.

He stood alone in the long hallway, hands locked behind him, brow creased. He gazed at portraits in heavy gilt frames and large tapestries without any awareness of their presence as he alternately berated and defended himself for the outburst. As he began to walk back and forth, shaking his head dismally and wishing he were already on the other side of the Sabine River, Whiteside emerged.

No word was spoken between them as they left the house. They were nearing the steamboat that would land them downriver in Natchez next morning when Jackson said, "If you don't mind, Brother Whiteside, I'd just as soon you'd admonish me in words as in silence. That way I won't be confusing what I'm thinking with what's on your mind."

Whiteside made no reply for some time. Then he stopped suddenly, looked up at Jackson, and said, "You've got a point there, Horatio. Now in the first place, you opened your mouth when you could have kept it shut. You weren't asked to air your views on the advantage of bad grammar after being caught up on 'a preacher don't.' Besides, those churchmen couldn't comprehend such. In the second place, you could have waited to see if they were going to ordain you before poking a finger at them and declaring you were off to Texas. In the—"

"It would have come up anyhow."

"And in the third place," Whiteside went on, ignoring the interruption, "maybe you should have realized we're running out of church groups that can ordain you. You do beat all, Horatio Jackson."

"Yes, sir."

"And in the fourth place, despite your stubborn insistence that your call is to Texas, which was a strain on the imagination of mild-mannered ministers, plus the fact that you retaliated to their suggestions for compliance to the church pattern with a fiery lecture that sawed against the grain, those men still wanted personally to ordain you. Now wipe that grin off your face, Horatio, and admit that a little restraint on your part and the merest show of conformity to the accepted rule might have turned the trick. But that's a little too much to expect of Hellfire Jackson, I suppose."

He paused there. Jackson said after waiting out a few seconds, "And in the fifth place, sir?"

Whiteside tried to suppress a grin. Failing, he placed a hand on Jackson's shoulder. "Well, in the fifth place, after you left the room, all of us decided that it wouldn't hurt us or the governing body of the church to start reading a little from your Bible, Horatio."

CHAPTER 16

On an afternoon some five weeks after the Vicksburg meeting, Jackson and Wash halted their animals at a creek on the Camino Real to let them drink. Having left Natchitoches, Louisiana, before daybreak, and with long miles still separating them from Gaines Ferry on the Sabine, Jackson decided to pitch camp in a forest some distance off the road and resume his journey to Texas with tomorrow's dawn.

"Reckon I'm just lazy, Wash. Maybe autumn's in my blood."

Breathing the pine-scented air, he moved from the shadows out into the early December sun. Its mild warmth was pleasant and he wished to lie flat of back and soak it up while taking in the change of colors in the oak and sweet gum trees. Since the frosts of late November, golds, reds, and browns stood out vividly against the always green backdrop of pines. It was a pretty time of year, a season that inspired Jackson and gladdened his heart with its promise.

As Wash shuffled off in search of a suitable camping place, Horatio stretched out on the ground. For a minute or so he watched a blue jay taunt a squirrel. The jay screamed and the squirrel pretended to ignore the teasing for a while. Then, shedding his dignity for play, he barked, ran up an oak, and sat on a limb swishing his tail at the swooping bird.

Jackson shifted his gaze to the blue sky and sent his thoughts back to Natchez, where after seven weeks of tutoring he had turned his pupils over to another man. Texas called and, despite the flattering offers of Mrs. Carstings and other parents, not to mention the pleas of the boys and girls in his classes, he left for Texas. Perhaps the letter from Velasco had prompted him to leave before Christmas. Jeremiah Whiteside had thought as much. "Come back with a wife to anchor you, Horatio," he had said, "and we'll have you ordained in short time." A wife would help, Jackson reflected now, and Miss Jane certainly qualified as far as he was concerned. But did he meet her exacting qualifications?

"A man never knows," he said, frowning. He removed Jane's letter from a pocket and read it again. Once past a short summary of events in Austin's colony, she replied in brief, forthright manner to his letter in New Orleans in mid-September:

> I do agree, sir, that your dignified employ as a tutor should influence the fulfillment of your aim to become an ordained minister. I can and do wish you well in both endeavors.
>
> I am also quite sure Mr. Austin cannot fail to appreciate your support of his constant bid for patience and understanding in matters having to do with Mexico. Nor can you, sir, censure him for compliance to his agreement with the Mexican government in religious matters. However, I am pleased to learn from you that you have pleaded your case in a letter to him. Do not for a moment think him lacking in gratitude and understanding of your position, despite the fact that your swath through Texas was something *sui generis* religiously, to say the least, and deserving of public admiration. Naturally you must expect defeat, circumstances being what they are. But one must realize also that defeat is often the foundation of success.
>
> I am in excellent health, and appreciative of your concern, as well as pleased to know that your memories of the Brazos are not all of a doleful nature.

Jackson studied the letter almost wonderingly. Fresh in his memory was the touch of his lips to hers, and for perhaps the hundredth time since that day in June he let his mind dwell on the kiss he had stolen from her on the bank of the Brazos. Now, in the letter before him it was not at all difficult for him to read into Jane's "pleased to know that your memories of the Brazos are not all of a doleful nature" her own fond memory of that kiss. And what he read into it he was content to believe true.

A grin spread across his face and he gave a moment's thought to the gift he had purchased and sent to her from Natchez so that it would reach her by Christmas. Then he was reading her letter once more. Upon finishing it again, he said:

"Miss Jane, you don't fool old Horatio one bit. I know you stopped the letter short simply because you were tempted to sign off with '*Tout à vous!* Wholly yours, Mr. Jackson'!"

The sound of something crashing through the underbrush cut his elation short. Scrambling to his feet, he saw Wash running toward him, hurdling bushes with the agility of a boy.

"Injuns, Rev'ren'!" Wash exclaimed, panting to a stop. "A

whole passel of 'em on de other side o' dem trees! Let's git goin' to where they ain't! Right now, Marse Jackson!"

"Now hold on, Wash. Most likely they're friendly. You stay here while I reconnoiter and see if they're Delawares, Shawnees, Kickapoos, or Cherokees." Despite the Negro's stout objection at being left alone, Jackson eased into the forest. He had not gone far when the sound of a twig cracking caused him to whirl.

There stood Wash, a sheepish look on his face. Joining Horatio, he whispered, "Thought maybe ole Wash better he'p yo'all reck-a-noit, Rev'ren'. I'se heard tell it's a heap better fo' two of us not to be alone than fo' just one of us to be together."

Jackson eyed him a moment before shaking his head in hopeless manner and moving forward again. Topping the rise several minutes later, he parted the bushes and surveyed the Indian camp. Their behavior and regalia told him much. This was a Cherokee hunting party, and not a war party; they were expecting others to join them; there was no fire water to craze them. Jackson waited the better part of an hour. Then he saw another dozen bucks riding in. Two were Shawnees, the remainder Cherokees of Chief Bowles's tribe. The presence of Antonio Yellow Bear was proof.

"Friends, Wash," he said. "Now let's get back to our animals and see if we can find a few gifts that will make us welcome to partake of roast venison they'll be serving up at nightfall."

Just before the sun disappeared Jackson and Wash walked their mounts into the Cherokee camp. Horatio's greeting in their language put them at ease. "I am Red Fox," he added, "and I see my friend Yellow Bear, to whom I bring gifts." Inquiring of "The Bowl," their chieftain, he got off his horse and walked among them, grinning, pausing here and there to feel of braves' muscles and comment on same. After presenting Yellow Bear with a new hunting knife, he sat cross-legged and talked of things that interested them.

"We hear of you many time, Red Fox," Yellow Bear said. "You speak from magic book to many people, but you never let the Cherokee listen to your magic. Maybe Red Fox tell us about Great Spirit in book on this night."

Jackson rubbed his jaw thoughtfully. Aware that the suggestion was virtually a command, one which must be obeyed if he wished to sustain the friendship of the Indians, he said he would do just that after all had eaten. Throughout the meal he pondered his subject. Knowing the braves would be satisfied with nothing less than conflict and action, he decided at last on the story of David and Goliath. That should stir them up considerably, if of course he put it to pantomime, maybe using a hatchet instead of young David's sling. While this was a deviation from the truth, Jackson believed the Lord realized that a preacher had to improvise at times.

When nothing was left of the venison but bones, Yellow Bear wiped greasy fingers on his buckskin pants and told his people that Red Fox would pull a story out of his magic book. "You listen," he told them. Turning to Jackson, he said, "You talk."

Jackson obeyed. He read from the Bible, translating the story in essence into Cherokee. He pantomimed, he looked up at the giant Goliath, and he looked down at David. When the stage was set, and he had Goliath backed up against an oak tree, he squatted down to little David's size and let go his hatchet. It sped fast and true. The blade was buried in the trunk. Goliath fell. The braves yelled approval. They wanted more.

As the yelling continued, Jackson's attention was drawn to a large white man who sat on a horse behind the Cherokees. In the dancing firelight Horatio could not be sure of the man's identity, though he thought he recognized him. However, it seemed improbable that the visitor could be the prominent lawyer and statesman from Tennessee whom he resembled. But the Cherokees were clamoring for another exhibition from the magic book, and Horatio could only comply to their demands.

He read from Genesis. He told them how the Great Spirit created all things. He named them, from land, sea, and heavens to birds, fishes, animals, and men. He pointed to the slice of moon hanging in the western sky. "Great spirit made that," he said, before turning the pages of the Bible and reading of the coming of Christ. "The Great Spirit came down to earth in the shape of a man. He was called Jesus."

All the while the man on the horse, who bore a striking resemblance to the ex-governor of Tennessee, leaned on the pommel of his saddle and listened to Jackson's story of Jesus.

"Now Jesus didn't look like the Great Spirit. And the people didn't know that He could hurl forked tongues of fire down from the sky, and make the heavens growl with thunder, and send rain to water the corn, pumpkins, and melons of the Cherokees and White Eyes. But He did not do much of this while on earth. He lived as men live. He taught goodness and kindness to men, so their spirits would go to the happy hunting ground when they died.

"Now He had twelve chiefs under him. They were good men, like Yellow Bear, all except one. His name was Judas. When the great chiefs of the people wanted to get rid of Jesus, they offered Judas thirty pieces of yellow metal to point out the Great Spirit to them. And Judas was thinking about the things he could could get at the trading post for this gold, like hunting knives and blankets."

Jackson was soon telling and enacting the betrayal of the Great Spirit by Judas following the Last Supper. Then he told of the trial of Jesus before the mighty chieftain Pilate. Next, he was chopping down an imaginary tree and making a huge cross. He talked on, playing the parts of Pilate and the angry Jews. The Indians sat entranced, awaiting the climax. But the planned climax was never reached, for as Jackson began to nail the hands of the Great Spirit to the cross an ominous murmur sounded from the Cherokees.

It grew in volume until every Indian but one joined in the chorus of angry defiance. Only Yellow Bear sat in silence, arms folded at his chest, as became his rank. He continued to sit there when a brave leaped to his feet and brandished a knife. Nor did he move to quell the disturbance when others rose and amid hideous yells waved knives and tomahawks and began hopping about the campfire in what Jackson knew was the Cherokee war dance.

Surprised and perplexed by it all, Horatio raised a hand and cried for silence. When his attempt to stop the warlike demonstration failed, he strode to where Yellow Bear sat and asked his assistance. Receiving only a stern look, he asked what had brought this about.

"Time for Cherokee to save Great Spirit, Red Fox. Yellow Bear not stop them. Pretty soon they catch little chief and mighty chief who do that to Great Spirit. We fix them."

Jackson shook his head in dismay. "You mean Judas and Pilate?"

"That them."

As Jackson stood there in shocked silence, his brain ticking fast for a way to stop his righteous uprising he had started some eighteen hundred years too late to save Jesus, the man out there on horseback began to laugh. He continued to laugh while Jackson tried to convince Yellow Bear that Judas and Pilate had died many moons ago and gone to their just rewards.

When Horatio finally made Yellow Bear understand and order was restored, the rider nudged his horse forward. Reining to a halt, he spoke to Yellow Bear and said in Cherokee:

"I am Co-lo-neh, the Raven. For many moons I lived with

our brother Cherokees up in Arkansas. Chief Oo-loo-te-ka is my old friend."

Jackson was certain of the man's identity even before he turned to him and said, with a twinkle in his piercing eyes, "Whoever you are, Red Fox, accept the compliments of Sam Houston. You're the first white man I ever heard preach in Cherokee, and if you do it as well in English, the devil might as well close up shop."

2

Early next morning Jackson, Houston, and Wash were riding toward the Sabine. Houston had never been to Texas before, and he told Horatio his mission to the province was to buy land. "Among other things," he added. He was very interested in Texas and his curiosity provoked a maze of questions about the American settlers and Mexicans, their attitudes toward each other, disturbances of the summer of 1832, as well as social, religious, and political conditions, especially in Austin's colony.

"Well, Governor, I ought to know a little about the religious and political, seeing as how I got caught up in both last summer." After relating his experiences in both Brazoria and Nacogdoches, Jackson waited for the expected laughter from the other. To his surprise, only a chuckle was forthcoming. Houston appeared more interested in the calm but explosive relationship between Anglo-Texans and the Mexican government.

"You know, Horatio, all you've told me bears out what I wrote a New York financier in August. I quote: 'A population like that of Texas is in perpetual liability to commotion, and though it may be tranquil today, a storm may arise tomorrow.' Do you agree?"

Jackson admitted that the past seemed to prove the future.

They rode on, silent for a time, Houston sitting ramrod straight on the fine horse he called Bucephalus, a name that "worried" Wash. Jackson was more curious of the man who rode the spirited animal, and his thoughts went back to last evening: After Horatio had introduced himself and said he had practiced a little law in Nashville, Tennessee, Houston had remembered him as the son of John Schuyler Jackson. Next Houston had narrowed his sharp eyes on Horatio and said, "Since you're a friend of the Cherokee, I suppose you know what they called me when I lived with them up in Arkansas." Jackson did. The Cherokees had named him the Big Drunk. "Well, I earned it, Jackson."

Horatio knew why Houston had taken to drink. In 1829, thirty-six-year-old Sam Houston suddenly resigned his office as governor of Tennessee and left his bride of less than three months. Nashville was shocked by the scandal that still remained a puzzle. There was gossip but no explanation. Houston, former Congressman, fiery speaker, close friend of and political heir to President Andrew Jackson, went from Nashville to Arkansas, where the tribe of Chief Oo-loo-te-ka, with whom Houston had lived as a boy, had moved. There for almost two years he lived and dressed like an Indian.

And now he was on his way to Texas. To buy land for a New York financier? "Among other things," he had said. Jackson had overheard his remark to Antonio Yellow Bear, "I'm on a mission to Texas for the Great White Father Andrew Jackson, to make peace with the Comanche Indians." A statement which caused Horatio's brow to lift. Besides this, as Houston mounted his horse at dawn, papers had fallen from his pocket. As Jackson had picked them up, he had seen a passport issued to Samuel Houston by the United States War Department.

All rather puzzling in a way, Horatio thought. And when one recalled President Jackson's admitted interest in Texas, it was not difficult to believe that Old Hickory had sent Houston to Texas to probe Mexican power and influence. But that too was wrapped in mystery. Horatio shrugged and dismissed it from his mind. Houston himself constituted the greater puzzle, for he left no doubt in any man's mind that he was as strong as he looked to be, and ambitious.

Horatio eyed him and saw a man who had emerged from the furnace of despair a bigger man than the "Big Drunk" of the Cherokee nation. Tall, stately, forceful, with the eyes of an eagle, he seemed endowed with springs of steel; and however mysterious and reserved, and at times vain and raffish, he impressed one as being a man capable of making every bit as big an imprint on the future as he had left on the past.

"Well, Governor," Jackson said, "are you ready to get off and stretch your legs a bit?"

Houston seemed resentful of being jerked out of profound thought. "What the hell for, Jackson? I'll stretch when we get to Texas."

"Then I'll catch up with you later, sir. Old Wash needs a rest, and the straps on my pack mule need tightening. Wouldn't want to scatter Bibles where nobody can read them."

Houston rode on without any reply, his gaze fixed on the road ahead.

Jackson and Wash did not see Houston again that day. After crossing the Sabine late in the afternoon, Horatio inquired of him and learned from Gaines that Houston had stopped at his place only long enough to rest his horse before riding off toward Ayish Bayou.

"Seemed mighty quiet and restless to me, Hellfire, but I suppose being a governor taught him when to keep his mouth shut. But what's he comin' to Texas for?"

"To buy land, he said."

"That's what he told me. But it don't exactly make sense. I figure it this way, once a politician always a politician. But how do you figure it?"

"I don't. But how are things in Texas, Mr. Gaines?"

"Weather's too dry, politics too quiet. Need a norther to cool things off so I can kill hogs. The only news I've heard lately is that Alcalde Elisha Roberts is holding court on his front porch tomorrow. Tryin' a horse thief, I hear. Stole one of Wyatt Hanks's mares."

"Planning to go?" Jackson asked.

"No. You know I don't get along too well with Elisha. On the strength of that I might be on the side of a horse thief, and favoring a horse thief is next to criminal in Texas. Now if the man had stole a hog or goat, I might just go and pull for him. But not a horse. Now back to Governor Houston, he's a whoppin' big man in size, and reputation."

They talked for some time, about Texas, her past and future, about Émile Fozatte, who continued to smuggle merchandise and slaves into the province, but always the topic of conversation swung again to Sam Houston, whose very presence in Texas provoked questions that had no answers.

Jackson and Wash left Gaines's place before sunrise next morning. A weak norther had pushed in during the night, and there was a pleasing chill in the dawn air. They rode unhurriedly toward the Ayish Bayou settlement and shortly after lunch sighted the house of Elisha Roberts. Wagons and saddled horses out on the campgrounds advised of a large gathering. Once beyond a screen of trees that hid the long porch, Jackson saw the body of men and recalled what Gaines had told him about the trial of a horse thief.

Leaving the animals in care of Wash, Horatio moved toward the crowd. There sat Roberts on the porch, a keg and hammer before him. At his left the jury sat on benches. Among them was John Cartwright, who kept a country store, and Philip Sublett, Roberts' son-in-law, and other men whom Jackson knew and liked; fair men all, he realized. Off to the right of the alcalde stood the culprit, with hands tied at his back. Near him, with rifle in hand, sat the accuser, Wyatt Hanks, whom Jackson knew to be a good and industrious citizen, operator of a water mill and cotton gin.

Surveying the crowd of onlookers who stood on the ground facing the porch, Jackson saw many men whom he knew well. Quite a few of them had fought in the Battle of Nacogdoches. Soon his roving glance fell on Sam Houston. The ex-governor stood with hands in coat pockets, his gaze fixed on Roberts, who was now saying:

"We have heard the charges from the man whose horse was stolen. We have heard the defendant's testimony, which more or less corroborates the charges. In any case—"

"What you mean more or less?" Hanks cut in. "Didn't he admit he stole the horse?"

Roberts picked up the hammer, rapped it resoundingly on the hollow keg, and said, "Silence in the court! One more outburst and I'll hold whoever he is in contempt and fine him accordin' to his means. Now as I was about to say, in any case, the defendant is entitled to a few words in his own defense. So you there, Jim Boyd, face the jury and speak up. Better make it good, 'cause there's not a man here who don't know you're one of Hominy Baines's crowd."

Jim Boyd looked at the men out of red-rimmed eyes that alternately flashed defiance and sobered with fear. A small, wiry man, he looked to be under thirty, and he wore the expression of a man who now wished above all things for the opportunity to live another thirty years. Looking at the jury, he said quietly:

"Like I told you, I borrowed the horse to get away from Hominy Baines, and I was going to return it."

"That so?" Roberts said. "Now if that's true, then why did you ride the borrowed horse back to Hominy's camp?"

"I had a score to settle." His glance dropped under Roberts' steady look of disbelief. "But you got no right to try me. Mexican law don't allow it."

Roberts turned to the jury. "The man has a point there, boys. Reckon we might as well forget the formalities of a trial and go ahead and hang him."

Boyd suddenly favored a trial. "I got a right to have a lawyer!"

"So you have." Hammering the keg, Roberts asked if there was a lawyer handy. "Governor Houston, you qualify. Care to defend this man?"

"I do not, Mr. Alcalde."

Roberts slowly surveyed the crowd. "Since there's nobody to defend the culprit, I hereby request the jury to weigh the evidence and come up with a—"

"One moment, Judge! I'll make a plea in behalf of the defendant."

Every eye there fell on Jackson. Roberts leaned forward, eyes squinting. "Hello, Hellfire. Good to see you." As Jackson moved up the steps, Roberts stood and held out a hand. "Sure you want to do this, Hellfire? He stole Wyatt's horse, you know."

"No, Mr. Roberts, I sure don't want to, but I feel it's my duty. And every man here, you and the jury included, knows by now that this is Hellfire Jackson's year for taking the wrong side on issues. Course I've had my feathers singed, but as the farmer said after he finally chased a skunk out of his parlor, "I knew I wouldn't be popular for a while, but I seen my duty and I done it.' "

A ripple of laughter ran through the crowd. Roberts picked up his hammer and struck the keg. "Silence in this court!" Looking at Jackson, he said, "Proceed."

Horatio took the steps separating him from Jim Boyd and placed a hand on his shoulder. "The Lord as your witness, did you deliberately and with intent to steal take said animal belonging to Mr. Hanks? Or did you with intent to return said property borrow same? If the latter be the motive, as you have stated, I call upon you to acquaint the jury with the score you had to settle. Now the truth, the whole truth, Mr. Boyd, and remember that the fires of hell don't cool one bit for a liar."

Boyd stood a minute silent. A tear rolled down his cheek. "Reverend, I was one of the men who tried to break up your meeting down at Nashville. I can't lie to you. I stole that—"

"Animal," Jackson said hastily. Turning to the jury, he said gravely, "This young man erred. He is human. We all err. He is young in years. He has repented. You saw, you heard. His life is before him or behind him. There is good in him for the future. Will you give him a future?" Then he said, "Look at him, gentlemen."

Jackson paused there to search the faces of the jurymen for pity or its opposite. Seeing a hangman's noose in the eyes of the majority, he began anew:

"So the defendant erred and stole a domestic animal. Now let's say he stole a hog."

Roberts was quick to remind him that the defendant had stolen a horse.

"Thank you, Judge. Reckon I was thinking on the twenty-fourth verse of Genesis one, wherein God said, 'Let the earth bring forth the living creature.' He didn't call them all by name, so we mortals must be content to accept 'living creature' as animals all equal in the eyes of God. Therefore, as the Lord defines it, this man stole an elephant or a goat—or a hog. So let's don't argue with God. Just say the defendant stole a hog."

"For the second time, Hellfire, it was a horse!"

"Your Honor, I don't aim to rile the court. But if God's word don't count in this court, you just say so." With no reply from Roberts, Jackson raised a hand and said, "For the sake of argument, Jim Boyd stole a hog, and—"

"A horse!" Roberts shouted. Laughter from even the jury benches caused him to lower the hammer on the keg. With silence restored, he looked at Jackson. "If the lawyer for the defense don't wish to be disbarred, he'll stick to the facts in this case and henceforth refer to the stolen property as a horse and not a hog. Is that clear, Hellfire?"

"It is, Your Honor. But if the animal stolen had been a hog, Judge, this man would not be facing a hangman's rope to prove the unwritten law of the frontier inviolate. No siree Bob, he wouldn't! Steal a cow, steal a goat, steal a chicken, saith the voice of man, but woe be unto him who stealeth a horse! What says the Book of Exodus, verse fifteen, chapter twenty? I'll tell you. 'Thou shalt not steal,' sayeth God. But did God say, 'Thou shalt not steal, *especially a horse*'? No, but you, my friends, are thinking perhaps the Lord forgot that, forgetting yourselves that commandment which says to you, 'Thou shalt not kill.' You have a way clear, ye who judge and pronounce judgment, a verdict which you can sleep with and in peace with your consciences—judge the crime, not the object stolen. Now as you peer at this poor man with a hangdog look on his face, forget the horse and say as I did, he stole a hog—a hog—a hog!"

With that, Jackson concluded his argument and stepped aside, careful to avoid an exchange of glances with the alcalde. It was just as well, since Roberts was doing his utmost to restrain himself and maintain the dignity of his office.

"Gentlemen of the jury," Roberts began after a minute of strained silence. "I keep tryin' my best to bend my imagination and go along with Hellfire Jackson. And I do tol'ably well in seeing it his way until my imagination ups itself and says it just can't picture a saddle on a hog—a hog—a hog!"

3

Sam Houston's hearty guffaw sounded above laughter from the crowd. The hammer struck the keg again and again, though it was not the gavel that put an end to mirth. It was the upraised arm of Hellfire Jackson that evoked silence. When a hush fell over the scene, he lowered his head and reminded the Lord that it was His duty to touch the hearts of the men who would soon pronounce judgment on their fellow man with mercy. His prayer was very brief. With his "Amen," he stepped down from the porch and walked alone out to the campground.

He knew what the verdict would be. He could not argue that the decision of men in this new and untamed frontier was without certain justification. He was quick to realize that once a horse thief was acquitted in a land where men were forced to make and uphold laws to protect themselves such outlaws as Hominy Baines would prey on them as never before. So Jim Boyd by virtue of his crime must for the common good serve as an example to his kind. Sam Houston had known it. Horatio Jackson knew it.

That afternoon the Ayish Bayou settlers took Jim Boyd to a tree a mile east on the King's Highway and placed a rope about his neck. Hellfire Jackson said a prayer, asked the Lord to have mercy on the soul of a thief, as the Saviour Himself must have given mercy to the two thieves crucified with Him. Following the prayer, a man drove the horse out from under Boyd and left him hanging where travelers along the road, and particularly Hominy Baines's crowd, could see him and take warning.

It was over and ended. Justice had been done. The crowd broke up, and men took a last look at the still corpse dangling grotesquely at the end of a rope. They departed for their homes, aware that they left something of themselves behind. Jackson read as much in their expressions. He knew also that however painful the memory of this day, they could not dwell on the past in a society where a man was measured by his ability to survive and by his contribution to the welfare of his neighbors. One looked to the future and clawed and hewed and fought to tame the wilderness and rid it of its evils. This was Texas.

Jackson's sober observations were interrupted by Sam Houston. He shook hands with Jackson and Roberts and said he would be on his way to Nacogdoches. When he got on his horse and rode off, Roberts placed an arm about Horatio's shoulder and invited him to remain at his place a few days.

Looking at the position of the sun, he said it wouldn't be long before Martha began setting the supper table. And Martha knew how to serve up sweet potatoes, baked plain or fixed fancy. She would put hot corn bread on the table and plenty of fresh-churned butter to go with it, plus buttermilk to wash it down with. Besides all that, Jackson could carve himself thick slices of shoulder roast from a big fat . . .

"Well, it's pork, Hellfire."

This was Texas.

CHAPTER 17

The north wind blew in with vigor before Christmas of 1832. It howled through the pines of East Texas and wailed like a banshee about the cabins of colonists. It whistled over the hills encircling Nacogdoches, where Sam Houston had stopped for talks with the authorities, and raked an icy finger down the path he had taken to Austin's colony. It continued to blow cold in San Felipe, where Houston learned that Austin had gone to Mexico. The blue norther, as Texans called it, pushed the tides back from the mouth of the Brazos, and schooners heavy with goods from New Orleans sat it out in the Gulf waiting for an end to low water over Velasco Bar.

In the town of Velasco, the few merchants cursed the foul weather that tied up their merchandise at sea at Christmastime. Bucktooth Sal's turbulent reminder that they could have ordered goods earlier provoked excuses, which in turn invited such blazing rejoinders as, "If I ran a blacksmith shop like you do a store, I'd be nailin' December shoes on your mule next fourth o' July! Now what the devil am I goin' to give Jane and Cap'n Herrick for Christmas, a damn horseshoe?"

On the day before Christmas the jealous south wind drove in and pushed the norther upriver. Schooners crossed the bar and welcome cargoes were discharged in Velasco. By nightfall townspeople were opening gifts and celebrating Christmas. They talked of all the good things the year had brought to Texas. Certainly 1832, despite the clash of arms —rather, because of it—had been an improvement over 1831.

There were no Mexican soldiers, no Bradburns to harass Texans, and down in Mexico Santa Anna had won. The future looked very promising.

Even Captain Herrick and Bucktooth Sal were for once in agreement on this score. But they were on this evening both a little under the influence of wine. The schoonerman poked the logs burning in Sally's fireplace and told of meeting the ex-governor of Tennessee up in Brazoria the day before.

As Jane took a chair before the fire, Herrick said, "A big man, Sam Houston, in more ways than one. He told us he was in Texas to make peace with the Comanche Indians, that him and Colonel Jim Bowie was off to San Antonio right soon to meet with a delegation of Comanches. Got something to do with President Andrew Jackson."

"That's odd," Jane said. "I mean the United States sending a prominent man like Houston to a Mexican province to talk Indian peace."

"Yeah, I reckon," Herrick replied. "But he said he once lived with the Cherokees. Which reminds me, he told me about ridin' into a Cherokee camp on his way to Texas. And guess who was preachin' to the bucks in their own language. Hellfire Jackson."

Bucktooth Sal laughed. "Hellfire might come in handy at keepin' peace with the varmints, all right. If they listened to him they'd throw bows and arrows and tomahawks away."

"Well, accordin' to Mr. Houston, Sal, he sort of outdid himself on that night." Relating the story of Jackson's sermon as told by Houston, he concluded with, "There was them Indians all riled, lookin' for Judas and Pilate, and Hellfire standin' there wonderin' what kind o' war he'd started."

Bucktooth Sal bent double with laughter and Captain Herrick almost lost his breath. It was infectious and Jane was laughing with them. When Herrick finally said between gasps, "So finally Hellfire got the bucks to call off the hunt for the night," Jane added fuel to their mirth by saying they should be ashamed of themselves.

A rap at the door sobered them. Bucktooth Sal admitted a storekeeper's boy who brought a long package his father had overlooked. "For Miss Jane," he said. "It came from Natchez."

"Well, let's have a look at it," Sally replied, drawing from Herrick a salty reminder that it wasn't for her. But both hovered over Jane as she removed the wrapping, and both emulated her gasp of delight when a roll of pale blue satin was uncovered.

"A whole roll!" Sally exclaimed. "Now who but a rich man

would lay that in a gal's lap?" Seeing a note pinned to the roll, she grabbed it up before Jane could reach it. Then she was reading it aloud:

"To a maiden fair, with lovely eyes to match a southern sky,
Or dewdrop o'er a budding flow'r;
Pray accept from one who admires thee, fond sentiments
For thy every golden hour."

"From Hellfire Jackson!" Bucktooth Sal exclaimed. "By thunder, he sure sparks a gal pretty, Jane. Makes me all teary eyed."

As Jane snatched the note from her, Sally's eyes lost their dreamy expression. Turning to Herrick, she boomed forth, "Now why the bloomin' hell can't you write nice words like that?"

2

That same evening Horatio Jackson was some two hundred miles northeast of Austin's colony. He sat before Ben Osborn's fireplace in the Nashville community. As the cold wind howled outside, and corn popped in a skillet over the fire, he read from his Bible the story of Christ's birth in a manger. The children listened avidly but soon fell asleep. Then the Osborns decided to retire.

When all were in bed, Horatio began a letter to Jane Wells. He wrote of failure to be ordained in Natchez and of his return to Texas, his meeting with Sam Houston, and then more or less debated on his plans for the future:

At this writing, dear Miss Jane, I am thinking seriously of exploring new territory in my missionary work. Running crookedly northeast from Nacogdoches is the old Indian trail known as Trammel's Trace, named after a man supposed to have run stolen horses down from Arkansas back in 1813. Also north from Nacogdoches is the Cherokee Trace. Now should I, I ask myself often, carry the gospel in those directions or continue to shepherd my beloved flock in this area? There is work to do here, and Amen! One man in this vicinity is a challenge I feel the Lord placed before me. Somehow I must find a way into Abner Bowser's encrusted mind and soul, though it will be like cracking a seasoned hickory nut with my teeth instead of a heavy hammer. But I won't bore you with that. Now I intend to remain here until the heavy freeze lifts and until my faithful Negro Wash is fully recovered from pneumonia. In the interval I shall decide on my direction. More anon, Miss Jane, as it is getting late and I must rise early to help with the chores here.

It was mid-January before Jackson added more to the letter. Beginning where he had left off, he told of Wash's recovery, of his attempt once more to convert Abner Bowser—"I wrestled with the devil for his soul, Miss Jane, no holds barred, and again the devil won. I told the Lord Bowser was a stubborn cuss, and that next time I'd like a little help from up there, like He gave the prophets of old, and I named the Scriptures to refresh the Lord's memory."

Twice during February of 1833 he enlarged the same letter with accounts of his experiences up the Cherokee Trace and, finally, in early March completed it while in Nacogdoches:

You can imagine my surprise, dear Miss Jane, upon arriving tired and spent from a disappointing trip into N.E. Texas to learn that Texans, in the absence of Mr. Austin, were calling another convention at San Felipe for April 1 of this year, because nothing had been done to present the forthcoming President of Mexico, Santa Anna, with the resolutions of the Convention of 1832.

Now here in Nacogdoches on the 1st of March, after Adolphus Sterne and others had prevailed on Sam Houston to make his home here, an election was held and Houston was unanimously chosen as a delegate to the Apr. 1 convention at San Felipe. Also Mr. Sterne. And from Ayish Bayou my friend and alcalde there, Elisha Roberts, will attend the convention. Which calls to mind a little joke on me, stemming from my defense of a horse thief on Roberts' front porch, and follows me wherever I go. People greet me and always laugh about "A hog—a hog—a hog!" which incident I shall relate to you one day.

But to the present, Miss Jane. The people in this municipality are once more warming to politics as much so as they are to the lovely weather here that would appear (but don't let it fool you!) to mark the end of a hard winter and the advent of glorious springtime. They stand on the street corners and talk of all Santa Anna will do for Texas. Let us hope so. Indeed, let us do that, with our hearts and in our prayers.

It would please me greatly to be in San Felipe (and of course, Velasco!) during the convention. But, alas, I have been invited to hold religious services down on the Neches in April, and a camp meeting at Ayish Bayou in May. Thence, in June, I must return to Natchez to replenish my supply of Bibles and tracts. While there I hope to again take the examination for the ministry.

Perhaps from there, Miss Jane, I can once more journey to the Brazos, where I am sure that by now the mockingbird outside your door trills his sweetest springtime notes. (As well he should!!!)

Jackson, as all Texans, awaited news of the convention. Some were skeptical of the good that would come of it. These few held the 1832 meeting up for example. The majority were hopeful, and their optimism was based on the military support the province had given Santa Anna the year before in the overthrow of President Bustamante.

Upon Jackson's arrival at the Neches River shortly after mid-April, he stopped at the house of a friend and talked with a delegate who had just returned from the convention. Jackson learned that the fifty-five delegates had entered immediately upon the business at hand, because each had to pay his own expenses. William H. Wharton presided.

"We framed a state constitution, Hellfire," the delegate said proudly. "Assuming that our petition for statehood would be granted by the Mexican Congress. The pessimists said we assumed a hell of a lot. Anyhow, Sam Houston was chairman of that committee. A memorial was adopted, and it set forth reasons why Texas should be a separate state of the Mexican Confederacy.

"We asked for repeal of the anti-immigration law of 1830. We asked for tariff exemption, adequate Indian defense, trial by jury, habeas corpus, freedom of the press, and universal suffrage. Some of the boys wanted to ask for authority to establish banks in Texas, but Sam Houston argued that down on the grounds that Mexico would be suspicious of that and reject the constitution. Now that's what we did in San Felipe, and Wharton and Austin were appointed to take the constitution and memorial to the Mexican government. What do you think of all that, Hellfire?"

"What I think doesn't amount to a hill of beans. However, don't you think the delegates should have waited until Mexico granted Texas statehood before writing a constitution?"

The delegate gave him a most unequivocal answer: "Hell, no!"

Jackson let the matter drop, and for good reason—it was like whistling in the wind to argue political procedures with Texans.

3

On the road to Ayish Bayou in May, Jackson and Wash stopped at Abner Bowser's place. Thinking a day or two of plowing for the man might soften the heart of a disbeliever somewhat, he went to work. For three days he and Wash helped Bowser rid his corn and cotton of weeds and grass. On the third night Horatio made another attempt to remove the weeds from the man's soul, hoping that the Word of God might take root and flourish there.

Dawn of the next day found Jackson on the trail east. His continued silence worried Wash, who finally asked what troubled Marse Jackson. "I'm weary from wrestling with the devil, Wash. For two hours last night I tried to convert Abner Bowser. And when I got through and asked him to accept Jesus as his Saviour, he said to me:

" 'Hellfire, I like the way you walk a furrow and the way you weed cotton and handle a mule. I even like the way you sing—that is, until you make so goddam much noise a body can't think. And I'm beholdin' to you for cheerin' up Eunice and the young'uns so they set a better supper table. And I got no objection to you workin' on me, givin' me all that attention which I ain't used to. I'm a right appreciatin' man, Hellfire, so I hope I don't hurt your feelin's none when I tell you once and for all I ain't one damn bit interested in what them Jews done.' "

Wash tried to check his laughter but failed. Jackson glared at him a moment. A chuckle escaped him and then he was laughing as loud as Wash.

They rode on, reaching Ayish Bayou settlement on the following morning. There Jackson learned from Elisha Roberts that Stephen F. Austin had departed for Mexico in April. He had gone alone because there was not enough money to pay the expenses of the other delegates chosen to go with him.

Roberts had gathered more news. True to reports, Sam Houston had taken up residence in Nacogdoches and had been or was planning to be baptized in the Catholic faith at the home of Adolphus Sterne, where he lived. This meant, of course, that Houston intended to apply for a grant of land in Texas. "Which is good," Roberts said, "since he has the capacity to command confidence and arouse enthusiasm among all Texans in our dealings with Mexico."

Everywhere Jackson's work took him during the summer and fall of 1833 the subject of paramount interest was Austin's trip to Mexico City. Even in Natchez, where Jackson spent the month of July, and especially in New Orleans in August, Americans voiced hope that President Santa Anna would favor the Texans' bid for statehood. New Orleans businessmen predicted a great economic boom in Texas if this came to pass, and trouble of a serious nature if the Mexican Congress refused the plea.

Sam Houston's decision to remain in Texas also provoked considerable curiosity and speculation. There were few who did not recall the close friendship of Houston and President Andrew Jackson, and fewer still who failed to believe that Old Hickory had sent his protégé to Texas for some undisclosed and very important reason.

There were all sorts of rumors about Houston, and they were aired aplenty at Maspero's Exchange. One of these, supposed to have come straight from Major Rector up at Fort Jessup, near Natchitoches, Louisiana, was that the major had given Houston a razor while the latter was on his way to Texas. Accepting it, Houston said that when Rector next saw the razor "it shall be shaving the president of a republic, by God!" And from Nacogdoches it was heard that forty-year-old Houston, who had a Cherokee wife named Tiana Rogers, was courting the seventeen-year-old daughter of Colonel Raguet.

And right there at Maspero's somebody had asked Houston what was going to happen over in Texas. Houston replied, "What happens when you put a skilletful of popcorn over a fire?"

While in New Orleans, Jackson learned from a Texas schooner captain that a terrible cholera epidemic was raging in Austin's colony. Among the victims were John Austin, leader of the Texans in the Battle of Velasco, his wife and two children. Alarmed, Horatio asked the schoonerman if he knew Miss Jane Wells of Velasco. The man did.

"Is she all right, Captain?"

"Aye, that she is," the other replied, grinning. "She disembarked from my schooner here a few days back, and a well-dressed young man was on hand to meet her. Acted like a couple headed for a wedding as they drove off in a fancy carriage."

Jackson turned away. Feeling as though he had been struck by a bolt of lightning, he forgot to thank the Lord for sparing

Miss Jane from cholera. And when he did think of it, he was too hurt and angry to do anything about it. He resolved to show Jane Wells a thing or two. Yessiree! He would go upriver to Natchez and tell the churchmen he no longer wished to carry the Word of God to Texas but, rather, to take a church in Mississippi or Louisiana. Aye! Let the devil keep Texas! Furthermore, he would find himself a lady in Natchez and see to it that fickle Miss Wells got word of his squiring her about.

With his mind made up, he returned to Natchez. Arriving there he went straightway to Jeremiah Whiteside's house only to find that his sponsor had gone to Tennessee and would not return until late in October. To blunt his professional spear of resolve further, he was told by Mrs. Whiteside that a minister representing the American Bible Society had made a temporary visit to Texas during the summer and was desirous of conferring with Jackson on a matter of mutual interest. She suggested that Horatio stay at her house until the minister completed his tour of Mississippi. Perhaps her husband would be home by that time.

With no plans to the contrary, Jackson remained in Natchez. He found employment as a bookkeeper. Wash attended to chores for Mrs. Whiteside. A week and another went by, and a man born to the outdoors struggled to discipline himself to desk and never-ending work on the accounts of a shipping firm. He thought of Jane Wells often, and as often wished to stalk out of the office and either strike out for Texas or find a lady here and fulfill his vow to show Miss Wells that two could play her game.

Then one Sunday at church the pastor called on him to say the morning prayer and read the sermon text. While engaged in the latter, he found himself the object of a very attractive lady's attention. His glance returned to her, and he was certain that he detected interest in her expression. When the service ended, he made it a point to stand with the preacher in order to meet her. As a result, he was introduced to Miss Elizabeth Hamilton. Horatio executed his best bow and held her extended fingers a little longer than was proper, all the while beaming forth his pleasure.

Before the week ended, Jackson accepted her invitation to dinner at Cherryhill, the imposing plantation home of the Hamiltons. The following Sunday, dressed in his best, even the high collar that sawed ear-high at his neck, he escorted Miss Elizabeth to church. By the end of October, Natchez buzzed with talk of the growing romance, and in ladies' circles there was considerable speculation as to when the Hamiltons would announce the engagement of their daughter Elizabeth to "Reverend" Jackson. "Indeed, it's about time," said not a few, "dear Elizabeth is all of twenty-six."

Jeremiah Whiteside learned of all this on his first day at home. He took Jackson aside and plied him with questions, which evoked evasive answers. Eying Horatio, he said, "You couldn't marry better financially, son. And with a wife and a decision to stay here, you're certain to be ordained. However—"

He let it end there, aware that with the arrival of Reverend Benjamin of the American Bible Society within the week Horatio could no longer hide his true feelings behind a mask of evasion.

Reverend Benjamin reached Natchez in early November. At Whiteside's home one evening he told his host and Jackson that during his brief visit to Texas he had found a lamentable destitution of the Scriptures prevailing; that other than in the jurisdiction of Nacogdoches, where Jackson had exerted his influence, households destitute of the Bible numbered nine to one. Jackson was to be commended for his sale and gratuitous distribution of Bibles in East Texas. Now, since Reverend Whiteside had been appointed Southern agent for the Society, and since not less than five hundred Bibles were wanted immediately for distribution in the interior of Texas, would Mr. Jackson consider becoming the Society's first salaried agent in the province of Texas?

Horatio gave Whiteside a surprise when he failed to jump at the offer, and again when he came up with: "For nearly three years I've done that work for you, Reverend Benjamin. Forded rivers and floated Bibles across swollen streams on rafts, dodged ruffians and outlaws, plowed and swung an ax, and more to take the Word of God to the wilderness—all without compensation. Worse, the church refused time and again to ordain the man who did it, me, because I did it, and because I felt my call was to Texas. So I don't know whether I'm interested or not."

Whiteside combed his beard with fingers. He thought Jackson was trading for something. "Odd, Horatio, that coming from you," he said.

"I reckon it is. But it's colporteur Jackson talking. Now if I was Reverend Jackson, who would carry more weight in Texas and be able to organize Bible societies there, I might consider it. Might, mind you."

Whiteside chuckled. Big, strong persistent Benjamin took the cue. He proceeded to relate a tale he had heard in Texas, about Jackson's defense of a horse thief. Ending it with, "A hog—a hog—a hog!" he laughed until he shook all over. Then he played his trump card. Taking from his portmanteau a sheaf of papers, he handed them to Jackson, saying:

"Do these mean anything to you?"

Jackson's brow lifted as he read letter after letter from his friends in Texas who had addressed to Reverend Benjamin their honest opinions and recommendations of Hellfire Jackson as one who had performed and could perform the duties of minister and Bible agent. Ben Osborn, Elisha Roberts, Adolphus Sterne, Sam Houston, Wyatt Hanks, men from the Neches and—even that infidel Abner Bowser!—over twenty of them, and all expressing a desire to have "old Hellfire" back in Texas. And Benjamin had asked if all this meant anything to him! Touched deeply, he was too choked up to reply to the question. Finally he nodded his head and conveyed his gratitude and love for all those Texans in one word: "Yes."

"Then do you accept our offer, Jackson?"

"I'll need time to think about it. Even if I do accept, I won't be going to Texas until spring."

"Very well. Perhaps in the meantime you'll help Reverend Whiteside in Arkansas and Louisiana. On a salary, of course."

Jackson deliberated on this. He was tired of bookkeeping, and he was wondering also if it wasn't time he extricated himself from the romantic trap before it sprung on him and sent him to the altar with Miss Elizabeth Hamilton. But he wasn't sure that the jaws of the trap hadn't already closed on him or that he wished to extricate himself if they had.

But there was one thing he was sure of in the weeks that followed, and that was the devilish delight he felt upon telling a group of Texans from the Brazos in Natchez to purchase seed cotton, that he just might be married to the lovely Miss Elizabeth Hamilton the next time they saw him. And would they please convey his warm regards to Bucktooth Sal, as well as her niece of course.

4

On Christmas Day the Hamiltons sent a carriage to bring Horatio to Cherryhill. Elizabeth met him at the door with a joyous greeting and ushered him into the house. Again he took in the hand-carved spiral staircase, massive chandeliers, and fine imported rugs, all with the possessive eye of a mortal. Self-admonishment was futile. A Negro butler in red clawhammer coat bowed them into a large room where a fire burned in the hearth. "Season's greetings, suh," he said, placing a decanter of brandy on the table.

The day occasioned something more than just Christmas; it was in the air, suspenseful, and Jackson recognized it as a stage set, bedecked with holly and gilt, even to a velvet pillow on a love seat for a suitor to kneel on as he proposed. And Elizabeth looked more than lovely in pale green satin.

To bait the hook further, the Hamiltons excused themselves immediately after dinner and left their daughter and guest in the parlor. In their wake all was too quiet and still. Great-grandfather Hamilton seemed to stare out of his frame above the mantel straight at Jackson, as if he were about to say, "Well, are you going to just sit there, man?" Shifting his gaze to Elizabeth, Horatio thought he detected the same question in her expression. He squirmed, and he remarked on the mild unseasonal weather, and Elizabeth said, "Yes, isn't it?"

In the hour that followed they touched on various subjects, church, music, Texas, national politics, New Orleans, and plantation life, to name a few. Then she asked if Mr. Jackson planned to return to Texas soon, or did he intend to settle in Natchez? Mr. Jackson's answer was rather ambiguous. Could she serve him coffee? Why, yes, if she didn't mind. She rose, her glance on him, a smile on her face, and Jackson stood politely and smiled down at her. Her eyes quickened. He offered her his arm and escorted her into the long hallway. There she stopped before him and said:

"I'd enjoy hearing you sing and preach often, Mr. Jackson. Or shall I call you Horatio?"

"Please do, Miss Elizabeth."

Jackson did not follow her into the kitchen. He stood shaking his head and rubbing a cheek. Under his breath he said, "Lord, You better come down and lend old Hellfire a hand. And don't wait another hour or two, else—"

Elizabeth appeared with a silver tray on which sat a silver coffeepot and fine China. "See what I mean, Lord?"

Evidently the Lord was listening. At any rate, a carriage came to a stop before the house just as coffee was being served. When a number of Elizabeth's friends alighted with gifts and moved up the steps singing a Christmas carol, Jackson blinked his eyes in amazement. The wonders of the Lord! And in the moment's spell he thought he heard the Lord dressing him down good and proper before shaking a finger in his face and saying:

"Look here, Hellfire Jackson, you in that fancy rig! Come spring I want to see you in Texas, where I sent you in the first place!"

CHAPTER 18

Hellfire Jackson obeyed the command. Since the weather in Texas was about as uncertain as the tempers of her colonists, and since the Lord hadn't told him whether spring would be early or late, he and Wash set out for Texas in mid-February. A cold rain kept them company all through Louisiana and ice hung on the trees along the Sabine.

"I'se plum froze," Wash said as they approached Ayish Bayou. "It sholy ain't spring, Rev'ren'!"

Jackson agreed, adding, "Couldn't wait for violets to bloom, Wash."

They rode on, the cold wind whistling about upturned coat collars. Jackson's thoughts returned to Natchez. The new year of 1834 had not been two weeks old when the Hamiltons had bundled Miss Elizabeth off to New Orleans to spend the winter. Perhaps they hoped her absence would bring Mr. Jackson to his senses. In any case, she had written Jackson inviting him to visit her there. Instead, he had gone with Whiteside over into Louisiana to establish a Bible society. Upon his return to Natchez in late January, a letter from Velasco awaited him. The contents of Jane's letter continued to puzzle him. Beyond her account of the cholera epidemic in Austin's colony during the summer of 1833, she wrote:

> While visiting friends in New Orleans in August, I heard that you were in the city, and Robert and I tried in vain to locate you. (I refer to Mr. Robert Berry, of Berry & Son, N. O. shippers & merchants, Robert being the son, and my dear friend, with certain romantic inclinations toward me.)
>
> I did so wish you to meet dear Robert, if only that I might evoke from you an honest opinion of him. I value the judgment of a man who has by example and deed proved himself above petty jealousies; even as such a man as yourself would no doubt hold in high esteem the discernment of a woman, and close friend, in judging another of her sex! One must be cautious and sure in such matters. Don't you agree?

Reports from Mexico City vaguely express Mr. Austin's satisfaction concerning his mission for Texas. It is rumored that he will begin his journey home before Christmas. All Texans await his return.

Both Aunt Sally and I appreciated the warm wishes you sent from Natchez via our mutual friends from Velasco and Brazoria. At this time I wish to return your greeting, from both of us, and wish you not only the happiness of the Christmas season ahead but success in your professional and personal endeavors.

Sincerely & c.

Jane

Puzzling indeed, in a way, Horatio reflected. There was little doubt that the Texans had repeated his "I might just be married to the lovely Miss Hamilton the next time you see me," or that Jane retaliated with "dear Robert's" romantic inclinations toward her. And maybe she was telling him not to marry Elizabeth.

" 'One must be cautious and sure in such matters. Don't you agree?' Yes, Miss Jane."

"What you say, Rev'ren'?"

"By thunder, she was telling me not to get married!"

Then, to the amazement of Wash, he dug his heels into the ribs of his sway-backed horse and began singing, " 'Amazing grace, how sweet the sound . . . !' "

2

Jackson remained at Elisha Roberts' place for several weeks due to inclement weather. A hard freeze lay over the land. Limbs of trees heavy with ice fell to the ground, and livestock the colonists were unable to locate in the thickets froze. With the first hint of spring in the Redlands, Jackson and Wash rode up to the Nashville settlement. After a week there, Jackson departed for Nacogdoches, where Reverend Benjamin and Reverend Whiteside wished him to organize the first Bible society in Texas and dispense some five hundred Bibles they would send by wagon from Natchez.

Horatio's arrival in Nacogdoches late in April was timed to the disturbing news that swept up out of Mexico. Expressions of grave concern and anger mingled with shock and disbelief as colonists discussed the alarming report that Stephen F. Austin had been arrested in Mexico and thrown into prison.

Jackson admitted his surprise also. He listened. One man scoffed and said it was impossible. Wasn't Santa Anna President of Mexico? Sure he was, and he hadn't forgotten how Texans had chased Bustamante's troops out of Texas in 1832.

"Right!" another man spoke up. "And didn't a messenger arrive a week ago from Mr. Austin's secretary in San Felipe advising that Austin had in December succeeded in getting the anti-immigration law of 1830 repealed by the Mexican Congress?" Meeting with no argument on this, he said, "So how can we in the face of good reports believe Santa Anna would listen to Mr. Austin and grant reforms for Texas one day and imprison him the next? It fails to make sense."

While the majority agreed to this, many continued to believe the report true. They could only wonder and wait for news that would either confirm or refute the imprisonment of the representative of all Texans.

In the interval of waiting, Texans went about their work as usual. They tilled the land, cleared forests, built homes, planted crops, and operated mills and stores, even as Jackson preached under brush arbors and in rural homes and formed Bible societies in the area of Nacogdoches. He returned to Ayish Bayou and met with the committee of settlers who were selecting a site for the town they would call San Augustine. He went wherever he was invited. He was chased by outlaws and when they caught him, as frequently they did, he was warned to get out of Texas.

In late May, Jackson arrived in Nacogdoches again and found that the report of Austin's imprisonment in Mexico had been confirmed. He had left Mexico City in December after securing promises of certain reforms in Texas local government from the Mexican Congress. Other than the repeal of the anti-immigration law, Texans would be allowed greater religious freedom, trial by jury, more representatives in the legislature of Coahuila, and to write legal documents in English for the first time. That was well and good and encouraging. But what about statehood for Texas?

Santa Anna had refused to approve state government for Texas.

Austin had reached Saltillo on his return to Texas when he was arrested. He had written a letter to officials at San Antonio, advising them that due to conditions in Mexico nothing had been accomplished in securing statehood for Texas; that in view of this they might consider his suggestion to go ahead and establish Texas as a separate Mexican state. The letter had been intercepted and returned to Mexico City, and Austin was seized for being a dangerous man trying to incite insurrection in Texas. Returned to Mexico City, he had been placed in prison. From his dungeon he had written to his people, urging them to be patient and keep the peace.

Everywhere Jackson went that summer he found the people confused, bewildered, and a few angry. In the Redlands, up the Cherokee Trace and down on the Neches, colonists argued peace versus "timely intervention," as they had in 1832. Down on the coast in Matagorda, where he formed a Bible society and preached and sang, he found Texans less aroused by the injustice accorded their leader. It was the same on the Brazos.

Jackson rode into Velasco anticipating another meeting with Jane. As he entered the blacksmith shop, Bucktooth Sal dropped hammer and grinned. "Well, if it ain't Hellfire hisself!" she boomed forth. "Where's the bride?"

"What bride?"

"The gal you was goin' to marry in Natchez. Ain't that what you told our Brazos men when they were in Natchez last fall?" With Horatio's reply, that he had changed his mind, Sal burst into laughter. "Just like I figured. Tryin' to make Jane jealous, wasn't you?"

"Quiet, Miss Sally, she'll hear you!"

"Now that would be a miracle, all right, her being in New Orleans again." A moment later she said, "Don't look so sad, Hellfire. She won't be marryin' up with that Berry feller until I pass judgment on him." She winked an eye at Jackson. "I could be a right smart help to you, all right, but—"

She hushed suddenly and eyed him despairingly. "But it wouldn't do a damn bit o' good. Not with you traipsin' off to hell and back. A man has got to take time out to spark a gal, Hellfire. Now the way I see it—"

Jackson was still sitting on a nail keg, still looking glum, when she finished the lecture. He watched as she placed shoes on a mule, then he asked if any news of Mr. Austin had reached the Brazos lately.

"Father Muldoon wrote Mr. Williams that he was tryin' to get Mr. Austin free, but wasn't havin' much luck. The Mexicans are transferin' him from one prison to another. You know what I think? I think Santa Anna is a polecat!"

"Last time I saw you, Miss Sally, you were crying '*Viva Santa Anna!*' "

"That was a long time ago. Me, I'm rarin' to fight and get Mr. Austin back home. But I'll bet you couldn't raise a dozen volunteers on the Brazos. People are too interested in crops and business, and Santa Anna is a shrewd one, him givin' Texas a few of the things Mr. Austin asked for. He's got most Texans pacified, and pacified men don't reach for guns. Try to get a schoonerman riled and he says, 'What about? I'm runnin' past closed customhouses and empty forts. Free trade, good times. So why should I complain?' That's Texas, Hellfire."

Jackson nodded. There was no denying that Bucktooth Sal had her finger on the pulse of Texas. The political scene was minus war clouds, and for once the land and sea offered up security—enough to cause Texans to consider their imprisoned leader's request for peace timely words of supreme wisdom.

But now Bucktooth Sal was working on Jackson's sense of right and wrong. As he sat there, some of her righteous indignation spilled over and into him. She talked on, and he listened as she said, "And there we were entertainin' Colonel Almonte, Santa Anna's representative on a tour of inspection of Texas, while Mr. Austin lay in a damn Mexican dungeon! It's a shame, Hellfire Jackson!" Then she poked a finger in his face and placed a question that struck home, "Why the hell don't a preachin' man like you do something about it?"

Jackson thought about it all the way to Anahuac in late August. It was still on his mind as he struck out for Nacogdoches to the north in mid-September. He reached the Neches River crossing with his mind made up.

"Wash," he said, "I believe that public apathy in the wake of Mr. Austin's imprisonment is cause for alarm. I'm going to try and arouse the people."

"You mean you'se gwine politic a little, Marse Jackson?"

With no denial forthcoming, Wash shook his head sorrowfully and said, "Heah we goes ag'in."

3

During the months of October and November, Hellfire Jackson's voice rang in the Redlands of Texas with a clarion call for action. "There we were, calling ourselves Texans, wining and dining Santa Anna's aide Colonel Almonte, while down in the dark, damp confines of a rat-infested Mexican dungeon lay our pale and wan leader Mr. Austin, whose guilt was nothing more than carrying the wishes of all Texans to the Mexican government. Can you sit here complacent? Not if you're real Texans!"

"Pour it on, Hellfire!" a few shouted.

"No, you can't sit still any longer, Texans. Call a convention and draft demands for Mr. Austin's release!"

When a challenge rang out, "Who'll take it to Mexico, Hellfire?" Jackson leaned forward and replied, "Your servant here, sir!"

He preached an end to complacency from the Neches River in the south to Sulphur Creek in the north, from the Angelina west to the Sabine east, under arbors, in homes, and even on Plaza Principal in Nacogdoches. He stirred a few into talk of a convention. But talk was all that came of it. Many asked what had come over "old turn-the-other-cheek" Jackson of 1832, even as the aroused Jackson of 1834 wondered at the complete reversal of public political sentiment in Texas as well as his own.

Early in December he wrote Bucktooth Sal: "Texas has turned topsy-turvy. And while I have also, I'm again on the unpopular side. It *do* beat all!"

To Jane Wells he penned a vow "to keep my nose out of Texas politics, which is, my dear Miss Jane, as unpredictable as Texas weather, as unreasonable as a selfish woman, as fiery hot as mesquite coals stoked by old Lucifer himself, and as savage as a pack of hungry wolves."

He held his opinion in check when in mid-December the rumor was confined that Santa Anna had openly renounced his States' rights program, which had placed him in the National Palace, in favor of dictatorship. Again, in January of 1835, Jackson forced himself to remain silent when news swept through Texas that Santa Anna had placed customs collectors and garrisons of convict soldiers in Brazoria and Anahuac. Moreover, Captain Antonio Tenorio, commander of the garrison at Anahuac, let it be known that Texas schoonermen who refused to pay duty would be branded as smugglers and pirates and would be chased down and treated as such.

"Shades of 1832!" Horatio exclaimed upon hearing the latest. "History is repeating itself. Now that Mexico is touching our pocketbooks once more, it's highly probable that Texas will catch on fire again."

He said this to James Gaines, and when the ferry keeper on the Sabine agreed, Jackson added, "right now I've got to go to Natchez, but if things do catch on fire, ole Hellfire will be back and for once maybe he'll be on the right side at the right time."

CHAPTER 19

True to Jackson's prediction, Texas did catch on fire. The spark that caused it came off the water. It was maritime pure and simple, ignited by the death knell to free trade and fanned by Texan resentment against a dictatorial show of arms in the enforcement of a decree the colonists had no voice in making. Santa Anna's renouncement of republican ideals had also ended the colonists' dreams of statehood. The situation bore a striking similarity to that of the thirteen American colonies on the eve of the American Revolution. Taxation without representation provoked a Boston tea party, and in turn the Lexingtons and Concords.

Before Jackson reached Natchez in the spring of 1835, Santa Anna heaped further fuel on the kindling fire. Colonel Ugartechea appeared in San Antonio as province commander. He did not stop with a rattle of sabers on land but employed the Mexican schooner-of-war *Moctezuma* to patrol the Texas coast as revenue cutter.

But while the blaze was slowly being fanned by the prevailing winds off the Mexican Gulf, Horatio Jackson and Wash arrived in Natchez. As was customary, they went straightway to the house of Jeremiah Whiteside. There the bearded minister shook hands with Horatio and in the next breath said:

"Well, you lost her, son."

Jackson blinked his eyes. "Who?"

"Elizabeth Hamilton. She married a sugar planter's son from New Orleans last August. Too bad, Horatio. Too bad."

"Yes, sir, it sure is," Jackson replied, feigning dolefulness. "Seems I gad about too much. And it seems New Orleans has an eye on another lady I'm right fond of."

Whiteside eyed him sharply. "The way you talk leads a man to think you court a girl in every place you stop."

"Well, a Bible agent does get around. And you aren't lookin' at a dead preacher either."

" 'Lookin',' Horatio? I suppose I'll have to start grooming you all over again. Which reminds me—a group of churchmen will be meeting here within a few months. Now you still wish to be ordained, don't you?"

That night Jackson wrote Jane. He told her of the encouraging news upon his arrival in Natchez:

> The American Bible Society was more than pleased with my results in Texas, despite my unnecessary dabbling in Texas politics, as they put it. As I put it, pretty Miss Jane, you can tell your Aunt Sally I let her kindle a righteous fire in old Hellfire, which burned bright for a while and then fizzled out like a lone coal in an East Texas drizzle. But it seems Mexico rekindled the fire good and proper. Anyhow, it looks that way. But back to my chances of being ordained a minister:
>
> They, not I, suggest that I appear before them (body of churchmen) in early August with letters of commendation from the good people of Texas; as many as possible. I am hoping you can see fit to pen a line or two in behalf of this patient aspirant to the ministry, who is also your consistent and *devoted admirer!!!*

He posted the letter, sure that it would evoke a reply from her prior to the August meeting. While awaiting this, he traveled with Whiteside in Mississippi and in southern and central Louisiana. Their work in establishing Bible societies proved successful, and always wherever Whiteside preached on Sundays, Horatio led the singing. He was in Alexandria, Louisiana, when news of the first clash of arms between Texans and Captain Tenorio's garrison at Anahuac reached him.

A colonist had been wounded in a dispute over payment of duty on the twelfth of June. William B. Travis, whose imprisonment by Bradburn in 1832 had brought on a battle, aroused the Texans this time and on June twenty-ninth, with twenty-five men aboard a little schooner, fired on Tenorio's fort. The convict soldiers ran. Tenorio surrendered and left Texas with his soldiers.

That was the spark. Jackson knew it, and it was quite evident that Texans realized as much, for they began to form militias and issue calls for a general convention to be held in San Felipe in October. They wished to be ready for the inevitable, the arrival of more of Santa Anna's troops in Texas.

While in New Orleans in late July, Jackson learned of another justified flare-up of Texans' tempers. Mexico had sent the warship *Correo de Mejico* to patrol the Texas coast. She was commanded by an English adventurer, Thomas M. Thompson, who issued an autocratic proclamation declaring himself "commander of the coast from Tampico to the Sabine." So angered were the Texans by his blockade and orders that they disband their militias that they met and passed resolutions against Thomas "Mexico" Thompson. Even in inland Nacogdoches a public meeting was held and a resolution drafted by Sam Houston and Thomas J. Rusk was read.

With things warming up in Texas, impatient Horatio Jackson reached Natchez only to learn that the church leaders had postponed the meeting until mid-September. As he began preparations for returning to Texas, where, he told Whiteside, he was needed, a letter from Velasco addressed to Whiteside arrived. At last Jane had responded to his request for "a line or two" in his behalf. Her sincere comment on "Mr. Jackson's open loyalty to his convictions regardless of opposition," plus Whiteside's firm belief that he would this time be ordained a minister, caused Horatio to consider postponing his trip to Texas. Whiteside's argument that a Bible agent and lay minister could do little to win a war in Texas before the war started, evoked from Jackson:

"Well, since for once I'd be on the popular side, I'd like to stir amongst them with a prayer on my tongue and a rifle in my hand."

Whiteside threw up his hands. "All right, if you're so anxious to stop a Mexican bullet, then go on to Texas! I give up!" Rising, he took a few quick steps before turning. In softer tones he said, "Why don't you pray on it first?"

At the supper table that evening Jackson said he had approached the Lord on the matter, and Whiteside asked if the Lord had told him what to do.

"Well, sir," Jackson replied, "I've learned that it isn't so much what the Lord tells a man as it is what a man tells the Lord. Give Him all your reasons pro and con and pretty soon you'll find He's let you argue the thing out and come up with the answers yourself. I suppose it's because a man is a mite more honest with himself when he's talking up in that direction."

Whiteside meditated on this but made no comment other than, "And what did you talk yourself into when maybe you should have been listening?"

"Oh, I listened, all right, but I heard no objection when I told the Lord it might be better for both Him and me if I didn't go traipsin' off to Texas right away."

2

The news of increasing unrest in Texas found its way to Natchez, where Jackson waited for the churchmen to meet. As the hot summer days of late August and early September dragged by, he heard that Stephen F. Austin had been released from a Mexican dungeon and was in New Orleans preparing to return to Texas. While these truths or rumors merited keen interest and considerable speculation on his part, he could not forget that the church meeting at the imposing plantation home of the well-to-do spinster Miss Polly Fincher would decide his future in Texas also. He would return to the Redlands either a licensed minister or, again as many times before, lay preacher and colporteur.

He had presented numerous letters from people in Texas to the judging body, all commending his work as lay preacher and Bible agent and citing the need for a continuation of his work but as an authorized minister with license to preach, perform weddings, and the like. No personal letter had come from Jane Wells, however, and the absence of any word from her about her romantic affair with Robert Berry continued to nag at his peace of mind. He thought up all sorts of excuses for her failure to write to him as he waited for her letter, somehow feeling that her sentiments would give him the inner boost he needed for success. But no message from Jane reached him prior to September fifteenth, the date set for his examination by church leaders.

On the afternoon of the meeting Jackson was dressed in his best, stiff collar sawing at his neck, his unruly shock of hair plastered down. He rode through the plantation gates in the carriage Miss Fincher had sent for him. At his side sat Reverend Jeremiah Whiteside. As the white-columned pillars of Holly Lawn appeared at the other end of the tree-lined road, Reverend Whiteside said in confidential tones:

"Dear Miss Polly is quite taken with you, Horatio. You know of her influence on the others, of course." Jackson nodded, and rubbed his jaw thoughtfully as his old friend added, "Of course you know she wants you to attend theological school first, but what you don't know is that she is willing to pay the cost. So—"

"I do declare!" Jackson said. "Why?"

Reverend Whiteside shook his head and replied tiredly, "I don't know of a minister who wouldn't jump at the opportunity, Horatio."

"Then why is she so generous where I'm concerned when I'm not even a preacher yet?"

"Brother Horatio." The older man's hand fell to Jackson's arm. "Son," he added patiently, "there's a mule over at your right. Would you kindly tell me if he's white, black, or brown?" He paused for the answer. "Brown, you say? Then you aren't totally blind, thank the Lord."

Jackson looked puzzled. Then his eyes began to blink and he swallowed hard, his Adam's apple bobbing up and down. In the ensuing seconds his expressions of discovery ran the gamut, and before the liveried servant opened the carriage door at the broad steps of Holly Lawn he had the look of a curious animal appraising a trap, one designed to keep him out of Texas. And Whiteside had helped bait it with such talk as:

There was no denying that dear Miss Polly had an engaging smile, and a lurking kindness in her sharp, imperious gray eyes. If under his scrutiny she appeared more rail thin and hatchet faced than before, he should remember that true beauty emanated from within. Her charity was a virtue unquestioned. "A heart of pure gold," he had said.

Once inside, Horatio took in the gleaming crystal chandelier, rich draperies, gold cornices, sofas and chairs upholstered in silk damask, great mirrors in gilt frames, and the huge imported rug. The room in which the meeting was held bespoke the wealth of the mistress of Holly Lawn. Like the Hamilton's Cherryhill mansion, it dazzled the eye. "Indeed, a heart of pure gold," he said to himself.

Now Miss Polly was eying him intently, speculatively, and the chairman of the august body was clearing his throat. "Did you hear my question, Mr. Jackson?"

Jackson started. The required examination in Bible, ancient and modern history, and mathematics continued. Now would Mr. Jackson please complete the second verse of chapter twenty-four, Leviticus, in which "the Lord spake unto Moses, saying, Command the children of Isra-el, that they bring unto thee pure—"

" 'Olive oil beaten for the light, to cause the lamps to burn continually,' " Jackson said matter-of-factly.

"Excellent! Amazing!" Miss Polly declared. She said the same when Jackson gave correct answers to questions in arithmetic and history.

At last the examination was completed and one by one the ministers probed the mind and heart of the applicant. Then came the final question. In his other appearances before this body he had declared that his call was to Texas; did he after more than four years in that uncivilized wilderness still hold to this erratic belief?

Jackson got to his feet slowly. He bowed in the direction of first Miss Polly, then each of the gathering, calling them by name as he did so. All the while he was carefully assembling his reply and urging himself to speak with prudence. The stakes were high. Reverend Jackson could be a dream realized or once more jerked out of his reach. But there was more to consider now. The imported vase that caught his eye was probably worth twice as much as his horse and saddle, two mules, and Bibles combined. It symbolized the world that might be his if he shaped his reply to Miss Polly's liking. But the churchmen were waiting for his answer to the question.

"An uncivilized wilderness, indeed," he said. He told of the coastal Indians who resorted to cannibalism, the restless tribes of East Texas; of outlaws, would-be assassins, and fugitives; of wild buffalo herds roaming the country; and wolves, panthers, and bears in the forests.

"How terrible! How very terrible!" Miss Polly said, coyly lifting an open fan to her chin. "Pray continue, sir."

"That's one side of Texas. There's another side." Now Jackson was telling them that San Felipe published a newspaper, as did Nacogdoches; that Stephen F. Austin had attended Transylvania University in Kentucky, and his secretary and manager, Mr. Williams, was of a family that boasted of a Yale College president. He named a dozen more Texans with college educations.

"I heard the Lord call me to Texas. He didn't say it would be easy for me. It hasn't been easy. I've gone hungry, nearly froze, swum rivers, fought bears, outlaws, thieves, been chased by all three, I've been ridiculed and jeered at. My life has been threatened. I've known hurt, anger, frustration, heartache, and bitter defeat in Texas. To pay my way I've cut wood, gathered corn, mended and made harness, blacksmithed, plowed, doctored, tutored, chopped, picked vegetables, ginned and hauled cotton, carpentered, and more, not to mention selling Bibles, Testaments, and tracts."

"Heavens!" Miss Polly exclaimed, touching a handkerchief to her eyes. "Such persistence! Such courage in the face of adversity!"

"Indeed," said the chairman. "A Christian soldier home from the wars deserves a rest, a reward for—"

"Begging your pardon, sir," Jackson broke in, "my reward was constant. The day I came upon a family from Georgia whose children were thirteen and fifteen years old and had never heard the Word of God preached, their eagerness and joy were my reward. The time I doctored an old man with tea I made of roots and herbs and prayed at his bedside for days, his recovery and praise of God were my reward. I could go on and on, but to answer your question, I took the Word of God to the wilderness as I was told to do. In obeying the call, I brought lost sheep into the fold."

He observed a pause. A frown creased his brow as he

looked from the faces of his judges to the symbolic vase on the marble mantel. The struggle inside him was then this piece versus the vicissitudes of turbulent Texas. Ease, recognition, esteem, and a fine church to preach in versus hunger, opposition, Mexican bullets, and no end of trouble. He had a choice. The intent gaze of Miss Polly Fincher seemed to be imploring him to choose the former.

"The people of Texas needed me." He paused. "They still do, more than ever now. Trouble is brewing in Texas and the Lord never told me to desert people in trouble."

Miss Polly's face fell. Reverend Whiteside blew out his bearded cheeks. The other gentlemen exchanged hopeless glances before looking toward their hostess for any suggestion. None forthcoming, the chairman asked Horatio if he wished to say more.

"Just one thing. Seems I've done it again. Mention Texas as my call and my chances fly out the window. But it's like I told the Lord every time it's happened. 'Sir,' I said, 'as long as You figure I'm doing a pretty good job of preachin' the gospel, I don't suppose You're frettin' too much about me not havin' the word 'Reverend' tacked onto my name.' "

A heavy silence followed. It ended with the chairman's request that Jackson wait outside while they reached a decision.

Jackson bowed himself out of their presence and moved to the long porch of Holly Lawn. There he paced back and forth past the tall massive columns. A half hour went by. A lone rider entered the gates and walked his mule toward the house. The mule looked familiar. Then Jackson recognized Wash, and wondered what brought him here. He soon learned that his own anxiety regarding a letter from Texas had not escaped Wash, who was delivering a message fresh off a riverboat. It was from Jane, and it had been written in New Orleans in August:

> I embark for the Brazos today aboard Mr. Thomas F. McKinney's trading schooner *San Felipe*, which is also returning Mr. Austin to his colony in Texas. After long months of imprisonment in Mexico, he was released and sent from Vera Cruz to New Orleans. He is pale and appears weary, but he is less the pacifist now. Also sailing are Mr. Wm. H. Wharton who, as you know, advocates energetic opposition to Mexico, and Lorenzo de Zavala, former secretary to Santa Anna, as well as Mr. Robert Berry of New Orleans, who is to represent his uncle's shipping and cotton interests in Texas. He had been a dear

friend for many years. Now he has asked for my hand in marriage. I pray that my decision in a matter as important as life itself will be a wise one. Whether I shall make up my mind aboard ship or wait until Aunt Sally expresses . . .

There was more, but Jackson did not read it then. He felt his heart skip a beat and a knot forming in his stomach. It was a sickness flooding him and he could do nothing to relieve its heaviness. Every memory of Jane that he had carried under sun and stars and moon to buoy him up and comfort him now seemed laden with a whip-tailed stinger. He wished to cry out in protest, and he felt the veins of his neck and forehead standing out like cords.

He called out after Wash, now disappearing through the distant gates. Then he struck out on foot, vowing not to stop until he reached Velasco on the Brazos.

But he did stop at the big iron gates of Holly Lawn and stood there a minute in debate and another in indecision. So great was the temptation to return to the house and accept Miss Polly's generosity—perhaps he'd even marry her, if only to show Jane Wells a thing or two—that he began walking in that direction. He suddenly whirled and ran when his imagination conjured up pictures of Miss Polly extending her arms to him, her eyelids fluttering sixty to the minute.

When Reverend Whiteside reached Natchez-Under-the-Hill an hour later and told a ferryman that he was the bearer of important news and must deliver it to Mr. Jackson posthaste, the man said, "If he's the lanky fellow with a swaybacked horse and a nigger on a mule, then you better high-tail it across the river after him, mister. He struck out for Texas like a bull bat out o' Hades."

3

Unaware that his faithful friend and sponsor was pursuing him through Louisiana, Jackson pushed relentlessly on, sparing neither animals, Wash, nor himself. Reaching Natchitoches far ahead of Reverend Whiteside, he paused only long enough to replenish supplies for the trek through the vast pine forests extending far into Texas. He and Wash passed Fort Jessup with merely a wave of a hand at the sentry and urged their tired horses on toward the Sabine. James Gaines told Whiteside days later that Jackson's Negro Wash had said, "Marse Jackson am wearin' me down to a nub, him runnin' lak de spirits was after him."

Gaines said, "You won't catch up with him this side of the Brazos, Reverend."

At Wyatt Hanks's gristmill in San Augustine, a colonist said to Whiteside, "Old Hellfire went through here like a blue norther was on his coattail, mister. You ain't about to catch him."

Weary of the fruitless chase, the Natchez minister left a letter for Jackson with Elisha Roberts and departed for Mississippi. On the day Whiteside crossed the Sabine on his return to Natchez, Jackson forded the Trinity River and rode on toward Austin's colony.

At the house of a colonist he added to his store of news that had come to him piecemeal since reaching Texas. In San Augustine he had heard that the irate Texans at Velasco had on September first at the insistence of Thomas F. McKinney boarded the latter's small steamboat *Laura* and crossed Velasco Bar to engage Lieutenant Thomas "Mexico" Thompson's becalmed Mexican warship *Correo de Mejico.* Protected by bales of cotton on the maneuverable steamer's deck, they had inflicted considerable damage on Thompson's crew and ship with rifle fire. While the battle raged hot, a sail on the horizon drew the *Laura* out to investigate. It was the *San Felipe,* heavy with munitions, returning Stephen F. Austin to Texas. The steamer escorted the vessel to the bar and her passengers into Velasco. Early on the morning of September second, with the *San Felipe*'s cannon to augment the Texas rifles aboard the steamer, and the still becalmed Mexican vessel unable to train her guns on the Texans, the one-sided battle ended with Thompson's surrender. And since the arrogant Thompson had no copy of his Mexican commission aboard the captured vessel, he had been taken to New Orleans, where he was charged with piracy and jailed.

Jackson had already heard of the August fifteenth meeting of the colonists at Columbia, in which they declared that they had been deceived by the sly, untrustworthy dictator Santa Anna and had resolved "that a consultation of all Texas through her representatives is indispensable." The consultation was to be held at San Felipe on October sixteenth.

Jackson pushed on toward the Brazos. His arrival in San Felipe was timed to alarming news of further Mexican aggression: General Cos, Santa Anna's brother-in-law, had landed in Texas with more than four hundred well-trained soldiers, heavy artillery, and huge military stores. Jackson found the Committee of Public Safety in closed session and the Texans of three opinions, one faction in favor of fighting for independence, another known as the Peace Party who believed it unwise to defy Mexico, and still another of the opinion that Cos was marching on the Brazos to avenge the *Correo de Mejico* and that it would be expedient for all Texans to return to the United States before the Mexicans arrived.

Before Jackson could adjust in his mind all that had happened to the prevailing excitement in the capital of the colony, members of the Peace Party surrounded him on the porch of a general store and asked him to make stump speeches in favor of peace and help save Texas from war and devastation.

In this group Jackson saw a few men who had walked out of the tabernacle when he had preached for peace and patience back in June of 1832, and he knew they were now afraid. However, they were the minority. The majority of Texans were in favor of fighting for their rights. Jackson's first question to the pacifists in reply to their request was:

"What is Mr. Austin's stand?"

Reluctantly they told him about Austin's speech of September 8, in which he declared that Mexico had been unfair to the settlers, and that Santa Anna had deserted the program which placed him in office; and that he was in favor of the consultation of Texas. But Jackson should realize that Mr. Austin was not a violent warmonger like that rugged, contentious schoolteacher in the canebrakes of the Brazos, Henry Smith, who headed the Independence Party.

Jackson heard them out. As he sat on the porch of the store listening patiently, more settlers arrived. By the time the Peace Party members completed their arguments a sizable crowd had gathered. With the question "Will you preach peace for us, Hellfire?" Horatio got to his feet.

"All of you folks know I'm an advocate of peace," he said slowly. "But there are two kinds of peace, the earned and honorable kind and the kind enforced at the point of a bayonet. Depends on which one a Texan wants to live under. First, every man here ought to look at his hands and tell himself how he got them scarred and calloused, and think about why he came to this land and tamed it with the sweat of his brow, with a gun handy as he cleared trees and tilled the soil, a gun to protect himself and his family from Indians and outlaws.

"He came on a promise. He came with hope in his heart, and trust in the promise of the Mexican government that had in 1824 adopted a constitution patterned after the ideals of the republican form of government that are written into the Constitution of the United States. That's the promise that brought all of you to Texas. As a further inducement to get you to settle here you were offered duty-free trade, freedom from taxes, and more. It looked good and the promise of good things was made better when immigration and the right to use slave labor were granted. So every scar and callous on your hands is a badge of faith and trust in the promise made by Mexico.

"And—" he struck a palm with a fist, "—every bullet you fired in the battles of 1832 was your protest against a Mexican dictator who turned his back on the promise made by Mexico, and for the man who declared himself in favor of the principles written into the Mexican Constitution of 1824! Santa Anna was then the champion of the promise that brought you here to claw the ground and create a society of freemen of Texas, loyal to a constitution you could approve and prosper under.

"So Texans met and asked Santa Anna for schools and protection from Indians, and an extension of free trade and trial by jury, and statehood. He shrewdly gave a little, but he took too much in return—our leader Mr. Austin first. And second, he tore that page out of the Mexican Constitution that upheld the rights of the individual and the states. He turned dictator, and he sent soldiers and warships to Texas to catch the Texan smugglers and pirates, as he calls them. And when you once more resisted, he sent more troops to subdue you. And he's going to send more, because a dictator can't hold his seat unless he does subdue you. And that's a fact.

"Now look at your hands, Texans, at the scars and callouses on them—at promises fulfilled or at promises annulled—and choose the kind of peace you want. The peace of slaves. Is that what you want? The peace of a wronged people enforced by bayonets. Is that what you want?

"You ask me to preach that kind of peace? Me, whom you once called old peace-at-any-price Jackson? Well, Hellfire Jackson sees no peace until we earn it. I see a struggle between aroused and wronged people and an unprincipled dictator who tore the promise and the hope of promise from us.

"So the kind of peace I'm going to preach is over the sight of a rifle."

With that, he left them. Some cheered and others stared thoughtfully after him. He followed the river trail down to Brazoria, scene of his first great defeat in Texas. He stopped his horse at what was left of the tabernacle and said to Wash, "Should have preached them a hominy-and-grits kind of gospel, I reckon." Riding on, he said, "Though I reckon a man should do what he feels compelled to do."

This brought his present and short past up for inspection. He was riding down to Velasco a red-eyed, sun-seared, saddle-weary, brush-whipped man. All because a pretty schoolteacher had unwittingly bidden him to travel almost four hundred miles. What he would do or say when he saw Jane Wells next he did not know. He knew only that she had held him in the ravenous grip of pain and suspense every hard mile of the way; that he could now, as at every sunrise and sunset and moonrise, summon her out of memory without closing his eyes; that he could hold her a moment in all her beauty and womanly splendor and then watch her vanish as always like a wood nymph.

He glared at the trail ahead, at the image that flitted teasingly before his eyes, and tightened his jaw muscles until they played in hard ridges at the corners of his face. Then he blew out his cheeks savagely and gave his horse an unwarranted kick in the ribs.

CHAPTER 20

The clang of hammer on anvil and the familiar smells of Bucktooth Sal's blacksmith shop would have been welcomed by Jackson at any other time. On this midafternoon of October first, 1835, he stood outside nervously shifting his weight from one foot to the other until Bucktooth Sal looked up from the forge and cried out in amazement:

"Well, if it ain't old Peaceful Jackson! Get in here, you scarecrow-lookin' Bible peddler and help shoe these hosses!"

"I'm looking for Miss Jane. She up at the house?"

"Probably. Then she might be down at the river in the shade with Mr. Berry. Why you wince when I tell you that, Jackson?" Before Horatio could reply, she knotted her big hands at her hips and walked toward him. "So that's it? Well, well! So you didn't come all the way down here to preach love and kindness for old Santa Anna, eh?"

"Well—I made record time from Natchez. Maybe I got here too late. Did I?"

She continued to shake her head, her expression hovering between pity and mirth. "He's got money, Hellfire, and he's a damn sight better lookin' than you. But I'm wonderin'."

"Wonderin' what, Miss Sally?"

"Nothin'! Nothin'! Unless it's why I'm standin' here jawin' with you when there's work to be done."

"Reckon I'll help you."

"Oh no you won't! A man in your condition is as apt to nail a shoe on a mule's rump as a hind foot. You get on and find Jane and get it out of your system, Jackson."

He nodded, darted a fearful glance toward the oaks lining the riverbank, and began walking bravely but slowly in that direction. He had not gone far when he saw her. She sat on the grass, alone, he observed thankfully, gazing at the opposite bank. A twinge of guilt assailed him. It was followed by a sharp stab of fear. He stopped still, mustering the courage to go on. Then she turned her face his way, and he saw the shock in her expression, saw it rise and fall away. Then she seemed a study in arrested motion. He felt the impact of silence until she said:

"Horatio! I wasn't expecting you—Mr. Jackson."

"I've scarcely stopped since I received your letter in Natchez, ma'am." With hat in hand he moved toward her. She wore a white dress, very plain except for sleeves ruffled at the elbows, and her hair was piled on her head. The same brown ringlets danced in the light wind at her forehead.

"You mean you—?" She did not finish the question but bit her lower lip and studied him. "You do look done in," she said in detached manner.

Her eyes were blue and deep and curious. He searched them for something he wished to see before saying, "I came on account of the letter you wrote. About Mr. Berry's proposal of marriage, Miss Jane."

He stood a few paces away, his eyes demanding, troubled, and fearful all at once. He waited patiently, and he saw she was looking level with him, as if she too were making demands of him. He felt strangely out of place and then he knew a desperate sense of entrapment. "Well?" he asked, aware that he rasped the question.

"Well, what?" she replied, and he tried to detect the presence of laughter or mockery in the question. She revealed nothing but the same firm attention, and that seemed well guarded. All of which left him as confused and oddly bedeviled as before. A wave of anger swept through him and he said more sharply than he intended:

"Well, are you going to marry him?"

He stood before her tense, awkward, his tall figure stamped with a kind of ruthless dignity that reminded her of a weathered oak. While she resented his tone of voice, she could not forget that she held the initiative, which, because she was a woman, pleased her. "Why do you ask, Mr. Jackson?"

"Because I came all the way from Natchez to find out!" he thundered forth. "And don't just sit there smiling at me, Jane Wells!"

"Suppose I said I was not going to marry Robert?" she asked, quite unperturbed.

"Then I'd say—I mean that's fine! Fine!"

"And supposing I said I was betrothed?"

"That, ma'am, I wouldn't like one little bit! And I might not even accept it."

"No?" She got to her feet. With a touch of mocking humor in her sweeping glance, she sauntered toward the landing. "Just what would you do?"

"I—why, I don't know," he replied, his militant attitude suddenly giving way to puzzlement. "But like I said, I wouldn't like it."

Reaching the shade of another moss-covered oak, Jane whirled to face him. "Seriously, Mr. Jackson, you keep repeating yourself and saying nothing. Why not begin at the beginning and say what's on your mind?" Tilting her face, she said, "So far you haven't, you know."

"I know," he replied meekly, moving to her side and taking her arm as the ground sloped down to the old pier. "And so far you haven't answered my questions, just kept me jumping like a grasshopper on a hot skillet. Now are you promised to this Robert Berry or not?"

"Almost. I kept putting him off because I couldn't be sure —until today." Her glance narrowed on him and she said, "Incidentally, I was expecting Robert, not you." Under his intent, hard glance, she looked at the river. "We can still be friends, Horatio."

His eyes were bitter, flashing, and his mouth thinned into a brittle line. Controlling himself, he said, "Friendship is something different. It would have taken me twice as long to get here for friendship. Understand?" When she did not reply, he said, "It's all or nothing between us, Miss Jane."

"Really! Aren't you presuming a lot, sir?"

"No, I'm not, and you know it! You knew how I felt the day I kissed you back in thirty-two! Sure, I'm a big, unpolished, stubborn, backwoods excuse for a preacher, and I know I'm unworthy of your glance, much less your romantic attention—and I wasn't invited here! I know my station, ma'am, like I do my ambitions, trials, troubles, and dreams, and I feel humble and out of place in the company of so beautiful and wholesome and refined and sensible and tolerant a woman as you, Miss Jane. Now, I would in all dignity and honor and sincerity and love get on my bended knee and ask for your sweet hand in marriage, but I won't stand for your mockery!" His fist pounded into a palm and his voice rose with anger. "Not for a minute will I be laughed at!"

His words ran out and he was standing with a fatuous look on his face. Jane had heard him out amid expressions of mounting surprise, genuine interest, and contained admiration. Now, gazing at his blinking eyes in a startled face, she could not put down the overwhelming desire to laugh. It burst into the open, unbidden, necessary, satisfying. She tried her best to tell him between spasms that she was not laughing at him or his sentiments revealed, though each attempt seemed to make him and the situation appear even funnier.

Then suddenly his dark and threatening expressions seemed to explode into violence. Jane felt herself being scooped up into his arms. Her laughter turned into protest. As she squirmed in an effort to go free, he simply flung her over his shoulder as he would a gunny sack of field cotton and moved in great strides toward the river landing. When her cries of "Put me down!" went unheeded, she demanded to know where he was taking her.

"To dampen your merry spirits and drive the imps of mockery from your soul, ma'am! And I pray the Lord you can swim!"

Despite her frantic cries and the pounding of her fists at the small of his back, he reached the pier's edge. Then a man's voice sounded an order for him to stop. Turning, Jackson saw a fashionably dressed, hatless young man, his handsome face twisted in anger, advancing toward him with hands knotting into fists.

As Robert Berry raced onto the pier with a shout of "Put Jane down!" which he augmented by a threat to whip Jackson within an inch of his life, Horatio met his swift advances by sidestepping and thrusting a foot forward. Berry tripped over it and, with a yell, went sprawling into the river.

Just as Jackson drew his foot back, Jane heaved mightily and threw him off balance. A moment later she loosed a scream that ended when she too splashed into the Brazos.

As Jackson watched her go under, then come up spitting water and threshing about, he stood on the pier the most surprised and bedeviled man in all of Texas. To make it worse, he wasn't sure of how it had happened. Was it an accident, or had he tossed her into the river as he had meant to do?

Jane's pinched and strangled cry from the river, "I despise

you, Horatio Jackson!" left little doubt as to her opinion of how it happened. In another second a yell followed by a deep-throated laugh from the riverbank advised that Bucktooth Sal had witnessed the whole affair:

"By damn, that's what I call a real Texas baptizin'!"

Then Horatio Jackson did a strange thing. He turned slowly and moved in dazed manner to the riverbank, where he sat down with his hurt and contrition and emptiness and did nothing to stop the tears that streamed down his weather-beaten cheeks.

2

In the days that followed, colonists along the lower Brazos were given more to talk about than a small six-pound cannon which the angry Texans of Gonzales refused to turn over to Mexican Colonel Ugartechea. Hangers-on at the blacksmith shop in Velasco heard the story of the unscheduled baptizing of Miss Wells and her New Orleans suitor from Bucktooth Sal and quickly spread it upriver.

It had not been a "gospel dippin'," Sal declared. Vengeance and not eternal salvation had prompted Hellfire Jackson. "Him as red-eyed as old Nick one minute and cryin' like a baby the next, and Jane and Berry madder than two wet hornets. Berry wants Hellfire to get up and fight, but poor old Jackson he says the fight's all gone out of him, that when he's restored he'll take Berry on, no holds barred."

When the tale reached Brazoria, Hog-Trough Jones cocked an ear. He had not forgotten Jackson's threats to whip him as soon as he returned from Anahuac back in 1832, or that when he had reached the Brazos, the "loud-mouthed preacher" had vanished. Now Mr. Jones bristled, all two hundred and fifty pounds of him, and began looking for Hellfire Jackson again. His search took him down to Velasco. Entering the blacksmith shop one afternoon, he demanded that Bucktooth Sal tell him where Jackson was hiding; he knew the preacher was somewhere about, because there was his "nigger" out there working for Sal. So she might as well "trot Hellfire out."

"Jackson ain't here, Hog-Trough, and you ain't liable to be here long either," she replied, advancing toward him with a heavy hammer in hand.

As Jones backed out the door apologizing and protesting, a rider leaped from his horse with a joyous yell: "We won! We chased the Mexicans toward San Antonio!"

They soon learned that he had ridden from Gonzales,

where on October second the Texans met a hundred Mexican dragoons sent by Colonel Ugartechea from San Antonio to take a small six-pound cannon which the colonists had refused to surrender. This time the Texans filled the cannon with chains and scrap iron, mounted it on an oxcart, crossed the Guadalupe River with it, carrying a flag on which was printed "Come and Take It." When the cannon was fired once, the Mexican commander suggested a parley. After the Mexicans refused to surrender and defend the principles of the Mexican Constitution of 1824, the cannon let go another blast. Ugartechea's dragoons retreated then.

"Yes, sir, we won!" the rider said again. "And I've come for more volunteers. Met Mr. Austin and his men at the Colorado River. They're marching for Gonzales, thinking to ambush General Cos and his Mexican troops before they can reach San Antonio."

Bucktooth Sal boomed forth a loud cheer, then gave Hog-Trough Jones a menacing look. "Since you come lookin' for a scrap, why the hell don't you volunteer and fight where you can do some good?"

"Well, now maybe I'll do just that. Too bad a war had to interfere with my pussonal scrap, but I reckon that preacher Jackson will keep until I chase them Mexicans out o' Texas."

The rider from Gonzales said, "If you mean Hellfire Jackson, he's already volunteered. He was riding alongside of Mr. Austin when I met them."

3

Just how many men there were in the cornfield that October afternoon, Jackson could only guess. From the noise they made the number could be one thousand instead of only a few hundred. But they were Texans, he realized, and on this occasion they were engaged in their favorite sport, arguing among themselves—hotly, discordantly, over who would be elected commander in chief of the Texas forces.

Jackson sat on a tree stump, his feet in the stubble of dried cornstalks. Close by the clear Guadalupe River flowed serenely on. Beyond a screen of live oak trees lay the sleepy little town of Gonzales. A dozen yards to his right stood the adobe *jacal* where Mr. Austin and his little staff were quartered. And scattered over a few acres were a dozen or more groups of Anglo-Texans. On every side rang loud protests, jeers, vows, and "by Gods!" and "by damns!" and closer to Jackson the argument was growing more explosive:

"Sam Houston? Hell, no! He's too high and mighty. Maybe

he was a colonel back in Tennessee. So what? Wasn't Ben Milam a prisoner in Mexico? And ain't he a scrapper? You damn tootin' he is, and he's got my vote to lead us!"

Another dispute drew Jackson's attention. Captain James W. Fannin of the Brazos Guards had his following. He had come to Texas from Georgia in 1834. He was supposedly a plantation owner, and it was known that he was also a trader in slaves. But he was a militant leader and had attended West Point. His champions swore he had the spirit and knew how to chase Cos out of Texas. Disputing this were the followers of Edward Burleson, whom the Army had only the day before elected colonel of Austin's regiment.

Fights broke out here and there, and the snarls and shouts of debaters continued, all without restraint, and minus any mention of Stephen F. Austin as the man to lead them. A ragtag lot, Jackson observed. Men in greasy, saddle-worn buckskins mingled with others in homespun, hickory cloth, and dungarees. A few wore Mexican jackets and shakos taken from the retreating enemy earlier. Some wore coonskin caps and moccasins. One man had sack wrappings on his feet and a wide-brimmed beaver hat sat on his head.

"Bearded men and whiskerless boys," Horatio observed. "From the Sabine to the Comanche country." Philip Sublett picked it up from there, adding, "Englishmen, Americans, Germans, Irish, Poles, Swedes, and free Negroes. And don't forget the platoon of friendly Texas Mexicans."

Indeed, here was proof that the tide of revolution was flooding strong across Texas. Minus enough food to sustain them one day, lacking blankets, medical supplies, and doctors, aroused Texans were still arriving in Gonzales. Untrained, undisciplined, they caused one to think of disaster in the making and to pity the man they chose to command them. They had rifles and the will to fight, so what else mattered?

"All in favor of Ben Milam form a line over here!" The shout had scarcely begun than the faction favoring William B. Travis of Anahuac drowned it with, "Travis men, line up!"

Sublett had no sooner left Jackson to join the outnumbered Sam Houston enthusiasts than a courier rode in on a sweat-lathered horse and leaped from the saddle before Austin's adobe. In the moment of silence this evoked, Jackson heard the bell of the little Gonzales church clanging wildly. Several minutes elapsed, however, before Mr. Austin appeared and made an announcement that drew a round of cheers and firing of guns that would soon ring all over Texas.

Another Texan victory had been achieved. However small, it was significant. Captain George Collinsworth, a Matagorda planter, had organized a group of colonists and marched on the garrison General Cos had left at Goliad. After a brief fight the Mexicans had surrendered.

So now Collinsworth, whom few of the Gonzales army had ever heard of, was hailed as the man to command the Texans' forces. Jubilation over victory soon gave way to politics in the ranks. The arguments continued another hour or so and came to an abrupt end in true Texas fashion. Since the men could not agree on any of the nominees and refused to give ground to opposing factions, they settled on a nonmilitary man as their leader.

Upon learning that he had been elected commander in chief, Stephen F. Austin stepped outside the *jacal* and in a brief speech accepted the honor and all the heavy responsibilities that went with the office. Another rousing cheer broke from the rank and file.

Then it was all over, and the men began to think of their stomachs. They were forming groups to spread out and forage for their supper when Colonel Edward Burleson approached Jackson and said, "The general wants to see you, Hellfire."

Looking at the forty-two-year-old Indian fighter from Tennessee and seeing no hint of humor in his face, Horatio moved toward the adobe house wondering what on earth "the general" had in mind for him. He went inside and stood while Austin finished dictating a letter to a secretary. His desk was a plank table. On it were papers, quills, an inkhorn, and bottles of medicine. As Jackson observed how pallid and worn the small, neat bachelor appeared, a servant came with coffee. Austin looked at it, and offered it to Horatio.

"Now, Mr. Jackson, sit—if you can find anything to serve as a seat." After Jackson drew up a keg and very carefully tested its strength before sitting, Austin began telling of his need for doctors. "Once we engage the enemy around San Antonio we'll need doctors to attend our wounded. I've heard you were versed in the art of healing. Are you?"

"Not much, General, sir. I'm a poultice-and-herb man mostly. Probed a few bullets in my travels, but I qualify more as a preachin' man than physician."

Austin sat thoughtful and silent, as was characteristic of him, a minute. "Then just do your best, Dr. Jackson. I'll assign you to the medical corps."

Jackson frowned and rubbed the stubble on a jaw. "I had in mind usin' a rifle, sir. So with your permission I'll fight and doctor too."

Touching a finger to his pointed chin, Austin said, "In a military sense that's irregular, isn't it?"

"Well, General, it could be, I reckon. But in a military sense, wouldn't you say everything about this army of yours falls into the category of highly irregular?"

Colonel Burleson, who had remained silent, suddenly stuck a palm to his thigh and burst into laughter. Austin's secretary chuckled. Then Austin himself began to laugh.

As Jackson stood awaiting further instructions or an end to the interview, Austin lapsed once more into study of the campaign ahead. He weighed his present position at Gonzales, roughly fifty miles east of San Antonio de Bexar, the same distance north of Goliad, and twice that from the Brazos, weighed his ability to intercept General Cos, and balanced the scales by discussing the wisdom of not chasing the well-armed Mexicans but, rather, considering a siege of San Antonio. Burleson agreed, since more volunteers were necessary.

Also, guns and supplies were necessary to any army; and too, as Jackson had intimated, a look at the fighting force out in the cornfield would cause any military man to ask if this wasn't a hastily organized buffalo hunt.

"But they have that one thing that wins wars," Jackson spoke up, unbidden. "And that's the spirit of freemen to fight for their rights."

4

That was the army of volunteers that moved toward the Mexican stronghold of San Antonio in October. An army of men without uniforms, and many had not even a coat; no tents, no change of clothing, no food other than the land gave up. More volunteers overtook the outfit along the way: Milam's, Fannin's, and Collinsworth's men. Riders in from San Felipe advised that because so many of the delegates had joined the Texan volunteers the consultation scheduled for October sixteenth had been postponed to November first.

"First things first," the Texans declared. "Fight and then consult."

Jackson meditated on this. He sat his sway-backed horse in silence. Ahead and behind him the army volunteers rode and walked, argued, sang, and raised the cloud of dust higher. A scout had just ridden in to advise that the San Antonio River lay a few miles ahead, that by nightfall the army could camp north of the town.

"Well and good, *Doctor* Jackson," Horatio said to himself. Then the present, with its sounds and dust and sights, faded. He was once again back in the Brazos, holding Jane in his arms there on Bucktooth Sal's old pier. The memory of his doing so put a grimace on his face and a sadness in his heart, as it had done in strong backlash a hundred times since that day. Fool that he was, he had tossed the woman he loved out of his life; but worse, right into the arms of Robert Berry. And after he had recovered his senses and tried to adjust the loss in his mind, he had moved as in a trance to the blacksmith shop for his horse. There Bucktooth Sal had tried to both comfort and encourage him.

"Am right proud of you, Hellfire. They both needed a duckin'. And word got down here about the speech you made to the Peace Party up in San Felipe. Seems it done some good. Now I won't be callin' you Peaceful Jackson no more. So you stick around and give this Berry feller a run for his money."

"Won't do any good, Miss Sally. I'm licked here. Maybe I'll have a fighting chance with the Mexicans. Anyhow, I'm off to join Mr. Austin's volunteers."

He had ridden off with Bucktooth Sal's "Damn fool! Don't you know nothin' about women?" ringing in his ears. But that had faded, as a bit of idle talk slips from a mind, and in its place, sounding over and over, was the strangled cry of Jane Wells:

"I despise you, Horatio Jackson!"

It continued to haunt him. With every step of his horse, every breath of the dust-choked air, it kept him company. It was still a part of him, a heavy burden on his mind and heart when the army pitched camp north of San Antonio late in the afternoon.

CHAPTER 21

The day of October twenty-eighth broke bright and clear. About a mile from the position the Texan detachment had taken on the San Antonio River the evening before the old Mission of Nuestra Señora de la Purísima Concepción de Acuña stood out in the early morning sunlight like carved alabaster. In the Texan camp bivouac fires were dying, though the smells of burned grease and bacon hung in the still air. Sentries remained motionless, their eyes fixed on the mission grounds where the enemy camped. Though all seemed well at present, Colonel James Bowie and Captain James W. Fannin, whom Austin had sent with ninety men to find the Mexicans and secure a camp for the main army, expected the enemy to try and dislodge them from their position before they could be reinforced.

Not far from the little knoll where Bowie and Fannin discussed matters of the day, Jackson sat with rifle across his legs staring at the bleached morning sky and next lowering his gaze to buzzards circling the offal of cattle slaughtered the day before. As the wind came in weak it wafted in the stench of both human waste and the remains of animals. He got up and moved. In passing the command, he saw a scout now talking to Fannin and heard him say:

"I say again this is the best ground for the main army. And for us too, since Cos will call mighty damn soon." This from a scout as well known as Erastus "Deaf" Smith simply erased all doubt. Captain Fannin agreed with Smith, and next with Bowie that they should send a rider to General Austin at once, advising that they had found both the enemy and a camp. But who should go?

As Horatio moved on toward the sentry post in the north, Bowie's glance swept in a half circle and halted abruptly on a tall, lean man with the stamp of the frontier on his face. "He'll get through come hell or high water."

"Who?" Fannin demanded.

"Hellfire Jackson."

Bowie scrawled a brief message to Austin, which he and Fannin signed, then walked toward Jackson. He was still some fifteen yards from Horatio when the sentry facing the mission to the south gave the alarm: "Mexican cavalry!" In the opposite direction a sentry's cry rang out, "Cavalry charging our position!" The alarm sent all men into action except Jackson, who acknowledged the order from Bowie rather bleakly, accepted the message, and eyed the Mexican riders coming on fast. When Bowie said it seemed they were surrounded and asked if he thought he could get through, Jackson replied:

"The Lord willing, sir!"

The thunder of the Mexican charge caused the very ground to tremble. It rolled closer, a hundred horses on each side of the Texan camp, four great walls of hoof-thrown dust rising skyward and hiding all but the advance columns behind a curtain of pale tan. Only the lead horses and the barrels of muskets glistened in the sun, and only those Pedros, Antonios, and Manuels whose red and blue uniforms raced ahead of the dust were visible to the Anglos looking down their rifle barrels. A sharp report, a puff of smoke, and a Mexican fell from his horse. The dust swallowed him. The agonized scream of a mortal or horse, the cracking of guns, the swerve of a repulsed charge, the scuffed-up alkali dust, and the yells, the shrill, savage cry of the Texans, all declared that the battle had begun.

"There's a gap in the dust, Hellfire!" Bowie cried. "Take it —zigzag and lie low on the pony's off side!"

Jackson had long ago learned how to ride a pony Indian style. He got on the horse Bowie had ordered brought up, dug his heels into the ribs, bent low, wheeled the animal, and rode at top speed toward the disappearing wheel of a Mexican column in retreat. He tore on, unaware that in the wall of dust to his left another fresh unit of General Cos's crack horsemen was galloping fast in his direction.

The roar, like that of a buffalo herd, increased to warn him. As he jerked the reins to avoid a meeting with overpowering numbers, he saw the ranks split, leaving a void of choking dust to blind him. There was no place to go but into it, for to turn back or to the left or right meant certain death or capture. He raced into the split, praying that he would not ride into another cavalry wave. For a run of seconds his prayer seemed to have been answered. Then, as if out of nowhere, Mexican soldiers on foot appeared before him. A rifle barked and a saber flashed, both close.

"Too close, Lord!" he cried aloud, instinctively falling flat on the back of his horse and digging his heels into the animal's flanks.

Then he was in the clear and there were no more Mexicans that he could see. He felt a stinging sensation at his upper left arm. He thought nothing about it until a bullet screamed past his ear and another spat at his hat brim. Placing a hand at his upper arm, he felt something sticky, then he saw it. He had been shot!

In another second even that was forgotten. A Mexican on horse was suddenly riding down upon him crying, *"Alto! Alto!"* As the enemy reined in to ride parallel with him, saber drawn and lifting for the downstroke, Jackson threw himself at the soldier, catching him about the chest and hauling him from his horse. With the speed of a cat, he leaped back from the Mexican, who lay stunned, grabbed up the saber, and began looking for his horse. Several minutes passed before he was in the saddle again, his arm now red with blood.

He rode into Austin's camp an hour later, a little giddy and weak, and praising his horse for getting him to Austin's camp after he had lost all sense of direction. Refusing to stay behind with the rear guard, he moved with the main army up to the scene of battle and on to the old mission grounds where the combined army set up its camp.

Lying in the shade of the old mission, Horatio listened to Bowie's account of the Battle of Concepción. It had lasted only a half hour. In that brief lapse of time ninety-one Texans had repulsed four hundred crack Mexican cavalrymen.

"The enemy lost sixty men," Bowie said. "We lost one."

"Don't forget one wounded," Horatio replied, pointing to his bandaged arm. Even as he spoke a lanky, bearded Texan winked an eye at Bowie and said dryly:

"Jackleg preachers don't count, do they, Cunnel?"

2

Volunteers from all over Texas and parts of the United States swelled General Austin's ranks. They arrived almost daily, each man bringing his own gun, lead, and powder. While the army waited expectantly for the order to move in and take San Antonio, the consultation at San Felipe began on Austin's birthday, November third. When it adjourned on November fourteenth, the fifty-eight delegates had voted to remain a part of Mexico and fight for the Constitution of 1824, even to using the Mexican red, white, and green flag, but replacing the eagle, snake, and cactus in the center field of white with the numerals 1824. They set up a provisional government, naming Henry Smith, head of the War Party, governor, and Sam Houston commander in chief of the army; proclaimed a Texas Navy and, among other things, named Stephen F. Austin, William H. Wharton, and Branch Archer commissioners to the United States to borrow money and obtain aid to carry on the fight against the dictator of Mexico.

The army was rather displeased with the delegates for not declaring for independence from Mexico. "If we're going to fight, let's fight for total freedom," the men argued. The flag that had flown at the Battle of Concepción had a bloody arm holding a sword, thirteen stripes, and the word "Independence." Designed by a Brazos schoonerman, Captain Brown, the flag had flown in battle and it spoke their sentiments.

"Now it's odd as all hell," they said, "that Sam Houston, head of the Peace Party and the man who argued against a declaration of independence, should head the army." When advised that Houston's argument for remaining within the Mexican nation was to gain the active support of Mexican liberals in overthrowing Santa Anna, the men said it made sense but they still didn't like it. Nor did they approve General Austin's departure for the United States.

"We're contradictions down to the last man, us Texans," Horatio Jackson declared on the day he left the army to become a member of Austin's escort to San Felipe late in November.

Austin readily agreed to this, adding, "Myself included." He not only looked relieved but admitted his pleasure in turning over his command to Colonel Burleson, who was by far more experienced in military matters. As they rode along, he said, "I know where I can best serve Texas, Jackson. So did the delegates to the consultation know that also."

Jackson realized then that Austin had no doubt worried over his earlier decision following the Battle of Concepción to launch an immediate attack on San Antonio. Whether Burleson, Bowie, and Fannin had changed his mind, it was not revealed. But much had happened in the weeks since the battle.

One event to remember was the arrival of a company of New Orleans Greys. They had marched in with drums rolling. Smartly uniformed, each man carried a rifle, saber, pistol, and knife. In their baggage wagon were tents. In contrast to the Texans, they were something to see, and they were welcome. Of particular interest to Jackson was the origin of this company. It stemmed from a speech made by Adolphus Sterne of Nacogdoches in Bank's Arcade in New Orleans. The Texas merchant had helped finance the formation of the company as well as its trip by sea to Texas.

"And another company of Greys is to follow by land," their spokesman had declared proudly.

The Texans had also cheered the arrival of a brass siege gun. Then shortly after that the cold rains came, and the soldier-colonists, many without even coats or blankets and no roof over their heads, shivered. Many became ill, and Jackson laid down his gun and turned doctor. He was glad that episode in his life had ended. And he was gladder still when they approached the Brazos with ex-General Austin safe and sound.

Also in the escort party was Hog-Trough Jones, who vowed Jackson had purposely "got hisself wounded so's not to battle pussonel with the Bull o' the Brazos." Arriving in San Felipe, Mr. Jones remarked on his distrust of Hellfire Jackson for the way he talked about the Lord and prayed: "Hell, I ain't got nothin' agin goin' to heaven when I die, but damn'd if I want that jackleg to pray all the fight out of me by the time his arm gets well!"

In San Felipe, Horatio encountered Henry Augustin, delegate from San Augustine to the consultation, who handed him a letter. "Some preacher from Mississippi who was chasing after you left it with Elisha Roberts a few weeks back, Hellfire."

Soon Jackson was reading Reverend Whiteside's letter. It opened with "My Dear Exasperating Friend, Horatio," and continued with:

> Just what strange seizures of mind, body, and spirit prompted your sudden departure from Holly Lawn (while we of the council listened to Miss Polly Fincher's kind and sincere plea in your behalf), none of us can fathom. Perhaps it is just as well, my boy, that we are deprived of the power to know what actually moves you; else we might thank the Lord for good riddance! Who knows?
>
> In any case, I hastened after you, all the way to San Augustine, in Texas, where I pen this and convey to you the following: The body accepted you at Holly Lawn and set the date of your ordination sermon, which I was to deliver, for Sunday, October third. However, when I was forced to report your unannounced departure for Texas, the body naturally decided to reverse its decision; but, at the behest of Miss Polly and myself, the body stands ready to reconsider, provided you appear in Natchez before the year ends with a satisfactory explanation for your conduct and some assurance of your future dependability.
>
> My prayers for you are constant. God go with you.

Jackson crumpled the letter in his hand and moved in detachment to the river. There he tossed it into the Brazos, wishing he could as easily rid himself of the bitter memories Whiteside's message evoked. Now he supposed he must always remember that he had, after years of striving to become an ordained minister, finally realized his ambition only to fling it aside for an uncaring woman.

Jane Wells clung to his mind. Her every look, smile, frown, word, and gesture since that day on the Sabine over four years in the past paraded out of his memory into sharp focus if only to torment him. The desire to see and talk to her despite his shameful behavior was stronger than he had imagined.

But so was the fear that he had tried to put down every day since he had last seen her, the fear that she was now Mrs. Robert Berry.

Jackson asked questions in the stores that day, dreading the answers. He heard that the New Orleans shipper Robert Berry had purchased considerable Brazos cotton; also it was rumored that he was going to marry a schoolteacher on New Year's Day. A schoonerman from Velasco verified this later that day, saying he had it straight from Bucktooth Sal herself.

"Well, that was that. However much it hurt, he had expected it and, he told himself, he was prepared for it.

He had a choice now. If he returned to Natchez without further delay, perhaps he could salvage something of the past. On the other hand, the road to San Antonio and battle was open, well traveled, and inviting. To himself he said: "The sword or the cross. Choose your weapon, Jackson."

He knew that either was a worthy choice in itself. The pages of history were red with the blood of men with a desire for freedom in their hearts. Texans would never submit to anything less than full freedom because it was not in them to do so. Self-government, freedom of the press, speech, worship, and more must be theirs or the Anglo would not, could not remain in Texas. The cause excused the sword.

And the cross? Surely in the struggle for freedom there must be a place where a preacher could actively serve in his capacity. Yes, he believed there was, and that the Lord would show the way, but only to those who were interested enough to go out in search of it. However, the sword was handier. Through it, he felt, he could better search for his place to serve actively as a lay preacher.

Jackson and Wash set out for San Antonio on a cold, rainy day in late November. On the following afternoon they met a dozen volunteers who were returning to their homes and families. In reply to Jackson's questions, they said the shortage of food and warm clothing had nothing to do with their departure; the apparent decision of the leaders to retreat and sit out the winter had caused them to leave the army. They had gone to fight, not sit.

Jackson invited them to make camp and join him in partaking of sowbelly and beans and honest-to-God coffee. Around the fire that night he talked to them about freedom, its worth, its cost. He told them also that whether or not the rumors out of Mexico were true—that Santa Anna was assembling eight thousand troops to put down what he called the "piratical *Yanquis*" in Texas—Santa Anna's future in Mexico depended on his conquest of Texas.

And what did Texas have to stop the tyrant? Jackson reminded them that Texas was without funds to fight a war, minus guns and ammunition, without a naval vessel, and it had an army not one-tenth as powerful as that of their foe. And besides, Provisional Governor Henry Smith in his first address to his Legislative Council had stated that the government was at the start clogged and impeded by conflicting interests.

"So this is no time for freedom-loving men to quit. Me, I'm going to San Antonio with my Bible in one hand and a rifle in the other."

The colonists and ex-soldiers thought about it as they looked into the fire, at the arm Jackson still carried in a sling, and at each other. Finally one of them spoke up and said he was returning to the army next day. Before the campfire died all of them decided to take the road back to Bexar with Hellfire Jackson.

CHAPTER 22

Toward noon of the day before Christmas the wind freshened out of the north, driving the low-hanging gray clouds over the Brazos back into the Gulf of Mexico.

Captain Herrick, a few miles above Velasco, welcomed the push of a following wind and set his schooner's sails for the "river romp down." Business was brisk, with cotton from upriver Columbia bound for Velasco sheds, thence to New Orleans, and armed volunteers from the States moving upriver. Given a couple more months of war and prosperity, he might pop the question to Bucktooth Sal. Indeed, with her anvil and his hull they should make a fair wind of it! Anyhow, a letter for Miss Jane would give him an excuse to tie up at Sal's landing.

As he had expected, Velasco was still celebrating the news from San Antonio de Bexar. One week ago word had reached the Brazos of the surrender of General Cos to the Texans on December ninth. Over eleven hundred Mexican regulars had been driven from house to house in San Antonio to the plaza and on to the Alamo, where they gave up and pledged themselves never again to oppose the Constitution of 1824.

There were many accounts of the siege of San Antonio, and Captain Herrick, not knowing which one to accept as the truth, decided to believe them all. Especially the one in which Ben Milam had upset the decision of army leaders on the fourth of December to retreat to Gonzales and establish winter quarters there. It came about when a Texan volunteer captured by the Mexicans in October escaped San Antonio and reached the Texan camp with news of weaknesses in the enemy's defenses. This information provoked a timely shout:

"Who will go into San Antonio with old Ben Milam?"

Two hundred and fifty volunteers joined him on the spot. The attack began the next day. For four days the Mexicans resisted and for four days the long rifles of Texans picked them off with deadly accuracy. Then the plaza belonged to the Texans, and next the Alamo was theirs. Cos had been thoroughly beaten.

"Too bad old Ben Milam was killed," Herrick said. "But he didn't die in vain. Not a damn Mexican soldier left in Texas."

Lowering and furling sails for coasting in at the landing, Captain Herrick helmed the small craft gently alongside the dock and secured her fore and aft to bollards. Grabbing up a few gifts and letters for delivery, he bent his sea legs up the bank to the tune of an improvised rollicking sea chantey which he ended with "For she's a gal from Texas, and they call her Tops'l Sal!"

Soon he greeted Jane at her door with, "Christmas Eve gift—and she's goin' to blow cold! Now what have ye got for a brave hearty who brings ye a letter, girl?"

"A hug and a warm tot of spirits—which I was saving for your Christmas gift, Captain."

With his departure, Jane opened the letter. It was from Horatio Jackson, written from Gonzales on the twelfth of December. He advised that he had left San Antonio on the morning following the surrender of Cos and was en route to Natchez, where he hoped to be ordained; his wound had mended nicely; he wished to apologize for his behavior at the pier to both Jane and her husband to be, and to wish them happiness in their forthcoming marriage. He had closed with:

"I shall love you always."

Jane read the letter again. It ended all too soon, leaving her a little shocked and more curious than she wished to admit. "It sounds so final," she said, moving to a window that offered a view of the wind-whipped Brazos through the scattered live oak trees.

Watching Captain Herrirk's schooner straining at her moorings, Jane recalled the many times her aunt had said at the supper table, "A feller in the shop today had news about Hellfire Jackson." It had been Aunt Sally who told her he had been wounded in the Battle of Concepción, who had brought her news relayed from Bexar regarding his ability to scout the enemy and skirmish by day and "sing and doctor the army to sleep" at night.

In the shop one day Jane had heard an ex-soldier on crutches tell how Jackson turned the tables on a smart aleck while making a speech to a group of disgruntled volunteers. When they began to heckle him as he talked of the things Texans were fighting for, and their leader asked what was in it for a "river-bottom man like me if we whup them Mexicans," Jackson replied, "Well, instead of the Mexicans hangin' a real sharp bully like you for stealin' hogs, the Texans will do it."

Jane learned that wherever men met or camped they welcomed Jackson or some new story concerning him. He spoke their language and he wove himself into the true fabric of Texas homespun humor and philosophy. True, they often made sport of him and mimicked his pulpit mannerisms down to fist pounding palm, arms swinging, and more, but they listened to him and took lessons. Even the great Sam Houston alternately laughed and turned serious as he defined freedom in the words of Horatio Jackson.

Houston had come upon a gathering one night and had heard a colonist ask Jackson to explain what he meant by this freedom he "harped on so dang much." To which Hellfire replied, "I can describe it two ways. Do you want it highfalutin or Texan?" When the crowd roared "Texan!" Jackson said:

"Freedom is your right and joy to sweat while drivin' a nail in a statehouse to pass your own laws in, in a public schoolhouse to educate your children in, and in a church house you want to worship in."

Jane knew that his short speech on freedom had been repeated from one end of Texas to the other. She realized also that he was less the uncouth backwoodsman and more a man of the people, a symbol. However natural it was for him to be just that—and she admitted he did not have to work at it—he was greater because of it.

And this was the legendary figure who had in a fit of jealousy and anger tossed her into the river out there. She still resented it. He had been a savage, no better than an untamed Indian fighting for a squaw. And why she had defended him to Robert Berry she continued to wonder. But she had, and they had quarreled about it. Her aunt had made it worse by telling every Tom, Dick, and Harry how Jackson had baptized them. Even now, months later, she felt herself a laughingstock. But the one thing that puzzled her was the fact that she had actually forgiven Jackson in her heart even as Robert nursed his resentment.

Robert had little sympathy for the Texans. He had said they were fools of the first water to risk all they had worked for just to humor their tempers. Why, Santa Anna would drive them out of Texas before they could plant a cotton crop. "So we're moving to New Orleans as soon as we're married, Jane," he had told her in no uncertain terms. She had not argued this, at least not with him; nor had she spoken her mind when he left for New Orleans to pursue a business idea at a time when Texans and men from the States were marching on San Antonio against the Mexicans. It had been when he returned and told her of his scheme that she rebelled:

He had talked to the Mexican Consul in New Orleans, as well as a big shipping firm doing business with Mexico, about a cotton monopoly on the Brazos once Santa Anna had conquered Texas.

What did he mean by that? "Wealth beyond your imagination," he had replied, citing the big Eagle Island Plantation of William H. Wharton as an example. Once the militant Wharton was driven out of Texas, his holdings, as well as the property of many others, would be Robert Berry's in partnership with Mexican officials.

When she had broken their engagement because of this, he had finally agreed to pass up "the greatest opportunity of the century" if she would marry him. She had not made up her mind as yet whether to become his wife or not. True, time was growing short. He had much to offer her, position, wealth, travel, and he was handsome. Beyond these things he had agreed to give up his scheme of a fabulous Texas empire. He asked, "What more do you want?" She continued to reply to the question with another: If despite his sacrifice he still harbored the scheme with no qualms of conscience whatsoever, then just what sort of a man was he?

And always, with the question Horatio Jackson appeared unbidden out of memory to stand before her.

2

In the bottom land of the Sabine River the pines bent their green heads under the cold breath of the north wind. The bleak, leafless limbs of oak, elm, and pecan trees seemed to conspire with the gray skies in an effort to chill one's spirits as well as one's body on this Christmas Eve. At least Jackson thought so. Then he realized that he too had joined in the conspiracy by allowing his thoughts to meander down to the Brazos and linger on the woman he would always love. In self-defense, he said:

"Go 'way, Miss Jane."

Wash started. "How's dat, Marse Jackson?"

"Said it was goin' to rain."

"Yassuh." A minute passed by. "But I remembers one time when it never did rain, Marse Jackson. Way back—"

They rode on, through mud, and on up out of the lowlands into the Louisiana pines. Seeing fresh tracks, they left the road and picked their way through the forest on one side of the trail and then the other until the hoof marks disappeared down a narrow Indian file. Then Jackson came upon twigs stacked and pointing east, which advised in Cherokee sign: "White men camp not far away."

Since the Indian sign was fresh, as the droppings of a pony advised, Jackson decided to proceed cautiously just off the trail. This he and Wash did for an hour or so, until the thickets forced them back to the road and into the company they had so diligently tried to avoid.

There were six white men, four on horseback, two dismounted, all with rifles up. They were unshaven, flinty eyed, grim mouthed, and rawhide clad. They looked mean; were mean, Jackson realized. He had seen them before, somewhere. As he racked his brain for the answer, one of them said:

"Figgered it was you, Jackson. But you beat no doctor at all, and you better pray you got a potion that works. Now get movin'."

Half a mile off the Sabine-Fort Jessup road on the banks of a twisting creek they came to a camp. A half-dozen men awaited them. "Yore nigger's safe as you are, Jackson, if you can cure our leader. Now let's get over to his lean-to."

When the canvas flap was thrown back from the front of the crude pole-and-thatch shelter, Jackson looked down into the fevered face of the man lying on a blanket and exclaimed, "Fozatte!"

A faint smile animated the face. *"Dieu vous garde, Dieu*

vous bénisse!" Next he asked if he was going to die. He tried to say more, but he was too weak. Jackson asked him where he hurt and how long he had been ill. All the while Fozatte's lieutenant stood by. Finally Jackson said:

"My friend, you've got a bad case of gallopin' pneumonia —*la grippe.* I can doctor you and pray, but unless you and your men help me you're a gone goslin'. Maybe you'll die anyhow." When Fozatte ordered his man to obey the preacher, Jackson said, "Get me fresh eggs and turpentine, a jugful; and the same of good red whisky; and the same of good apple vinegar; and some axle grease and red pepper; and a pair of stockings—oh, yes, and a few pinches of snuff."

The lieutenant simply stared at Jackson. "Maybe you could kill him quicker with a rifle," he said.

"You might fetch me a gallon of molasses while you're at it," Jackson replied.

"What's that for?"

"My flapjacks."

While the smugglers swore they would rather run a hundred slaves past the American Army than fill the order, they came up with every item on the list within the next three days. They saw Jackson force raw eggs down Fozatte's throat, rub his neck with axle grease and wrap it with a stocking, place a rag soaked in turpentine on his chest after applying axle grease to the skin to prevent blistering. At his order they boiled vinegar, salt, and red pepper in a pot, strained the liquid, and added it to one-fourth the measure of whisky. Two tablespoonfuls were given the patient every half hour.

One of the band finally admitted that his curiosity had the better of him; he simply had to know what the snuff was for. Jackson said, "I dose him with snuff so he'll sneeze out a cold. Course it's better if he sneezes in a mirror at his own reflection, but we'll just have to do the best we can and pray."

The last day of 1835 found Jackson sitting inside the lean-to listening to the slow, cold rain and the labored breathing of the Frenchman. It was a time when he should be in Natchez, as Jeremiah Whiteside had ordered if he wished to become an ordained minister. With the gray dusk, Horatio asked if it was God's will or his own stupidity that had trapped him here and once again left him staring at the ashes of his perennial dream. Why Fozatte chose the moment to ask, "Why you do all this for me, *mon ami?*" he didn't know, unless the Lord was reminding him to put selfish ambitions aside. To the sick man, he said:

"Because the Bible here tells me to. In the Book of Matthew, chapter ten, Christ said to His disciples, 'Heal the sick.' "

Bleak skies ushered in the new year. The day was dreary enough without a memory of what he had heard would take place in Velasco on New Year's Day of 1836: Jane would say "I do" and become another man's bride. Staring into the blazing campfire, he surprised Fozatte's men by saying, "The Lord says, 'Thou shalt not covet,' but He didn't say a thing about kickin' the livin' tarnation out of this fire!" After giving the burning brqnches a mighty feel of his boot, he stalked off into the woods alone.

Fozatte chuckled. Wash looked worried. "Marse Jackson am sholy in a fix, Mistuh F'zatte. He sholy am, him wantin' to go down and jine up with Mistuh General Houston's army and de Lawd tellin' him to git on to Natchez, and purty Miss Jane her marryin' up wid somebody else. He got a heap mo' miseries than yo'all is, suh."

Despite his pain, the smuggler laughed. It was a sign that he had passed the crisis, Wash told Jackson that night. When Fozatte began to show concern for his doctor's condition, Wash was sure the patient was on the road to recovery. Within a week Fozatte was able to sit about the campfire a few hours each day. But he overdid it and suffered a relapse. He could still give orders, however, and knowing of Jackson's interest in what was happening in Texas, he sent his men out to stop and question any travelers along the King's Highway. They returned with much to report, and none of it encouraging:

The civil and military leaders of Texas were quarreling. Provisional Governor Smith and the General Council were barking at each other, and there was talk of impeaching Smith. The military heads didn't like Houston and refused to accept him as their superior despite the fact that he had been elected to command the Texan forces. The Council ordered Fannin and other leaders to invade Mexico. Houston not only opposed this but was threatening to dissuade the army itself from taking part in it. Besides this strife among the leaders, it was reported that Santa Anna himself was preparing to invade Texas with over eight thousand crack troops.

Then one day Fozatte's Lieutenant rode in and told of meeting a company of armed men in fine new uniforms. They called themselves the Newport Rifles, volunteers from Newport, Kentucky, and Cincinnati, Ohio. Their leader, Sidney Sherman, advised they were on the way to aid the Texans in their fight for freedom.

Jackson was pleased to hear this. He was also glad to see Fozatte recovering rapidly. The Frenchman was once more sitting about the campfire. Several days later he began to move about the camp. By the end of the third week in January, he told his men they would break camp and resume their business in Texas.

On the following morning he approached Jackson and extended a pouch of gold coins. When Jackson refused to accept the gift, he thundered forth:

"Have you such a poor memory, *mon ami?* Once you refuse the hand of Jean Émile Fozatte! Now you do not accept his purse! *Dieu m'en preserve!*" When bluster failed, he said with friendly persuasion in his voice, "It is only six hundred dollar, m'sieur. You take it and do some good with it, no?"

Jackson finally accepted the pouch and said a parting prayer for Fozatte and his band. A half hour later he reached the King's Highway and looked in both directions before telling Wash they would ride east toward Natchez.

Two weeks later Reverend Jeremiah Whiteside sat at Jackson's bedside, chin in hand, elbow on knee, his large dreamy eyes lost in troubled thought. For almost a week the council of churchmen had waited for their most exasperating applicant to the ministry to recover from chills and fever and appear for examination again. Whiteside said it was too bad that he, Jackson's sponsor for years, had been unable to escape his Christian duty and withhold from the judging body what had transpired down on the river front shortly after Jackson arrived in Natchez.

The incident had taken place in Natchez-Under-the-Hill, where the boats docked. This was the cotton port and market. It was crowded with business houses, taverns, brothels, and gambling dens, and made livelier by flatboatmen, scented quadroons, slavers, thieves, and smugglers. It was also a jumping-off place for volunteers from the North on their way to Texas. Here the Sabbath was no different from any other day.

Despite the fact that Jackson had on his first Sunday in Natchez set a precedent by preaching a sermon from the bar of a notorious saloon, which resulted in the conversion of more than a dozen river pirates and painted ladies, such unauthorized behavior by an unlicensed minister was frowned upon by the elite of "Natchez-on-Top-of-the-Hill." However, the churchmen admitted that Jackson had displayed both bravery and religious zeal and was above censure. But a public brawl, out of which he was stricken with a severe case of *la grippe,* was another matter.

It happened on a cold afternoon when a steamboat just in from New Orleans began disgorging passengers and cargo. A handsome man in Burgundy coat and gray beaver had stopped in midstride on the gangplank and exclaimed, "Jackson!" Hastily removing his fine coat, he said, "I've looked forward to this meeting a long time!"

Surprised, Jackson backed a step. "Look, Mr. Berry, I've waited some time to apologize to you in person for what happened on the Brazos. And I want to wish you and Jane—Mrs. Berry, I mean—all the happiness in—"

"Thanks to you, she's not my wife!"

Jackson's jaw hung slack. Amazement and disbelief left him defenseless. As he said, "How was that again?" Robert Berry leaped at him, fists swinging. Jackson went down with the other on top of him, with the crowd of passengers and hangers-on yelling and cheering. Finally he managed to get astraddle Berry and hold his hands to the ground. Then, unmindful of his bleeding nose and fast-closing eye, he said:

"You mean you and Jane didn't get married?"

"We didn't. Now if you'll get up and fight—"

"Why didn't you get married?"

"Because I didn't fit the pattern of a damn backwoods preacher, that's why! And," Berry added, "I'm going to throw you in this river if it's the last damn thing I ever do!"

To the surprise of the crowd, Jackson spread a grin across his face, released Berry, shouted "Glory hallelujah!" and threw his hat high in the air. Robert Berry seized the moment to lift Jackson bodily and hurl him into the Mississippi. But even that failed to dampen his joy. Streaming water, Hellfire Jackson walked to the bank shouting:

"Hallelujah!"

CHAPTER 23

As a thin, emaciated, but hopeful aspirant to the ministry stood before the churchmen at Natchez on a morning in mid-February, a man equally as tall and more imposing than the lay preacher sat in a meeting with the leading citizens of Nacogdoches at the Stone Fort. He was Sam Houston, whom the provincial governor of Texas had sent to East Texas to cultivate friendly relations with the Indians. Now that he had visited with various chieftains, Houston told the group, he was satisfied that the Mexicans were doing their utmost to start an Indian uprising to coincide with Santa Anna's conquest of Texas. It was rumored that the outlaw band headed by the notorious Hominy Baines had been employed by the Mexicans to foment Indian trouble.

"What we need here is a man who can keep the Indians on our side," Houston said.

The Texans nodded gravely. They knew that Santa Anna, at the head of several thousand trained soldiers, was advancing on San Antonio; that the Texas Army had in January refused to accept Houston as commander in chief; that constant political squabbles had resulted in the impeachment of Provisional Governor Smith. Without harmony among the leaders, without money or supplies with which to equip a small ragged, mutinous army, which had no recognized leader at a time when the enemy moved in, Texas was in serious trouble. Even if the Indians honored the treaties made with Houston it seemed that only a miracle could stop Santa Anna. But if the Indians sided with the Mexicans, the situation would be hopeless.

Houston said at last, "I know only one man the Indians trust. He might be able to keep them peaceful."

Even as Houston named Hellfire Jackson and asked if anybody knew where to find him, Horatio was explaining to the church body why he had engaged in a public fight with a prominent New Orleans merchant's son. With each mention of Jane Wells, Miss Polly Fincher winced and caused Jeremiah Whiteside to squirm in his chair. Besides this, Jackson had frankly replied to the question of why had he failed to report in Natchez before the end of the year by saying he had doctored, nursed, and prayed the sick smuggler Fozatte back to health. So what sort of man was this applicant? Was he friend of savages and thieves and saloon hangers-on who would embarrass, perhaps disgrace, the church, or was he a better Samaritan and Christian than they who sat in judgment of him? Whatever he was, he remained a problem of the first water.

In the hour that followed the words "brawl, embarrassment, rules, discipline, dependability," as well as "the dignity of the church," were tossed back and forth, then flung at Jackson like so many flying swords. Although his brain ticked fast, he was hard put to answer each question or charge with a suitable verse from the Bible. Finally the spokesman asked if he still felt that his call was to Texas.

"I do." Even as he said it, he read the verdict in their expressions. It was not in his favor. When he was asked to retire and await the decision, he said, "I know what it will be.

For a man who must shape your rules to the pattern of the wilderness, who is disciplined by hardships, pain, and sorrow, who beneath the dignity of the church and to its embarrassment finds a pulpit even in a saloon, and who believes the soul of a thief is precious in the eyes of God—for that man your thumbs are down. But on the subject of dependability, you know from the past that Hellfire Jackson can be depended on to be back again." At the door he said, "Good-by and God bless you."

He had scarcely turned his back than Miss Polly cried sharply, "Horatio Jackson, you come back here!" Then, rising and shaking a finger at the astonished churchmen, she said, "How can you refuse such a good man?"

The body could not and did not. After considerable harangue and a clearing of throats, the members decided to license and ordain Jackson. However, and it was so noted in the minutes of the meeting, such action was not to be construed as a precedent in the future. The ordination sermon would be preached by Reverend Whiteside the following Sunday.

Prior to that important sermon Jackson received word that Sam Houston needed him in Texas and had asked that any person who saw Jackson should advise him to ride fast for Washington-on-the-Brazos, the site of the 1836 convention of Texans, scheduled for March first.

Curious, eager to serve Texas again, Horatio broached the matter to Jeremiah Whiteside, who in turn spoke to the churchmen. As a consequence, due to the rising feeling in the United States for Texans in their fight for liberty, plus the element of time, it was decided that the ordination sermon should be postponed indefinitely in order that Reverend Jackson could be off to Texas.

Elated by this news, Jackson loaded his pack mule with Bibles, tracts, and a supply of gunpowder and struck out for Texas. Once across the Mississippi River into Louisiana, Horatio said to Wash, "If General Houston said ride fast, I reckon he meant it." They set a pace that taxed their mounts to the fullest without exhausting them and reached Nacogdoches early in March.

There Jackson heard that Colonel William B. Travis, the frontier lawyer who had been imprisoned by Bradburn in Anahuac back in 1832, and one hundred eighty-seven men had decided to defend the old mission called the Alamo in San Antonio de Bexar against Santa Anna's invading army. Among the defenders were the famous James Bowie and

David Crockett of Tennessee. According to the latest dispatches, Santa Anna had on February twenty-fourth begun the siege of the Alamo.

While all Texas waited anxiously for further news from the Alamo, the people took encouragement from the fact that their delegates had pledged to declare for independence as soon as they convened. Also, Houston was at last in command of the army. The arrival of volunteers by land and sea and the ability of the four small schooners of the Texas Navy to keep the coast clear of Mexican vessels of war bolstered public morale also, though few could forget the presence of Santa Anna in Texas with an avenging army of thousands.

In Nacogdoches, Jackson dipped into the six hundred dollars Fozatte had given him and bought two horses before taking the road toward Washington-on-the-Brazos. Late on the following day he and Wash were chased by a band of painted Kickapoo Indians, and only Jackson's ability to read and cut sign and hide his own tracks as he doubled back on the trail enabled them to escape. While he and Wash hid in a river-bottom thicket, Hominy Baines and a Mexican officer in the company of the Kickapoo chief rode within a few yards of them.

Delayed by flight from the warring tribe, Jackson did not reach Washington-on-the-Brazos in time to meet Houston there. The commander in chief of the Texas Army had left the convention for Gonzales on the sixth of March with a few hundred men in answer to an appeal for help from the defenders of the Alamo. However, Almazon Huston from San Augustine, now Quartermaster General of the Army of Texas, relayed Sam Houston's message to Jackson.

But before he got around to it he proudly announced that the delegates had on March first agreed on a document, a Declaration of Independence, and on the second, amid great pandemonium, it had been read section by section and signed. "We're electing an ad interim government of the Republic of Texas, and it looks like David G. Burnet will be president." Then he delivered Houston's wishes regarding Jackson:

The greatest service Hellfire could render Texans in their fight for freedom would be to prevent an uprising of the Indian tribes while the small army of the new Republic of Texas was trying to halt the advance of Santa Anna.

"I suppose so," Jackson said, somewhat crestfallen at being unable to join up with Houston at Gonzales or Fannin's command at Goliad. Then he was wondering how he, armed with Bibles, tracts, and a lone rifle, could deal with the marauding

Kickapoos or other restless tribes. "Perhaps the Lord will point out a way," he said.

Two days later the Lord and circumstances did just that, though Hellfire Jackson didn't realize it at first. A running shower had drenched the Trinity River bottom land and raced on upriver. Finally Wash got a fire going, though he wasn't too hopeful, "cause it sholy smokes wet, Rev'ren' Jackson. *Rev'ren'!* Hear dat? 'Rev'ren'' sound good when it am real, don't it, Rev'ren'?"

"I reckon." Jackson sat on his haunches, skinning knife in one hand, a rabbit in the other, his gaze fixed on the red band that rimmed the western horizon. Above the color was turquoise; below, indigo. It was that time of day when his thoughts always searched out Jane. She came as she had the evening before and as she had hundreds of other evenings before in all her beauty and dignity and womanly wisdom. He smiled and forgot rabbit and knife and hunger and urgency of the mission that kept him from her until Wash cried out:

"Lawdy! Run fo' yo' life—!"

Before Jackson could reach his rifle an arm closed about his neck. Then a laugh sounded in his ear and he was released. "*Mon Dieu,* no! *Mon ami,* I am please, yes!"

Jackson gave the Frenchman a hug of genuine relief and welcome before greeting his men. They brought venison and real coffee and sugar, luxuries indeed. After all had eaten, Jackson and Fozatte sat over pannikins of coffee talking of their experiences. Fozatte admitted to Horatio's surprise that he had found religion rather costly. He could no longer cheat or steal without a twinge of conscience, which was "mos' regrettable." Beyond "thees terrible thing, m'sieur, my *coquines* they wish to turn hones'! *Sacrebleu,* it is bad!" To which Jackson replied casually, "If religion pointed out no difference between right and wrong or called for no sacrifice, what good would it do you, Fozatte?"

"Eh! Say that again! Maybe it soon sound good."

They talked on, about Fozatte's friends Fannin and Travis and Bowie, the war, and the outnumbered Texans' chances of winning it. When the time came for them to turn in for the night, Jackson asked where the other was headed and learned the band was on its way to Contraband Trace with scarce items for the people of Louisiana and East Texas.

"But Fozatte is hones' smuggler, *mon ami. Oui!*"

Jackson got to his feet, all the while looking the Frenchman in the eye. "Sure," he said finally. "While your friends

Fannin and Travis starve, the selfish sinner Fozatte sells coffee and flour at a profit to fatten his purse."

"*Non, non!*" Fozatte was on his feet, his face troubled. "Do not scold, m'sieur!" When Jackson turned his back, the Frenchman said, "I do anything you say, my good fran."

Only then did Jackson think of the task Houston had assigned him. He seemed to know then that the Lord had guided him to perhaps the only man in the Southwest who could serve Houston and Texas in severing the link between the Mexicans and Indians. But would Fozatte leave his profitable business long enough to deal with Hominy Baines, the real agitator? Very carefully he approached the Frenchman, and after presenting his case, he placed the question.

"Try me, m'sieur!" Fozatte replied.

A quarter hour later Fozatte pledged his support in helping drive Hominy Baines and his rowdies as well as the Kickapoos out of Texas. He would begin next day, *oui!*

Jackson smiled, raised a hand and lowered his head. When all had bared their heads, he thanked the Lord briefly in the tongue of his friend: *"Dieu merci, grâce à Dieu."*

2

Jane stretched luxuriously as the first light of day reminded her that this was Saturday and there would be no school. She could sleep another hour or so—that is, if her Aunt Sally would stop singing in the kitchen. Putting a finger in each ear, she closed her eyes. Sleep eluded her, however; a dozen and one things tried to dominate her mind at once. Her pupils, the epidemic of colds, the waiting for reports from the brave men defending the Alamo, speculation on what would happen if Houston's army did not arrive to help them in time, these things and more provoked questions she could not answer. . . .

Had she married Robert she would be where and doing what on this fifteenth day of March, 1836? Where was Horatio Jackson, and why did he always crop up out of memory when the moon shone large and ripe and the pulse of spring surged in her veins?

Her eyes opened slowly and she was staring at the ceiling, wondering, wondering, almost forgetting to scold herself for once again letting her thoughts channel themselves around to the backwoods preacher. How often had she told herself, and her aunt as well, that if he were one of a row of unattractive, ordinary men, he would be the last she would select? Often. And yet, despite her wishes, he was etched deeper in her memory than any other man. Perhaps it was because he had been so persistent these five years she had been in Texas.

"I'm goin' to the shop, Jane!" Aunt Sally's voice caused her to jump. "Sowbelly and coffee on the stove—only the flavor's boiled out of the coffee after the fourth day."

"Fifth!" Jane corrected, rising. She sat on the edge of the bed for some time watching the sun break through the clouds. When the gray overcast warned of more rain to feed the already swollen Brazos, she got up and stretched the muscles of her arms, legs, and back.

She had no sooner dressed and sat down to breakfast than Bucktooth Sal arrived with two letters addressed to her. One was from Natchez, the other from Washington-on-the-Brazos. Both were from Horatio Jackson. She read one, put it down and said, "So he let Robert throw him in the river! He was that happy!" She wasn't sure that this pleased her, so she read again about his tending the sick Fozatte and missing his chance to be ordained.

"You're as irresponsible as a child, Horatio Jackson!" she charged.

Then she was reading of his being accepted for the ministry, of his hurried trip to Texas at the behest of Sam Houston, of his escape from hostile Kickapoos, and next, the reason Houston had sent for him. After scanning his next line, "I am writing this after Fozatte has agreed to help me with the Mexican-Indian trouble," Jane bit her lip and grudgingly admitted that he was not so irresponsible after all. Then she said, "*Reverend* Jackson," as if she were trying to get used to the word. The letter closed with:

> We go in search of Kickapoos tomorrow. When this job is done, and when and if peace comes with Texas free and rejoicing, I shall come to you on bended knee and ask that all important question. Be thinking about your answer, my dear sweet Miss Jane. While I have so little to offer you in worldly goods and small promise of ever giving you the fine things you so truly deserve, I do proffer my faithful heart in love and devotion.

"Well!" Jane exclaimed. Rising, she went to the window, drew in her lower lip, released it, and said "Well!" again, and read the proposal once more.

As the day wore on, she admitted to herself that Jackson's letter troubled her, angered her, puzzled and pleased her. Certainly she had never known such ambivalence of feeling in all her life. Horatio Jackson was certainly assuming a great deal and he should be ashamed of himself for upsetting her day. Nor would she ponder the matter any longer. There were more important things to occupy her mind.

Jane was very right in her last assertion. She and every resident of Austin's colony on the Brazos were given something to think about that afternoon when a courier from General Houston arrived with news of the fall of the Alamo. The guns had been silenced late in the afternoon of Sunday, March sixth, and of the one hundred eighty-seven defenders not a single man survived. When they refused to surrender, Santa Anna had ordered the *Degüello,* no quarter, sounded and sent five thousand soldiers to storm the walls.

Bucktooth Sal for once looked worried. Alarmed, she left the charcoal-blackened walls of her shop and joined other shocked and dazed Texans who gathered in small groups. Jane heard her ask the courier what Houston could do to stop Santa Anna now that so many of the Texas leaders had died at the Alamo.

"He's got three hundred seventy-four half-starved men. Half of them are unarmed. Santa Anna has over five thousand well-fed, trained soldiers moving in this direction. Houston's doing the only thing he can do, ma'am. He's retreating to the Colorado River."

By nightfall in Velasco, shock had given way to grief for the Alamo's dead and their living kin. By morning, sorrow was contained in silence, but anxiety and fear were fast taking its place. Again people met and talked and went home to pack belongings. The blacksmith shop was crowded with men demanding that their animals be shod in a hurry. Families were melting lead in pots and molding bullets, readying wagons, and baking bread, just in case the war came closer and they should be forced to leave their homes.

Next day fear subsided somewhat. Settlers felt this was no time to panic. Not a few returned to their plows. Some left to join Fannin at Goliad, while others rode toward the Colorado to aid Houston. Bucktooth Sal went about her work as usual. In the days that followed she watched as a few wagons heavy with household goods departed the Brazos for Harrisburg in the north. And where one family left Velasco a dozen arrived from the west, the latter fleeing from the Colorado River to the safety of the Brazos.

"Hell, it don't make sense," Bucktooth Sal told Jane one evening. "Every place but the one where you're at seems safer. But I ain't about to run. Nosiree, I ain't. I'm countin' on Fannin to stop General Urrea down at Goliad, and Houston to scorch old Santa Anna's tail feathers when he gets to the Colorado. How you feel about it, Jane?"

Jane said nothing. She did not wish to reveal what she had heard at the store a half hour earlier, that up at Washington-on-the-Brazos the delegates had upon hearing the news of the fall of the Alamo broken up the convention and decided to move the ad interim government of the Republic of Texas to Harrisburg above Galveston Bay.

Her aunt was saying again, "How you feel about it, Jane?" when rapping sounded at the back door. Bucktooth Sal rose and flung the door open.

There stood Wash.

Upon seeing him standing there, his clothes ragged and torn, his expression both weary and sad, Jane started inwardly. As her aunt said, "Where's Hellfire?" Jane felt sure Wash was the bearer of bad news. Finally the Negro replied:

"He ain't heah, Miss Sally. No he ain't."

"Then where the devil is he, and what brings you here lookin' like you tangled with a bear?"

" 'Cause I done rode fast in the bushes to git heah like Marse Jackson say do. He say, 'Wash, you skedaddle on down to Velasco and help Miss Sally and Miss Jane while I tell de chief I got de job done in a hurry.' Well, heah I is."

"What job?" Sally demanded.

Jane knew of the mission Jackson had been assigned to, but she knew also that Wash was hungry. Relieved to know Jackson had completed his task and was alive, she told Wash to come inside and eat. Then he could talk.

The Negro obeyed. He fell to the food like a starved animal. He apologized, but said he had not eaten since the day before. All the while Jane sat every bit as curious as her aunt as to how Jackson had put down the Indian threat. Finally, when Wash had eaten his fill, she asked him to tell all that had happened.

"Well, ma'am, dere we was layin' in de cold rain on de bank o' de Neches, wid mean Kickapoo Injuns on one side and some o' dat outlaw man Hominy Baines's men on de other, and Marse Jackson him tryin' his best not to sneeze—"

Wash talked on. He told of how Jackson had enlisted Fozatte's aid in the job Houston had given him. The smuggler had sent a man to ask Chief Bowles of the friendly Cherokees to join in the fight against Baines and the warring Kickapoos. Wash continued, saying:

"Den Marse Jackson he sneeze and dat Mexican lootenant wid de Kickapoos starts shootin' at where we is at. But we ain't dere, 'cause we's runnin'. But we runs right into Hominy Baines. And while he tyin' us up dem Kickapoos surrounds Mistuh F'zatte and his boys and guns is poppin' all round us. 'Bout a hour later mo' shootin' comes in from de nawth and den it gits quiet. Pretty soon, a whole passel o' Injuns rides in and Marse Jackson he say 'Praise de Lawd!' fo' dere was Chief Bowles hissel. We done won. But—"

Wash paused, "But it am sad. Real sad. Don't mean 'cause old Hominy Baines gits killed. I'se thinkin' o' po' Mistuh F'zatte. He shot up bad and he dyin' and he ask Rev'ren' Jackson—he a regular orderlydained preachin' man now—to pray fo' him. Marse Jackson do and po' Mistuh F'zatte him die and we bury him and Marse Jackson he write on a plank that heah lies Émile F'zatte who died a hero fightin' fo' Texas. And Chief Bowles he say he keep de Injuns peaceful and fo' Marse Jackson to tell Mistuh General Houston dat."

"Then what?" Sally asked.

"Well, heah I is, like I been told to do, and Marse Jackson last I seen o' him when he sent me back heah yestiddy from halfway to de Col'rado River was diggin' his heels into dat hoss o' his goin' west."

Bucktooth Sal looked from Wash to Jane. "Well, I'll be damned! And that's the man you despise, girl!"

"Is he?" Jane replied. "Or is he the man I once said I despised? There's a difference, you know."

As a wise grin formed on Bucktooth Sal's face, Jane gave her a sharp look of defiance and turned to the Negro. "Did Reverend Jackson send any message to—to us, Wash?"

The Negro scratched his white head a moment, then chuckled. "Well, ma'am, in a way I reckins he did. He say to de Lawd like he do—he always tellin' de Lawd a heap o' things—anyhow, jes' befo' he leave ol' Wash, he say, 'Lawd, Yo'll knows ol' Hellfire don't ask much fo' hisself, but dere's one thing I wants Yo'all to do while I'se busy fightin' Mexicans and dat is take keer o' de woman I loves.'

"Dat's what he say, Miss Jane. I reckins he done mean yo'all, 'cause he send me heah to help de Lawd out whilst he busy fightin' dem Mexicans."

Before Bucktooth Sal's laughter fell away, Jane turned and left them. She went outside and walked slowly down to the old pier, wondering why Horatio Jackson seemed to reach out to her more strongly than ever before. Perhaps, she told herself, it was because he had never stopped flicking at her curiosity, like an exasperating puzzle she could never quite solve; and Wash's arrival with Jackson's further declaration of love in a prayer only heightened the puzzle. But that was only a partial answer, and she knew it.

Gazing up at a slice of moon peeping through a veil of running clouds, she spoke in low tones, "It was kind of you to send Wash, Horatio." Then she closed her eyes and said, "Lord, if You'll allow me to talk to You as that gangling preacher does, I'm going to tell You to watch over Reverend Hellfire Jackson."

3

While Jane Wells sat on the pier watching the moon sinking in the western sky, some ninety miles to the northwest Jackson stood outside Houston's headquarters at Burnham's Crossing on the Colorado River awaiting an audience with the general.

For almost an hour he had waited. Twice he had heard Houston's outburst. It was, rather, his voiced puzzlement at the strange conduct of the man he had appointed a colonel in the Texas Army back in December, James W. Fannin: "On the eleventh I rushed an order to Fannin to retreat from Goliad to Victoria and to send me one-third of his effective force to Gonzales! And now I learn he divided his force three ways to skirmish with General Urrea's detachments, even after having one command annihilated on the Agua Dulce!"

Whether Houston voiced his unequivocal opinion of Fannin in plain Tennessee language, Jackson didn't know; loud talk about the bivouac fires drowned out the general's comment. The men groused openly, voicing disapproval of both Houston and Fannin. "Hell, Fannin got Colonel Travis' plea to come to the Alamo! Why didn't he go instead of shilly-shallyin' around doing nothing?" As for General Houston, "Him at Gonzales arrestin' and jailin' them Mexicans who brought the news of the Alamo's fall as spies and liars! Done it to restore order, he said. I say different, say he was tryin' to fool us. Well, we ain't blind men."

A courier entered the tent and departed. Then Horatio heard Houston boom forth to his aide: "Hellfire Jackson? Impossible! I've got him busy in East Texas! But send him in."

Houston did not speak when Jackson entered the tent. He stood tall, straight, arms folded at chest, feet spread apart, his fierce eyes flashing like polished saber points in the light of the small enclosure. It was not at all difficult to realize that this man carried the weight of a new and weak and impulsive nation on his shoulders. But this and other realizations faded quickly when he opened his tight line of mouth and said in clipped tones:

"I gave you a job to do in East Texas. What the hell are you doing here?"

Jackson stood a moment speechless under the glaring scrutiny of the general. Then he opened up and told of the skirmish on the Neches and next of Chief Bowles's message. "The Bowl asked me to tell you he would keep the Indians peaceful in East Texas, General."

Houston did not so much as nod his head. There was no sign of gratitude or relief, no expression whatsoever. Jackson knew he was the type of man who refused to reveal his true feelings to anyone.

In the moments of disconcerting silence, Jackson said, "I reckon I did my job, sir, so with your permission I'll join the army and do my bit. I've got a rifle, powder, and lead."

Colonel Burleson entered, gazed at Jackson, said, "Hello, Hellfire," then spoke to Houston. Deaf Smith, the army scout, came inside and stood with arms resting on the barrel tip of his rifle. Minus any semblance of concern, he spat lustily, lifted a hand, said, "Hi, Jackson," and looked at Houston, who eyed him thoughtfully before saying:

"Well?"

"General Sesma's cuttin' a dido to the north of us, like he might be tryin' to get behind us. He's movin' up to the river across from us."

"What do you think?" Houston asked.

"I don't," Smith replied. "I reports, General."

Houston looked at the excuse for a desk in his tent. On it sat a bottle and a cracked glass. He poured generously, handed it to Deaf Smith, who refused, then drank it down as though it were spring water.

"By God, it's Fannin that's got me worried!" Houston exclaimed. "That and the lack of reinforcements. And the men out there aren't too happy."

Deaf Smith shifted his cud to the other cheek. "Who is, General?"

Ignoring this, Houston picked up a paper and said, "The quartermaster general says we haven't enough money in the treasury of the Republic of Texas to buy coffee for the army, much less cannon, shoes for the men, or any medicines. I just wrote to him, telling him to beg, borrow, or steal, and I don't give a damn which, but get us supplies." Glaring at Jackson, he said, "Can you raise any money in Natchez or New Orleans? If you can, get going and bring back shoes, medical supplies, gunpowder, blankets, and—"

Jackson lifted a hand. "Hold it right there, General, sir. I've worn out a horse and two mules between here and Natchez. If the Republic needs money, there are better men than old Hellfire at raisin' it. I came to fight this time and I'm going to fight."

Before Houston could reply, Horatio drew a packet from underneath his buckskins and spread money on the crude desk.

"There's over five hundred dollars here, sir, and if the general will give me a receipt for it, consider it a loan to the Republic of Texas."

Deaf Smith blinked his eyes, leaned forward, and said, "I be goddamned! Beggin' your pardon, Rev'ren'."

Houston showed no surprise whatever. He wrote out a receipt for the money, ordered a secretary to send it by courier to Quartermaster General Almazon Huston posthaste, then looked at Jackson. "Just who the devil did you rob?"

"Nobody until now. If I'm robbin' the Lord for the Republic, I reckon the bookkeeper up there will just have to charge it to old Hellfire's account until this scrap is over. Now, General, if you'll assign me to the ranks, I'll be right obliged to you."

Houston sat down, scrawled a few lines on a sheet of paper, and gave it to Jackson. "You'll get your fill of fighting soon enough, Hellfire. But first you'll take this order down to Colonel Fannin at Goliad."

CHAPTER 24

Jackson sat tiredly on his horse, staring at the midafternoon sky out of red-rimmed eyes. Whether he heard gunfire ahead or imagined it, he wasn't sure. Two days of continuous riding since leaving Houston's camp, pausing only to change horses and catch a wink of sleep, had dulled his senses considerably. He seemed rooted to saddle, growing out of it, his back and legs turned to leather. And now thirst was making demands on both rider and horse. The bay mare was tossing her head and foaming at the bit. She smelled water ahead.

Again the sound of a shot reached over the tree-dotted hill. He drew his mount up sharply and listened. The sound came again, no mistaking it this time. Reining his horse off the Victoria-Goliad road, which he had reached only the hour before, he angled up toward the crest of the hill for a look. Topping the rocky incline, he paused under a live oak tree and looked to the west. A quarter mile away rifles barked. Beyond the little draw a detachment of cavalry moved in. The uniforms, though far away, were without doubt Mexican. Which meant that the defenders of the draw were Texans.

"Let's go join them," he said, nudging the mare forward.

As he approached the Texans, a bullet cut through his hat crown. Another whistled past as he leaped from the horse, gun in hand. Then he was lying behind a rock and looking down the barrel of his rifle. The man next to him said, "Welcome stranger, whoever you are." This was no time to talk; the enemy was now forming a charge.

Then, suddenly, it seemed time to do some talking. The expected charge was held in check with the arrival of more Mexican cavalrymen. The Texan leader looked at his seven men, including Jackson, down at his three dead, and again trained his shocked eyes on the enemy.

"Hold your fire, men. They're going to ask us to surrender. Do we or don't we?"

"What's our chances if we don't?" one asked.

"Sixty or seventy to us eight, Bob. What do you think?"

A uniformed soldier on a horse approached with a flag of truce. The Mexican rattled off a demand for surrender in his language, wheeled his horse, and rode off.

"Gave us five minutes," the leader said. "Told us if we decided to fight, they would take no prisoners." Looking at Jackson, he said, "Friend, seems you got here just in time to get shot or captured. Suppose you vote first."

"Yeah," Jackson replied. "Happens I'm carrying an important message from General Houston to Colonel Fannin. So I'm going to make a run for it. Maybe I can get it to the colonel in time."

The leader stared at Jackson. "I reckon you don't know what happened a few miles ahead yesterday. No, reckon you don't. Tell him, Bob."

A dejected silence held for long seconds. "Cunnel Fannin began his retreat from Goliad day before yesterday mornin'. On Saturday it was, the nineteenth. Said General Houston ordered it. Sent out a scoutin' party ahead to find a crossin' to Coleto Creek. We got cut off by Mexican cavalry and when we tried to get back a battle had started and we couldn't get through the Mexican lines to join Fannin. It went on all that day. General Urrea circled Fannin with about a thousand soldiers. Next day Urrea had another thousand men."

He stopped talking and scratched his head in a perplexed manner. "What I can't figure out is why Cunnel Fannin halted his three hundred on that bald, dry prairie to fight when Coleto Creek and water and woods lay ahead. But he did. And on the twentieth it happened. Yesterday. It was Sunday."

"What happened?" Jackson said impatiently.

"If they had got to the woods they could have picked off them Mexicans, all right. Or if the cunnel had moved up to the trees of Encinal del Perdido, it might have been different. But he didn't. And on the twentieth the cunnel's army made a good target for the twelve-pounder cannons old Urrea brought up. The Mexicans outranged the Texans. So Cunnel Fannin surrendered."

"Surrendered!" Jackson exclaimed.

"Now what else could a happened, mister? Didn't we see Fannin's boys being herded back toward Goliad? Probably surrendered on the same terms we just heard, and which we got about a minute left to accept or reject. And that's surrender at discretion without any guarantee whatever."

Jackson stared at the ground. "Fannin beaten," he said dejectedly. His next thought gave him a start. "I've got to notify Sam Houston!"

"You're a little late, mister. Our time's up."

He spoke the truth. The Mexican was riding toward them for their answer, and the Texan leader was now asking, "Who wants to live and who wants to die?"

That was the choice, and all eight knew it. While not a man of them wished to die, not one wished to be the first to vote for unconditional surrender. The enemy horseman came to a halt. He demanded an answer. With none forthcoming, he reined his horse about. It was then that the Texan leader asked him to wait a minute. The Mexican did so.

"I vote we fight," the man called Bob spoke up.

"I second."

"I say we might escape on the way to Goliad."

"I go along with Hiram on that."

The next man spat on the ground and wiped blood from a bullet nick on his cheek. "By God, I want to pick off a few more o' Santa Anna's bloodthirsty bastards here and now!"

"I vote we live maybe to even the score."

The leader looked at Jackson. "Tied at three and three, which leaves me and you, mister."

"After you, sir," Jackson replied.

"The devil with you! You know I can't condemn my men here to certain death!"

Jackson nodded. "I didn't think you could, sir. And since I figure the Lord might find some use for a few of us, I'm votin' right with you."

They laid down their guns and raised their hands. The Mexican cavalry rode up, seized arms and horses, then ordered the prisoners to march west. The man called Hiram began to limp. Jackson saw blood dripping from his foot, and stopped to look at the source. A bayonet point pricked at Jackson's back, and as he began to protest the guard swung the butt of the rifle around, knocking him off his feet. Then, amid oaths in both Spanish and Anglo, both Hiram and Jackson's hands were tied at their backs. With ropes about their necks and the lines fastened to saddles, the march continued. A few of the Texans began to sing "Ole Zip Coon" at sunset. They too were tied and led by ropes all the way to Coleto Creek, where the Mexicans pitched camp for the night.

At daybreak of Tuesday, March twenty-second, the march continued. Upon reaching the site of the battle, the cavalry commander halted to take in the scene of Urrea's victory over Fannin's Texans. Jackson's nose and eyes had already warned him of the close proximity of the battlefield. The stench of death was in the air, and vultures circled and swooped down to earth.

The ground was littered with the dead, many in Mexican blue, others in buckskin and homespun, Texans; and there were bodies in the uniform of the New Orleans Greys. Dead oxen, horses, and mules, bullet-pocked, overturned wagons and cannon-scarred earth and broken muskets, together with the paths dug by the feet of circling horses—and there were the improvised trenches where Fannin's men had huddled —all told the story of wild confusion and death. Coleto had been a sad and bloody day for Texas.

Jackson lowered his head and spoke a prayer. The man called Bob voiced regret that all had not voted to fight the day before. Hiram looked down at his bloody foot. It was turning a frightening blue-green color. The Texan leader of the scouting party said he was glad to be alive to one day even the score. Then the ropes jerked taut and a cry of "*Viva* Santa Anna!" sounded. The hard march to Presidio La Bahia continued. It seemed endless, but at last the short Spanish church steeples, each with a cross on it, came into view, and then they were wading the San Antonio River, and next marching through the wagon entrance of the fortified patio wall of the fort as darkness fell.

"Right where we was before," one of the men said. "Cunnel Fannin named it Fort Defiance. Wonder what he calls it now."

A Mexican colonel ordered the prisoners taken to the storeroom some one hundred fifty feet from the chapel. There they were placed under guard, served a weak beef broth, and left to ponder their fate. But all were too tired for this. There would be time for such dismal conjecture tomorrow. For the present sleep was a luxury. But sound sleep was denied all but the most exhausted of the lot.

2

Jackson dozed, started, came instantly awake at every cry of the officer of the guard's *"Centinela alerta!"* The rasp of bugles and the marching of troops on the parade continued until far into the night. At around midnight the guards ushered in about twenty more prisoners. They were New Orleans Greys. In the light filtering through the barred windows, Jackson recognized several men he had met at the siege of San Antonio. One of them exclaimed:

"Doctor Jackson!" Then he said, "Reverend, you doctored my wound at Bexar. My brother here is cut up pretty bad, but the Mexican officers won't allow Texan doctors to attend our wounded until the Mexican wounded are cared for."

A growl of outrage at the enemy rose from Jackson's companions. The man called Bob asked Horatio if he was the preacher called Hellfire Jackson. "Well, I'll be—!" he said. "And you a doctor too? Well, I'll be—!" Jackson told him to go ahead and complete his sentence; a good "be damned" or two was appropriate under the circumstances. To the New Orleans Grey he said:

"I'll talk to the guard. Maybe he'll let me have a little medicine and clean rags."

The guard was too alert and suspicious. He pointed his bayonet at Jackson and babbled forth ominous Spanish. When the guard was changed a few hours later, Jackson appealed to the captain of the guard, who said he would talk to the colonel at once.

The morning of the twenty-third broke with a heavy mist obscuring the sky. Still no word had come from anyone regarding the wounded. Hiram groaned constantly and held his swollen foot with both hands. The New Orleans Grey continued to bleed. The prisoners met the leaden day with fear in their eyes. The same fear was on their tongues before cold beef broth came.

"Ever heard of Santa Anna's decree of December thirtieth, 1835?" a man asked. All had, including Jackson. They knew it stemmed from an attack on Tampico in November by exiled General Mexia and volunteers from New Orleans. Twenty-eight Americans had been captured, tried as pirates, convicted, and shot. Santa Anna had issued a bloody decree thinking he had found an excellent deterrent to Americans seeking to aid Texas.

"The decree says that all foreigners taken in arms against the government shall be treated as pirates and shot." Following a minute of heavy silence, the speaker said, "I reckon we're all going to be shot."

Jackson got to his feet. "The Lord gave man hope. Use it, men, else you'll die a thousand foolish deaths. Colonel Fannin didn't surrender you to a firing squad."

"The cunnel didn't have no choice, Jackson. Besides, he was wounded bad in the thigh when he dickered over surrender terms."

Further talk was interrupted by the arrival of troops. All prisoners except the wounded were herded out and moved to the west side of the fort. The wounded were taken to the *cuarteles* on the west wall. Jackson's request to remain with the wounded went unheeded. He shuffled along with the majority and was marched at bayonet point into a room already overcrowded with Fannin's soldiers. There the day dragged by, each hour seeming to lengthen into two or three. The smells of sweat and excreta and the oaths of the angry and the voiced despair of the hopeless all blended into a terrible nightmare that promised no relief.

Dawn of Thursday, March twenty-fourth, ushered in more of the same. A man dreamed and reviewed his life, shared a little of it with his fellow man. A soldier thought about a wife and a boy back in Tennessee or Alabama. Jane Wells and Wash and Jeremiah Whiteside and the open Pineywoods of East Texas played about in Jackson's head and then departed and left him once more a caged animal; left him wondering what had happened to the preacher who was supposed to influence men and console them in time of trouble.

That afternoon a priest came and walked among them and spoke of their return to the United States as soon as transportation by sea was available. He left cheer and hope in his wake, and Jackson felt that the Lord had reprimanded him. Rising, Horatio introduced himself and asked the padre to have him placed as a hospital attendant.

Later a group of Tennesseans, part of Major Miller's seventy men captured when they landed at Copano, were pushed inside the packed room. The major had offered his services as medical aide to Dr. Bernard, Dr. Ferguson, and Dr. Field. On Friday, March twenty-fifth, Colonel Ward and his Georgia battalion arrived at the fort under heavy Mexican guard. They had surrendered to General Urrea on the twenty-first of March.

"Well, Urrea's got the New Orleans Greys, the Alabama Red Rovers, and now the Georgia battalion," a lieutenant said dolefully. "We're all rounded up. It wouldn't surprise me to see him bringing in Sam Houston and his army next."

Jackson shed his dejection with a convincing "Don't ever believe that, sir! General Houston is playing this game to the north. Smart as a fox, he is. Not about to be trapped by Santa Anna's generals!"

He talked on and when he had finished there were cheers, however weak, and men began to take fresh hope for Texas. Lest they fall back into the old ruts of despair, Jackson began telling of his experiences in Texas. "Was always on the unpopular side. Preached for peace when Texans wanted war back in 1832." Men laughed, and they laughed louder when he completed his story of defending a horse thief with "A hog—a hog—a hog!"

Toward noon of Friday, Jackson purchased coffee and bread from the camp followers. Although it took his last money, the enjoyment it brought to the prisoners gave him a feeling that it was the best purchase of his entire life.

The sun was scarcely one hour above the horizon on Saturday, March twenty-sixth, when the priest came for Jackson. With him were one of General Urrea's officers, Colonel Guerrier, and Dr. Bernard of Fannin's army. The colonel, a man of benevolent face, said in English:

"Reverend Jackson, we are in need of medical aides for both our army and the Texans. I place you in the service of Dr. Bernard and Dr. Shackleford."

This marked the beginning of an eventful day at the fort. Dr. Bernard took notice of Jackson's ability to cheer the wounded Texans even as he applied medicines and bandages with experienced hands. Dr. Shackleford, captain of a company of the Red Rovers and surgeon and physician by trade, was also impressed, and when at noon Colonel Guerrier asked if the preacher qualified, both doctors admitted that he did indeed.

Early in the afternoon Dr. Bernard took Jackson to a small room in the chapel. There Horatio saw Fannin, who had just been returned from Copano. While they dressed his wound, Fannin spoke of the kind treatment accorded him by Mexican officers. "Especially Colonel Holzinger," he said, almost smiling. "The colonel thinks after talks with General Urrea that we may all be given a speedy release and returned to New Orleans."

Dr. Bernard smiled. "Do you believe it, sir?"

"No," Fannin replied. "But it's the best news I've heard in a long time."

Almost in the same sentence he said to Jackson, "So they got you too, Hellfire. Never will forget you the day we fought off four hundred Mexicans at Concepción. But why are you here?"

Jackson then handed him the message from Houston. Fannin read it, winced, and finally said, "I hesitated too long. I should have obeyed Houston's order of the eleventh. But I divided my forces and—" He fell into dejected silence and Dr. Bernard began to talk of other things.

It was idle conversation for the weary, wounded, and troubled Fannin. He seemed to relive his military errors before saying, "In the terms of capitulation on the battlefield I was told that as soon as possible we would be sent to New Orleans under parole not to serve against Mexico again. Moreover, I think you, Dr. Bernard, heard General Urrea assure me that there was no known instance where a prisoner of war who had trusted to the clemency of the Mexican government had lost his life, and that he would recommend to General Santa Anna acceptance of the terms proposed by us and that he was confident of obtaining Santa Anna's approval within eight days." He added:

"This is the sixth day."

Dr. Bernard said quietly, "There is talk among the men that you surrendered at discretion without any guarantee whatsoever."

Fannin almost shouted, "You tell them I did no such damn thing!"

"Good." Bernard grinned. "That outburst should help your circulation, sir."

3

The chapel bell was tolling the hour of four when a carriage rolled through the gates past the sentries, its smart escort riding ahead and at the rear.

Jackson was carrying supplies at the time, and as his guard paused at attention he stopped also. A handsome officer alighted, then handed down a lovely Spanish woman. Pretty of face and figure, she seemed at the moment all eyes. Large and curious, they took in everything about her, from walls to officers, troops at stiff attention, and on to the round-faced, short-statured Colonel José Nicolas de la Portilla, Commander of the Post of Goliad, who stood with his aides to greet one of General Urrea's officers and his lady just arrived from Urrea's headquarters at Refugio.

Then she and her husband were ushered into the fort. The guard nudged Jackson forward, and he moved on with a memory of her spirited face. It was as if a cool refreshing wind had blown in to relieve the fort of its depressing stillness. He thought no more about the arrival of Señora Francisca Alvarez, as Dr. Bernard identified her later, until just before sunset when he and Dr. Field entered a prison room to carry a sick man to the hospital.

To their surprise, the taffeta-clad beauty was there also. Eyes flashing, she was dressing down Colonel Guerrier in rapid Spanish for allowing these prisoners to lie there so tightly bound with cords that their blood circulation was checked.

"Mother of God!" she exclaimed. "I will not allow it!" To prove it, she began to unbind the Texans with her own small hands.

The colonel thereupon ordered all cords cut and, at her insistence, demanded food and drink be served the prisoners at once.

"*Gracias! Gracias*, Angel!" a Texan cried as she departed.

Turning to the colonel, she said in English as they passed Jackson and Dr. Field, "These Texans have been described to me as rebels and heretics, the worst and most abandoned of men. But I'm beginning to wonder about our own people. Such barbarity!"

By nightfall she had visited every prison room in the fort. She looked down her imperious nose at the guards and her officer escort and ordered sanitary measures in effect at once. Also the prisoners should be given better food than just thin beef broth. She earned the title prisoners gave her that night: "Angel of Goliad."

At nine that evening all doctors and aides were working on the Mexican wounded. Some were dying. Others cried out in pain. The reek of human flesh and waste and sweat seemed unbearable to doctors and helpers. A few of the latter did retch. One of the Alabama volunteers tried to reach the outer door. A musket butt floored him. As Jackson and all the medical staff looked at the fallen man, Señora Alvarez appeared and bent over the lad. A minute later she said:

"You are all Americanos! Yet you are merciful to the enemy. May God bless you."

As she rose, Colonel Guerrier appeared, very agitated of face and manner. He said something to her in low tones. She paled and stared at him in speechless amazement a moment.

"No! Oh no!" she cried out weakly, clutching at his arm. *"Es imposible!"*

"Colonel Portilla just received it, Señora," the colonel replied gravely.

She stood weakly, as though she were about to faint. Then she turned her gaze from him, made a sign of the cross, accepted Guerrier's arm, and walked away.

4

Jackson awoke early next morning. It was Sunday, March twenty-seventh. "Palm Sunday," he said to himself. "A good time to speak to the Lord." He moved quietly to a window, so as not to disturb the doctors and aides who were quartered in the same room, and knelt to pray. His dawn prayer was never finished. . . .

The sounds of marching feet and orders flung in English and Spanish suddenly drew his attention. He rose curiously and looked outside. The prisoners were being marched outside the walls in columns of twos. On each side were dismounted cavalrymen of the crack Tres Villas Battalion. From the Texan ranks came a joyous shout:

"Goin' after beef! No more broth, just good meat."

Then the body of men were marched off on the Victoria road. The prisoners included the New Orleans Greys. No sooner were they halted a hundred yards away than another group of prisoners appeared in the same formation with the Battalion of Yucatan as guards. Jackson recognized many of the prisoners. They were from the Georgia Battalion, and were pointed up toward the San Antonia River ford crossing toward Bexar. They too seemed in excellent spirits, and Jackson gathered from the scrambled bits of talk they were out to gather wood and considered the trip a lark.

Suddenly the door to the doctors quarters opened and Colonel Guerrier appeared. His normal geniality seemed lacking as he told Jackson to rouse Dr. Bernard and Dr. Shackleford at once. Jackson thought his expression unusually grave, but said nothing. The doctors got up immediately, as did all aides, including Jackson's friend and medical helper, William Scurlock of San Augustine. When all stood before the colonel, he said, frowning and staring at the window:

"Come with me."

That was the extent of his speech. The medical staff accepted his laconic order, a signal departure from his normal greeting, in silence but with exchanges of puzzled glances. They followed him to the gate of the fort, where Major Miller and his seventy Tennesseans were assembled. Again Guerrier faced them, pointed to his quarters some three hundred yards from the fort.

"Go to my place with Major Miller's company and wait for me there. Do not leave until I get there."

So saying, he turned and walked away. The medical staff then followed Miller's company to the place. Along the way Dr. Bernard said he supposed a number of sick or wounded had been transferred to the colonel's spreading quarters. Dr. Shackleford agreed, adding that it was odd that the entire staff should be shifted there. Then Dr. Field joined them. Striking Jackson a friendly tap on the back, he said:

"Taking them out for a Palm Sunday morning prayer, Hellfire?"

"Not a bad idea, Doctor. But a Protestant preacher prayin' in this place might put all of us before a firin' squad."

Then the group noticed the two long companies of prisoners under strong guard, one on the Victoria road, the other on the Bexar road. As the doctors and aides entered Colonel Guerrier's low-walled patio, sounds from the fort behind them drew the attention of all to a third company of prisoners moving out the gate. This group was marched southwest down the San Patricio road. As the medical staff paused to listen to a song Shackleford's own men were singing, the doctor-captain voiced his curiosity:

"Now what the devil are my boys so happy about this morning?"

"Maybe they were told they'd be going home in a few days," Dr. Field replied. "I heard a few officers of Colonel Portilla's staff hinting as much at the other hospital this morning."

"Then let's pray it's the truth," Shackleford said earnestly.

Then all three companies, on a given signal, began to march. Bugles blasted the early morning quiet. They hushed as suddenly. The rent healed and the tramp of marching feet sounded less raucous and more rhythmic. The doctors and aides entered the spacious stone house of Colonel Guerrier.

A young Mexican officer in immaculate uniform bowed them in as Miller's men were directed to the rear buildings. "Welcome, gentlemen," he said in English. "I am Lieutenant Martinez, educated in Bardstown, Kentucky." Smiling, he turned and clapped his hands twice. "Coffee for the gentlemen! *Pronto!*"

He kept up a lively run of talk, about the weather, the work General Urrea had ordered in the rebuilding of the town. Coffee and small sweet cakes were served. A mockingbird sang just outside the window. The day seemed to be off to a good beginning, Jackson decided, despite the chatter of young Martinez. Then Dr. Bernard managed to inject a question:

"Where are the patients, Lieutenant?"

"Patients? Oh, I see. Do not concern yourself with professional duties at this time, Doctor. There are no patients here."

Dr. Bernard put down his cup and made as if to rise. "Please, Doctor," Martinez said. "Colonel Guerrier's instructions that you are to remain here were most positive. He will arrive soon, so I suggest you be patient. Now shall I order more coffee?"

At that moment two sheets covering something in a corner of the room stirred. Jackson started. Martinez observed this, and calmly ordered the two concealed men to end their masquerade. When two Texans emerged, the lieutenant said, "Colonel Guerrier was quite pleased with their carpenter work yesterday and decided to give them a rest."

If the early morning was full of surprises—and it seemed they were fast overlapping—another came fast on the heels of the last one to give the prisoner doctors and aides a start that brought them to their feet:

A rapid volley of gunfire sounded from beyond the fort. Shackleford asked, "What's that?"

"Oh that?" Martinez smiled. "Just some of the soldiers discharging their muskets in order to clean them."

As shouts and cries in English followed the volley, Jackson rushed to a window. Through openings in the trees he saw prisoners running in every direction, Mexican soldiers in swift pursuit. Rifles continued to bark. The Texans were being shot down. Men on their knees, pleading for mercy, were run through with bayonets.

"Oh, Lord, no!" Jackson cried out. "It can't be, Lord!" He closed his eyes, praying that when he opened them again the horrible scene would vanish. It did not, however. He stared, still unable to reconcile the sight to reality. Piercing screams rent the air of Palm Sunday. Powder smoke hung like a devil's pall over La Bahía. Closer, a Texan grappled for his life with a Mexican soldier until another Mexican cut him down with a saber. It was impossible, but it was so. The butchers kept up their work.

Suddenly Colonel Guerrier appeared. He was every bit as
pale and distressed as the terribly shaken doctors and aides
who were witnessing the slaughter of their countrymen. He
slumped into a chair and gazed out of unfocused eyes a moment. Then in the distance, from up the Bexar road, came
the muffled sounds of gunfire. He crossed himself, grimaced,
then met the shocked glances of the doctors and aides.

"I had no part in this. This is not my order, nor did I execute it. You are safe here, because we need doctors. That is
why I ordered you to come here."

Then he told them the order had reached Colonel Portilla
last evening. It came from Santa Anna himself: The "perfid-
ious foreigners" should be executed immediately. A conflicting order had reached Portilla two hours later from General
Urrea in Refugio: The prisoners should be teated with consideration, especially their leader Fannin, and should be used
in rebuilding the town. But Santa Anna was the man to obey.

As the sounds of gunfire reached their ears from the direction of San Patricio, Jackson felt a tightening of his throat
muscles. His hands closed into fists and opened only to con-
strict again. The desire to do something, to cry out, to run,
to go to the aid of the prisoners, anything but stand there in
helpless agony, was overpowering. Now Dr. Bernard was saying, "And Miller's men?"

"They did not bear arms against Mexico. They are safe."
Shackleford said, "The wounded prisoners?"

"Surely they won't be shot," Colonel Guerrier replied. "But
I don't know."

Jackson could bear no more. He broke and raced to the
door. Oblivious of shouts from the colonel and the doctors to
stop, he flung the door open and ran as fast as he could toward the fort.

5

Jackson reached the gate of the fort just as the soldiers began dragging the wounded prisoners out to the parade. He
stood utterly dazed by what met his eyes and ears. Then he
turned away from it. The screams of men unable to rise and
run, the crack of rifles and stabs of bayonets were more than
he could bear. He sat down and lowered his head.

When he looked up again they were marching Colonel
Fannin out to the parade. All guns ceased firing. The troops
stood at attention. Colonel Portilla stood a little apart from
the firing squad. Fannin stood erect.

Then someone touched Jackson. He recoiled instinctively

and leaped to his feet, suddenly aware that he was in danger. As he turned to see who had touched him, expecting to be shot or stabbed in the next second of time, he saw Señora Alvarez. In her face was horror and alarm, though she was no longer looking at Jackson. A volley sounded, and she covered her face with hands.

Jackson saw Fannin fall; saw his body picked up and tossed into the heap with the Texan wounded who had just been murdered. Señora Alvarez broke Jackson's fixed gaze with:

"Are you a fool, sir? Why aren't you with the other medical men at Colonel Guerrier's quarters?" Without pausing for any reply, she said, "Come with me—quickly! Perhaps I can hide you!"

She raced toward the door of Colonel Portilla's quarters, Jackson at her heels. They had no sooner reached the interior than the colonel and his staff rounded the corner.

CHAPTER 25

The chapel bell of Presidio La Bahía was tolling the hour of noon. The day, Tuesday, March twenty-ninth, 1836, was bright and peaceful. All was quiet at Goliad. The fires that burned the Texan dead still smoked, though the sounds of bugles and marching feet were missing on the parade. The day before Colonel Portilla had departed with his troops for the coast, leaving only a small garrison to guard the fort and attend the hospital.

As the last stroke of the bell sounded, a carriage appeared at the entrance of the command's quarters. Señora Alvarez moved toward it, her hand at her husband's arm. She smiled up at him and scoffed as he once again urged her to double the escort of two cavalrymen. Then, as he handed her into the carriage, she turned her glance on the cart that carried her belongings. A saddled horse without rider stood a few lengths behind the cart with a lead rope about its neck; just in case she grew tired of the carriage, she said, smiling disarmingly.

"My best to all in Matamoros, Francisca," he said. "And General Urrea will see that you secure swift passage."

Carriage and cart rumbled through the gate and took the road south to Refugio. As they disappeared from view, Dr. Bernard turned from the hospital window and heaved a sigh of relief.

"That's the way I feel also," Dr. Field said. "So far, so good. We can only hope now that he gets through the Mexican patrols and reaches General Houston."

While the pair talked of the great lady whom the Lord had sent to bloody Goliad in time to save at least a dozen lives, the "Angel of Goliad" scanned the road ahead and behind the carriage for any signs of a Mexican cavalry troop. Although Colonel Portilla was nowhere about, she did not trust him even in his absence. He was not only executioner in cold blood, he was a most suspicious man. Twice she had felt his cold eyes upon her—once just after she had hidden several of Fannin's men on the parapet the night before the massacre, and again after she had pleaded with Colonel Guerrier to go against orders of powerful Santa Anna and save as many lives as possible. What a terrible enemy Portilla could be!

"Especially if he learned of what's in the cart," she said aloud.

The cart was far behind. It was better that way. Manuel, the driver, would be blind. Of course, a Mexican patrol might open his eyes and loosen his tongue. She decided to keep the cart in view for another hour or so, and advised her uniformed driver accordingly.

"*Madre mia!* Why do I do this thing?" she said to herself, glancing back toward Goliad. "Just because a foolish preacher-doctor refuses to remain a prisoner and vows he will never accept release under parole not to serve against Mexico again. These Americanos! But one must admire them."

The miles were long and time passed slowly. She was sleepy, but sleep was impossible until she got rid of her cargo. She looked at her watch. It was almost three. Then she began to wonder if old Manuel back there was dozing with the reins in his hands. A hill separated the carriage from the cart. A quarter hour later the cart poked up into view. The saddled horse was no longer tied to the cart.

Señora Alvarez drew in a deep breath and smiled. "*Válgate Dios,* Señor Jackson! Now I can relax."

2

Once in the saddle, Jackson gave the wrinkled old Mexica a "*Gracias,* Manuel!" and struck out due east. Not daring t move up to the Goliad-Victoria road and risk encounter wit ranging Mexican patrols, he picked his way cautiously ove hills and through wooded areas. Often he paused to scan hi horizon in every direction before moving on.

For company were memories, both horrible and good. Th massacre at Goliad preyed on his mind. It angered him anew The slaughter of three hundred forty-two defenseless me continued to leave him sick and weak. But not all Mexican were Santa Annas and Portillas. He thanked God for that thanked the Lord for Señora Alvarez and Colonel Guerrie who had saved many of the prisoners from the butchers. An to the senora, for the risk she had taken in his behalf, wen his eternal gratitude. He would never forget to ask the Lor to bless the grand lady.

The powdery dust fell away behind him and the ground be came muddy. Each stream he came to was swollen. He forde Coleto Creek just before nightfall and made camp in a dra on higher ground. Before dawn next day he was in the saddle Impatient of time and tempted to cut due north, he though of his capture in this area and decided to ride on east. Finding the Guadalupe River a raging torrent far out of its banks and with no way to go but north or south, he headed nort and crossed the Goliad road east of Victoria, hoping to for the river ahead. Several hours later the crossing was effecte but as he topped a small rise just beyond the east bank of th river he almost stumbled into the camp of a Mexican cavalr detachment not fifty yards below.

A shudder played up and down Jackson's spine. Althoug the Mexicans were not mounted and their muskets wer stacked, they had him between them and the river, with impossible terrain in any direction but straight ahead. Fortunately they had not seen him. Pondering the situation, he sai under his breath:

"Lord, if You were caught between the devil and the Guadalupe old Hellfire would sure help You out. So You'd bette do the same for me, 'cause I'm riding down amongst 'em."

Digging his heels into the horse's flanks, he loosed an unearthly Cherokee yell and charged down the slope with musket up and firing. Before his bullet struck a Mexican in th shoulder and spun him about, the surprised troop began t scatter in all directions. Cries of "Me no Goliad!" reached Jackson's ears. Then, to his amazement, he saw them raise hands over their heads. They were surrendering! The Lord had really come through, but in doing so had created a problem. Just what would Hellfire Jackson do with a dozen prisoners?

He didn't pause to answer the question, but raced toward the Mexican horses picketed close ahead. They broke loose and he chased them to the top of the next rise. As he nudged his mount over the hill, a Mexican fired. Jackson heard the whine of a bullet, and almost as suddenly a popping sound at his right ear. He was down into a draw when a stinging sensation registered in his mind. Touching his ear, he felt blood, and next, a hole neatly drilled through the concha. A close call, but . . .

Now that would be something for Miss Jane to see! Wouldn't it now? And laughing Texans would no doubt ask him if it whistled in a norther.

Wiping blood, he looked back often to see if he was being pursued. He saw nothing and slowed his tired horse. As the afternoon wore on, a cold rain began to fall. His ear burned and he winced. He rode on, now wondering where Sam Houston's army would be. The news of Fannin's defeat at Coleto had no doubt reached the general by this time. If so, Houston would probably fall back from the Colorado.

There was a house ahead. He would stop and ask questions. He found the place not only deserted; it was partially burned. A table had been set and stale food filled the plates. It told a story of hurried flight from Santa Anna's armies. In the smokehouse Jackson found hams. He was hungry, and a hungry man takes chances. He built a fire and fried ham. He was eating when something jabbed him in the back.

"Sit still, stranger, and you won't get shot." Jackson obeyed. "Now who the hell are you and what you doin' here?" When Jackson answered, the gun was removed from his backbone and the man slumped into a chair. "So you're Hellfire Jackson. Have you got any more ham?"

"I have. But who are you?"

"One of Deaf Smith's scouts. Was detailed to watch for the approach of Mexican troops down in this neck of the woods after Houston got news of Colonel Fannin's defeat. Houston heard about it on the twenty-fifth, five days back."

Jackson learned that Houston's force on the twenty-fifth of March numbered over twelve hundred men; that he camped on the east bank of the Colorado, with Mexican General Sesma on the other side of the river with about fourteen hundred men; that the Texans were clamoring to flight and threatening to depose Houston because he refused to attack Sesma.

The scout learned of the massacre at Goliad. Unable to believe it at first, he finally shook his head sadly and said, "Well, that leaves only Houston's army. With Sesma backed up by General Gaona to the north and General Urrea with no opposition to the south, and Santa Anna ready to head his own army to support them, it don't look good. No it don't. Reckon you know what's bound to happen, don't you?"

"What?" Jackson asked.

"General Houston's going to retreat to the Brazos. Got to. And when he does all hell is going to break loose. Houston's army is in bad temper with him already, and more'n likely the men will mutiny. They're rarin' to fight. And whether they do or not, everybody on the Brazos will join up with the folks from the Colorado already running from the Mexicans and rush like mad toward the Sabine. Like I said, it don't look good, does it?"

Jackson frowned and gazed forlornly at the cold rain outside. He could not argue against all the scout had said; he could only hope that the man erred in his prediction. He thought of Sam Houston and next of Jane, and of both in flight. Then he was on his feet and moving to the door.

"Where you going?" the scout asked.

"To find out whether you're right or wrong, mister."

3

On the morning of Thursday, April first, Jane did not go to the schoolhouse. There was no reason to go. The day before only one child had appeared. With more bad news from upriver late Wednesday, school was out of the question.

The slow chilling rain still came down, and the Brazos River continued its rise. She looked up at the low gray skies, then moved to a window across the room. The road fronting her aunt's blacksmith shop was clogged with wagons and carts, some with wooden wheels. Refugees from the west, families who had left their land and crops and homes, all fleeing from the advancing Mexican armies, now reported to be on the east side of the Colorado; fleeing because Sam Houston had sent word that they should burn their homes and take their belongings and move toward the Sabine and to the safety of the United States.

Jane stood with forefinger massaging the cleft of her chin. A shiver of dread ran through her as she recalled the happenings of the last five days.

The Saturday before, Houston had begun his retreat from the Colorado. On Palm Sunday the army had risen up in protest of Houston's leadership. Captain Moseley Baker had led the uprising. Colonel Sidney Sherman had joined in. As the men groused and waited, Houston had put an end to their ominous threats, for a time at least, by marching them all the way to the Brazos. Then a recurrence of mutiny. On Monday, March twenty-eighth, the army, camped a mile from San Felipe, had refused to obey Houston, had thrown down their guns, demanded to be marched out to fight General Sesma instead of retreating upriver. Houston had ignored their shouts and insults and had marched them upriver.

"And yesterday," she mused aloud, "the word came that Houston was setting up a permanent camp up at Groce's Plantation. Why, when we downriver are left unprotected from any Mexican advance?" There was no answer to this, so she turned her gaze away from the street, wondering what sort of news would reach Velasco on this first day of April.

"Miss Jane!" Wash yelled from the front porch. "Oh, Miss Jane! Jes' heared Marse Jackson done got sent to Goliad by Mistuh General Houston back a spell!"

Jane started. The news of Fannin's defeat and surrender had reached Velasco last Monday. She was hoping, fervently, that Jackson was alive and not a prisoner.

"You can hear anything, Wash," she replied.

"Yes, ma'am, I reckins. But what Miss Sally done hear a few minutes ago sholy got her upset some. She say tell yo'all ebberbody done decided fo' to git out o' Velasco right now. She say fo' us to git to packin' up things and put em' in de wagon."

Jane felt herself go cold all over. She bit her lip and tried to put down the fear creeping over and through her. Managing to keep it out of her voice, she said:

"Why, Wash?"

"Mexicans comin' she say. What I do fust, Miss Jane?"

A few minutes later Bucktooth Sal entered the house storming forth her opinion of Sam Houston: "A hell of a general he is! Him upriver and General Sesma's Mexicans movin' toward the lower Brazos! Why don't he fight? And why are you standin' there doin' nothin', Jane Wells? You, Wash, hitch them mules to the wagon and pull up for the things we can take! Don't just stand—!"

In the hour that followed she flung orders right and left; she put Captain Herrick to work loading bedding, clothing, and provisions. Then she left the house and doused the fires in the blacksmith shop. She returned, mouthing her regard for the fool townspeople who had hauled their furniture to thickets along the river and covered it with brush. Captain Herrick finally said:

"All right, Sal! Calm down! The water ain't shoalin' you yet and it's a good hull you got under ye for the trip."

"Is that so?" Bucktooth Sal flung back at him. "Well, I'm tellin' you one thing, mister schoonerman, and that's to get a gun and go fight them damn Mexicans! Understand?"

Before the sun set their covered wagon joined the seemingly endless train of wagons and carts filled with meager possessions, panic-stricken women and children, slaves and old men, all moving north into the night toward Harrisburg some fifty miles away.

They kept going all that dark night. Jane and her aunt and Wash took turns driving. Not a one of them could sleep. They moved at a snail's pace into and out of ravines, following a bobbing lantern ahead, gazing at the muddy road and overcast sky, the two women trying to forget that all they had worked for in their years in Texas had been abandoned. Bucktooth Sal broke the silence with:

"I'd like to wrap a damn anvil around Santa Anna's head!" A minute later she was asking what had happened up ahead to stop the wagons. One had lost a wheel. Soon the wagons behind were cutting a path around it. A little girl sobbed and clung to her mother's dress as the people moved on past. She was afraid the Mexicans would arrive any minute.

Morning broke clear, but soon after the stop for a hasty breakfast the sun gradually disappeared once more, this time behind a cloud of dust to the east. Soon a sound like distant thunder rolled across the prairie. As it drew closer, the very earth seemed to tremble. Slaves on foot at the sides or behind their owners' wagons fell to their knees in fear and prayed until a man astraddle a mule rode down the line to advise that the dust and rumbling noise was caused by a moving herd of buffalo.

That afternoon it began to rain. At first it came down hard pelting the animals, wagons, slaves, and roadway, and shutting off visibility. It increased with flashes of ragged lightning and a bombardment of thunder. Then the battle of the winds ended and the rain blew in cold out of the north. By dusk it had settled down to a slow, steady drizzle that seemed to chill one to the bone.

There was little rest that miserably cold night. A frightening rumor ran the train that Santa Anna's General Sesma had outflanked the retreating Texas Army and was crossing the Brazos in swift pursuit of the civilians. As a result, slaves began to moan and cry out to the Lord, and drivers flung whips frantically at their oxen and mules in an effort to go around wagons ahead. As mud flew and sucked at the feet of plodding animals, two wagons ground together, one losing a wheel, the other turning over on its side, spilling belongings and a baby sleeping in a barrel bed. A mother's piercing scream quivered off into the night.

Bucktooth Sal had scarcely jerked her mules to a halt and cried, "Holy hell!" than Jane leaped to the ground with lantern in hand. A great blob of mud struck her when a horse veered past, but she reached the baby and was wiping its face with her skirt when the mother appeared. Jane learned that the poor woman had lost her husband at the Alamo. Now her wagon lay in twisted ruins. Jane and her aunt took the mother and child aboard their wagon and moved on with the fear-driven, panic-stricken refugees until the disorganized train ground to a stop near daybreak because the weary Texans were minus the strength and the will to continue the flight.

The gray dawn revealed slaves asleep in the wet bushes alongside the deep ruts, and women and old men staring out of tired, uncaring eyes. Through the heavy mist that fell cold and collected in beads on every surface, Jane saw a man sitting bare of head in a hide-bottom chair, elbows on knees and staring forlornly at his overloaded wagon. He continued to sit in silence after men unloaded it and shoved and pulled with the mules to free it and finally told him it was no use. The poor man was Jonathan Mundy. Jane went to him and asked about his wife.

"I buried Nora back a ways."

Jane looked from the beaten man to her own mud-splattered skirt and hands, then to the fire her aunt had somehow got going. Suddenly she forgot that she was weary and troubled and afraid. There was a pot over the fire and the tangy mesquite-wood smoke should warm and cheer one. "Come, Mr. Mundy," she said. "We'd be grateful if you'd ride with us."

The cold mist continued to fall. The train finally began to creep forward, leaving many broken and mud-fast wagons behind. With the weeping mother and baby and the widowed Mundy in their wagon, Jane emulated scores of other women whose conveyances were running over. She got out of the wagon and walked. Mud tugged at her ankles and sucked at her shoes until she could hardly lift her feet. She trudged on, leaving the road only long enough to pick a lonely wild flower that dared raise its head to announce spring in the midst of the terrible thing that was happening to Texas.

Late that afternoon the wagons stalled and clogged the road a mile from a swollen creek. Camp for the night was forced upon the refugees. Wash foraged for wood and, finding none, returned to the wagon dreading Bucktooth Sal's scolding voice. She only glared at him, however, then proceeded to take a rocking chair she had brought with her to Texas and told Wash to use it for firewood. "It was my mother's chair," she said, wiping a tear from her eye. Then, looking at Wash, she yelled:

"Well, what the hell you waiting for?"

When the last of their bacon was frying, a rider in fringed buckskin stopped his horse and eyed the skillet longingly. Finally he said, "It sure smells good to a man who hasn't et a bite all day."

Bucktooth Sal ran him up and down with a sharp eye before asking who he might be.

"Army scout. One of Deaf Smith's boys. And he don't give a man no rest, ma'am. No sooner I hit the lower Brazos after a ride back from the Guadalupe than a messenger down from him and General Houston heads me for Galveston Bay to look for a schooner with supplies for the starvin' army."

"Well, you see what we got here, scout, so if you're a mind to eat it up from me and my bunch, get down and help yourself."

The scout joined them about the fire, but only after taking a ham from a sack tied to his saddle. He presented it to Sally "in swap" for a bite, drawing from her a vow that he was more an angel than scout. As they ate, Sally said it was too bad that Fannin had to surrender, that if he had held the Mexicans at Coleto she'd still be shoeing mules in Velasco.

"Reckon you would, ma'am. But you don't know what happened to Fannin's men on Palm Sunday, I reckon." Sally didn't, and the scout launched into the story of the massacre at Goliad. As Jane and Wash listened with horror, he said:

"It's hard to believe, but over three hundred of Fannin's men were shot down in cold blood. Even the wounded. All killed in one hour that Sunday mornin'."

"Where the devil did you hear that cock-and-bull yarn?" Bucktooth Sal demanded.

"Heard it first from a preacher I come up on this side of the Guadalupe River. He saw it and two days later escaped.

The only reason he weren't shot was because he helped doctor the Mexican wounded. Then I verified it from—"

"A preacher?" Jane said. "Know who he was?"

"I do, ma'am. He was Hellfire Jackson. You've heard of him, I reckon. Most folks have. Anyhow, the day I come up on him he had a hole shot in his ear. Last I seen of him he was ridin' northeast, up toward Houston's army, I reckon."

"Praise de Lawd!" Wash exclaimed. "Marse Jackson he still alive!"

Jane rose. She looked at the flower she had plucked earlier, smiled, and told her aunt the nightmare of flight would surely be over soon.

"Yeah? Reckon you think Hellfire Jackson will stop the war."

"He will help," Jane replied. "You can count on that."

Bucktooth Sal ignored this. She was telling the scout that with Houston taking it easy up in the canebrake thickets of the Brazos, and that since Texas had nothing to stop Santa Anna, it appeared to her that the horrors of the runaway scrape had only begun.

CHAPTER 26

Shortly after nightfall of April sixth, a tall lean, mud-splattered man, with a week's growth of matted beard on his face, rode into General Houston's camp at Groce's Ferry. He looked neither to the left nor to the right, but walked his horse through the slow, cold rain past the few bivouac fires the dejected soldiers kept going. Men gazed curiously at him and one soldier called out, "Now, who the hell be you, stranger?" There was no reply, and the man said, "He looks as done in as his hoss, so I reckon he's a Texan." The rider moved on toward a tent where a lantern shed its yellow glow through the rain. Reaching the tent, he slid off his horse and said to the guard:

"I want to see the general. Tell him I'm the bearer of important news from Goliad."

"The general's busy. And he's madder'n a wet hornet."

"You go tell him anyhow."

"He'll chew you up, mister."

"Son, did you ever hear of a man named Daniel in the Bible? Well, they tossed him to the lions long before my time. So you go tell the general I want to see him right now."

The guard entered the tent. He returned shortly. "General Houston will see you, Mr. Daniel."

Houston stood with back to tent flap, hands behind him holding a sheet of paper. He slowly brought the paper up and read the message aloud: " 'Sir: The enemy are laughing you to scorn. You must fight them. You must retreat no farther. The country expects you to fight. The salvation of the country depends upon your doing so.' " Turning to his secretary, he said:

"You'll reply to President Burnet's urgent demand as follows: 'When my men wanted to march downriver instead of up the Brazos, I consulted none—held no councils of war. If I err, the blame is mine.' "

Pausing there, he glanced at the visitor. He took a closer look. When the light of recognition played in his eyes, he said, "What's the important news from Goliad, Jackson?"

"Maybe you'd better sit down, General, unless you've already heard about what happened at Goliad on Palm Sunday."

Houston did not move. His piercing eyes remained fixed on Jackson. Nor did he speak. He stood with no change of expression whatever as he listened to Jackson's account of the massacre of three hundred forty-two prisoners. What he was thinking, he kept to himself, hid it behind his flinty, inscrutable mask. That it struck as a terrible blow to this the one man who carried the hopes and the burden of Texas in her darkest hour, one could not for a moment doubt. And the fact that he could contain himself in all dignity and poise was, as Jackson admitted later, something to see. When the story had been told in full, Houston continued to stand silent a long minute. Then he said:

"I don't believe a word of it."

Jackson started. "It's the truth, sir."

Houston called the guard. "Arrest this man and see that he talks to no one."

"But, sir—!" Jackson protested.

"I deem it expedient to do this, Hellfire."

2

Jackson accepted his arrest and confinement in stoic silence. While he thought the general had thanked him in rather high-handed manner for plodding across rain-sheeted prairies and quagmires of almost bottomless mud to advise him of the massacre, he realized also that Houston had wanted to suppress the news lest it precipitate another panic. Jackson didn't think it would. But then he wasn't a general of the army either. So he shrugged it off and thought of Jane and Wash, wondering if they had been caught up in the flight of colonists toward the Sabine. Most likely they had, he reflected, since it was common knowledge that all settlements on the lower Brazos had been evacuated.

Jackson was released two days later and assigned to Dr. Labadie's staff to care for the sick. Within minutes he learned why Houston no longer held him under guard. Stragglers who had escaped the firing squad at Goliad had arrived in camp with the story of the massacre. The men reacted in various ways once the shock left their faces. Some simply sat down and stared vacuously at the wet ground. Others, realizing that nothing stood between their fleeing families and the advancing Mexicans to the south, simply picked up their guns and left the army to go to protect their loved ones in flight. But the majority were angry, very angry. They wanted vengeance and they let it be known that they were going to fight and soon. They would not be put off again. Whipped into a frenzy, they decided to call on General Houston.

Jackson saw them stop at Houston's tent, saw General Thomas J. Rusk, Secretary of War, emerge with Houston, and he heard a man say after saluting Houston, "Hello, Boss. What do you intend to do with us? Will you march us across the Sabine and give up the country? Or will you stop somewhere and fight? We want to know, so we will know what to do. We have families, and if we are going to give up the country we want to convey them back to the United States where the Mexicans can't hurt them. But if we are to fight, we want to stand by you to the death."

A hushed quiet hung over the group. Houston stood bare of head looking at their spokesman. "You men are too impatient," he said. "I am done retreating. I am going to encamp you here a little longer. Victory is sure, and you shall have as much fighting as you can eat over."

The promise to stand and fight spread throughout the camp. It was met with doubt by many. The majority believed him, however, and around the campfires a gleam of hope was in evidence. It held, suspenseful, when late in the day scouts rode into camp with news that Santa Anna himself at the head of an army of twelve hundred was building barges to cross the Brazos at San Felipe. Here was Houston's chance to fight. But would he fight?

The question was tossed back and forth for two days. Meanwhile scouts arrived from downriver and reported that Santa Anna had been unable to cross the swollen Brazos, that Captain Moseley Baker's company had kept up a steady fire against the Mexicans, causing the thwarted Santa Anna to bring up artillery to shell Baker's position, but without any success whatever. Then Santa Anna took five hundred men and moved downriver to find an easier crossing, leaving Sesma with about seven hundred troops.

"Now's the boss's chance to go down and mop up old Sesma!"

As Houston continued to drill his men and reorganize his dwindling army, Jackson doctored the malaria patients as best he could and wondered as all in camp when the general would attack the enemy. Then one day the order to break camp was received. The army marched a little distance southeast and made camp. On the morning of the sixteenth, Houston began his march to the east. The road was clogged with refugees rushing in the mud toward the Sabine and safety. The army plodded on through the rain and mud, grumbling, mutinous. The leaders had made a decision, and Colonel Burleson and Colonel Sherman and Captain Baker and Captain Martin were prepared to execute it the next day.

The road ahead forked at Spring Creek. One direction would take the army east toward the Sabine; the other pointed southeast to Harrisburg, the destination of Santa Anna, the scouts reported. If Houston took the upper road, to the east, he would be abandoning Texas. If he did this they would depose him. It was that simple.

Jackson had overheard this and more. The leaders believed Houston was treating President Burnet, who had sent Secretary of War Rusk to order him to fight, with utter contempt. They had access also to Santa Anna's note of threat to Houston, that he was going to Harrisburg to "hang the president of the so-called republic and his cabinet and smoke Houston out." They knew that should Houston desert the government at this time to the fate Santa Anna had promised he was not the man Texas needed, nor was he fit to command the army of Texas.

Jackson heard, wondered, and worried that night. He walked back and forth when not attending the sick. He approached Houston's tent only to turn back. A preacher, a mere private in the army, didn't advise a general. Then who could talk to Houston? The answer came:

"The Lord can, that's who."

Horatio walked to the edge of the camp. When a sentry

challenged him, he advised that he wanted to catch up on his "out-loud" praying.

The sentry studied him a moment. "What you gonna pray for?"

"Well, now, brother, I might be prayin' that this war will end soon in a Texan victory and that I'll marry the woman I love and take her to Natchez to my ordination sermon, and that on the way back I'll be able to bring a man named Abner Bowser to the Lord. But that's not what I'm prayin' about tonight."

The lonely sentry asked, "Why not?"

"Because I've said it so often the Lord would probably say, 'Look here, Jackson, I know that prayer backward and forward.' "

"Yeah, I reckon it's hard to think of things to pray for, all right."

"Ever try?" Jackson asked.

"Not much."

"Which means you're the kind who's really got a lot to pray about and for—your soul, brother. Now the folks who think of plenty to pray about don't need half the prayin' for that you do."

"You don't say!"

"I do, and you listen. You've got to get into the spirit of prayin', brother. Got to get out of your callous shell and talk to the Lord real earnest until you feel Him drivin' the gospel into you like a spike being hammered down your throat. Now you think on that, friend."

Jackson left the bewildered sentry staring after him and moved on out into the dark night. He got on his knees and talked to the Lord about conditions in Texas. Next he told the Lord that Sam Houston could use a little help on this night; that old Hellfire would greatly appreciate it if He would sort of ease up to the general and tell him that when he came to the fork in the road next morning to be sure and take the road to Harrisburg; and while Houston might have already decided on that road, it was better to take no chances.

"I reckon that's about all for tonight, Lord. I won't overdo it by remindin' You again to watch over Miss Jane and Wash. Course You might slant an eye their way while You're workin' on the general."

3

Just before daybreak next morning Colonel Sherman, officer of the day, called his regiment into line and began the march to Spring Creek and the crossroad. Colonel Burleson's regiment followed, as did all other groups. The march eastward continued.

The road was littered with wagons of refugees, some drawn by cows. Weary old men and tired women and forlorn-looking children stared at the army in retreat. Many shook their fists and called the soldiers cowards, but most of the bedraggled lot stood silent. Scattered along the road and over the deep-rutted prairie were household goods, bedding, and provisions. Feathers from torn beds dotted the countryside for miles. Everything from the faces of the civilians to bogged, broken, and overturned conveyances told in grim reality the story of flight, panic, hunger, sickness, distress, and exhaustion. They could not stop, for they knew the measure of Mexican mercy.

Jackson trudged along with the medical corps, occasionally looking in on the four sick men in the cart he followed. But always his anxious eyes roamed the host of refugees in search of Jane, Wash, and Bucktooth Sal. Ahead a woman in mud-soiled calico uttered a cry and ran toward her husband, who was marching past. The man stepped from the ranks, took her in his arms, and held her close for a minute before joining his company again.

Now General Houston was riding up to the left of the column. A few civilians greeted him with weak cheers. Their voices were drowned out by those angered by his retreat. One old man cried out, "Think you'll get to the Sabine today, General?" Others yelled, "Why don't you stand and fight?"

Houston made no reply. He looked straight ahead and rode on up the line of troops. Jackson watched him closely as he passed Burleson's regiment and moved on. He was moving toward the head of Sherman's regiment when the woods lining Spring Creek came into view.

"Show 'em, General!" Jackson kept saying under his breath as the army moved closer to the fork in the road that would reveal Houston for what he actually was, a leader searching for the enemy or a false leader bent on abandoning the country to the merciless enemy.

The entire army seemed to crane its neck for a look ahead as the crossroad drew near. The secret was out in the open, if there was any secret as to the resolve of Colonel Burleson and Colonel Sherman. The one flag of the army, brought by Sherman from Cincinnati, Ohio, and carried by flagbearer James A. Sylvester, alternately drooped and rustled in the wet wind, as if the goddess painted on a field of white were also caught up in the anxiety and suspense of waiting.

The slosh of mud by marching feet seemed to join every other sound in that last eighth of a mile to beat rhythmically in every head: "Which road will Houston take? Which road will Houston take?" Over and over.

Jackson's jaw hung slack when he saw the general falling back toward Burleson's regiment. His hopes fell and he was trying at once to excuse Houston and silently urge him to take the lead. But Houston had stopped his horse, as if to resign leadership when it was needed most to those under him.

"Lord, didn't You talk to him last night? If You didn't get around to it, I hope You're stirrin' amongst us now!"

A minute and another dragged by. Then the officer of the day was nearing the fork in the road. To the left, the Sabine and safety; to the right, Harrisburg and a joining with the enemy in battle. Which? Colonel Sherman's regiment moved on. Houston still sat his horse.

Then, suddenly, General Houston urged his horse forward. He stopped in the middle of the crossroad. He looked to the east. He turned his gaze to the southeast. As the army held its breath, he lifted a hand and pointed.

A cheer lifted from the ranks and rolled across the prairie. Houston had taken the road to Harrisburg!

"Thanks, Lord! You kept old Hellfire hoppin' like a barefoot boy in a bed of hot coals, but we finally got the general headed in the right direction!"

4

As Houston sat his horse watching the army move past, cries of anguish from the refugees lifted and drew his gaze. Cries of "Are you going to leave us to the robbers and Indians, General?" and "Do you want us to go on to the Sabine without any protection?"

Houston eyed them until the noise subsided, then called Captain Martin to come forward. As Jackson drew near, he heard sixty-year-old Wylie Martin shouting his protest. "General, what have you got against me? You sent me to hold back the enemy down on the Brazos with a mere handful of men, which I haven't forgotten. And now you want me and my company—all of us itchin' to fight—to nurse all those refugees across the Trinity River! I don't like it, and I'd sooner resign from the army!"

"Captain, you'll do as I say."

As Martin fumed and called his company of horsemen out of the formation, Houston sharply eyed Dr. Labadie's pitiful medical corps.

"You, Hellfire Jackson. I've got a job for you."

Jackson's mouth fell open and he began to stir up his defense against any mission that would take him out of the ranks. As he opened his mouth to speak, Houston said, "And I don't want any argument. You stay with those poor civilians and cheer them as best you can."

"I came to fight, General!"

"You've got a hole in your ear to show it, Jackson. Now those refugees out there are Texans. They need the help and comfort and prayers you can give them, and you can do a damn sight more good for the country with a songbook and a Bible than a gun."

With that, he turned his horse and rode away, leaving Jackson staring after him. "Yes, sir, General," he said at last. "I reckon you're right."

As Horatio stood there lost in thought, torn between duty and desire, and trying to adjust himself to the former, he became aware of excitement in the ranks ahead. It ran down the column of troops like a chill wind. It rose up in angered cries and it left shock and dismay in its wake:

The day before Santa Anna had burned the town of Harrisburg, the seat of the Texas government!

Hellfire Jackson looked at the army and then at the destitute civilians in flight. He felt anger and he felt pity. Wrath collided with sympathy inside him, and he trembled under the ambivalence of feeling that racked him. A gun or a Bible? It did not matter what Houston had ordered him to do; the battle now was between soldier Jackson and Reverend Jackson. And no matter which man won, a part of him would go in spirit with the side that lost.

Fragments of talk penetrated his torn mind: "President Burnet and his Cabinet escaped before Santa Anna arrived." Jackson looked at his rifle. He heard next: "The government is fleeing to Galveston." Then a cry from ahead ran down the line: "The boss says march on the double for Harrisburg!" The men let go a long cheer and stepped faster.

Jackson took a step forward, to join them. Then he heard again fresh out of memory, "You can do a damn sight more good for the country with a songbook and a Bible than a gun." He stopped in his tracks. He touched the Bible in his pocket. Reverend Jackson walked toward the refugees.

CHAPTER 27

Bucktooth Sal stared at the hundreds of wagons ahead that had waited for three days to cross the San Jacinto River. "Fully five thousand people!" she said incredulously. "All scared and running for their lives with Santa Anna on our coattails!"

News of the burning of Harrisburg had struck terror among all early that morning. Santa Anna had put the torch to the town. Reports had him moving up toward the San Jacinto River to meet Houston. Hundreds of families seemed to go wild that day. With no room on the road for their wagons, they had rushed blindly off into the impassable quagmires of the prairie. And still more were coming, beating their mules and oxen, cursing all who got in their way.

"Runnin'! Everybody frantic and runnin', Jane! And nowhere to go! Can't move on and can't turn back!"

"I know, Aunt Sally. But the soldiers General Houston sent to escort us to safety did restore a little order." She added glumly, "That is, before they moved on to help those ahead of us."

"Yeah! Runnin' from Santa Anna! And leavin' us, five or six thousand people back here, helpless."

She did not mention the sick and those who would never cross the muddy San Jacinto. There was no need to, for tragedy, like fear, stalked the seemingly endless train. Mud had taken a toll of wagons. Every mile of the way was dotted with them, wheels sunk hub-deep. Most of them were deserted, though a few were not. Their owners and families had given up and were content to sit and watch the awful parade of frightened people despite the news that Santa Anna was approaching. But now all wagons on the road were motionless, each waiting its turn to be ferried across the San Jacinto. The ferryboat never stopped night or day. Earlier that day Wash had heard a man traveling behind them say:

"Only a hundred and ten wagons ahead of us."

Jane sat under the wagon with her aunt while Wash tried again to get a fire going. Food had long since become so scarce that it caused further panic and no end of theft. Even as they sat there, a party of hunters returned empty-handed. Dee and buffalo had gone north, they said. Now the small rabbi Wash had brought in looked bigger to Jane. As she looke at Mr. Mundy and the mother with the babe, she saw then staring at the rabbit also.

"Miss Wells! Oh, Miss Wells! Come quick!"

Startled, Jane cried, "Yes, Mrs. Mills!" scrambled int the open and ran to the wagon in which the ten-year-ol Mills girl lay. Esther needed a doctor badly. There was none Nor was she the only sick child in that part of the train. Al most every wagon had its case of measles or whooping cough The former had reached the epidemic stage, as had sore eyes Esther Mills had pneumonia.

Toward three in the morning Jane broke the terrible new to Mrs. Mills. She tried to comfort the weeping mother. B noon there was another grave marker along the clogged an torn muddy road that stretched from the Colorado and Brazo to the San Jacinto.

The wagons moved up slowly all that morning and after noon. Another day ended with news from the river ahead. I traveled from wagon to wagon and finally reached Jane an Wash, both now burdened with another worry—Bucktoot Sal of all people had been put to bed in the wagon with chill and fever. When Mrs. Pugh, their neighbor back in Velasc came at Jane's request to help with Sal, she brought the news

There was a report that fighting had broken out amon the wagoners who had reached the river. In the struggle t see who would cross first, two men had been injured badl and one had drowned. When it seemed that the fighting wa spreading, a man on horseback had appeared out of no where.

"They say he rode amongst the fighting men," Mrs. Pug went on, "pulling them apart and shouting, 'Blessed are th peacemakers; for they shall be called the children of God.'

Wash froze in his tracks. "Maybe Marse Jackson don come!"

Morning ushered in a spring storm. While it made the road worse, it filled buckets and pans with precious drinking water Then the sun came out and wild flowers burst into blossor along the roadside. After breakfasting on cold corn brea Jane decided to grant Wash's request to ride ahead and lear if the man Mrs. Pugh had told about was Jackson.

Wash returned several hours later in the company of Mr Pugh, who related what had happened. His story was punc tuated at regular intervals by Wash's exclamations of "Amen Praise de Lawd!" and "Dat's de gospel truf!"

Pugh continued his story:

On the way to the San Jacinto they had ridden through water standing in the road and forded ravines that the storm had filled with raging water. Driftwood and snakes were common sights. Mosquitoes swarmed out of the thickets and the stench of dead oxen and mules filled the air. News that the ferryboat had grounded caused weeping among the women along the way. Others wept because of their sick on the verge of death, and still others because death had already visited their families. As they neared the river, a cheer had sounded. The ferryboat had been put into service again.

"Wagons moved," Pugh said. "Slowly, but they moved. Then I heard a man's cry of 'The sick go first! If you have no sick, pull aside!' I recognized the man then. He was the same Hellfire Jackson who held that camp meeting at Brazoria. Well, a big bully of a man rode up ahead of his wagon and said he had waited two days to cross and, despite the fact that he had no sick folks, he was crossing. To which Jackson said, 'Sir, before you bare your head and thank God for His goodness, have your wagon pulled aside.' And when the man refused, Jackson jerked him off his horse and said, 'Brother, this ain't no time for me to persuade the hard of heart. Now you do as I say, or else!' We waited while he checked each wagon, prescribed for the sick, and said a short prayer for each. He didn't have to use his fists but once during the hour and a half we had to wait."

"Yassuh!" Wash said, beginning where Pugh left off. "And he done come rushin' up to me, Miss Jane, and he put his arms aroun' me and he say he sholy glad to see ole Wash, and how is Miss Jane, he say, and I say as how yo'all is quite tol'able but Miss Sally she got fever bad, and he say fo' us to wrap her in a wet sheet and de fever will break. He sholy did, Miss Jane!"

"Why didn't he come with you?" Jane asked.

Pugh replied, "He couldn't leave right then, ma'am. Said he had to doctor the sick and preach a funeral first."

Jane bit her lip, then suddenly left them, saying, "And that's probably the way it would always be! No thanks, Reverend Jackson!"

Pugh scratched his beard and looked puzzled. "Now what on earth is the matter with her?"

2

Jackson preached more than one funeral that morning, and in between funerals he doctored a sick family and helped

a pair of Captain Martin's men give chase after rowdies fror
the badlands who made a habit of holding old men, wives
and slaves at gunpoint while they plundered wagons. Th
outlaws were trapped in a thicket and a gun battle followed
One of Martin's men had been killed. Then the three outlaw
who survived moved into the open with their hands up.

Martin's corporal politely informed them that surrende
was out of the question, that they were not equipped t
handle prisoners. So they would just have to hang them.

One of the ruffians looked at Horatio. "Ain't you Hellfir
Jackson? You can't let them hang us—Reverend!"

"Brother, the Good Book, which you have neglected, say
the way of the transgressor is hard. What you men have don
calls for a rope, and since the corporal here decided on
rope, may the Lord have mercy on your souls."

With that, he wheeled his horse around and rode towar
the ferry crossing. He had not gone far when he turned an
went back to the scene of skirmish and surrender. Sur
enough, the corporal and his men were fastening ropes abou
the necks of the rowdies. Jackson waited until all was read
for the hanging.

"Corporal, I've got an idea that might save us this job and
the memory of it. Why not pitch these sinners in the Sar
Jacinto River and let them swim it if they can. It's only a
mile wide here."

The corporal heaved a sigh of relief. The outlaws were
duly heaved into the swirling water, and the last they saw of
them they were being swept along in the current, and, as Jackson put it, "repenting of their transgressions."

Only then did he find the time on that busy morning to allow his mind a minute or so of rejoicing and thoughts of Jane.
She and Wash were safe. It gladdened his heart and turned
the overcast sky into the sunlit blue of spring. Despite his
aches and pains of body, he smiled. He thanked the Lord
again for watching over dear sweet Miss Jane in his absence. He began to sing and a joy seemed to flood his being
anew. He told himself that as soon as possible he would write
out an appropriate poem and send it down the line of wagons
to her. That he would, and she would read:

For such a lovely maiden as thee, my dearest sweet Miss
Jane,
'Tis my fondest wish in thy behalf, to drive away the cloud
and rain;
To bring into thy sweet life the every perfumed blossom—
of love and spring!!!

"Or should I say 'dewdropped blossom'?"

Further thought on that score was interrupted by a rider streaking toward the corporal's detail. He came on, jerked his horse to a stop, and asked for Captain Martin. Upon learning that Martin and most of his men were helping refugees cross the Trinity River far ahead, the man said:

"Can't go that far after him. Got to get back to the army. There's going to be one more hell of a battle, boys. Deaf Smith learned where old Santa Anna is—down at Lynchburg on the San Jacinto, not fifteen miles downriver. And the boss, God bless him, is movin' down after him!"

Again the urge to spur his horse downriver gripped Jackson. For a minute he thought he would give in to it and charge after the now departed rider. Then Houston's words about a songbook and a Bible checked him.

He rode on toward the ferry, cheering Houston on into battle. When it seemed that he had done all he could from this distance, he picked up his trend of thought the courier had interrupted and said to himself:

"Might as well make it real pretty while I'm at it and say perfumed and dewdropped blossom.' "

3

At around two that afternoon the wagons began to move forward again. Jane's wagon was finally third in line. Then it was on the ferry. Once across the raging San Jacinto, she moved on as she had been told to do, on toward the Trinity River in order to make room for the wagons that would follow. The wagon had not gone far when a man on horseback approached at a gallop crying, "Run for your lives! Mexicans!"

Although it was another of the many false alarms, panic in its worst form again stalked the train. Frightened drivers seemed to go berserk, wrecking their own wagons and those who got in their way. An ox fell dead and the fear-crazed owner began to whip the others instead of cutting the dead animal loose. Women with infants in their arms left their wagons and began to run and weep aloud. Some were without shoes. The mud grew stickier and deeper and the rain came in a torrential downpour. The road ahead and behind Jane was dotted with stuck wagons. When the excitement died down many of the people were begging for shelter, others for food, and all for help.

Jane tried to shut out the sight and sound of it all. With her wagon already overloaded with passengers, she nevertheless wished to pick up a mother and a baby. She knew better, and she drove on. An old man with watery, red-rimmed eyes stood almost to his knees in sticky mud holding on to a mule. "Ain't much use to go on, girl," he said. "They say the Trinity is five miles wide at Liberty and still rising."

Wash trudged alongside the wagon, sneezing and coughing. "Don't let nobody scare yo'all none, Miss Jane. Marse Jackson gonna save us."

"I wish to God I had your sublime faith!" she flung back, causing him to blink his eyes in perplexity. When he gave her a meek "Yassum," she said, "Forgive me, Wash," and swallowed hard in an effort to choke back the tears that seemed determined to break through.

The refugees continued on without any stop for nourishment. It was just as well, for there was little or nothing to eat. Then a swollen bayou forced the wagons to halt again. When Mr. Pugh said he was going to kill one of his mules for food Jane felt a sickness in her stomach. When a tale of horror rippled down the train—that a man had been knocked into the bayou ahead by the tail of a big alligator and had failed to come up—Jane shuddered and clutched her face in her hands until her fingernails broke the skin. How she managed to bear up and still attend the sick in her wagon and others, when hunger gnawed at her stomach and fear preyed on her mind she did not know. She could only pray that the ordeal would soon be over.

Then word reached them that if they ever got to the Trinity River there would be no way to cross. The ferryboat was grounded. Again a feeling of utter frustration assailed the fleeing colonists. The fear that had accompanied them every foot of the way was still a part of them, as were terrible memories of tragedy, personal and otherwise. And now, besides these things, flood and hunger. They stared hopelessly at one another as if to ask:

"What can we do to survive? There's nothing left to eat."

A partial answer to their question came out of the west late on that April afternoon when the bawling of cattle and shouts of drovers drew the attention of the refugees. Soon a man stopped his horse and said a few words. A rousing cheer went up, and within minutes the whole train was buzzing with activity.

Mr. Pugh brought the news to Jane and Bucktooth Sal. Grinning happily, he said, "The cattle are for us to eat! He told us so, and said, 'Don't ask me, a minister of the gospel how I got them, folks. Just sharpen your knives and say the Lord works in manner strange.' That's what he said!"

"Who?" Jane demanded.

"Hellfire Jackson, that's who!"

"Oh!"

There was a great feast that night. Jane went with the Pughs and Jonathan Mundy. She stopped short when she saw Jackson over by the fire serving the people big slices of beef. How long had it been since she had seen him? It didn't really matter, for she was looking at him now, unable to take her eyes off of him. The feeling that assailed her was strange and in a way discomforting. Then he was looking at her. He held her glance and he saw her look of wonder and he smiled at her. He stilled her pulses and quickened them at the same time. Then people were clamoring for him to serve them. He obliged them, grinning from ear to ear.

When the feast ended, Jackson sang to the crowd. A few joined in the hymn and soon it seemed that everybody was singing. Jane was one of them. It felt good to be able to sing again. It shut out fear and worry, if only for the time being, and made one glad to be alive. It restored one's faith in things, even kindled hope for the future in a heart.

Then Jackson was telling them he was going to visit and doctor the sick as best he could, as well as help the able-bodied men build rafts to get them across the Trinity when they reached the swollen river.

After the meeting broke up, Jane returned to her wagon. Suddenly Wash appeared out of breath and finally said, "Marse Jackson say fo' me to ask Miss Wells can he visit her a spell and fo' me to come right back wid a answer."

Jane said quickly, "Oh, no! Not the way I look!"

As suddenly Bucktooth Sal's head emerged from the canvas. "Go tell him yes, Wash! Get! And you, Jane Wells, fetch that lantern in here and pretty yourself up! *Pronto,* girl!"

Jane turned her back in defiance, walked to a large oak beside the road and watched the late misshapen moon peer warily over the horizon at turbulent Texas. As she stood there giving her thoughts free rein, she heard in detachment the approach of two men engaged in conversation. It was only when she recognized one of the voices that she listened to what they were saying. . . .

Almazon Huston, Quartermaster General of the Army, was telling of the urgent need of supplies for the army. The soldiers had to have shoes, food, blankets, and munitions. The government had no money, and he had personally sold his watch and saddle to buy coffee for the soldiers. He was on his way to New Orleans to borrow money to buy more supplies.

"I wish you'd go with me, Jackson. It would help a great deal if—"

"Hold it, Almazon. You know I'm needed here a lot worse. You know how these poor people are going to panic if we don't fight a battle and win it. So I belong here. You and me and the Lord know it, Almazon. But maybe I can help in another way. This morning we chased the outlaws who were robbing these refugees. I took some money off of them, for the Lord, I thought, but I reckon Texas needs it worse right now. It's all here except what I spent for the—" He paused there, then said, "Well, I spent about a hundred dollars, and what I bought with it don't matter."

"The cattle these people ate tonight, Jackson. I know about that."

"You do, eh? Well, I sure don't want these folks to know about it! Understand?"

"I understand, Hellfire. These folks are a breed known as Texans. Let 'em think a preacher purloined the cattle and they'll laugh about it on the sly for years. But if they ever learn you bought 'em, they'll pry up hell with you for making them objects of charity. Right? But what's all that got to do with the money you took off the robbers?"

"It's what's left," Jackson replied, handing him a pouch. "You take it and buy shoes and food and supplies for the soldiers. Just say I'm loaning it to Texas."

Huston voiced a low exclamation, then said, "You mean you've got that much confidence in the future of Texas?"

"In the language of the realm, Almazon, I sure as hell have."

Jane stared at the moon and shook her head in despair of the man who gave his all to Texas even as he came to ask her to be his wife. "That's the way it would always be, going from pillar to post married to a penniless preacher," she said to herself. Then she was eying him narrowly, a scolding smile on her face. "How on earth does one deal with such a man?"

Her question, a mere whisper, was given to the balmy April evening. As if trouble and fear and flight were over or never had been, the night answered. It seemed to declare its elemental wisdom in all things, even affairs of the heart. It painted out pictures one saw by day in good judgment and painted in the clean pride and hardheaded goodness of this lean scarecrow of a man who challenged both her sound judgment and her emotions. A warmth flamed up in her and a strange peace and gladness filled her.

Suddenly it all frightened her. She wanted to run from him, run far away where he could never find her. Or did she?

Some answer was due at once, for the sounds of the night were drowned by her aunt's foghorn voice:

"Jane! Hellfire Jackson's here!"

She stood stock still except for the trembling of her body. She was afraid, of him, of herself. And yet somewhere in her heart a bell was ringing. Whirling, she looked at him. He stood across the road in silhouette. In the burning intensity of her gaze, he stood a tower of strength, a man a woman could honor and cling to.

"Oh, Horatio!" she said in a vibrant whisper. Then, driving out all fear and restraint, she raised her voice to him:

"I'm over here, Horatio."

He came toward her. Then she was running toward him.

4

On the following afternoon a low booming noise far to the south was borne on the Gulf wind up to the refugees' camp. All eyes searched the horizon for storm clouds. There were none. Then the word spread that the noise was the sound of distant cannon. Perhaps Houston had decided to quit running and fight. But that was hard to believe. It was easier to believe that Santa Anna was drawing near, that it was time to run for their lives again toward the Sabine.

Before the sound of cannon ended, runners were sent out to learn what had happened. Night had fallen when they returned with the glad tidings: "The Texans won! The war is over! Houston's men defeated Santa Anna at San Jacinto!"

Praise God, they could all return to their homes! It was all over. Texas had won her independence from Mexico.

The frightened, despairing, and tired refugees of minutes earlier were suddenly transformed into a mass of jubilant people. Torches and lanterns were lit. Men slapped one another on the back, leaped into the air, and loosed yells of delight. A man grabbed a woman and began to dance and sing. The slaves emulated their masters. Bucktooth Sal, who swore she had not shed a tear in twenty years, broke down and cried. Jane looked at her and said this was a time to rejoice, for now she could return to the Brazos and open her blacksmith shop again in a free and independent Texas.

"So be happy, Aunt Sally."

"Hell, I am happy! And if Cap'n Herrick toted a gun in this fracas, I'm going to make him propose to me if I have to coax him with a hot horseshoe in one hand and an anvil in the other. But where you going, Jane?"

"To find Horatio, that's where."

Jane threaded her way through the hundreds of dancing, yelling colonists. Ahead huge bonfires burned. On one side of her a man sawed away on a fiddle and another blew on a jug. Men beat the ground with their feet. A few scooped up their children and loosed deafening yells all about her. Mr. Pugh let go of his wife and hugged Jane. Jonathan Mundy eyed them and looked rather bewildered. Then a smile appeared on his face, and he caught Jane's arm and asked if he could "cut just one dido" to the music with her.

"Why not, Mr. Mundy?" Jane smiled and let him swing her about a few turns. Then she saw Wash and broke from Mundy, saying, "Thanks for the dance, sir." Almost in the same breath she cried, "Wash, help me find Reverend Jackson!"

"Sholy, ma'am! He over dere singin' to de folks. He done send me fo' to look fo' yo'all."

"Where, Wash?"

"Mean yo'all can't hear Marse Jackson? Jes' lissen, Miss Jane!"

Jane pushed through the crowd with Wash until she could hear Horatio's baritone voice. Soon it came through clearly with: " 'Am—az—ing grace—how sweet the sound—' " She worked her way closer to where he stood, recalling all that had happened between them the night before, from his outstretched arms to her promise to marry him once the refugees were safely beyond the reach of Santa Anna. How tenderly he had held her even as he stammered forth: "Will you—marry me, dear sweet—Miss Jane?" And how sincere his thanks to the Lord had sounded when she replied, "I most certainly will, Horatio Jackson!" And he had picked her up in his arms and kissed her. Then, still holding her, he had kicked up his heels in a little jig and shouted, "Hallelujah! Hallelujah!"

And now Wash was pointing. Jane stopped still and stared at the man she would soon marry. He stood tall and strong in the light of a bonfire, and the very sight of him seemed to cause bells to ring in her heart. He was leading the people in the last stanza of "Amazing Grace." She lifted her voice and sang also: " 'Tis grace that brought me safe thus far, And grace will lead me home.' " The song ended, and she was listening to what he was saying to the gathering:

"The last courier in just handed me some more news, folks. Last night General Cos's army of over five hundred men joined Santa Anna's force of about seven hundred. General Houston knew it was happening and he let Cos get through —maybe so he wouldn't have to take two bites at the same cherry. Anyhow, today, while twelve hundred Mexicans were snoozin' through their afternoon siesta, the boss turned his Texans loose on them with cries of 'Remember the Alamo! Remember Goliad!'—their battle cry. The battle lasted less than thirty minutes, folks. Imagine that! The Lord was on our side, and—"

Long, rousing cheers silenced Jackson for a minute or so. When he could be heard again, he said, "And now it's time to thank the Lord. You musicians over there! The Lord's got good ears, boys, but I don't want Him sayin', 'Will you repeat that, Hellfire? Can't hear you for that dadblamed fiddle and jug.' "

Jane listened to the people laugh. She laughed with them, all the while watching Horatio as he stood behind a tree-stump altar awaiting the end of mirth. Then he lifted his arms high and all bowed their heads. She and Wash did likewise.

"O, Lord," Jackson began, "if we ever did have thanks in our hearts it's now. Some of us have been a little too busy complainin' and cussin' General Houston, I reckon, but You know how that is, Lord. We got a mite discouraged and riled up when it seemed You were pushin' us a little hard and it looked like General Houston was going all the way to Alabama or Georgia before he put up a scrap."

"Amen!" It lifted in a chorus.

"Yes Sir, Lord. But it's like I told You right often, us Texans do a lot of talkin' we don't exactly mean. We've just got to howl about something or other. What we're going to howl about next, I reckon You're wonderin' Yourself, Lord. But we'll come up with something, so don't You get worried about us if we seem tol'ably peaceful for a spell. But we're a grateful people, Lord, and right now we want to thank You for endowing Sam Houston with the patience and wisdom that enabled him to choose his place to fight and give us victory, and—"

"Amen! Amen, Lord!" the people cried.

"And we ask Thee to heal the wound Houston got in the leg today. And we ask Thee to bless every man in that Texas Army that charged the enemy today in battle."

"Amen! God bless 'em all!" a man near Jane shouted.

"And," Horatio continued, "bless the families who lost loved ones in all battles with the enemy, and all who lost loved ones during the terrible flight of the civilians. Put cheer in their hearts, O, Lord, and a promise of a great and God-fearing Texas! Old Hellfire down here is going to help You with that promise, Lord. He's going to take for a wife one of the finest, fairest, and sweetest women You ever laid eyes on, Lord, and he's going to take her to his ordination sermon in Natchez, and he's going to come back and with her at his side spread Thy Word in this new and great Republic of Texas, where there are no longer any religious restrictions!"

"We sholy is, Lawd!" Wash cried.

When the prayer ended and the Texans clamored for Jackson to preach them a sermon, Jane noticed that Horatio looked tired and spent. But the people persisted and he finally consented. A short sermon followed. It was all too brief to quench the excitement in the gathering on this night, however, and when Jackson had finished, a man deep in the crowd yelled forth:

"What's the matter, Hellfire? You ain't so sharp tonight!"

As laughter rippled through the throng, Jane looked at Horatio and wondered just how he would answer the man, as he surely must to satisfy the crowd. She was silently cheering him on when he said so all could hear:

"Brother, I reckon you're right about that. You see, old Hellfire is like a grindstone. He ain't so sharp himself, but he's mighty good at sharpenin' others."

Amid the laughter that followed, Jane cried out, "That's my man!" and moved toward him.